Prince
of the
Vale

Kelly R. Michaels

Prince of the Vale
a novel by
Kelly R. Michaels

The Silver Crown Chronicles
Part 2

Cover by
Sarah Foster
Sprinkles on Top Studios

Map by
Arbor Winter Barrow

Edited by
Kelsa Warner
&
Andy Arnold

2018 Edition

Copyright © 2015 Kelly R. Michaels
www.kellyrmichaels.com

Little Owl Publishing
ISBN: 0-9894685-4-2
ISBN-13: 978-0-9894685-4-1

In loving memory of
Lady Kimberly Michaels,
the Fairy Singer and this era's Tragedy.
I love you, Momma.

CONTENTS

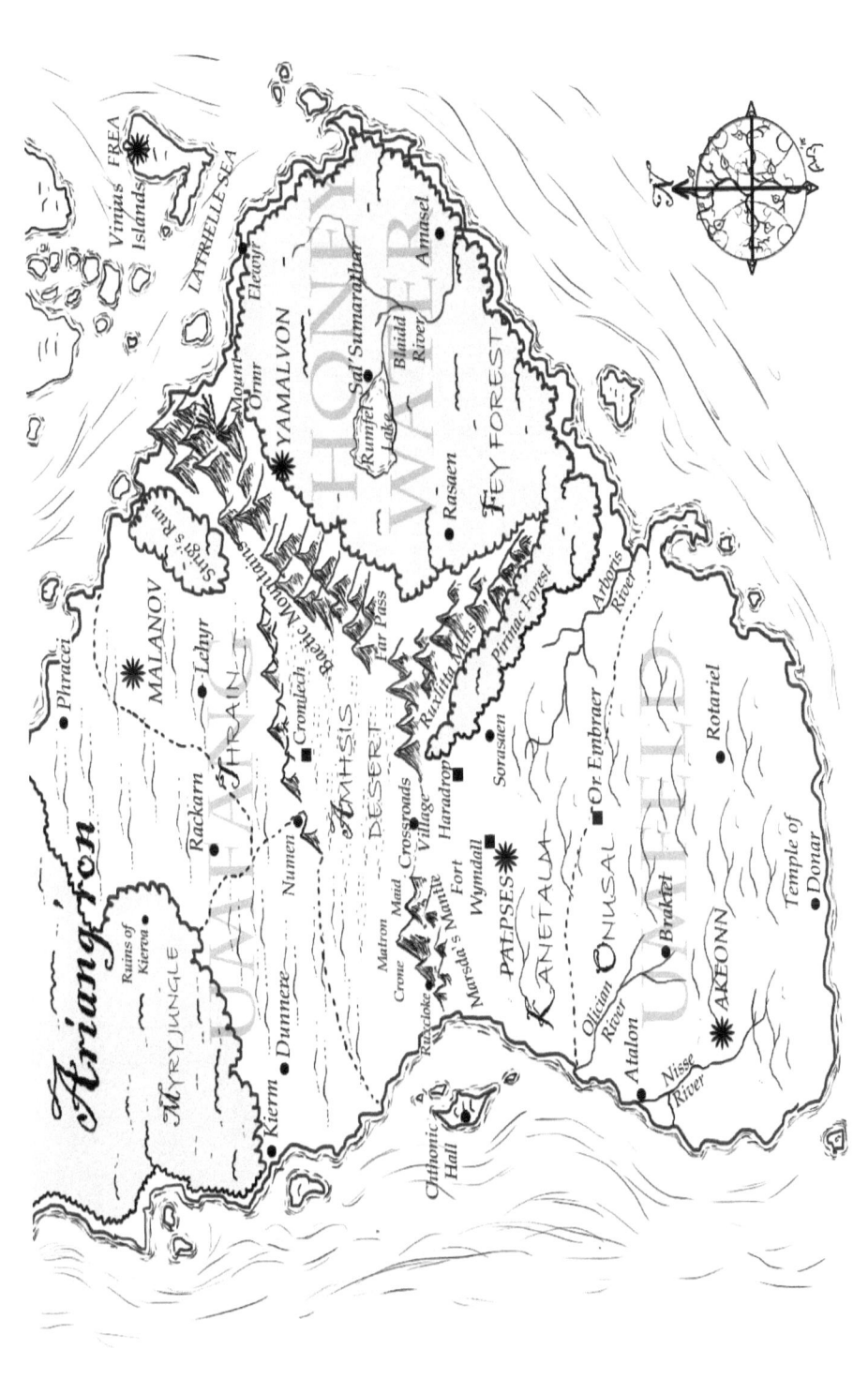

Prologue

"**M**other would never make me clean out the chicken coop," Reuthe grumbled to herself, shovel and bucket in hand.

Though in truth, Reuthe didn't have a mother and had never known one. She had her father, Ólff, who was keeper of the temple at Sorasaen and mostly a loving parent throughout her life. Sometimes, however, he would put his foot down and insist that Reuthe go do her chores, and it was times like these that Reuthe would fabricate the mother she had always yearned for. Her mother would never force her to do chores, especially now, a few years shy of her twentieth year. Her mother would understand things that her father never could. After all, Reuthe must have gotten her brilliant shock of snow-white hair from someone, and it definitely was not inherited from the mousy-brown head of her father.

But there she was, dragging her feet to the chicken coop as she made her way to the farmhouse across the road from the Temple of Saint Hubertus. Mucking out the nest houses was not her favorite task. It hurt her back and made her shoulders sore. The smell was an atrocious matter of its own.

She shoveled, careful not to breathe through her nose, and noticed that while the hen house should hold ten chickens, Reuthe could only count eight. She paused and counted once more, coming up with the same result. She looked around the fencing for any sign of entry made by a fox or other predator and saw none. No stray feathers or other sign of the missing hens. Reuthe finished her work quickly and rushed to inform her father. Her shovel and bucket were left abandoned next to the coop, and as she ran across the road, her eyes darted suspiciously between the various villagers of Sorasaen.

Reuthe needed no harbinger to enter. She burst into the temple library where she had last seen her father. "Two of our chickens are missing! I think someone has stolen them," she informed Ólff. It was only when she was met with a stern silence and a hard gaze did it dawn on Reuthe that she had interrupted something.

Ólff was entertaining a visitor, and Reuthe immediately recognized the battle-scarred leather armor. She was easily familiar with the visitor's blood-brown stubble and the pale white scars on his left cheek. His name was Freki, and Freki was from the fortress-village of Haradrop, a half-day's journey from Sorasaen. He often visited Sorasaen for food and supplies for his family. And he was often met with resentment and occasionally open hostility from the Sorasaen merchants and grocers, for Haradrop was a suspicious place full of wizards and dangerous werefolk. No one knew if Freki was one of those, but his money must have been good enough, because the merchants and grocers still sold to him.

And secretly, Reuthe fancied him, because, despite his rough appearance, he was kind and gentle. Suddenly, she found herself acutely aware of the smell of chicken dung that clung to her clothes and hair. Freki held her eyes as Ólff scolded her for the interruption.

"Reuthe, please leave us for the moment," he said.

She reluctantly turned her eyes to her father as her expression fell into a scowl. She loathed being dismissed. "But the chickens—"

"*Leave us,*" he snapped.

Reuthe glared and made sure to slam the library doors behind her to show Ólff her temper. She returned to the chicken coop, kicking up the dust with her boots as she cursed her father's inability to listen to her.

She counted the chickens again, but this time she noticed a trail of large wolf tracks leading away from the coop. Reuthe examined them closely before deciding to investigate. If her father would do nothing for their plight, she would have to take matters into her own hands.

The tracks led her into the Pirinac Forest, where she hesitated before pursuing them further. Father had often warned her against the evils of the forest, but Reuthe decided if there was such evil, an absence of trees would not stop it.

Her path turned beyond the trees, and she suddenly found herself facing a man, tall with thick, dark coils for hair. Ultimately though, he was nude. Reuthe stopped, checking herself. She modestly diverted her gaze to the ground, and there she saw the mangled carcasses of their two missing chickens. Blood and feathers surrounded the man's feet. And quickly, her modesty gave way to rage. She squared her shoulders, meeting his gaze, and ignored the condescending smile he used with which to greet her.

"Those were *our* chickens!" she informed him angrily, pointing.

"You are either brave or foolish to come into the forest."

"I do not care much for thieves," she hissed, crossing her arms. "My father will find out, and we will get the Kanetalm Guard—"

But he was laughing, unimpressed with her display of bravery. He began pacing around her. "Your father? The guard? It matters not, because they are not here. *No one* is around to hear you *scream*—"

And at this, he lunged, tearing into Reuthe's shoulder with newly enormous fangs.

1. Deceit

Caelfel Gyssedlues was far away from home, stuck in the company of a cantankerous she-elf, and wandering in a direction that stretched further than the huntsman they spoke to had initially indicated. Tired and ill-tempered did not even begin to described her mood. She trudged onward, her friend Garvanna Hunithrae close at her heels.

"I don't see why we have to go to Palpses," Garvanna complained, not for the first time.

Caelfel sighed impatiently as she recited her answer again. "The humans are holding a celebration for one of their goddesses. When I asked you to come with me to see the world, the humans and their culture were some of the things I wanted to see."

"You said we were going to the *coast*. The sea. The ocean. Not some dirty forest."

Caelfel sighed again and decided not to answer her friend this time.

It was true. When Caelfel had first invited Garvanna along, she'd promised the coast. But the coast was still some distance away, so Caelfel had decided that a few detours to see other things would not be a misplaced venture. Unfortunately, she was having trouble getting Garvanna to see that.

It had been two weeks since they left the Cromlech Palace, the desert fortress where Caelfel had been kidnapped and held prisoner. Due to the efforts of her family, Garvanna, and others, she had survived the incident. But there was one elf to which she owed everything, for he had crossed the desert alone and faced the Admiral Grimault and his malicious sorcerer on his own.

And his name was Feraan.

But Feraan was an elf that she was, at present, trying her best to forget, though her broken heart kept the memories far too fresh. She took a deep breath to brace herself against the flow of emotional pain and pushed Feraan from her mind. She knew that Garvanna had noticed her anguished expression, but the other she-elf refrained from commenting on it because she too suffered similarly.

Garvanna plowed through an uncharacteristically cheerful commentary on their dank surroundings, which helped distract Caelfel sufficiently.

The worst of the two weeks' journey had been crossing the Amhsis desert, which was unforgiveable in its heat with a bleak landscape that was nearly impossible to navigate. A week later, they found themselves at the opening to the Farpass, a mountain pass in the Baetic Mountains. It led them to the border of their own Fey Forest, the mainland for the Honey Water Empire, the realm of the wood elves. They continued south to the Pirinac Forest, and it was there that they chanced upon the huntsman who inquired if they were on their way to Palpses, the capital of Kanetalm, for the Celebration of Strigi, a venerated goddess of the forest.

And so Caelfel had decided on this destination, while Garvanna could be counted upon to voice her quarrels with the idea. Once Caelfel had mentioned a feast, Garvanna's complaints had mostly quelled. They weren't starving, but Caelfel could admit that a meal other than foreign roots and berries would be much welcomed. Elves were ultimately food-foragers by nature, so there had not been a need to pack very much in the way of sustenance. Even so, Caelfel and Garvanna had learned in their two weeks together to appreciate the convenience of food readiness in the city.

And Palpses was a city, promising all the luxuries of one, so Garvanna soon exhausted her supply of arguments to the notion. Even she would take a human city over the wilderness. So they made their way through the rugged landscape of Kanetalm, one of the provinces of Umfeld.

"There is supposed to be a pass somewhere," Caelfel noted, consulting a worn map the huntsman had given them. "The Ruxlitta Pass, in the mountains."

Caelfel glanced around. This forest was unusually dark, so much different than the forest of their home. The Fey Forest had great trees, taller than the evergreens in the Pirinac Forest. Here in the Pirinac, very little light reached through the spindly needles to the forest floor. And there was an unfamiliar and unsettling smell of mud and pine, spruce and juniper. And though spring had arrived a few weeks previous, the air of the forest was still damp and chilled. Had Caelfel not known any better, she would have mistaken it for autumn or even winter.

Garvanna offered nothing in the way of counsel. She leaned against a tree and glared at the oppressive foliage around them. "This forest is disgusting."

Caelfel found she could not disagree but thought a different description for the Pirinac would be better suited. "This forest is *deceiving*."

And it was an uncomfortable truth she could not deny. Upon entering the woods, a sense of danger had settled on Caelfel, which only intensified the further they ventured into the Pirinac. It made the hair rise on the back of her neck, and she constantly had a hand on her bow. Garvanna made a curt laugh, drawing Caelfel away from her reverie. "The forest isn't alive, youngling," she said, shrugging herself off a tree.

Caelfel frowned, detesting the name, for she was no longer a youngling. Younglings were elf children who had not passed their half-century year. Caelfel was seventy-six, mature by all means, but being the youngest of her community, she had often struggled to surpass the designation of a youngling. What bothered her more was Garvanna's casual dismissal of her apprehension. Garvanna may have been centuries older than Caelfel, but Garvanna was ultimately a mage, specializing in the use of magic.

Meanwhile, Caelfel's father had trained her since the summers of her youth in the skills of hunting and archery. Caelfel was familiar with forests and predators. She knew the difference between paranoia and being hunted. "We are being watched," Caelfel said, eyes flitting around in the dimness.

Elves had superior abilities and strength, including their eyesight, but this forest was unfamiliar with its dark depths and eerie silence. Caelfel was wary.

"Stop that," Garvanna snapped. "You are making me nervous."

She held her hand out for the map

"Perhaps you should be nervous," Caelfel muttered darkly, passing over the map without protest.

Garvanna kept them moving, and Caelfel was content to follow, keeping watch. She recalled the huntsman with his suspicious narrow eyes and ominous scar that disfigured one of them. He was eager to point them into the forest, warning nothing of any dangers that her instincts now alerted her to. He had recommended cutting away from the road, for it was the quickest way to the Ruxlitta Pass. Caelfel began to suspect a duplicitous motive in his suggestion.

"There," Garvanna pointed, interrupting Caelfel's thoughts.

Caelfel followed Garvanna's gaze to a crumbling, weathered stone statue. She approached it, recognizing a feminine shape. The runes on the pedestal below it faintly spelled out the name of the Ruxlitta goddess. Half of her face was missing, and the defining features chiseled in her dress were mostly eroded away. The statue was no taller than Caelfel's shoulder when she straightened and turned back to Garvanna. "The Ruxlitta goddess. The pass must be near."

They shared a smile before the snapping of a twig interrupted the never-ending silence of the forest. The two she-elves were instantly alert, pressing their backs together. Caelfel drew her bow and nocked an arrow, feeling the heat of Garvanna's aura behind her. They waited two painful minutes before lowering their guard. Garvanna's yellow aura disappeared, and she scoffed.

"You are so jumpy, Caelfel," she sniffed. "Always paranoid."

Caelfel only scowled, keeping her bow and arrow in hand. They continued past the Ruxlitta statue, Caelfel praying that they were heading in the right direction. "I will be much happier once we leave this forest," Caelfel said.

"Do you miss home?" Garvanna asked, attempting conversation.

Mindless chatter did not settle Caelfel's nerves like it did Garvanna's, but Caelfel complied with Garvanna's attempts. "I do not think we have been gone long enough to miss it."

Though, that wasn't entirely true. Caelfel harbored a deep longing for her parents. For her beautiful mother, who was a fierce battlemage, personally bringing down the walls of the Cromlech Palace in search of Caelfel. For her father, the greyling who knew a millennia's worth of stories. And also, for her friend Thoroth, who had carelessly broken Garvanna's heart.

And as always for Feraan, who had carelessly broken hers.

She swallowed past a dry lump in her throat. No matter how tight her chest felt, Caelfel took a small comfort in knowing that her situation was better than Garvanna's. While they both suffered from the sickness known as rejection, Caelfel still had her parents. Garvanna had lost her entire family in a massacre nearly a century ago. So that was something.

"I do miss my horse, Rowan," Caelfel admitted at length. She hadn't tired of walking yet. Only, riding horseback would have seen them through this accursed forest at a much faster pace.

Garvanna laughed quietly in agreement. Caelfel remembered her bay horse Nerium. After the battle with the desert army, for which they both had volunteered before Caelfel's kidnapping, Caelfel suspected their horses were returned to Sal'Sumarathar, their woodland city in the Fey Forest.

"I had heard a rumor," Garvanna said after emitting a noise of disgust when she avoided a pile of what seemed to be decomposing shrubbery. "If our horses were to leave the Fey Forest for an extended period of time, they would quickly die."

This bit of news horrified Caelfel. "Why is that?" She bent down to inspect the smelly refuse Garvanna had stepped over, for it did not smell like plant decay.

"From my understanding of it, the Fey Forest is magical, and just as our lives prove to be quite long, it also extends the lives of our steeds." Garvanna paused, wrinkling her nose when she glanced at what Caelfel was doing. "*Apparently*, normal horses do not live quite so long."

Caelfel catalogued that information in the back of her mind but was too preoccupied with the putrid mess before her. She rose slowly. "This isn't shrubbery," she said quietly. "This is an animal, specifically a wild boar."

Garvanna, though not familiar with the subject of game, at least sensed that something was amiss with Caelfel's report. "Then why does it smell so *funny*?"

Caelfel wouldn't call the odor of rotting flesh normal by any means, but Garvanna was perceptive. The scent was *off*. Caelfel showed her two fingers coated in a clear, thick fluid. "I think this is saliva, and it seems to be masking most of the smell."

Garvanna graced the carcass with another glance. "So it was

eaten?"

Caelfel nodded in affirmation. "It was a large boar, so I'm not sure what would be big enough—"

But the howling of a nearby animal immediately silenced her. Caelfel turned, barely bringing her bow up in time to see a large wolf hurtling through the air toward her. She had no time to release her arrow before it knocked her to the ground. Caelfel felt its massive paw digging into her stomach.

She would have cried out in pain, except the wolf had pushed all the air out of her lungs. She smelled its rank breath and heard the low growling from its throat, but Caelfel could not inhale until Garvanna sent a blast of orange magic to throw the beast off of her. Caelfel staggered to her feet, catching her breath.

"I told you we were being watched," Caelfel gasped. The wolf stalked, pacing as Garvanna held it at bay with magic.

"*What* is it?" Garvanna asked.

Caelfel would have given the obvious answer—that it was a wolf. But this creature was much larger than a normal wolf, standing taller than either of them. A distant memory, a name came to her, and Caelfel uttered it. "A dire wolf?" she suggested.

Then it howled, and more howls responded to it. Caelfel realized with horror that they were nearly surrounded by the beasts. She held her bow up defensively.

A sharp snarl came from behind, and Caelfel spun towards the sound, releasing her arrow. The point lodged in another wolf's shoulder, and this one staggered in obvious pain. Caelfel realized grimly she had only injured the creature as she prepared another arrow. But even while the wolf limped in its prowling, more snarls ripped through forest.

It was evident that their only chance for survival was escape, so Garvanna cleared a space in their barricade with a blast of fire. Then the two she-elves ran for it.

Elves were prodigiously quick, faster than the other races. As they ran, Caelfel was alarmed to see the wolves shadowing close behind. Their exchanged growls only seemed to spur each other on faster. Despite the renowned elvish abilities, these wolves were easily keeping pace.

Caelfel veered away from Garvanna and used her momentum to scale a tree. The branches were sharp and stung her hands with sticky resin. But it was enough to distract at least half of the pack, and soon eight wolves paced around the tree she took refuge in.

She drew her bow and fired three arrows at once. It was enough to fell one of them.

"*Caelfel!*" In the distance, Caelfel saw the glint of Garvanna's copper hair circling back for her.

"Just go! They can't climb trees," Caelfel called back to her as she shot another three rounds, injuring another wolf.

The remaining six seemed to understand her words. Two of them backed up, ran, and jumped for the tree. Their large claws were strong enough to keep them tethered to the trunk, and they continued to ascend towards her. Caelfel's eyes widened as her heart hammered painfully in her chest.

"Forget what I said!" she yelled back to Garvanna. "They *can* climb trees."

She dropped to the branch below, using the former to swing forward and kick at one of the climbing wolves. It gave a high-pitched whimper as it fell heavily to the ground. Caelfel landed beside it, and in its confusion, she used an arrow to pin one of its paws to the ground. At least she could immobilize it.

"I'm coming for you!" echoed Garvanna's voice through the trees.

Caelfel's eyes met those of a wolf in front of her. Its upper lip pulled back in a growl, revealing yellow fangs. But Caelfel found herself transfixed by its shiny, intelligent eyes. They were not the eyes of a mindless beast. Perhaps—

"Just keep running," Caelfel told Garvanna as the five unharmed wolves forced her back against the trunk of the tree. She didn't break eye contact with the creature but realized that with the way the others flanked behind it, this dark wolf, so much larger than its brethren, must have been their leader, their alpha. "I think I've found the alpha. If we take him out, we should be fine," Caelfel yelled back to Garvanna, struggling to keep her voice even.

"Are you sure that will work?" Garvanna asked, sounding alarmingly close. Caelfel heard the rustle of magic through the trees and she wondered how well Garvanna was defending herself.

"It's basic pack mentality," Caelfel tried reassuring her. She raised her bow, aiming for the center of its chest.

Then its mouth moved again, and the wolf appeared to be smirking. Caelfel faltered at this as she involuntarily lowered her bow.

"*Caelfel!*" came Garvanna's shrill voice again.

The alpha wolf raised its paw, and Caelfel's vision flooded with bright orange light before a searing pain cut across her stomach. Her head hit the tree before falling to the damp forest floor. And Caelfel saw no more.

2. Hollow Bones

Caelfel didn't expect to wake, and had, instead, resigned herself to fading quickly into oblivion. There had only been a slight possibility of survival, a possibility so small that Caelfel had not even considered it.

But here she was, blinking groggily, which could only happen if she was indeed alive. Various visions shifted in and out of her focus.

A man hovered over her as she felt her body ascending. Her eyelids fluttered to catch glimpses of his striking face. Panic clouded his features, but she did not have the strength to register his concern.

The world tilted as her vision fell to darkness once more. A sudden jolt caused her to open her eyes again. She was reassured by the face of the same man. She focused on his strong jawline with its shadow of brown stubble. His throat moved, shouting soundless commands. A faint ringing pulled her back to the darkness.

A third time she was briefly roused to see his brown, shining eyes as he mouthed inaudible comforts and promises. Without knowing him, she stared blearily back into his eyes and placed an enormous amount of faith into him without fully realizing it. Her head fell back against his cradling hand.

She slept, and upon awakening, her body felt stiff. Her eyelids held a new heaviness that she had not known previously. It took an effort to open her eyes and an even greater one to lift herself and assess her surroundings.

She was in a tent, where orange light filtered through the thick, red canvas. The cot was hard and splintery beneath her. When she sat up, a sharp pain flared across her stomach in protest. Her hand went to it, touching the scratchy bandages. Then Caelfel realized the shirt she wore didn't belong to her. The pants were hers, but her bow was also missing. She specifically remembered having her bow when she had been attacked.

Caelfel tried to stand, but the pain in her abdomen was too great. She sank against the cot, lifting the strange shirt to inspect her injury. She had removed most of the bandages when she was interrupted.

"She's awake! Hey, stop that now. Do you want to bleed to death?"

Caelfel snapped her head up to see a human—a grisly *man*—poking his head through the tent flaps and peering sternly at her. It was the not the faint visage she recalled from her half-conscious state. She glared and in her indignation, she forgot her pain as she attempted to stand once more.

The attempt proved unsuccessful when she buckled to the floor, clutching her abdomen as she gasped for breath. The man's eyes had gone wide when she rose but now they changed into an expression of pity. Caelfel's mind raced, trying to determine what had happened. All she could remember was being attacked by the wolves, and Garvanna—

"Where is Garvanna? Where is my friend?" she asked the man desperately.

He looked reluctant to answer. "All in good time, miss. I believe he wants to speak to you himself."

Caelfel was about to protest that she did not have the patience when a second man entered her tent. The first one disappeared outside as the second introduced himself, "My name is Brenin."

She remembered his face. Brenin had been her savior. He was evidently much younger than his companion, judging from his bright, eager eyes. His brown hair framed either side of his face, and his build was tall and lanky, if the first man was any comparison. But what surprised Caelfel the most was that, despite his youth, his mere presence commanded an authority that the first man, although older, obviously deferred to. Brenin was who she should take all her problems to.

"Where is my friend? The other elf I was with?" Caelfel asked him. She had already deduced that these humans had rescued her, so they could be marginally trusted. Her faith in them was only corrupted by her previous—and first—experience with humans.

But Brenin's eager face turned perplexed. "There was no other elf. I found you in the woods alone and unconscious."

Caelfel's breath stuck in her throat. "Then she must still be out there. We must find her." Caelfel wondered what a sight she must have been, giving this human orders from her crumpled state.

But Brenin did not look as confident. He placed his words delicately, "I don't think your friend—proved as *fortunate* as you were."

Caelfel eyed him sideways, taking in his suddenly tense frame. "Then you must know what is out there."

Brenin's nod came, though reluctant and curt.

She tried getting to her feet, but the feat proved too much for her waning strength. Brenin crouched next to her, compensating for the height difference. She gripped his arm covered in layers of leather armor as she pleaded. "You know what lives in those woods, so it is imperative I find her as quickly as possible. I do not think she could last very long on her own."

More pity flashed in this man's eyes, and Caelfel understood his unspoken answer. But Caelfel would not accept that answer. She would not give up on Garvanna. Certainly, this human could see that.

And she smiled triumphantly when he did, shoulder slumping as he wordlessly yielded to her request. But he did not give up entirely. "You are in no condition to enter the woods again."

She grew impatient. "If you would *heal* me, then I could stand on my own," she countered sharply.

More confusion clouded his eyes. "My physician has already treated you. There is nothing that can be done except for you to heal on your own."

Caelfel released him, belatedly realizing a small yet crucial characteristic of the humans. The humans were not elves so therefore they lived without magic. Healing for a human would take time and was not instantly curable by means of magical healers. At that moment, Caelfel acutely missed Thoroth, the healer that had broken her friend's heart.

"I can manage," Caelfel told him stiffly, hastily reattaching the bandages around herself.

Brenin gave a small smile before summoning a man named Edilon to her tent. The man who entered the tent had yellow hair and a beard to match. He was a human healer, yet for all the reverence Brenin offered him, Edilon's skills only allowed him to deftly rewrap her bandages. Caelfel did not thank him, seeing no need as she could have easily performed the job herself, and Edilon left as silently as he had entered.

So Caelfel stood, pushing out and ignoring the pain that burned through her. She followed Brenin out of the tent to see a small army camped around them. Caelfel was stunned for a moment as she stared at the soldiers with plated armor and smelled the curling smoke of firepits. The scene knotted painfully in her belly. Her last encounter with humans had been in the company of an army that did not treat her so well. Caelfel could not help but be apprehensive.

Noticing her hesitation, Brenin turned. "Something wrong?" Caelfel quickly shook her head and followed him.

The Company of the Prince, as Brenin called this band of soldiers, camped just out of reach of the Pirinac Forest, and Caelfel took comfort in the fact that the forest made them wary as it did her.

"I will take you to the place where I found you," Brenin said. "I do not think you will find anything else there, and it would be wise not to tarry in the woods."

Caelfel nodded at this, grateful for anything they could offer her. But she *would* find Garvanna. She steeled herself against the gnawing pain that spread through her chest. Four more men accompanied them, and Caelfel noticed one to be the first she had encountered upon waking in the humans' camp. Brenin identified him as Cyrus, and Cyrus stood out from the three others, mainly because he did not wear any armor. Brenin noted her puzzled glance and continued.

"Cyrus is my steward. He takes care of me."

Caelfel's polite acknowledgement turned suspicious. Of *all* of the humans she had encountered, a certain steward had been the worst. Lisiek had been Admiral Grimault's steward and as well as a powerful sorcerer. He had physically tortured Caelfel, and she still had scars branded on her hip from the ordeal.

Cyrus quailed awkwardly under her suddenly wrathful gaze. He looked away first, but eventually Caelfel tore her eyes away from Cyrus. She could admit that Cyrus did not have Lisiek's menacing air. He was older than Brenin with broader shoulders. While Brenin had a dusting of stubble on his face and Edilon had a beard to boast about, Cyrus maintained well-groomed patches of hair beneath his nose and bottom lip.

Brenin introduced the other three soldiers as Huwel, Turre, and Melker, and Caelfel assumed they were present for protection against the wolves.

They entered the woods. Caelfel did not miss the odd looks that passed between the other soldiers, and the familiar eeriness prickled the back of her neck. She would have commented on her uneasiness but Caelfel did not feel comfortable enough to reveal her thoughts around humans. During her kidnapping, she had uttered no word to her human captors, and while Brenin and his soldiers did not seem to mean her any harm, habits of self-preservation were hard to break.

She couldn't stop herself from voicing one question, "You found me in the forest, correct? What were you doing?" She thought for a moment and then amended, "How did you know to find me?"

Brenin glanced at her from the corner of his eye. Normally, Caelfel would have been taller than him, but in her current state, the pain from her injury made her shoulders hunch. She was unable to stand to her full height. "There have been various reports of these wolves attacking people. My men and I were scouting the area, fortifying defenses. We chanced upon you, mostly. I had a man tracking them, and he came back to say that *something* had diverted their attention. They were being aggressive, so we hurried to aid whoever they might have been attacking." Brenin's eyes briefly flickered to where Caelfel pressed a hand to her stomach, an attempt to stem the surge of pain. "I am only sorry we did not reach you sooner."

He was kind enough, Caelfel could admit, and it reminded her of someone else who had performed a unsolicited kindness. But she pushed that stray thought aside; she would not be satisfied until she had Garvanna.

The walk did not feel long, and Caelfel wondered why she and Garvanna had not escaped the wolves sooner. Brenin gestured toward the base of a tree. "You were lying here."

Caelfel inspected the tree. It looked like the one she had climbed, before she had been surrounded. Then she had jumped to the ground. Then—the *alpha*.

Caelfel stroked the rough bark of the tree where claw marks had defaced it. She remembered the lumbering wolf, the largest of them all. She had no doubt now that he was the alpha. He had swung at her—then she fell.

As she recalled these events, she gently reached up and touched the side of her face. Sure enough, the skin of her temple was tender, and her fingers lightly brushed against four faint scratches. Caelfel was only surprised that they were not deeper.

Then other memories came to her, and she searched around the trees for the bodies of the fallen wolves. Evidence of their skirmish was clearly visible, but wolf corpses were markedly absent. Caelfel could not even find her discarded arrows. She looked to Brenin. "Were there no wolves when you arrived? Not even dead ones?"

Brenin shook his head. "There was only you."

Caelfel tapped her chin and did not understand. If the wolves she thought were dead had survived, she assumed that they would have finished her off, eaten her, whatever they wanted. Then the only explanation that made sense—

Garvanna.

Caelfel reached to climb the tree. The humans around her started, and she heard Cyrus mention to Brenin the poor judgment of her decision. But Caelfel gritted her teeth through the pain and climbed high enough so that she could see a large expanse of the forest.

"*Garvanna!*" she called through the dank and desolate trees.

The only response that greeted her was the flapping of startled birds. The rest of the forest was silent, the humans below her tense should the wolves reappear.

But Caelfel was heedless of this. She called Garvanna's named repeatedly, louder each time, until finally some time later, her voice gave out to choking sobs that racked her body. Caelfel finally accepted the conclusion that the humans had already gathered hours before, but they could in no way understand the sadness welling through her throat.

She was trapped in an accursed forest with an incompetent healer. Her friend, her only companion was gone. And she was *alone*.

She could choose to return to the Fey Forest, return to her home city of Sal'Sumarathar and be greeted warmly by her parents. But now that she was weakened by her grief, the injury that plagued her abdomen slowly began to overcome her senses. She could not travel with it. She would never make it back to Honey Water. She would have to heal first.

And deciding this, she swallowed the last sob and slowly descended the tree.

Time must have passed differently for the humans. The soldiers had scattered, wandering off in a perimeter. Cyrus had a small book that he now returned to his front pocket. Only Brenin seemed to have the patience of the elves, waiting loyally next to the tree for her. She glanced at his face that had so many questions.

But Caelfel was not ready to speak. Her silent acceptance was indication enough for them to leave. They departed the Pirinac Forest in a reticent procession. Only when leaving the shadow of the trees did Brenin brave the unknown and attempted conversation with an elf.

"Was Garvanna the name of your friend? Was she an elf too?" he asked.

Caelfel nodded numbly. "Her name was Garvanna Hunithrae, and she was beautiful and powerful," she said, whispering the last words in reverent fondness.

"What is your name?" Brenin pressed.

"Caelfel," she sighed.

Brenin, doing nothing for human intelligence, paused at this. "Cow field?"

Caelfel's energy returned to her as she angrily rounded on him. "My name is *Caelfel* and it sounds *nothing* like *cow field.*"

He raised his hands in a peaceful gesture. "Caelfel. My apologies." She did not think his accent did her name justice but accepted it over his first effort. The metal-clad soldiers dispersed, but Cyrus remained with them until a nod from Brenin dismissed him. Caelfel didn't comment on the exchange, the pain from her wound was now worse than ever. She breathed slowly, hoping it would subside. It did not.

"Those weren't normal wolves," she said once they reached her tent.

The dark expression that flashed across Brenin's face confirmed this. "They are werewolves."

"Why did they attack us?" she asked. "I am not sure how we provoked them." Caelfel gripped the wooden post that tethered her tent to the ground for support.

"They are very protective of their territory. I can only assume that you and your friend wandered just within their territorial bounds." Brenin sighed. "But they are still human and they know the laws. I cannot understand what has made them so aggressive."

"They've attacked other people before?" Caelfel asked.

"There was a girl from Sorasaen that has recently gone missing. We suspect it was them, though Sorasaen does not lie within their territory."

Caelfel frowned. "And you have done nothing about this?" She couldn't keep the accusation from her voice.

"We have done everything we can for the moment," he snapped, showing whatever strain he felt. When Caelfel flinched, he added in a softer tone, "That is why the Company is here, but an elusive pack of werewolves is not a force I am quite so ready to confront."

Caelfel could not blame him but did not say so. Her wound throbbed painfully, and her knuckles turned white as she gripped the wood post tightly.

Noticing her discomfort, Brenin said, "Perhaps you should go and rest. Your injury looked very serious."

Caelfel nodded and disappeared behind the tent flap. She was relieved that he did not follow her. She shuffled slowly towards her cot but collapsed onto the dusty ground before she reached it. A groan of pain escaped her lips, but she quickly silenced it. Biting down on her tongue, she lifted her shirt and peeled away the bandages, becoming alarmed when she felt how slick and sticky her skin was beneath them.

Her breath stopped when she saw her wound. Her abdomen was sliced open from ribs to hip, and the threads that appeared to have, at one time, stitched the opposing pieces of skin together now hung loose and ineffective at the ragged edges of the wound. Her previous, ill-considered activity had ripped apart the stitches, and a liberal amount of blood poured from her reopened wound. The sight caused her to freeze, helpless as more blood flowed over her hands. With shallow breaths, she slowly reached up and gripped the edge of her cot. Black spots danced in front of her eyes, and she prayed to Mother Ewyn to spare her from this humiliating death. She squeezed her eyes shut and sluggishly counted the seconds as all the energy drained from her body.

In her semi-conscious state, what happened next seemed like an unlikely miracle. Someone entered her tent with a half-uttered question on his lips before seeing her collapsed on the floor. He shouted for someone to get their useless healer. When Caelfel opened her eyes, her head swimming with nausea, she saw Brenin's face in front of her. He pressed two fingers against her neck and ran his other hand across her brow.

"What have you done? I should not have allowed you to go into the forest," he said angrily.

Caelfel could only offer him a half-hearted glare, which was the most vehement response she could muster in her critical state.

The healer, Edilon, reentered with a hot needle in his hands. It only had to touch Caelfel's skin twice before she passed out from the pain.

When she awoke, the tent and the cot were the same. She tried to move, only to find that leather straps kept her bound to the bed. The room seemed to tilt as she struggled against her restraints. Her frustration escaped her lips in a series of grunts, and when she looked up, she found she was not alone.

"Be still," Brenin told her. "You don't want to reopen your wound."

"I don't want to be tied down," she said, thrashing.

"We have to make sure you don't move—"

"*I don't want to be tied down*," she hissed again. She had been bound before when she had been kidnapped by humans. The memory sent her into a frenzied panic. "Please, I promise I won't move. Just untie me."

Brenin looked taken aback by the sudden urgency in her voice and he must have understood that there was something wrong, because he nodded and went to free her. She sighed in relief once the leather straps were removed, and rubbed her wrists where they had been bound. She felt smug to see that Brenin looked to be ashamed of himself.

"I'm sorry," he said and paused. "You almost died, again. Please, just keep good on your promise."

Caelfel didn't say anything and refused to look at him. He lingered in her tent, however, which made her think he had more to say.

Eventually, he did. "There is something that I would like to ask before the Company leaves. What were you doing out here?"

"How do you mean?" she asked curtly.

"What brings you to the Pirinac forest? I know it's not my business, but elves haven't been seen around here in centuries. We know you exist in Honey Water, but elves are the stuff of legend to humans. Unless your race usually travels in secret and you were only exposed this time because of the werewolves?" His suggestion held a note of hope.

Caelfel looked down at her hands. "No, the elves do not like to wander. My race prefers to stay within the boundaries of the Fey

Forest. I seem to be the exception. I wanted to travel, and my friend and I were headed to a city called Palpses. We had heard there was a celebration for one of your goddesses."

Brenin stared at her for the longest time. "You want to go to Palpses?" he repeated slowly.

Caelfel nodded, wondering if something might be wrong. "Have you heard of the city or the celebration?"

Brenin cracked a smile. "How have I not? Palpses is the capital of Kanetalm, and the celebration is the Festival of Strigi. As it happens, the Company of the Prince is headed to the capital for that very festival. You are welcome to travel with us."

"How can I travel if I cannot even leave this bed?" Caelfel asked irritably.

The amusement did not leave Brenin's face. "It seems that you will have to be carried, Lady Elf." He left her tent, laughing at her indignant expression. His laughter reminded her of Feraan, and Caelfel wished the comparison had not come to mind, for this man was nothing like Feraan.

The Company of the Prince had dismantled their camp and were ready to depart by the time the sky began to brighten in the east. Caelfel could only lie there helplessly as, true to Brenin's word, she was placed on a litter supported by two men. One of them was the healer Edilon, and the other was one of the soldiers, a brute of a man who identified himself as Huwel. Caelfel remembered him from the ill-fated excursion into the forest the previous day. Then the Company of the Prince set off.

She had always heard of the inferior qualities of humans. They were weaker, slower, and infinitely more stupid than their elvish counterparts. Despite this knowledge, Caelfel had no desire to experience it first-hand, and the slow pace of the Company exasperated and infuriated Caelfel. Travelling in itself was a maddeningly boring pastime. However, travelling while being physically incapable of doing anything was much worse. The landscape was boring and monotonous, offering nothing but gently rolling farmland. When they passed cow pastures, Caelfel turned up her nose at the plodding beasts.

When they stopped for a break around noon, Caelfel would wager they had not even covered twenty-five miles and she did nothing to disguise her irritation at their slow progress. Edilon merely gave her a puzzled look and scratched his beard before retrieving food for the three of them. Huwel, Caelfel noticed, was a man of good spirits, often laughing at everything she said, and her comment on their speed was no exception.

"It is not funny," Caelfel persisted, rubbing her side. "I've never met a slower army, and the two of you walk like cows, always jostling me about. You've provided me nothing but discomfort."

Huwel laughed some more. "For all of their bluster, I do not think elves have built up much tolerance against pain. You are so short of temper, my lady."

Caelfel frowned at him, but Huwel ignored her and eagerly dug a spoon in the bowl of gruel Edilon handed him. The healer offered Caelfel an identical bowl, but after a suspicious sniff, she declined it with as much grace as she could muster. Edilon would not even allow her to sit up, and though she was ill-tempered, she acquiesced to his demands lest he decide to tie her down again.

Brenin approached them after some time, hovering above where they sat. "How is the lady elf getting on?" he asked.

"She is tired," Caelfel informed him crossly. "These soldiers are slow. *This* one," she started, pointing at Edilon. "Is nothing but an overbearing bull, and the other one laughs all the time."

A hint of surprise flashed through Brenin's face as he looked between the accused men. "I assure you, Lady Elf, they are nothing but admirable company."

"*My name*," she said, exasperated. "My name is Caelfel. I am not a *lady*. I am not royal; I am only a ranger," she sighed dramatically.

Brenin suffered a grin. "And their names are Edilon and Huwel, and they are good men," he countered. "We have done nothing but help you. Your callous treatment of them is unwarranted."

Caelfel felt as though she had been smacked in the face as a wave of shame passed through her. She averted her eyes but told Brenin in a low voice, "I have a good reason to be leery of humans."

"I assure you, Miss Caelfel, that the Company has given you no such reason," he said lifting his chin. "Try to be gracious for our efforts."

At this, Huwel gave another laugh, jabbing his dirty spoon towards Caelfel. "At least she is light. I would expect even someone of her size to weigh much more."

Caelfel glanced at Huwel sideways, and her lips curved into a half-smile. "It is said that the elves have hollow bones, like a bird. Mother Ewyn gave them to us so that we might fly."

Brenin staggered at this, his interest immediately piqued. "Is that true?"

Caelfel's smile faltered slightly. "No, it would just make our bones easier to break. Besides, we can't fly."

Brenin's eyes glazed over as he nodded, cataloging the information. Caelfel watched as Edilon and Huwel respectfully inclined their heads as Brenin departed. Caelfel wondered at the authority Brenin's retreating back held.

"Who is he?" Caelfel asked, pegging him for some sort of lord or thane.

Edilon, the ever-silent ox, kept his eyes on his bowl as he stirred the contents. "That is a man forced into the wrong path in life." The spoon was brought to his mouth as Edilon considered his own answer. "Perhaps not a wrong path. He will do well but he will probably be unhappy."

Before the Company of the Prince continued on their path, Edilon removed her bandages to check her wound. His mouth fell open as he marveled at it.

"It is healing rather quickly," he said.

Caelfel looked down at the puckered, broken skin and the dried blood that still caked around the edges. It still hurt her immensely and did not look any better to her. "Should it not be washed?" she asked.

"I did not want to risk opening the wound before, because you were bleeding so much," Edilon said but he instructed Huwel to fetch some water. When Huwel rejoined them, Edilon expertly dabbed at her wound with a damp rag until he was satisfied with the cleanliness. Then he carefully pulled out the stitches as Huwel issued a low whistle at the sight.

Then they were moving again, and Caelfel sighed, resigning herself to the long, tiresome journey ahead. When she asked how far away Palpses was, Edilon said that they had another day before them. Caelfel put in an effort to hide her groan.

"Do you have a mate?" Huwel asked suddenly.

Caelfel's eyes flew open. Their road now wound through a field that still lay fallow from the previous winter. Caelfel could see a provincial hamlet with mud huts and thatched roofing dotting the horizon of the afternoon sun. Though lackluster in appearance,

Caelfel would take this quiet scenery over the desert. "Excuse me?" she asked sharply, responding to Huwel's question.

"Do you have a mate?" he repeated. "You know—a husband? Betrothed? A lover, even?"

Caelfel's stomach clenched and not from her injury. The painful memory of a handsome face lingered at the fringe of her mind, but she pushed it away. "I have none of those, not that it is any of your business."

"So you are available for suitors?" Huwel pressed.

Edilon intervened on Caelfel's behalf. "Do you plan to beguile her, Huwel?"

"You cannot blame me for trying," Huwel said.

Caelfel lifted herself slightly to look at Huwel, who held the side of the litter her head was on. She laughed as he winked at her. "I am probably nothing but an old hag to you," she told him gently, remembering their differences in aging.

Huwel grinned, and his mouth stretched too big for his square face. "You look like a fair maiden to me, miss."

Caelfel's smile turned sad. "And I will continue to look this way, even when you are dust in your grave."

The idea did not deter him. "All the better, for they will all envy me for having such a pretty maiden in my bedside."

Caelfel found herself laughing again. She asked Edilon, "Is he always like this?"

She could hear Edilon's smile in the healer's voice as he answered, "You mean arrogant and shameless? Yes, he is."

As Caelfel laughed a third time at their antics, she discovered that perhaps she could grow fond of humans. But the deep ache for Garvanna still throbbed in the center of her chest and even deeper was the ache for the lover who had refused her, so her laugh was short as she solemnly lowered her head back to the litter. Huwel would never be able to compare to Feraan, and Caelfel was beginning to doubt anyone ever would.

3. Kingly

The Company of the Prince stopped the next day at a place Edilon named as Fort Wymdall. It was customarily used as a barracks for soldiers like the Company of the Prince, and Edilon told her many would not continue onto Palpses.

"But how much further is the city?" Caelfel asked, surprised to feel herself growing panicked at the thought of losing the loud soldiers she had grown accustomed to.

In answer, Edilon and Huwel turned Caelfel in the litter and pointed to a sprawling city on the horizon. "Not even an hour's ride. And I suspect many of us will go to attend the Festival of Strigi." Caelfel eyed the distant capital for a long minute before her carriers took her into the stone walls of Fort Wymdall.

They deposited her in a dark and drafty room, where the only thing not made of stone was the wooden bedframe and its straw mattress. Edilon checked her injury once more with Huwel lingering nearby. The skin on her stomach had knitted itself together, with nothing to show for it save a puffy, pink scar.

"I am not familiar with the ways of elves, but it appears that you heal much more quickly than we do. You should be fine to walk on your own now, but do not overexert yourself and rest when you begin to feel tired."

Caelfel breathed a sigh of relief, swinging her legs over the mattress as she sat up.

Edilon stood to leave. "Do not look so impatient. That was a remarkable recovery time. Most men would be bedridden for weeks."

Huwel laughed at Caelfel's horrified expression.

"But stay put," Edilon instructed. "It is not a clever idea for an elf to wander around this fortress."

"I can handle myself," Caelfel sniffed.

"I've no doubt, but try not to exert yourself. Huwel will bring some dinner up for you if you will finally eat something."

Caelfel nodded, and they left. She sighed impatiently once she was alone.

The fort was full of noises, the boisterous sounds of competitive men. Caelfel guessed the kitchens must have been nearby. She stretched her arms behind her head just as she heard voices drifting into her room.

"We never made our rounds to Haradrop." The voice belonged to Cyrus, and Caelfel saw Brenin and his steward passing by her doorway.

Caelfel sat up. "I have heard of Haradrop," she called to them.

Brenin paused at her voice, and Cyrus obediently hung back to wait for his master. Brenin met Caelfel's gaze before his eyes swept across the room. He did not mention Haradrop as he asked, "Are you allowed to be up?"

Caelfel frowned. "Your healer has permitted it."

"Have you eaten anything?" he asked.

"Huwel was retrieving something for me to eat."

Brenin nodded, looking down the hall. "Please excuse us." Then Brenin disappeared with Cyrus at his heels. He returned shortly without Cyrus, a tray of boiled greens in his hands.

"What is that?" Caelfel asked, wrinkling her nose.

"I've told Huwel that I would bring you your food. I know that elves have peculiar diets and avoid meat."

Caelfel nodded slowly, taking the tray warily in her hands. "We usually eat fresh vegetables," she explained apologetically as she swallowed the greens. They were not entirely repulsive, but Caelfel still longed for the produce of her mother's garden. Besides, it would have been impolite to throw the food away with Brenin staring. But then she realized how much he stared at her and, deciding that that was not polite of him, Caelfel set the plate aside. "Can I help you with something?"

"I wanted to ask you a few things. Elves have always fascinated me."

Caelfel attempted a weak smile and made a gesture for him to continue.

Brenin settled himself on the floor, crossing his legs. "How old are you?"

Caelfel was taken aback by the question. She deliberated, struggling to remember how long the humans lived. "How old is the oldest person here?"

Brenin shrugged. "Around fifty perhaps."

This made Caelfel chuckle. "I am older than that. Fifty is the age an elf reaches maturity. Garvanna is centuries older than me."

"I *am* sorry about your friend. If I had known that there was someone else—"

Caelfel raised her hand to stop him. "What happened to Garvanna was not your fault. The only thing you can do is resolve the werewolf issue. What do you intend to do about them?"

Brenin ran his fingers through his hair. "We have tried negotiating, but I fear the Company of the Prince will have to confront them directly."

"Whatever happens, Garvanna's death must not be forgotten. That is blood that had no reason to be spilled. We were *attacked*," she said severely.

And Brenin, whose mere presence bowed the heads of the soldiers and whose steward loyally obeyed his every word, nodded at her words. "I know. It shall not be forgotten."

Caelfel looked at him curiously, before sliding to the floor to join him. "How old are *you*?"

"I am twenty-two," he answered slowly.

Caelfel couldn't help but laugh. "If you were an elf, you would not reach past my waist. What are you exactly? You don't look like much of a soldier to me, not even a fancy general."

Brenin offered her a grim smile. "It is not my preference but it is my duty."

"But *why* is it your duty?" Caelfel asked, leaning closer to him. "You are not even half the age of the oldest man here yet you make everyone bow their heads as you pass."

"I don't make everyone bow their heads. That is my birthright," Brenin answered evasively. At this, he rose to his feet. He made a move to leave but paused, turning back to her. "I must ask one last time before we enter the city."

Caelfel nodded for him to continue.

"Is it truly your desire to go to Palpses?"

"Yes, of course. That is where the festival is being held, is it not?"

Brenin struggled to say what was on his mind. "Then I must warn you. Once we enter Palpses, the king of Umfeld will learn of your presence. I am bound by duty to take you to him, and he may not let you leave."

Caelfel looked at her knees as she considered his words. "Why are you telling me this?"

"I am warning you of what to expect. You've been given reason not to trust men, and I don't want there to be a reason for you to not trust us, to not trust me. All men are not the same. We are not all brutal savages like you may think. You *can* trust me, Caelfel."

Caelfel was stunned by his words, recalling another lonely soul who had requested her trust. And, as she had then, she granted it now, hoping that this time it would not end with a broken heart. "That is noble and kind of you. Thank you, Brenin."

"Once we enter Palpses, I'll do everything in my power to keep you safe."

"I don't need protection," she snapped, remembering how Feraan had once called her an infant in constant need of attention and protection.

Brenin faltered. "Are you sure this is what you want?"

Caelfel was not afraid of entering the city and did not understand why he was being so unrelenting. "Would the king of Umfeld harm me?" she asked uncertainly.

Brenin's laugh was humorless. "No, he would merely be curious because you are an elf. Humans tend to hoard any treasures they might find, and the king isn't one to let something of value go so easily."

Caelfel nodded, absently rubbing the scar on her stomach. "I would like to have my bow back before we leave for Palpses and I want to practice with it, to build up my strength."

Brenin smiled, and this time it was genuine. "That can easily be arranged. Cyrus will visit you in the morning and take you to the practice range. Be sure that you are ready." He opened the door to leave.

"I will be," Caelfel promised eagerly. She expected him to depart then, but Brenin lingered in the doorway. "Was there something else?" she asked.

"Are you sure you are well enough? Your wound has healed completely?"

"Yes, it has. Your healer has permitted it. You worry worse than my mother. She nearly let me drown when she was teaching me how to swim." Caelfel laughed at the memory, but the sound was suddenly hollow to her ears as she was unexpectedly seized by a bout of homesickness.

Brenin laughed softly with her, and it made Caelfel feel slightly better. "That was a remarkably fast recovery. May I see it?" he asked tentatively.

"My wound?" Caelfel asked. Then without a second thought, she lifted the bottom of her shirt to show him.

Brenin closed the door again and sank to his knees for a better look. He lightly traced the lines of her scar as if he also did not spare a second thought. Her skin quivered beneath his touch, and Caelfel suddenly felt herself flush as she realized the intimacy of the situation. She held very still as she waited for Brenin's reaction.

"Amazing," Brenin breathed, neither ashamed nor embarrassed. He fluidly straightened up.

Caelfel considered remarking upon how Elidon was similarly amazed at her recovery, but she could not form the words as she silently pulled her shirt back down. Brenin finally left her then, bidding her a pleasant night.

When Caelfel was alone, she wrapped her arms around herself and returned to the bed. Brenin's light touch reminded her of someone, and she was once more unsuccessful at banishing Feraan from her thoughts that night.

Caelfel was awake by dawn, but Cyrus didn't retrieve her until a few hours later. Humans must be very lazy if they didn't begin their day until hours after dawn, but Caelfel followed Cyrus all the same, noticing how their circuitous route avoided the busiest corridors.

"Am I not supposed to be here?" Caelfel asked once she realized this.

"You are welcome here, miss," was all Cyrus would volunteer.

Caelfel pursed her lips and said nothing more. As a steward, she preferred Cyrus over Lisiek but she could not bring herself to fully trust him. Once they were outside, Caelfel paused to blink in the bright sunlight. As she looked around, she saw that Fort Wymdall was not like the Cromlech Fortress in the desert. The road the Company of the Prince had arrived on ran through the grounds of the fort, passing through two wide gates that stood open in either wall. The stones were not glossy black but the dull gray of limestone. And the grounds were larger than the barracks themselves and primarily devoted to training. Fort Wymdall had no palace, probably because it was not owned by an arrogant admiral who fancied himself as nobility.

To her surprise, Cyrus took her on the road that started to lead them outside the fortress. When they approached the gate, Caelfel saw why. The archery ranges were too big to fit within the walls of the fortress. Soldiers honed their archery skills by climbing to the top of the parapets and shooting at targets arranged in the field beyond the fort's walls. Cyrus turned just before reaching the gate and ascended a winding stairwell at the top of which stood Brenin and some other archers. Caelfel left Cyrus's side and approached Brenin.

"My bow?" she asked once she realized his hands were empty.

Brenin cracked a smile. "I hope you don't mind, but some of the others are testing it."

Caelfel suddenly noticed Huwel nearby, her bow in his hands. She watched him a moment and then laughed with Brenin when she realized why her companion was amused. Huwel was a large man with thick, brutish arms but he did not have the strength to draw her bow.

"Huwel is not an archer but he is one of our strongest soldiers. He wanted to give your bow a try. So far, no one has been able to use it," Brenin explained.

Caelfel was still chuckling as she approached Huwel. She held her hands out for her bow. "Shall I show you how it is done?"

Huwel handed it over begrudgingly along with a quiver of arrows fletched with brown feathers. She nocked an arrow and easily drew back the string. It took very little effort for her, but Caelfel supposed she was used to the weight of it. She released the arrow, and it landed in the center of the furthest target.

She lowered her bow to the sound of praise from the soldiers around them. "Why are your targets so close?"

Brenin was confused. "Those are the standard distances based on army regulations."

Caelfel shrugged, deciding not to press the matter. The elves were superior in every respect. It was why Caelfel had the strength to draw the string of her own bow and it was why the elven archers' targets were at least twice the distance of those at Fort Wymdall. But Caelfel enjoyed the praise, so she released a few more arrows to impress them. Huwel was the loudest of them all.

Caelfel turned to see if she had moved Brenin with her performance, but Brenin's attention was claimed elsewhere. Cyrus had approached him, and Caelfel could make out the steward's faint words. "My lord, we should really depart for the capital."

Brenin nodded in response and, when he caught Caelfel staring, asked, "Are you ready to go to Palpses?"

She nodded eagerly, shouldered her bow, and followed Brenin off the wall. As promised, only two guards prepared to escort them to the capital. Caelfel was disappointed that neither Huwel nor Edilon were among them. Brenin and Caelfel waited by the gates while Cyrus and the guards went to retrieve the horses.

"Are you certain of this?" Brenin asked again.

Caelfel rolled her eyes. "I am very certain, *my lord*."

Brenin stiffened. "You don't have to call me that." The discomfort was audible in his voice.

"Cyrus calls you that."

"Cyrus is my steward."

"But why do you need a steward? Are you some kind of general or something?" Caelfel paused. "Please tell me you're not an admiral. I've had a very horrid experience with one."

Brenin's discomfort vanished as he laughed at her statement. "I promise you, I am not an admiral."

Caelfel would have pressed for more information, but Cyrus and the guards joined them with the horses. Then they set off for Palpses.

As Edilon had said the previous day, the ride to Palpses took less than an hour. One soldier led their procession while the second brought up the rear. As they drew closer, Caelfel could make out the stone wall that surrounded the city, similar to the one at Fort Wymdall. When the gatekeepers guarding the entrance to Palpses recognized Brenin, they hurried to open the gates. Caelfel was surprised no one dismounted. She had expected that horses would not be allowed into the city.

"Shouldn't the gates be opened for the festival?" Brenin asked one of the guards. Caelfel glanced at a collection of colorful tents erected around the front gate.

The gatekeeper in question straightened, reassuring his grip on a spear when he was addressed. "The king has commanded that the gates not be opened until you returned, my lord."

Caelfel noticed Brenin's hand clench at that. "So he is already here?"

"Yes, my lord."

"When is the festival again?" Caelfel asked once they passed through the gate.

"In two days," was all Brenin could say before the five of them were enveloped by a surging crowd.

Caelfel's sharp eyes scanned the sea of faces that had so quickly accosted them. The main road of Palpses twisted to the crest of the hill where the palace sat. Currently they were at the bottom of the hill, where the small shops and dirty hems of the rabble suggested a working class. The people around them had kind faces and reached to touch their boots, their horses, or whatever else they could get their hands on. Caelfel was stunned into a numb silence and tensed when someone touched her ankle.

Brenin was not so stunned. He smiled at them and uttered soft, gentle words. Most of the crowd's attention was on him until Caelfel's eyes met the gaze of a young girl riding the shoulders of her elder. The girl's gray eyes went wide when she saw Caelfel, and she pointed directly at her. "Elf!"

The small voice instantly silenced the crowd as every eye turned to Caelfel. The crowd took two full seconds to process Caelfel's existence before they swarmed her.

Caelfel only heard a few requests to bless their infants and fields before more soldiers appeared to escort them to the palace. The people parted ahead of their group easily after that, and Caelfel wasn't able to admire the human city as she would have liked.

"I don't understand what just happened," Caelfel whispered to Brenin. She felt alarmed. "Why did they want me to bless their infants?"

They dismounted at the stables outside the palace, and Brenin answered, "It's like what I said before. Elves are mostly legend here."

"But I don't know how to bless an infant," Caelfel persisted, but her complaints went ignored as they were ushered inside the palace.

The walls were made of deep, rich mahogany. The tiled floor was polished to a mirror-like sheen. Caelfel could easily make out her own features in the blue-gray flagstones of the entrance hall. She had been too busy gazing at the floor that she nearly missed the various diplomats that approached Brenin with bent heads. Brenin sent them all away with a wave of his hand. Cyrus pushed past the guard and spoke softly to one of the people that had approached Brenin. Caelfel was too preoccupied eyeing the scenic carvings on the wall to listen to his words.

Cyrus turned to Brenin. "He is just in the keep, sire."

Brenin nodded and, without sparing another glance at Caelfel, he led them away from the entrance hall. Caelfel's mind whirred as she wondered what they were about to do, and she looked at Brenin more closely. His clothing, while humble in color, had a tailored quality she had not seen elsewhere. But the keep was just beyond the entrance hall, so she could not complete her inspection. The guards stopped before the door, and Cyrus hung back with them. Caelfel paused uncertainly, wondering if she should wait with them.

But Cyrus nodded encouragingly, so she followed Brenin into the keep.

The keep was much larger than any room Caelfel had seen before, reaching up far beyond her head and stretching a great length in front of her. One wall was comprised of magnificent glass windows that arched at the top. Through them, Caelfel could see the expanse of Palpses. Two banquet tables lined the room, and a raised platform at the end of the hall held a single, glorious chair crafted from a lustrous metal. A throne, Caelfel realized. Servants flew around the room with appropriated tasks.

But Caelfel soon realized that the flurry of activity revolved around the center of the room and a single individual. One man did not move. He stood in profile to them, facing the windows overlooking Palpses. He was tall for a human, though not taller than Caelfel, and he wore a long, black fur coat that draped to the floor. His overall countenance was severe, with a sharply aquiline nose and dark brown hair streaked with gray tied at the nape of his neck. One of the servants stopped, seeing them, and whispered in the man's ear who did not acknowledge he had heard anything. He sent the servant away with a wave of his hand.

"This is one of those times that I so dearly miss your mother. She loved organizing these feasts. I was never so good at it," said the man.

Brenin checked himself. He would have been as tall as the man, Caelfel saw, if he did not have a bad habit of slouching. "I miss her for other reasons."

"Of course. You think I am being insensitive." The man finally turned, his brown eyes briefly resting on Brenin before settling on Caelfel. He smiled at her, and Caelfel couldn't read its intention. "I heard about the commotion you caused when you entered the city. An elf comes to Umfeld."

Brenin turned to her. "Caelfel meet King Orrik of Umfeld, my father."

Caelfel had easily inferred that this man was the king, so it was not the former part of Brenin's introduction, but rather the latter that caused her to turn her eyes sharply to her companion. King Orrik of Umfeld was Brenin's father. This made Brenin a prince, not a wishful princeling like Grimault, but a full blooded prince. The prince of Kanetalm.

King Orrik continued speaking. "Welcome to Kanetalm. I assume you are here to enjoy the festivities. I apologize for my son's behavior. Prince Brenin is often discourteous and lazy, and I am sure he has made no exception in your case."

Caelfel squared her shoulders in defense of Brenin. "I've found him to be very attentive." She forced herself to smile at this man, for he was a king after all. "My name is Caelfel Gyssedlues. I am indebted to your son. Brenin saved my life."

Orrik continued to examine her. "Forgive me for staring. I am most curious about the reason behind your presence. You *are* staying for the festival, I presume?"

Caelfel nodded slowly, unwilling to divulge any more information as she recalled her earlier conversation with Brenin concerning the king.

"Marvelous," Orrik purred. "I will have someone show you to your rooms shortly. It is my wish that you find everything to your liking. You are most welcome here, Lady Elf."

Caelfel was about to correct King Orrik, for she was not a noble, but Brenin silenced her with a slight shake of his head.

King Orrik turned to his son. "And you are very late. You were supposed to be back days ago."

"I didn't finish my tour. We encountered some problems," Brenin began to explain.

"I don't want to hear your excuses and I would rather not disagree with you here. Just get everything ready for the festival. We have dignitaries coming for tomorrow night's feast. Try to be on your best behavior."

Brenin exhaled sharply through his nose. "What sort of dignitaries will be visiting the palace?"

There was something in Orrik's face that resembled amusement. "Mostly your brother and his court."

Something changed in Brenin. Caelfel felt him tense beside her. "*Madoc* is coming to Kanetalm?"

The amusement grew in Orrik's face. "Yes, and he should arrive tomorrow. You would not be so surprised by this if you had arrived back in the city when you were meant to." The air between father and son was charged uncomfortably, and Caelfel felt uneasy witnessing a family dispute and a royal one at that. But then Brenin seemed to force himself to relax, as if he suddenly remembered Caelfel standing there. "If there is nothing else, your majesty," he said.

Orrik waved them off. "There isn't. Show our guest to her room."

"Which room should she take?" Brenin asked.

Orrik considered this before a wicked smiled touched his features. "She will take the queen's rooms."

Taking the queen's rooms sounded inappropriate even to Caelfel, but the reaction of everyone in the room made it feel as though she had committed a mortal sin. The servants all froze in their tasks, eyeing this foreign thief who would take the rooms that had belonged to their beloved queen. Brenin asked, "Mother's rooms?"

Orrik leveled his gaze. "Your mother is dead. She isn't going to need them."

This didn't make Caelfel more receptive to the idea, but arguing with a king would be rude and in poor taste. She followed Brenin out of the keep, and as they passed Cyrus, Brenin told the steward to prepare the queen's rooms for Caelfel. Cyrus concealed whatever reaction he may have had and left with a nod. This left Caelfel alone with Brenin in the entrance hall, all the guards having disappeared. She turned angrily to Brenin.

"You did not tell me you were a prince," she said.

Brenin frowned. "I did not think it mattered."

"Secrets are not conducive for a friendship." Caelfel shook her head. Feraan had kept many secrets from her, though now that she considered it, Brenin's nobility seemed glaringly obvious.

"Would it have changed anything if I told you?"

"It matters that you lied," she countered.

"I did not want you to think differently of me just because I have had the fortune to be the son of a king."

She sucked in a breath, calming herself. "The Company of the Prince? That means it's *your* army?"

Brenin looked away, probably feeling ashamed of himself.

Caelfel playfully pushed him. "A prince, then? I knew you didn't look like a soldier." They laughed, and then Caelfel hesitated. "I am sorry about your mother and her rooms."

He shrugged. "She died years ago in Onusal, so you don't have to worry about her ghost haunting you."

Caelfel gave Brenin a confused look. "Ghost?"

Brenin shrugged. The bedrooms were on the second floor of the palace, so they climbed a grand staircase that Caelfel couldn't keep her eyes off of. "You are so fascinated by everything," Brenin said laughing at her.

"It is very dark inside your palace," Caelfel said, not addressing his comment as she removed her hand from the banister. Her stomach clenched when the dark halls reminded her of the Cromlech palace in the desert. She quickly changed subjects. "Madoc is your brother?"

And then Brenin's face darkened. "Yes."

"Are you angry with your brother?"

Brenin relented in a sigh, and it made his shoulders slump. "I could never be angry with Madoc."

"But he makes you unhappy?" Caelfel pressed.

"He doesn't," Brenin struggled, growing annoyed. "It's difficult to explain. Madoc is older."

"Ah," Caelfel realized, snapping her fingers. "So you are jealous of him."

"No," Brenin said weakly but he didn't put up a good argument against it.

"You should be thankful. I don't have any siblings but I've always wanted one." Caelfel sighed wistfully. "I am doomed to be an only child."

"Why is that?" Brenin asked, becoming amused.

"Father is very old. It was lucky that I was even born," Caelfel said. "They said it wasn't likely he could sire any children."

"But he sired you," Brenin prompted when she had fallen silent, lost in her thoughts. They were on the second floor and reached the end of the hall where a portrait of a beautiful woman hung.

"Who is this?" Caelfel asked, but she could easily guess. The woman in the portrait had the same soft brown eyes and straight nose as Brenin, and it was immediately apparent which parent he favored in appearance.

"That is Queen Fronia, my mother."

"You look very much like her. I take after my mother as well. Her name is Sylaera, and she is a very powerful mage. She nearly brought down an entire fortress on her own. She was born into the nobility of our city."

"Then we *can* call you Lady Caelfel," Brenin said with a grin.

"No, you can't. She disagreed with her parents, and they shunned her, exiled her from the family. She lost her inheritance, her birthright, her title. But it's all right. She says it doesn't bother her."

"Do you believe her?"

"Why wouldn't I? If it didn't happen, she would have never met my father and had me."

"How did she meet your father?"

"My father used to be a healer before I was born. Mother was injured in a goblin raid and he tended to her injuries. They didn't tell me the specifics of what happened, but I understand that Mother left his tent, vowing that Father would be hers."

She expected Brenin to laugh then, but his brow furrowed in confusion on a small detail. "A goblin raid?" he repeated.

"Yes, we have them regularly."

"Goblins?" he said, stunned.

"Yes," Caelfel repeated, impatient. "Tiny, nasty creatures that live underground."

She sensed Brenin was about to inquire further when a polite cough from Cyrus standing nearby interrupted them. The steward inclined his head toward his prince, and Brenin turned to Caelfel. "I will show you to your rooms."

Before being given the queen's chambers, Caelfel had expected one room, a bedchamber with enough space to hold the meager possessions she had with her. As a traveler, that was all she needed, but it occurred to her that a queen would have a personal space more lavish and luxurious than that. And when Brenin opened the door for her, she saw that the late Queen Fronia certainly had had rooms to boast about.

There was first the entryway that any visitors would be received in, a small room with a padded bench and large doors flanked by two guards in livery. Beyond that was a room Brenin described as a parlor, where guests were entertained or when the queen decided to conduct her business in private. The parlor was large enough to comfortably keep a sitting area, desk, dining table, and bookshelves with walking space to spare. The actual bedroom was revealed when Cyrus slid back the wooden doors next to the dining table. Brenin explained he did not have to accompany her there, for it was usually considered inappropriate.

Caelfel marveled at the size of the parlor, too dumbstruck to even venture into the bedroom. She recalled her own room at her parents' house with fondness, missing the comfort of a smaller room. "And these are all mine? No one else uses these rooms?" she asked uncertainly. She hardly expected to entertain diplomats in her chambers when she had only come to Palpses for a simple festival.

Brenin nodded. "They are yours to use until you decide you do not want them."

Caelfel didn't miss the note of anxiety in his voice but didn't remark on it as she wandered towards the bedroom. There was a light airiness to the room caused by the floor-to-ceiling glass windows that dominated the entire left wall. These windows did not overlook the city as the ones in the throne room had. Instead, these afforded a view of the desolate, yet starkly beautiful moors, which were so characteristic of Kanetalm.

And though he had already described it as inappropriate, Brenin wandered into the bedroom with her. Cyrus appropriately kept his distance, remaining in the parlor. Brenin joined her at the window. "There is actually a secret door that leads to my room."

Caelfel did not look at him, keeping her eyes on the gray countryside of Umfeld. The view stretched beyond the walls of Palpses and to the hilly landscape dotted with rocks and heather crags. "That doesn't seem appropriate," she mused, teasing him for his previous word choice.

"It is a tradition to connect the king and queen's rooms. Most married couples would share a bed. Royalty are held to a higher degree of decorum."

This made Caelfel look at him, and he did not suppress the amused grin that came to his face. "I would think your father would take the king's rooms."

"My father does not usually stay in Palpses. Kanetalm is my home, and I am the ruling noble over her. King Orrik usually allows me to keep the king's room even when he visits."

"And how often does he visit?"

Brenin struggled to give a diplomatic answer. "He tries to come every season."

"So then he visits Palpses four times a year?"

"And four times too many for my taste."

"You do not like your father," Caelfel noted. "You must be very lonely in your family."

"I was much closer to my mother," Brenin admitted, gazing out the window as a distant memory clouded his eyes. "She was kind and patient. She raised me on stories of fairies and elves."

Brenin's voice trailed off, but Caelfel watched him carefully. "What did she tell you about the elves?"

"She said that they were magical and beautiful."

Caelfel looked down sadly at her hands. Queen Fronia's description of Caelfel's people was not incorrect, but it no longer described Caelfel. All elves were born with a magical aura and thus the ability to perform magic, but Caelfel had lost that ability only a short time ago. Her aura had been taken from her in an incident that nearly cost Caelfel her life. "I would disappoint your mother then," Caelfel whispered to him.

But Brenin shook his head, misunderstanding her. "No, she wasn't wrong. She met an elf once, and it was why the subject fascinated her."

Caelfel perked up at this information. "Who was the elf?"

"She never told me his name, but I suspected she was in love with him. But he never came back for her, and she ended up marrying my father."

Brenin shrugged the conversation away, as if it had no bearing of any sort. He moved away from the window and went on to describe in great detail the consideration that went into choosing the draperies and furniture, but Caelfel was not listening. She stayed at the window, wrapping her arms around herself as if her wound from the werewolf threatened to burst open.

But it wasn't her physical wound that was causing her pain, because there was only one possibility for the identity of Queen

Fronia's elvish visitor. An impossible answer. But Caelfel knew the truth to her very center. She knew the elf's name, for there was only one other elf who ventured beyond the borders of the Fey Forest in the last one hundred years. There was only one elf whose extensive roaming had caused him to be widely recognized as the Wandering Elf.

And it was the same elf who had broken her heart.

4. Idle Whispers

It was in her parlor after dinner that Brenin told her about the banquet that would take place the next night, a feast for the dignitaries that were visiting. But for that night, they had been allowed to dine peacefully alone. Brenin had admitted his surprise, remarking that he had expected King Orrik to subject Caelfel to an evening of his company.

"You should be grateful he has not. Although, I anticipate the worst tomorrow night."

"The worst?" Caelfel repeated. She was lounging sideways on a very ornate, yet surprisingly comfortable settee, and her head hung off the cushions, causing her hair to fan out on the floor below her. "It is a dinner with your father and brother and some more guests. I don't expect that to be quite so terrible."

Brenin leaned on a chair across from her and for the past hour had been detailing the woeful events that would surely follow the next evening. Cyrus had brought food for all of them, the remains of which now sat abandoned on the dining table. The steward stood in the corner of the room, content to remain unnoticed. Caelfel had insisted he sit down and join them, but Cyrus had declined the offer.

When Brenin had said nothing to her previous statement, Caelfel continued, "I've sat in this palace all day. Can I not go into the city?"

"Not yet," Brenin said quietly. "It is dark now, and tomorrow you will have to prepare for the feast. You'll see the city when we attend the festival."

"Prepare for a dinner?" Caelfel asked. She sat up and turned to face him. "All you have to do is attend."

"The king has decided to throw a ball in honor of your arrival. A seamstress is coming in the morning to measure you for a gown."

"A ball? You mean dancing?" She looked down at her own

travel-worn clothes. No, it was true; they would not be suitable for the occasion. She frowned. "I'm not your prisoner. I don't have to go to these dinners or balls. I just came to attend the festival and then go my own way."

Brenin appeared affronted by her sudden protest. "No, you are not a prisoner. You don't have to attend. It is only courteous to extend the invitation." He stood from his seat. "When the seamstress visits you in the morning, inform her that her services are not needed. Good night, Miss Caelfel," he said shortly before leaving the room.

Caelfel stared after him, stunned by his sudden departure. She looked to Cyrus who was preparing to follow Brenin. "How could I have upset him so?" she asked the retreating steward.

Cyrus cleared his throat. "I'm sure elvish customs and courtesies are much different than ours, but it is considered rude to refuse an invitation from the prince."

Caelfel frowned. "I think it is rude to corner a guest into attending."

Cyrus offered a small laugh before excusing himself entirely, and Caelfel let him go.

As promised, the seamstress arrived the following morning, but Caelfel did not turn her away. She allowed this old woman to measure just about every length of her body, even taking off her boots at the woman's request. Caelfel fidgeted and curled her toes on the cold, wooden floor of the bedroom, thinking it was an awful lot of trouble to go to for one dinner. Around mid-morning, there was a knock on her door, and the sight of Brenin bearing a tray of food was a welcome relief. As if on cue, the seamstress excused herself to sketch dress designs at a small desk in the corner.

"I thought you might be hungry," Brenin said, setting the tray on her bed.

Caelfel stepped up to it cautiously and saw a bowl of fresh blackberries and a small metal pitcher of cream. She was not ignorant of the care Brenin took in selecting her dishes. It surprised her, because she was not considered a picky eater at home. The diet of elves must have been so strange to humans. She popped a few of the blackberries into her mouth, heedless of how they stained her fingertips purple. "This is rather generous of you," she said, swallowing.

"Generous, indeed," said the seamstress who had hardly said

anything to Caelfel. "I wish I had a prince to deliver my breakfast."

Brenin threw an odd look across the room to the seamstress who did not apologize for her unprompted remark. "I'm glad to see you decided to have the fitting. I thought I would have to face the court alone tonight."

"The fitting," Caelfel repeated. The seamstress had been there for over two excruciating hours. "When I was fitted for battle armor, the measurements took less than two minutes." She glanced at the seamstress in the corner, wondering if her comment would be perceived as unkind.

The seamstress gave a very short laugh at that. "What a cheeky one you are. I apologize if my old fingers do not have the same speed as those of elves."

"I trust Miss Caelfel proved no problem for you?" said Brenin, trying to break the ice between them.

"She was no problem. I've never had a client who stood so still, especially for so long. She did hum a few pretty tunes."

Caelfel was surprised at this. She had not realized that she had been humming.

"What were you humming?" Brenin asked her.

"I don't remember. I was just thinking of home," Caelfel said, her voice trailing off in thought. She fondly remembered her parents, and her chest ached for Garvanna, lost and forgotten in a forsaken wood. And perhaps it would be safe enough to admit that she missed Feraan, though she had no idea what had become of him after the battle in the desert.

"Is there any way I can send a message home?" Caelfel asked suddenly. "They have to know about my friend, that she won't be returning," she said softly.

Brenin considered her request. "There is a way." He cast a glance towards the woman in the corner. "If your seamstress can spare you, that is."

The woman waved them off. "She is finished. I have everything I need."

And this was excuse enough for Brenin to grab her hand and pull her quickly through the castle. To her surprise, he didn't retrieve Cyrus, even when it became apparent that they were going into the city. Before they stepped past the stables, he tossed her a cape with a wide hood and donned an identical one himself.

"I'm sure you don't want to be ambushed again," he said.

She nodded. "Where are we going?"

They started down the hill, and Caelfel was relieved when she noticed no one spared them a passing glance. Brenin explained, "The palace has several fine couriers available to deliver any manner of messages."

"Then why don't we use one of them?" she asked.

He turned his head slightly to offer a wink. "Because there are even better messengers in the city."

"Even ones that can send a letter to Honey Water?" she asked dubiously.

"I would not doubt it."

On foot, the city of Palpses looked to be full and overcrowded, much larger than she remembered when she had first entered. The streets were filled with vendors and shopkeepers and their patrons milling about in the street. Caelfel noticed the number of streets that crisscrossed at frequent intersections. Palpses was much larger than Sal'Sumarathar, the woodland city of her youth.

Along with the sights, the sounds and the smells were nearly overpowering. People seemed always to be yelling for one reason or another, and Caelfel often wrinkled her nose at the odor of cooked meat.

"It's because of the festival," Brenin explained. "Things are normally much quieter around here."

Caelfel looked curiously into the wide faces of the people around her. They were open and encouraging and obviously ignorant of the quiet life of an elvish forest. She found it endearing in this race who did not have millennia to spare. An elf could turn away for a brief moment, and all of these people would be dead. The morbid thought troubled her, and she frowned. Brenin already looked her age and he was only twenty-two, less than a third of her seventy-six years. He might not even see his half-century year if he had the misfortune to be seized by a sickness. Caelfel's stomach turned as she realized why elves did not make friends with the humans. The creatures were so *fragile*.

"Something wrong?" Brenin asked when she had not responded.

Caelfel was about to shake her head when a familiar face appeared among the horde. And the small girl likewise recognized her. Her lips parted as they had the previous day, and Caelfel ran to cover the girl's mouth with her hand. The girl's large gray eyes become even rounder in surprise and in wonder at being silenced by an elf.

"You were the one who ousted me yesterday!" Caelfel hissed at her.

The girl mumbled inaudibly through Caelfel's hand. Caelfel lowered it to let her speak. "I'm sorry!" the girl squealed. "I was just surprised!"

Caelfel looked around anxiously for the girl's guardian but saw no one. "Who are you with?"

"I'm by myself," the girl informed her proudly. She beamed. "Can I tell mama I saw you today?"

Caelfel sighed. "I don't mind. Just don't tell anyone else, all right?"

The girl nodded eagerly. "What's your name?"

"Caelfel," she said, smiling. "And yours?"

"Ameala. Will you be at the festival tomorrow?"

"Of course, I would not miss it."

Ameala grinned, and the expression looked much too large for her small face. She skipped away, humming merrily, and Caelfel couldn't help the small smile that came to her face.

"How old would she be?" Caelfel asked Brenin, who had watched the entire exchange in silence.

"I would wager she is around six years old."

Caelfel shook her head. "She looks much older. I do not understand your aging."

They continued down the street, and Caelfel followed Brenin until the road opened up on a wide plaza full of tents and wooden stalls for merchants. Caelfel was surprised to see livestock roaming about on leashes. Brenin pushed his way to the center of the crowd, where there was a small clearing. When they were closer, Caelfel saw a tall metal stake with perches for five birds standing in the center.

A woman with shortly cropped, black hair danced around the post, which was occupied by a single raven. A man sitting on the ground supplied her music with the use of a small drum. Caelfel watched the young woman. She wore a long, dark purple skirt that shifted and fluttered with her movements. When the skirt lifted, it revealed that she also wore stitched leather pants underneath. Her dirty red shirt hung loosely off her shoulders, showing creamy pale skin. When she turned, Caelfel noticed a tattoo branded on her back, just below her left shoulder.

But the hair, the quick, agile movements, and the woman's sharp chin all seemed familiar to her. Caelfel hesitated when Brenin did not step any closer to the woman. "What is this? Who are they?"

"The Morrígna sisters," Brenin answered in a low voice.

The drumbeats stopped, and the woman twirled to a stop before them, offering a wide smile. "And we are the finest messengers of all Ariang'ron," she supplied, specifically greeting the two of them and swooping into a low bow.

Caelfel blinked, naming the familiarity at last. "You are werebirds."

The woman straightened, and her smile turned proud. Her blood red eyes were not familiar to Caelfel. "What an accurate observation. My name is Badb, and this is my sister Anann," she said, gesturing to the perched raven. "Our maid Boogn is not a werebird. He just tends to things while we are away," Badb said, glancing at the sitting man. Caelfel noticed a silver chain tied around his ankle that bound him to their perch.

"Do you know someone named Macha?" Caelfel asked carefully.

Badb did not conceal the recognition that flashed through her eyes. "Macha is our sister. We have not seen her for some time. Where is she?"

"I'm sorry. I cannot tell you. I only saw her briefly nearly a month ago," Caelfel admitted apologetically.

But Badb only shrugged, not too concerned over her sister's fate. "May we be of service to you?"

Caelfel swallowed, unable to break her gaze from Badb's unnerving red eyes. She wondered if she could trust Badb or Anann with delivering a letter. When she had encountered Macha, the other sister had warned Feraan of the army that eventually kidnapped Caelfel. She wondered if the same integrity extended to the other Morrígna sisters. "Can you deliver a letter to the Fey Forest?"

Badb smiled, and her red eyes made it look wicked. Without warning, she reached into Caelfel's hood and touched her pointed ears. Caelfel recoiled from her touch. "I can deliver a letter anywhere, even if you do not know where the recipient is. I have already delivered one letter to the Honey Water Empire this week. A second will be no problem."

Caelfel was surprised at the extent of Badb's abilities and her eagerness to visit the Fey Forest. During her travels with Garvanna, she had noticed people acted as though they had feared it. "Give me a moment. I need to write it first."

The sisters' servant Boogn suddenly procured a roll of thick parchment and a piece of charcoal. Caelfel took it with a soft word of thanks and began writing with Badb watching her closely.

Dearest Mother,

I find myself safe in the city of Palpses in Kanetalm, however Garvanna no longer accompanies me. We were attacked in the Pirinac Forest by werewolves, and I lost her. I fear the worst, though I could not find her body.

As I am now alone, I plan to return home after a festival, the Celebration of Strigi. There is a man here, Prince Brenin, who has been very kind and helpful. He saved me in the Pirinac.

Please make the arrangements for Garvanna's funeral. When you tell Thoroth, try to be sensitive. In spite of everything, they were *close friends.*

With much love,

Your daughter Caelfel

P. S. Send Father my love

Badb cleared her throat as Caelfel tightly rolled her letter into a scroll. "Do you have a signet? Something to seal the letter, perhaps? So they know it was not tampered with?"

Caelfel thought of the Gyssedlues family crest and how her parents would often press it into wax to seal their letters. She had no such seal or signet ring with her but looking down, she realized she did have a necklace, a protection amulet in the shape of a crescent moon. It was too big for the drop of black wax Boogn dripped over the paper, but the imprint it left behind was distinctive enough. "It goes to Sylaera Gyssedlues in the city of Sal'Sumarathar," Caelfel said as she handed it to Badb.

Badb appraised the letter thoughtfully. "The distance from here to Honey Water will understandably raise the price," Badb said, raising her eyes to Caelfel's pendant. "Of course, we do accept trades. Your magical trinket there would certainly be more than enough to cover the expenses."

Caelfel protectively clutched at her amulet. It had been designed and crafted specifically for her, replacing the one her parents gave her at birth. Having no magic of her own, it was her only defense against missiles and magical assaults. "It is not for sale," Caelfel said thickly, though she realized with a panic she had no money of her own to pay them.

Badb had fashioned her features into an expression of mock sympathy before Brenin intervened. "I'm sure you will find his amount suitable."

He handed her a small, black velvet pouch, which made a *chink*ing sound as it was transferred, suggesting it contained a great many coins. Badb weighed it in her hand before a satisfied smile spread across her face. "That will do quite nicely, my prince. Does the lady expect a response?"

Caelfel shook her head. "No response necessary. I will see them soon enough."

Badb turned to Boogn and her raven sister. "I would very much like to deliver this one, Anann," Badb said to the bird.

The crow tilted its head in acknowledgment, and Badb turned to the crowd around them and offered one last bow very low to the ground. The raven on the perch took flight, and in a well-practiced, synchronized moment, the two switched places. Badb shrank in size, and Anann filled her abandoned clothes before they could hit the ground as she transformed into her human self.

"Oh sister," Anann complained. "Yours pants don't fit right."

Badb screeched in response before soaring high above them and out of sight. Anann picked up the discarded pants and fixed the skirt over her hips. She glanced at Caelfel, flashing golden eyes, and Caelfel realized that although all three sisters were identical at first glance, they could be distinguished by the color of their eyes.

"Are you always in Palpses?" Caelfel asked Anann.

"No, we move around all the time. We've just returned from Haradrop and we were in the court of Onusal." Anann paused, looking to Brenin, and bobbed a quick curtsy. "Your brother is in good health, sire. I'm sure this news pleases you."

Brenin gave a thin smile. "It pleases me very much." But Caelfel sensed he felt otherwise.

"They know the Prince of Onusal?" Caelfel asked once they had safely rejoined the throng of people in the market.

"Madoc uses their services often. He is quite sociable, and the Morrígna sisters are faster and more reliable than most couriers." Brenin paused by a baker and purchased two small cream pastries. He handed one to Caelfel who sniffed the sugar icing warily.

"You didn't have to spend your money on me. I would have found some way to pay them." She nibbled on the edges of the cake and, deciding it had a delectable taste, took a larger bite.

"Do you have any money?" Brenin asked, his mouth full of cake.

The small amount of money she and Garvanna had brought with them had been depleted long ago. The elves didn't carry much currency, if any, since they had a local economic system that revolved around trade and goodwill. The money they originally brought came from selling a few elvish possessions in the Amhsis Desert. Caelfel shook her head. "No, but I would have thought of something."

Brenin laughed as if he didn't believe her. "I don't think you would have liked giving away your necklace."

"I wouldn't have," Caelfel agreed, frowning. "I will have to repay your kindness."

"Just don't leave me alone at the feast tonight. That's all I ask." They made their way back to the palace, weaving through the crowd that began to thin as they left the market behind. Brenin cleared his throat. "Tell me about that pendant of yours."

Caelfel touched the crescent moon and spoke in a low voice. "My parents gave me a different amulet at my birth. I had to give it away, and my friend made this one to replace my first. It acts as a shield against most things, like magic and projectiles."

"Except werewolves," Brenin pointed out.

Caelfel sighed, having difficulty concealing her chagrin. "Except werewolves," she agreed.

They continued walking until they reached the palace, where they were confronted by a flurry of servants. Three of them pulled Caelfel away while the rest swarmed around Brenin with questions about that night's affair. Caelfel recognized Cyrus as he resolutely and purposefully repositioned himself at Brenin's side once more.

The three women took Caelfel to her bedroom, where there now stood an enormous wooden tub, lined on the inside with wool padding. It was filled with water, and steam curled off its surface. Caelfel looked to the women. "What is this for?"

The oldest one had left the room to fetch something. The youngest stayed silent, her eyes downcast. The one who looked to be about Brenin's age answered. "It's for your bath," she said sharply with a hint of amusement.

Without further prompting, Caelfel undressed and stepped into the wooden tub. The water proved scalding and turned her skin bright pink. She schooled her features so as to hide her discomfort.

"Now what?" Caelfel asked, grimacing. The women had kneeled around the tub.

"Now you soak and scrub," said the oldest, returning with blocks of soap and thick woolen towels. The two youngest plunged their arms into the water and began furiously scrubbing Caelfel.

"I can wash myself," Caelfel protested.

"It certainly smells like it," quipped the one around Brenin's age sarcastically.

Caelfel fumed silently and allowed them to have their way. Soon they acted as if Caelfel was not even there and began conversing among themselves. Caelfel learned that the oldest was called Nari. The middle was Forra, and the youngest was Pieta.

"What shall we do with her hair?" Pieta asked eagerly. She was the only one who seemed to be enjoying their task.

"It will be tied up, of course," Nari snapped, putting an end to the discussion. "All highborn ladies wear their hair up, and a guest of the prince will be no different."

Caelfel frowned, disliking this idea. "I prefer wearing my hair down. It is customary for elves unless going into battle."

"The ladies of Umfeld wear their hair up. As a guest of his grace, you will do the same," Nari said with finality, putting an end to any argument.

"There have not been any ladies in Kanetalm for some time, not since the queen passed," Forra mused. She shook her head. "I don't care who you are. It still isn't right."

Caelfel kept her mouth shut during this topic change, and the other two fell into a silence that allowed Forra to continue.

"In Umfang, we would not so easily welcome an elf after they proved of no use to us," grumbled Forra, glaring at Caelfel. Caelfel ignored the girl, dipping her chin into the water. They had stopped scrubbing her, and Pieta began massaging oil into Caelfel's scalp.

"Forra, this lady is a guest of Prince Brenin," Nari warned in a tight voice.

"Don't get me started on that useless prince," Forra said, voice rising. "He goes on tour for weeks and can't even take care of werewolf rumors. He can't even take care of the people in his own city." Forra began brushing out Caelfel's tangled hair mercilessly.

"Forra, it is dangerous to speak ill of your prince," Nari pressed urgently. There was something new in Nari's voice that made Caelfel look up at the old crone. Nari stared at her, terror lining her face.

But Forra did not heed Nari's terror. "What an archaic method to rule Umfeld anyway. Why should King Orrik or Prince Brenin get to decide everything just because they had the gods-given fortune of being born?"

"Because that is their birthright," Nari said tightly.

"Umfang does not work in such a primitive way. They govern themselves. They have democracy and councils. Their lives do not depend on the whims of one person," Forra continued animatedly.

"Then perhaps you should return to Umfang," Nari said lightly. But she did not have such skill in ending a conversation with Forra as she had with Caelfel.

Forra smiled wickedly. "I should think not. We will get our turn in Umfeld. The rebellion is going to bring us democracy—"

"Forra!" Nari's face had completely paled. "You are speaking in the presence of Prince Brenin's guest who speaks to him regularly."

Forra's brushing stopped. "She's a foreigner. She doesn't understand what I'm talking about."

At this, Caelfel rose to her feet and turned to face Forra. The steaming water rolled down her naked body in great rivulets as she towered above the maid. "I understand perfectly. What you speak of is treason."

Forra's face paled to match Nari's. "Please, do not tell the prince. I meant no harm—"

"I would be more worried about King Orrik learning of your words. He is the more ruthless of the two."

Forra's bottom lip quivered. "Please, I am most loyal to our king and prince."

Caelfel watched the previously snide girl grovel for mercy at her feet. She had every right to inform Brenin of her traitorous words and Caelfel would have sent for the prince at that moment if it were not for her sudden surge of pity. Even so, Caelfel could not risk Brenin's life at the suggestion of a rebellion. Brenin had saved her from the werewolves, which meant Caelfel owed him a life debt.

"Please, my lady. Forra is all talk. She meant no harm," Nari pleaded when Caelfel remained silent.

Caelfel deliberated for a long while. She continued staring at

Forra. "Have you heard of the Vinius Islands?"

Forra rapidly shook her head. "No, my lady."

"They are a cluster of islands off the northern coast of the Fey Forest. We, the wood elves, conquered them many centuries ago. Not twenty years ago, they rebelled against the empire. The rebellion was quickly neutralized. It was the first time I had ridden a ship. I didn't fight in the battle, but my father did. I volunteered to help reconstruct the city. I do not think the number of bodies that littered the streets and fields could have been worth any rebellion."

Forra's eyes remained wide. She didn't respond, and Caelfel settled back down into the water, thinking of how to handle Forra. When her bath had finished, Nari quickly rose to dry her.

"Pieta, would you fetch Cyrus for me?" Caelfel asked, tossing her towel to the floor when only her hair remained damp. Nari went to pick it up.

Pieta nodded and hurried to leave the room.

"I will go and get your dress from the dressmaker," Forra volunteered.

"No," Caelfel said quickly. "You will stay here. Nari will retrieve my dress."

The two exchanged uncertain expressions, but Nari was quick to obey. Cyrus and Pieta entered as soon as Nari disappeared. Cyrus started upon seeing Caelfel's nude body and he discreetly hid his gaze.

"My lady, I did not realize you were undressed."

Caelfel, growing tired of being called a lady, folded her arms but made no further move to cover herself. "Perhaps you should have knocked."

"Of course, the fault is mine. You wanted to see me, my lady?"

"Pieta, leave us." Pieta quickly bobbed her curtsy before hurrying out of the room. "Thank you for coming, Cyrus. Is Brenin busy at the moment?" Caelfel asked.

"Prince Brenin is currently besieged with responsibilities that have been neglected since his tour. He should be finished in time for tonight's feast," Cyrus explained.

Caelfel nodded. "Can I trust you with something? Can you keep a secret and tell no one, including Brenin?"

Cyrus hesitated, choosing his words carefully. "If it was a matter that concerned the prince's safety, I would not be able to keep your secrets, my lady. Otherwise, you have my confidence. Perhaps you should not divulge them before household staff."

Despite Caelfel's previous experience with stewards, she felt like she could trust Cyrus. It gave her satisfaction to feel Forra squirming beside her. "Is the prince aware of any sort of rebellion in Umfeld or Kanetalm?"

Cyrus eyed Forra suspiciously but did not comment when Caelfel refused to dismiss her. "Officially, I cannot reveal matters of state to you. I might, however, hint that the Captain of the Guard works tirelessly to ensure the prince's safety."

Caelfel frowned, unsatisfied with Cyrus's answer. If they were not currently aware of a rebellion, then they needed to be. "If the Kanetalm guard discovered a member of this hypothetical rebellion, what would happen?"

Cyrus continued staring at Forra, as if realizing the source of Caelfel's curiosity. "If their guilt was proven, they would be hanged for treason, my lady," Cyrus said in a hard, unforgiving voice.

Forra made a small gasp. Caelfel turned her head slightly. "Hush, girl. I am speaking to the steward." Forra nodded weakly.

"My lady, have you discovered any information of such a rebellion?" Cyrus asked, still averting his eyes from Caelfel's nakedness.

Caelfel considered Forra's fate for a long minute as she looked back to Cyrus. "I just overheard the idle chatter of the staff. Nothing of substance."

Cyrus nodded slowly. "My lady, if you've heard of anything—"

"There was another matter, Cyrus. I'm not sure how appropriate my request will be but I would like to make this woman my personal handmaiden."

Cyrus straightened, shoulders rising. "Of course. I am sure the prince will have no objections. Is there anything else?"

Caelfel turned to Forra. "Go and help Nari with my dress."

Forra nodded and all but ran as she fled the room.

"That girl," Caelfel said once she was alone with Cyrus. "Her name is Forra. She needs to be watched, followed any time she is not in my sight."

"If you suspect something, Caelfel, she can be arrested," Cyrus pointed out.

"She doesn't need to be hanged just for being stupid. Now she knows her life is in my hands."

Cyrus excused himself, and the three women appeared in a single wave with Nari carrying the dress. Nari and Forra avoided meeting Caelfel's gaze as they smoothed out the diaphanous fabric on her bed. Caelfel gripped a handful of blue silk, feeling the fluid material through her fingers. It was not the spyder silk of Honey Water, and Pieta explained it came from a special worm from Umfang, which Caelfel thought strange.

Pieta set the silk aside as something about Caelfel caught her eyes. She stared unabashedly at Caelfel's naked frame. "Where did you get that scar?" she asked, pointing to Caelfel's belly.

Caelfel looked down. The long, jagged scar had almost faded completely. "A werewolf gave me that. I can tell you they are certainly not rumors." She glanced up at Forra to see if the girl registered her words. Forra acted as though she didn't hear.

"Pieta, you are being rude," Nari reproached lightly.

Caelfel smiled at the youngest girl. "I don't mind. It was quite a story."

But Pieta's attention had already shifted to something else. She pointed to Caelfel's hip. "How did you get that one? Are those letters?"

Caelfel did not need to look to see which scar Pieta referred to. She had only one other telling mark on her body, a scar that refused to go away. Two dark brown runes marked the skin on her hip, branded by fire and magic. No matter how much Caelfel would like to forget the incident, they remained. "That one was given to me by a very cruel man," she said solemnly.

Even Nari and Forra could not ignore the grimness in her voice. They paused their work to look at her. "I am sorry, my lady," Forra whispered hoarsely.

Caelfel shook her head, but Pieta, oblivious to the effect of her questions, asked, "What does it mean? What do the letters say?"

Caelfel's fingers subconsciously went to trace the runes. Its memory sent a cold shiver down her spine and an icy stab through her chest. "They spell a name."

"Whose name?" Pieta pressed. "Not the one who put it there?"

Caelfel sighed, and her chest felt heavy. "No, this is the name of an elf. His name was Feraan."

Pieta cast her companions a puzzled expression. She did not understand Caelfel's somber silence.

But Forra understood. "Did you love him?"

It took Caelfel a moment to find her voice. "Not anymore," Caelfel answered, unsure if that was a lie. She sighed again and attempted a smile for them. "I think I should like to wear my hair down tonight."

Nari did not argue with her this time.

5. Brothers

After her bath, Caelfel received a lesson on manners from Nari, who mostly lectured Caelfel on keeping her silence. Caelfel acknowledged her instructions with occasional nods, practicing for the feast. It suited her; Caelfel didn't really have an interest in speaking to Umfeld nobles and diplomats. She wasn't in Kanetalm in an attempt to establish foreign relations between humans and elves. Regardless, King Orrik insisted on her presence at the dinner.

Forra helped her to put her gown on with shaking fingers. She avoided any eye contact with Caelfel, which was unsurprising. What did surprise Caelfel were the timid compliments Forra uttered about how the dress fit.

"Blue is definitely your color," she offered in a small, quavering voice.

Caelfel stepped to the mirror and examined herself. She owned a blue dress at home. Her mother had made it in a single night to wear to a trial. Caelfel thought about remarking about the memory but ultimately decided she was not in the mood to answer questions about it.

The dress was dark blue and floor length. The front had a corset opening, revealing the white bodice beneath, and the skirt was decorated with bronze brocade that glinted in the light. A similar bronze band cinched her waist. The skirt was ridiculously and impractically heavy, hanging from her hips. The neck of the dress was also wide, almost falling off her shoulders, and the sleeves frilled out at the elbow. Caelfel did not like the dress and decided human fashion was gravely misguided.

She kept her silence though and didn't complain. Pieta and Forra insisted that it was a beautiful dress, so Caelfel only hoped she would not stand out conspicuously among the rest of the guests. And though Nari appeared obviously disgruntled, Caelfel's hair remained loose. It was a small victory, but she took great satisfaction in it.

It was an hour before sunset, and Nari's work was done. She excused herself to go home, and Pieta and Forra followed Caelfel as she went to find Brenin. Pieta directed her to the keep, so Caelfel hurried down the stairwell before stopping midway when she noticed an audience had gathered below.

Brenin sat on the throne, his brow knotted into an expression of discomfort. As she watched, one man stepped forward from the crowd and sank to one knee before addressing the prince. The clothes of the man were not bright and ridiculous like her dress, so Caelfel assumed he was not there for the feast.

"What's going on?" Caelfel asked the two women who had stopped behind her.

"The prince is listening to supplicants. Petitioners come to him with their problems, and Prince Brenin does what he can to solve them," Forra answered quietly. No one had noticed them on the stairwell, so Caelfel continued watching.

"Where are you from?" Brenin asked the man.

"I live on Crone Mountain, my lord in the town of Ruxcloke," said the man. "My name is Ralfric, son of Rhinedal."

"Tell me the problem you are facing on Crone Mountain," Brenin said patiently.

"People are missing, being kidnapped from their very homes."

"How many people?"

"Two, my lord."

"But one came back?"

"Yes, that is correct," Ralfric said, nodding.

Brenin sighed. "I don't think one missing person is the work of a kidnapper. They probably got lost in the snow."

"No one gets lost on the mountain, my lord. The girl who came back said things. She spoke of a sorcerer who has been kidnapping people, not only from our village. The sorcerer has been experimenting, practicing black magic."

"Is this girl with you?"

"No, my lord. I did not think she was in a well enough state to travel all the way to Palpses."

"How did she escape from this sorcerer?"

"Runa says the sorcerer let her go. He wants the world to know that he is here."

Brenin sighed again and seemed to sink further into the throne. "I can send three men to search for the missing person and perhaps investigate the whereabouts of this sorcerer."

"Only three? But my lord—"

"Ralfric, I am sorry, but the only evidence you have given me is the word of a lost, snow-crazed girl who is not here. Kanetalm at present suffers from other ailments."

Ralfric squared his shoulders, and his sharp chin seemed to shake as he confronted the prince. "My lord, the other missing girl is my niece, Remly. She is only eight. My own daughter Runa is a capable warrior, easily worth five of your men. If she was unsuccessful in searching for her cousin, I do not think three men will suffice."

"Then perhaps you should have taught her how to milk goats instead of playing with swords," cut across a new voice. King Orrik, Caelfel realized. Everyone in the room inclined their heads, except Brenin and Ralfric.

Brenin stood up, brushing past his father who had appeared beside him. He crossed the floor to stand before Ralfric and placed a hand on the older man's shoulder. "I am most sorry, Ralfric. My men will do their best to return your niece to you. That is all I can promise."

Ralfric hung his head in defeat. King Orrik dismissed the commoners from the keep, and when everyone had left, Caelfel approached Brenin. The prince and his father were having a disagreement in hushed tones, and Brenin pinched the bridge of his nose in obvious exasperation.

"You don't believe in this sorcerer," Caelfel guessed, interrupting their conversation.

King Orrik did not acknowledge her presence, but Brenin seemed relieved and was quick to turn and face her. "Do you?" Brenin asked.

Caelfel hid a grimace, recalling Lisiek torturing her. "I've encountered a human sorcerer before. From my experience, they are too dangerous to be ignored."

King Orrik suffered a smile at this. "I have seen more elves than sorcerers, and you are the only elf I have ever met. I try not to be swayed by mountain tales."

Caelfel frowned, turning to the king. "You do not feel that one person missing in the mountains is worth saving."

"It is not worth risking three good soldiers," the king said dismissively.

Caelfel glared and straightened her back, grateful that she was taller than Orrik. "I went missing once, kidnapped by some Umfang admiral. My friends, my family, and nearly all of my regiment risked their own lives to save me. Would you like to know who ended up killing this pompous admiral?" Caelfel pointed to herself. "Me, the one who went missing. Perhaps this Runa *would* be worth more than all of your soldiers."

"You have a remarkable way of looking at things, my lady." King Orrik turned to Brenin then. "Your brother and the Onusal court should be arriving soon. Be sure you're there to greet them."

Brenin gave a single, curt nod, and King Orrik left the room, his long fur coat sweeping the floor behind him.

"He shouldn't stay around long after the festival," Brenin said encouragingly, but it seemed more for his benefit than hers.

"It is sad that you and your father should disagree so." Caelfel paused. "But I think that he should not be so disagreeable." She glanced meaningfully at Forra behind her, who avoided her gaze.

A courier burst through the keep's doors with breathless news of Prince Madoc's arrival. Brenin called for Cyrus, and the court of Kanetalm assembled in the keep to greet the court of Onusal. The court of Kanetalm was relatively small, Caelfel realized, with Brenin positioned at its head and King Orrik shadowing his left. Other than the two of them, there was only Caelfel who stood next to Brenin as his guest and Cyrus who respectfully kept his distance from the royal family. Caelfel was surprised at this small turnout because she had always heard that humans had such large families compared to the elves.

And so they waited, like a scene worthy of a portrait. Caelfel began to despise the dress for making her back hurt in strange ways.

The doors to the castle opened, and a liveried pageboy announced Prince Madoc of Onusal, the Prince of the Vale.

The man that stepped into the hall was tall like his brother, and she recognized the older prince's grin and bright eyes as being inherited from the late Queen Fronia.

However, Madoc bore no further resemblance to the portrait Caelfel had seen outside her rooms, and he shared no features with the king at all. There was a haunting familiarity in his dark hair, the shape of his jaw, and the touch of grace that surrounded his movements, suggesting an altogether more scandalous parentage. She caught her breath, and the air burned her lungs as the truth of Madoc's parentage became clear to her, despite the prince's ordinary rounded ears.

Madoc did not stand as stiffly as the others, with nothing of the uncomfortable rigidity that Nari had schooled Caelfel to expect. He crossed the room in long, easy strides and embraced his brother in a fierce hug.

"It has been too long, little brother," Madoc rumbled in a great voice, also reminiscent of someone that was not King Orrik.

"You did not wait until the rest of your court was introduced," Brenin admonished gently, but Caelfel caught him smiling in spite of it. She smiled at their affection.

Madoc released his brother. "Ah, forgive me. I'm not one to remember such customs. It is good to see you here, Father," Madoc said, turning to the king. He did not offer his father the same hug, but respectfully inclined his head.

"I am pleased to see you in such high spirits," King Orrik said. "I hope this means you have good news to share."

"Only the best news for the king," Madoc said, but there was an audible strain to his voice. Without another word, Prince Madoc turned to wait for the rest of his train.

The pageboy introduced a Lady Saffir of Atalon. A raven-haired beauty with an emerald green dress entered the keep and went to stand next to Madoc.

She was followed by a Prince Orren. Brenin leaned towards Caelfel and informed her that Orren was King Orrik's younger brother. Orren resembled his brother, except he kept no hair on his face and was much younger, looking just slightly older than Madoc. After Prince Orren, there was a Lord Barad of Akeonn, who Brenin explained was the brother of the late Queen Fronia. Barad looked to be the age of Caelfel's own father, but she doubted Barad was thousands of years old, despite looking so battle-weary. After Lord Barad, a girl much younger than Brenin entered and was introduced as Lady Anissa of Akeonn.

"She's Barad's daughter, my cousin," Brenin explained.

"Where is her mother?" Caelfel asked. Lady Anissa looked nothing like the other members of the royal family with her rose-red hair and small nose.

"The late Lady Eira died giving birth to Anissa."

Caelfel nodded, her stomach clenching for a race that was so familiar with death.

The rest of the train included a number of noblemen and ladies that Brenin did not feel obligated to point out to Caelfel. They all greeted Brenin and the king, and the atmosphere tangibly relaxed once the initial introductions were over. Cyrus began directing everyone to their seats when Madoc suddenly noted Caelfel's presence.

"What's this? My brother has a guest. It is an honor, my lady—" But Madoc stopped short, Caelfel's hand halfway to his lips when he saw her pointed ears. Madoc dropped her hand and straightened. "Brother, you did not introduce us."

And Brenin surprised Caelfel by turning bright red. She spoke to cover his embarrassment. "I would rather not be introduced by Brenin. His mispronounces my name. He called me cow field the first time we met."

Madoc laughed at this, and it was a sound that easily filled the large hall. Even his laugh sounded exactly like another's, and Caelfel wondered if anyone else suspected that the oldest prince was, indeed, not a prince by birth. "And what is your name, my lady?" he asked.

"My full name is Caelfel Gyssedlues. You may call me Caelfel or Lady Elf if that proves too difficult for you," she said with a newfound bluster.

Madoc laughed again. "I should like hear the story of how you arrived at Palpses."

"It is not a very exciting story, I assure you," Caelfel said.

But this did not sway Madoc. Despite previous seating arrangements, Madoc was bent on doing what he wanted and planted himself firmly in a seat next to Caelfel, and it only reminded her more of an elf she had been so determined to forget about. Lady Saffir quietly took the seat on Madoc's other side.

"I am sure my brother has spoken very highly of me in my absence," Madoc said, settling down.

"Prince Brenin has actually said very little of you," Caelfel said.

Madoc gasped in mock offense and then laughed her words away. "How did my brother come across you in the first place? Did you find him wandering around the Fey Forest? Did you have to save him from a few goblins?" Madoc's words were met with laughter from everyone in the room. Caelfel glanced at Brenin beside her and saw that he looked to be in great pain. Caelfel pitied him, thinking she understood Brenin's reluctance to meet Madoc. She wondered if all older brothers teased their younger siblings so relentlessly.

Caelfel turned back to Madoc. "Actually, Prince Brenin saved my life," Caelfel said, raising her voice so the rest of the room could hear her. "If it were not for him, I would be dead."

Madoc's expression softened. "You must be very grateful for him."

"It's more than that," Caelfel insisted severely. Even as the oblivious son of an elf, Madoc should be made to know such things.

"The elves have a tradition. If you save someone's life, you owe them yours. It's called the life debt, and I will not be released from it until I return the favor."

"So you're his new bodyguard?" Madoc guessed.

Caelfel flashed a dangerous grin. If she was not wearing that silly dress, she would have looked much more intimidating. "An elf is the best sort of bodyguard to have."

The conversation mercifully shifted from her and Brenin, and Caelfel leaned back in her chair. She had not intended to declare herself as Brenin's bodyguard, and she realized belatedly that her hasty words would require her to stay in Kanetalm a while longer.

"You didn't have to do that," Brenin whispered under his breath to her.

Caelfel kept her eyes trained on Prince Orren as he spoke about some business on army recruitments. "Do what?" Caelfel innocently asked Brenin.

"Defend me against my brother."

"Perhaps you should not look so injured when he teases you."

Brenin laughed. "Did you mean what you said about being my bodyguard?"

"Of course, I would not lie about something so serious." She changed topics. "How much older is Madoc?"

"Only a few years. Why do you ask?"

Caelfel studied Brenin's brother and, ever so slowly, transferred her gaze to Brenin's father. It was so obvious to her that Madoc wasn't Orrik's son, though she had no proof outside of her familiarity with

Feraan. But as she scrutinized the King of Umfeld, Caelfel could admit that Orrik also had dark hair and wide shoulders like Madoc. With no reason for suspicion, it would not be difficult to accept Madoc as the king's son.

The courses were then served, and as the Prince of Kanetalm, Brenin's attention was always claimed someplace else. Caelfel eyed the nobles that filled the hall and picked at her food. It seemed strange to her to think that, only days ago, she and Garvanna dreamed about such an abundance of food. Now that she had it, Caelfel found she had mostly lost her appetite. Humans prepared their food in a way that made even ordinary things smell strange.

Madoc noticed the way she pushed her food around her plate. "Are you not hungry, my lady?"

Caelfel attempted a smile. "No, the elves have a rather particular diet."

"A diet without meat, I've heard."

"You have heard correctly." She wondered how a half-elf fared on a human diet.

"How is Grandfather?" Brenin suddenly asked Madoc. "He did not come with you?"

Madoc's face quickly turned grim. "Grandfather Bared has been ill for quite some time. He only grows worse and prefers to spend his days at his home in Akeonn." Madoc struggled to speak for a moment, and Saffir placed a comforting hand on his arm. "I would suggest, little brother, that you should come to Onusal and see him before it is too late."

Brenin received this news of his grandfather with a silent horror. His mouth opened with soundless words, and something stuck in Caelfel's chest for him.

King Orrik filled his second son's silence. "If he can ever finish a week's duties, he might have a chance to leaving Palpses," the king said coolly.

Madoc rose to his feet in anger. Caelfel was once again struck by the uncanny resemblance to another elf. "Grandfather Bared has very little time left. You've not let Brenin leave Kanetalm in years."

A thick and dangerous silence fell over the keep as prince challenged king. Orrik calmly finished off whatever was on his fork before speaking. "It's 'your grace,' *boy*. That's how you address your king."

"Excuse me, your grace," Madoc said thickly.

"And Brenin has his duties here. Kanetalm will continue with her problems even after your grandfather dies. You should do your best to understand that before you become king."

Madoc slowly sank into his seat without concealing the fury in his face. Caelfel realized with surprise that Madoc hated his father just as much as Brenin.

Conversation did not return in the keep, so the king continued to make his own. "How are the wedding plans proceeding, Madoc?"

Caelfel would have thought this was a preferable subject change and eagerly turned to Madoc and Saffir, having easily guessed their companionship. But Madoc remained furious and unyielding. "What wedding plans, your majesty?"

King Orrik's knife loudly clattered against his plate. "You know damn well what plans I'm talking about. You have been arranged to marry Anissa ever since her birth, and here you insult your cousin by eating next to this whore you insist on parading everywhere."

"Lady Anissa is only twelve. She is just a child," Madoc said in a hard voice.

"Lord Barad has assured me that she bleeds. Wait a year if you must, but you will marry her."

Caelfel realized she was gaping and turned her appalled gazed to Brenin for an explanation. Brenin shook his head slightly, and Caelfel hoped that meant he would explain later. She could not believe King Orrik would speak of Anissa and Saffir in such a way as if they were not there to hear it.

Madoc grumbled something that was incoherent except for the *your grace* that ended it. Caelfel looked between Saffir and Anissa, catching their red, mortified faces, before drilling her own attention into her plate.

Caelfel was only a guest there. She shouldn't get involved. She should not interfere with King Orrik's commands or challenge his words.

Thinking quickly, she turned to Saffir and raised her voice, though it was not difficult to be heard in the silent room. "Lady Saffir, that is a very lovely dress."

"Thank you," she said timidly.

"You are very beautiful," Caelfel continued. "You remind me of a friend. Her name was Garvanna and she was tall and beautiful. She was one of the most powerful mages I have seen. She was formidable and often underestimated. You remind me very much of her," Caelfel said, looking at her pointedly. Caelfel did not know Saffir enough to liken her to Garvanna, and the noblewoman looked nothing like her elf friend.

But Saffir picked up on Caelfel's meaning and returned the intended compliment with a smile. "Thank you," she said warmly.

Then Caelfel turned to Anissa who sat some distance across from her. "And Lady Anissa? I only knew one elf who had hair as red as yours. She was fierce in battle and a splendid archer. She could shoot her arrows straight through large trees."

Anissa's face brightened at the thought. "Arrows can't penetrate trees," she said dubiously.

"You've obviously never seen an elf shoot," Caelfel said, winking. She was relieved that it was not too difficult to cheer the two of them up. She pointedly ignored King Orrik's reaction but imagined his eyes rolling.

"Can you shoot?" Anissa asked eagerly.

"I can," Caelfel said modestly.

"Will you be participating in the Tournament of Strigi tomorrow?" Anissa pressed.

Caelfel faltered, having not heard of such a tournament. She looked to Brenin who explained, "Strigi is the goddess of the forest and the hunt. There's always an archery contest in her festival."

Caelfel turned back to Anissa's awaiting expression and found she did not have the heart to deny the girl what she wanted. "I will enter the tournament then, even though it means everyone else will surely lose."

Caelfel's statement sent everyone in the room murmuring to themselves, their curiosity piqued. Caelfel suddenly felt uncertain, wondering if she had just made some social blunder. She turned to Brenin and whispered, "Did I do something wrong?"

But Brenin's delighted face rivaled with Anissa's. "Absolutely not."

The conversations in the keep wore on, and after all the courses were finished off, the servants came and cleared the tables from the room. A line of musicians entered the keep and began playing lively music. It was strange music to Caelfel, music she had never heard before, but she was too busy marveling at the sheer amount of food the humans had consumed to pay attention. Madoc's stomach had acted like a bottomless void, and she stared at his abdomen throughout the night, fearing it would burst.

There was suddenly a crowd forming in the keep, and they all started dancing. Caelfel watched them from the edges of the room. The elves danced much differently. The humans were so rigid and too afraid to stand too close to their partners. Perhaps their clothes made them that way. Caelfel ogled at their movements until Brenin approached her silently.

"Don't feel like dancing?" Caelfel asked him. "I wouldn't blame you. The elves have a better way of dancing."

"And how do the elves dance?" Brenin asked with a smile on his face.

"For one thing, our clothes don't restrict movement. We had a festival not long ago and the dress I wore fell down to *here*." Caelfel indicated to a spot just above her knee.

She looked up to see Brenin's reaction, and his face turned deep red. "And you leave that much of your legs exposed?" he asked, choking on the question. He didn't sound critical, only surprised.

Caelfel couldn't help the smirk that came to her features. "You humans are too modest. I happen to think I have very nice legs. Why can't I show them off?"

"I can't think of any reason to deny you that right," Brenin said, stammering.

"Nari claims it would not be appropriate here."

"She's right. Everyone here would be unable to handle your beauty," Brenin countered, but he still struggled to keep his blush at bay.

Caelfel laughed at Brenin's embarrassment, and the sound was enough to draw Madoc to their location. Caelfel had just seen the Prince of Onusal dancing with Saffir, but Madoc greeted them alone.

"I see my brother is doing a fine job of wooing you," Madoc said with a wide grin. Caelfel noticed Brenin shrinking back from his brother.

Caelfel said, "Brenin is very nice company, but I do not think he is wooing me." She thought back to Huwel's attempts at flirting and saw none of the same behavior from Brenin. Caelfel realized Brenin might have shared Feraan's method of displaying affection, quiet and intense.

Madoc looked at his brother, examining him over. "That surprises me. Brenin has always been so obsessed with elves, ever since we were children. He wanted nothing more than to enter the Fey Forest and live with your kind."

"I can't blame him. Once you set aside the politics, it's a nice place to live," Caelfel defended, but something in her voice strained. She imagined the source of Brenin's fascination with her as a source of childhood obsession. Madoc had probably set out to annoy his brother, and judging from the way Brenin clenched his jaw, it worked. But Brenin's face flushed a deeper red which made Caelfel think Madoc was not entirely exaggerating.

It should not have been a point of shame for Brenin. Caelfel had an equal interest in humans.

"Would you care to dance, Lady Elf?" Madoc asked her suddenly. "I am not familiar with your dances, my lord," Caelfel answered carefully, unsure if it would be against social decorum to deny a dance with a prince.

Madoc shrugged and took her hand anyway. "They are not hard. Make up your own dance if you like."

And Prince Madoc led her into the throng of rigidly dancing humans, and Prince Brenin watched them with an expression of muted rage.

She mimicked the others around them, placing a hand on his shoulder while he held onto her other hand, and soon concluded that Madoc had not inherited his true father's dancing talent. Caelfel was acutely aware of Brenin staring at them. "I believe he is jealous," Madoc observed with a snigger.

"You should not be so harsh on him," Caelfel told him evenly. They swayed with even, shuffling steps.

"I am only trying to help him gain his confidence. If he sees you with me, maybe he will act on his feelings."

"Act on his feelings?" Caelfel repeated skeptically, unwilling to admit so herself.

"It is obvious he cares for you," Madoc said, for once losing his humor. "Watch how he stares at you." Madoc turned them so Caelfel was suddenly facing Brenin.

And Madoc was right. Once their eyes met, they shared a strange intensity before Brenin hastily turned his attention to the floor. Madoc turned them around once more.

"Oh no," Caelfel groaned.

Madoc turned a quizzical brow at her.

"Is Brenin not also arranged to marry someone?" she asked.

Madoc shook his head. "I am the oldest, and we have only one cousin. Besides, I do not think Father would refuse an elf for a daughter."

"*Madoc.* I *can't.* I can't love him."

Madoc looked disappointed. "Heart pledged to another?"

Caelfel grimaced as she thought of Feraan refusing her in the desert, despite everything they had shared together. Caelfel found she could not so easily make herself so susceptible to disappointment and heartbreak. She stared solemnly into Madoc's face which, in another circumstance, would have easily passed for Feraan's. "Something like that."

6. Traitor of the World

Brenin said very little when she returned to him, his mood soured. Not long after that, Caelfel decided to retire for the night, and Brenin escorted her to her rooms. On the way, he spoke of the following day's festival, promising that it would be much better than that evening. It didn't take much to convince her; anything would be preferable to the rigid clothes, the rigid dancing, and the awkward conversations of that night.

"What happens at the festival?" she asked him.

He suddenly became animated. "There are games and competitions, dancing and eating. And when it turns dark, there are fireworks."

Caelfel nodded, having no inkling of what fireworks were. "What sort of dancing?"

He chuckled nervously at her question. "Nothing like tonight. There are musicians from everywhere that are always playing. Painters and craftsmen sell their art. Sometimes there are even people from Umfang. It will be much better than tonight," Brenin asserted, more for his benefit.

Caelfel did not doubt him and she waited as his words lingered, stuck in his throat. Her thoughts went back to what Madoc said, and something inside of her tightened, fearing what Brenin would say.

But mercifully, he only bid her goodnight and hurried away as if to prevent himself from saying something foolish. Caelfel smiled softly at his retreating back.

When she entered the queen's rooms, she expected to be alone.

She was surprised to find Forra waiting for her. "What are you doing?" Caelfel asked.

"I am your new handmaiden," Forra reminded her. "I am here until you dismiss me."

"Well, what are you supposed to do?" Caelfel asked, feeling rather stupid. She had never had a handmaiden before. When she spoke to Cyrus, it seemed like a good idea. Now she had no idea what to do with the girl.

Forra shrugged. "Change your sheets, braid your hair. Anything you ask of me."

Caelfel thought for a moment. "I don't want you to do any of that, but there is something you can help me with."

She instructed Forra to help her remove the dress, and the two of them set to work modifying it. When she dismissed Forra just after midnight, Caelfel was quite pleased with the results. Caelfel told her she could have the next day off to enjoy the festival.

When Brenin came to retrieve her the next morning, she was wearing her newly altered dress to show off to him. Caelfel felt a surge of pride as she beamed at his stunned expression.

"I don't quite remember your dress looking like that," he finally managed.

The most notable modifications were the shorter skirt and the absence of frilly sleeves. With Forra's help, she had also adjusted the tightness of the corset and the color patterns on the front. "Do you like the changes I've made? Forra insisted I wear the pants to cover my legs. She says no one shows off their legs in Umfeld."

The blush that rose to his cheeks was faint and adorable but it also made Caelfel hesitate. She enjoyed teasing him, but she did not think it would appropriate to encourage him while she still longed for Feraan. Before he had time to respond, she went to grab her bow.

"What are you doing?" Brenin asked.

Caelfel paused. "Isn't there an archery tournament?"

"Cyrus will bring your bow later. You don't want to have to carry it around all day." She set it down and hurried out of the castle with Brenin.

The sun was high enough in the sky that it cast a warm light over the sprawling city below. Caelfel and Brenin donned the same hooded cloaks to conceal their features, and Caelfel noticed that the city was even more crowded than the previous day. "Are any of your family coming to the festival?" Caelfel asked him.

"I'm sure they will all be down for the archery contest. Anissa couldn't stop talking about it last night," Brenin answered but he was distracted as they pushed their way through the solid wall of people.

Caelfel noticed even more smells in Palpses. Initially she was overwhelmed by the stench of sweaty bodies, which was a foreign, salty odor that burned in her nose. This was quickly replaced by the acrid taste of smoke, and Caelfel turned at the sound of sharp cracking. Noticing her gaze, Brenin took her to the source.

A boy and a man stood in an unoccupied pocket of space. The boy would grab handfuls of paper-wrapped balls and throw them to the ground. When they fell, they made a loud *pop* accompanied by sudden bursts of white light. Caelfel watched in awe. The boy threw more, and sometimes they were blue or red. He spun in circles, making a display of his fire poppers to the crowd that had gathered around them. The man behind him worked at a mortar and pestle, grinding fine gray powder.

The boy approached Caelfel. "My name is Pren, and I bet I can guess your favorite color."

Caelfel smiled and nodded for him to proceed. Pren retreated back to where the man sat and began fishing through a wooden box, tongue sticking out in concentration. He pulled out some colored pebbles and skipped to the center of his circle. He spun himself around, balancing on one foot before throwing the pebbles forcefully to the ground. When they popped, they produced a screen of thick, green smoke that curled in great billows to the sky. When the smoke dissipated, Pren was nowhere to be found.

But then he was suddenly perched on her shoulders. "Did I guess right? Is green your favorite color?"

Caelfel laughed, secretly aching for the loss of her green aura. "It is."

Pren beamed. "For guessing right, I deserve a kiss."

"Pren," the man at the mortar and pestle scolded lightly.

"I don't mind," Caelfel laughed again. She turned to give Pren a small peck on the cheek before he slid from her shoulders to continue his act. Caelfel and Brenin turned to leave the circle when Pren called out to them.

"Wait! Don't forget to visit the shop of Pyros, dutifully responsible for today's fireworks! You can watching our show before the Tournament!" Pren gave a bow and everyone clapped. Caelfel and Brenin moved on.

The perch of the Morrígna sisters was still in the clearing where they had visited it the day before, and through the bumping shoulders, Caelfel could see Anann dancing for everyone and Boogn faithfully plucking away on an instrument. They continued through, examining stalls of merchants and jewelers. Caelfel admired a bauble, a jeweled pin in the shape of a stag. She returned it to the table when she noticed Brenin had removed his hood.

"Don't you think someone will recognize you?" Caelfel asked, despite the fact that she had not even worn hers.

Brenin shrugged. "There are many people here. It is easy to go unnoticed."

The jeweler interrupted them. "Can I interest you in some rubies from the Myry Jungle in Umfang—" But someone else interrupted the jeweler.

"Lady Elf!" boomed a voice Caelfel easily recognized. Heads turned as Huwel barreled his way toward her. Caelfel barely had time to respond before he crushed her in an enormous hug. She tried to say something but her empty lungs brought no words to her lips.

"It's nice to see you, Huwel," Brenin said curtly, a hint of amusement in his voice.

Huwel released her to greet Brenin. "My prince," he bid before dropping into a respectful bow.

"No need for that here, Huwel," Caelfel said, laughing. "Brenin is trying to remain hidden." Despite Huwel's outburst, no one appeared to notice the Prince of Kanetalm standing among them. Huwel straightened, brushing himself off, and eyed the two of them before excusing himself to rejoin his family.

"I have a sister waiting for me. Perhaps we will see you in the contest, Lady Elf?"

Caelfel waved to Huwel before he disappeared.

"I believe he plans to enter the contest," Brenin said with a chuckle. "He likes to brag how he is the best warrior in the Company."

"The best warrior or not, he will still lose," Caelfel said, flashing a grin.

"You are very sure of yourself," Brenin noted as they left the jeweler without purchasing rubies from the Myry Jungle.

"You saw me practice at Fort Wymdall," Caelfel pointed out. "I was one of the best archers in Honey Water. I do not believe that any human will prove a match for me."

"You should not completely doubt Huwel yet. He may surprise you."

"I do not doubt his skill. Only, mine is better."

Brenin stopped them at the edge of the marketplace where there stood a line of dark-colored tents. He considered the painted symbols before each one before deciding on the largest tent.

"What is this?" Caelfel asked, eyeing it suspiciously. This one was completely black and the white symbols on its front depicted the likeness of an owl. She did not like the sense of foreboding the black tent gave her.

"These are fortune-tellers," Brenin said cheerily. He did not share Caelfel's apprehension. "For a few coins, they will tell you your future."

"Many elves don't believe in the art of prophecy, myself included," she said quietly. She remembered the Spring Festival she attended in Honey Water. She had been coerced into having her future read from Daemona cards by a priestess. "When you seek out the future, you only invite suffering."

Brenin waved her warnings away. "It's all in good fun here. The fortune-tellers tell you when you will meet your true love, which archer to bet on in the contest. Expecting mothers go to see if they are having a boy or girl."

"And what question would you have for the fortune-teller?" Caelfel asked him carefully.

Brenin ignored her question and pointed to the painted symbol on the front. "You see the owl? It means this fortune-teller is the best at what they do."

It didn't answer her question, but Brenin was so intent on having his future deciphered that Caelfel relented and allowed him to lead her inside.

The tent was predictably dark with a fire-pit smoldering in the center. The smoke that drifted from the embers filled the tent in a thick haze that made Brenin cough. Caelfel struggled to breathe as well, feeling her mind grow lazy in the darkness. The fortune-teller stood with their back to them just beyond the fire-pit. The nearly naked frame revealed a woman with a heavily adorned headdress. The woman did not yet turn at their entrance.

"So. You have entered my tent, Prince of the Vale." The woman's head turned slightly. "And the Archer of the Lake. I will make your time worthwhile." When she spoke, Caelfel was sure she could hear the distant sound of rolling thunder, and Caelfel's mind reared at being called the Archer of the Lake.

"What shall we call you?" Brenin asked.

The woman turned to face them, revealing eyes without iris or pupil. "I am the Blind Seer."

Caelfel's chest tightened, muscles tensing in the presence of the Blind Seer. Her jaw hurt as she clenched it shut. Her mouth filled with blood when she bit her tongue. Brenin, noticing her reaction, looked at her with concern.

The Blind Seer continued, "Do you have your bow with you? I know you won't give it to me yet, but I would very much like to hold it before it's destroyed."

Countless questions ran through Caelfel's head at the Blind Seer's cryptic remark, but Caelfel pushed them aside and ignored the Seer's words altogether. She swallowed the blood in her mouth, and its metallic taste left her grimacing. "The elves know you by a different name."

"Ah, yes. How could I forget? The Archer of the Lake is an elf. Now what is this name you know me as?"

Caelfel's hands were shaking at her sides. "Traitor of the World," she spat.

"Yes, Traitor of the World. But you don't even know why I have that name. It's from a time long ago, before you were even born. I know elves shy away from the prophetic arts, but there is no reason you should bear any ill will against me." The Blind Seer was smiling, but the orange light that flickered across her face gave her an ominous, rather than an inviting, look.

"You are evil," Caelfel managed through tight lips.

The Blind Seer laughed, and the sound rippled through her tent like a wind. "I am not evil, child. I am merely a constant in this ever-changing world."

"Not evil?" Caelfel repeated, her voice rising. "A season ago, I was nothing to you. But it was because of you that the desert princeling kidnapped and tortured me. You told him to do that. If it was not for you, those things would have never happened to me."

"You were never *nothing* to me."

"They beat me and burned me. They tortured me. And you say

you are not evil," Caelfel shot back at her, yelling.

"Those things had to happen to you."

"*Why?*" Caelfel hissed venomously.

The Blind Seer never lost her smile. "Because you would have never met me otherwise."

"I believe I could go on without meeting you," Caelfel said icily.

The Blind Seer tilted her head. "But your prince couldn't have gone on without meeting you."

It wasn't a question, and the statement hung awkwardly in the air. Caelfel didn't know how to respond; she wouldn't claim Brenin as *her* prince. However, she could admit that she would not be there without him.

The Blind Seer spoke when Caelfel said nothing. "I am sorry. Strangely enough, I had not anticipated that my presence would make you so upset." She turned to Brenin, another smile lifting the corners of her mouth. "But you came for a reading, a prediction. Isn't that right, my prince?"

Brenin glanced at Caelfel uncertainly, and Caelfel could do nothing to rein in her hostility. "Her *predictions* can only bring harm," she told him. "That's the only certain thing about the future—it's painful."

Brenin nodded and started to leave at Caelfel's indication. But the Blind Seer, despite being unable to see, was surprisingly quick. She reached for Brenin's hands and held him in place as he struggled against her obvious strength.

"I do have a prophecy for you, my prince," the Blind Seer insisted urgently. "And though you might try to ignore it, you cannot escape it. You might find it in your best interest to listen to a warning."

"A warning?" Brenin repeated, stunned. He did not glance at Caelfel, his curiosity too great. "What is it?"

The Blind Seer's eyes briefly glowed yellow as she recited, "The prophecy states, '*An era shall end when a king stops for a traitor in the wood.*'" Her eyes slowly faded back to their milky white color as she released his hands.

"An era shall end when a king stops for a traitor in the wood. What does that mean?" Brenin asked skeptically.

"I cannot say," the Seer dismissed airily. She retreated to the other end of the tent, appearing suddenly exhausted.

"It probably means nothing," Caelfel said, ushering Brenin out of the tent. "Seers have a fondness for being enigmatic."

Brenin nodded in agreement and ducked outside. Caelfel went to follow him, but the Blind Seer called her back in a different voice. A voice that did not belong to the Blind Seer. A voice Caelfel had not heard for several weeks. "Caelfel, dearest?"

Caelfel froze and turned slowly, almost expecting to see her mother standing there. Instead, there was only the Seer, her eyes burning a dark orange. Caelfel said nothing as she waited for the Seer to continue.

"I am so sorry for your loss, child," the Seer said in her own voice.

"I don't suppose there's anything you could have done to stop it," Caelfel said in a hollow voice. "Garvanna's been dead for about a week now."

The Blind Seer's eyes flickered back to normal, and for once, she hesitated. "Of course. Silly me. You don't know yet."

"Know what?" Caelfel pressed. "Do you know something about Garvanna?"

"Nothing. Forget I said anything. Please leave," the Seer commanded harshly.

And Caelfel left, feeling a new sense of foreboding. Brenin noticed her grim expression and asked what was troubling her. Caelfel assured him that it was nothing, but she was unable to shake her sudden, overwhelming paranoia.

She was surprised when he did not ask about her time in the desert, but he stubbornly avoided any mention of what had transpired in the Seer's tent. Eventually, he managed to shake her out of her dazed stupor with the mention of fireworks. He took her by the hand as they followed the crowd of people that streamed towards the fields outside Palpses's walls. The smell of smoked meats and grease-battered food followed closely behind with the throng. "What are fireworks?" she asked, thinking back to Pren's display. Her voice sounded muted over the excited rabble.

"I can't believe the elves don't have fireworks. Take Pren's popper trick and magnify it tenfold."

"So they are really loud?" Caelfel guessed irritably.

"Not only loud, but colorful. They will be much better tonight when the sun goes down."

The grass of the field had been cropped short, and in places, the ground had been churned into mud. The crowd began forming around several archery targets and a wooden stage. Brenin explained they also used the field for a sport called jousting which involved horses and long lances, which explained the muddy furrows.

"The pyrotechnics put on a show before the competition starts," he said, unable to extinguish his sudden flame of anticipation. Caelfel worked to keep her frown at bay as she attempted to drive the Blind Seer from her mind. She saw Pren with his father erecting long wooden tubes and stuffing them with round ammunition covered in paper.

"And here comes the royal party," Brenin grumbled, suddenly turning despondent. He tugged his hood over his face.

Caelfel turned surreptitiously to see a carriage bearing the king of Umfeld with his oldest son. This was followed by a smaller carriage, inside of which could be seen the eager face of Anissa and her father Lord Barad. Caelfel was concerned when she did not see Saffir and judging by Madoc's dark expression, she easily guessed that she wasn't the only one. "Won't they wonder where you are?" Caelfel asked Brenin.

He gave a noncommittal shrug. "They are not bothered as long as I don't embarrass them."

"You can't always hide the fact that you are a prince," Caelfel pointed out. "*Prince of the Vale.*"

Brenin shook his head. "The Blind Seer was wrong. I'm not the Prince of the Vale. That title is given to the heir of Umfeld. As the oldest, Madoc is the Prince of the Vale."

Caelfel might have found some relief in knowing the Blind Seer was wrong about something but she knew deep in her core that Brenin was wrong about Madoc. His older brother was not the Prince of the Vale. It did not settle her nerves.

"But what is the Archer of the Lake?" Brenin asked, noticing her faint smile.

Caelfel took a deep breath. "The Archer is the guardian of the forest. The elves pray to him when we go to war. His skill is so renowned that it is said he could still shoot his enemies with exact precision even when he was close to death. He's a reincarnation of Sal'Sumarathar, one of the sons of Mother Ewyn."

"The Archer of the Lake is male?" Brenin asked.

Caelfel gave a small smile. "I suppose the Blind Seer can be wrong more than once." She did not mention that the Archer of the Lake was her namesake.

"And who is Mother Ewyn?"

"She is the mother of all elves, the Creator," Caelfel explained. "She gave birth to the five original elves, and they were the warriors of Honey Water. They conquered the dragons and then went on to found the five major cities."

Brenin chewed his bottom lip while he considered her words. "We have an Ewyn in our pantheon, though there is very little said of her children. Our Ewyn is the goddess of grace and beauty, master of the sea."

"That is unsurprising since she is an elf. What are the other gods in your pantheon? Who is this Strigi that you made a festival for?"

"Strigi is the goddess of hunting and the forest and rivers, the mountains and archery. She is the Mistress of Animals and The Wilds. The Lady of the Moon. She has a twin brother called Donar who is the god of truth and intelligence. He is a soldier, also called Warrior of the Sun. He's the best fighter in the world and a genius at military strategy. Their father is Voten, Father of the World, a champion of goodness and the Judge of Souls. He is our Creator. Then there is his wife Queen Marsda who watches over the world and cares for the earth and trees, harvest and childbirth. Her sister Ruxlitta is the goddess of magic and witchcraft, the patroness of change and healing. Ruxlitta's husband Numen is the god of the Never World, the god of death."

"What's the Never World?" Caelfel asked.

Brenin looked stunned. "It's the afterlife, where your soul goes after you die."

Caelfel blinked. "Nothing happens after you die. That is why it is called death."

Brenin was taken aback by Caelfel's conviction, and she saw his lip quivering faintly. Caelfel wondered if she had said something to upset him but couldn't fathom how. She'd only been telling him the truth.

"You don't believe in the Never World? Where good people live in golden fields of summer and the evil ones freeze on mountaintops in eternal agony?"

Caelfel flinched at such a fate. She did not think humans or their gods could think of such cruel punishments. "No, I don't. When you die, you just fade into oblivion. You don't exist anymore."

Brenin glared at something on the ground, lips pursing as he mulled over her words. "Then what is the *point*?" he countered bitterly.

"What is the point of what?" Caelfel snapped. She struggled to keep her voice down as more people pushed around them.

"What is the point of living if you just die?" he asked, obviously upset.

"The point is to live!" she told him exasperatedly.

Brenin stepped forward as if to pace, but the number of people around prevented him from doing so. Suddenly he snapped his fingers, realizing something. "Then what is the point of being a good person if the evil ones are not punished in the end?"

Caelfel could only blink dumbly at him, not understanding his argument. "A person will be a good person because it is the right thing to do. Evil people will still choose to do evil things because it is what they want."

"But who determines what is good and what is evil if not for the gods?" Brenin argued desperately. "And there is a god who rules over the Never World and one who judges your fate."

Caelfel frowned. "Then your gods are petty and you are very selfish to think only a few individuals are deserving of your summer fields." She sighed. "The elves live such long lives that it is pointless for us to live even longer after death. Mother Ewyn reminds her children that our death serves a purpose. Like the forest fire that destroys the trees and animals, death paves the way for new life."

It was Brenin's turn to sigh, and he released it heavily. "You don't believe in our gods. You think your goddess is the only one."

Caelfel turned to look at him. "I think you humans give yourselves too many lords to rule you, too many shackles to bind you."

Brenin voiced a short laugh, but then said nothing more on the subject. "You have such a beautiful view on life, Caelfel."

A sudden, deafening *boom* interrupted them, sounding as if the very air around them had shattered. Caelfel looked around anxiously, instinctively reaching for her absent bow at the sign of a potential threat. But then she saw a shower of red sparks blossoming in the air above them. The sparks extinguished themselves quickly before falling back to the ground. The people of Umfeld cheered and clapped for a gleefully grinning Pren whose face was covered in soot. Caelfel relaxed her muscles as Pren set fire to another one.

It erupted with the same noise, bringing an array of colors this time. There was more cheering, and several men came forward to assist Pren in igniting the fireworks in quick succession. Caelfel stared at the sky in wonderment, her grin stretching aching lines across her face. Gray clouds blanketed the sky, obscuring the sun from view. She worried it might rain.

She felt Brenin tug at her arm and she allowed him to lead her through the crowd, keeping her eyes on the sky as she watched the blue and purple sparks. Red and green ones took the shape of a flower while gold ones formed a winged dragon. She realized that the looming darkness of the gathering storm clouds made it possible for this spectacle to be visible.

Brenin stopped then, and Caelfel glanced around long enough to see that they had come to a low, stone wall that divided one field from another. She sat on the wall and quickly returned her attention to the colorfully illuminated sky. Brenin joined her.

"This is the closest thing we have to magic," he began. "But I'm sure you're capable of even greater wonders. I don't want to say that I'm envious of elves for their magic but I've always been fascinated by it. My mother would go on about all the things her elf friend could do. He could make it rain or he could make a garden full of flowers grow. He could heal broken bones in mere seconds or produce a sword of black steel out of nothing."

Caelfel's gaze drifted from the fireworks down to her feet. Brenin was so captivated by her because he was so immersed in the idea of magic. Elves were magical; they *were* magic. But Caelfel had lost her magic not so long ago with very little promise of getting it back. There were some who might not consider Caelfel a true elf because of it. Caelfel was ashamed of her inferiority. She swallowed past a thick lump in her throat. "I'm afraid I would disappoint you, then."

A frown passed through his features. "What do you mean?"

Caelfel avoided his gaze as she struggled to voice her pain. "Elves are magic because they have auras. Every elf is born with an aura, including me. Only, mine was taken away from me. I can't perform magic any more. If I could, I probably wouldn't even be here. I wouldn't have left Honey Water. I would have stayed to study magic at the colleges, like an elf is supposed to do," she confided quietly, rubbing the side of her nose.

To her astonishment, Brenin took her hands into his. His voice suddenly sounded rougher. "I am very sorry that you had to endure that. If it is any comfort to you, I am pleased that you have lost it. I am glad for the way you are."

"Why would you possibly be pleased about my plight?"

Brenin carefully avoided her gaze. "Because otherwise you would not be here, and therefore I would not have met you."

Caelfel glanced at their clasped fingers as her stomach twisted at his words and his touch. She awkwardly reclaimed her hands. Cyrus approached them then, rescuing Caelfel from the dreadfully uncomfortable conversation.

"My lord. Caelfel," the steward greeted them, Caelfel's bow in his hand. He passed it to her silently. "The match is about to begin. I took the liberty of registering your name for the competition. You'll be the last archer to shoot."

Caelfel nodded and stood to rejoin the crowd, Brenin and Cyrus trailing closely behind.

"Has my father inquired after me yet?" she heard Brenin ask.

Cyrus lowered his voice, but Caelfel easily heard his reply. "He seemed satisfied that you were with her."

Caelfel frowned at this information, perplexed as to why the king of Umfeld would be satisfied that she was with his son. But she pushed the thought from her mind as they reached a wooden platform that stood above the heads of the crowd of spectators. A line of archers circled its base. Among them, Caelfel recognized Huwel, Turre, and a handful of nameless faces she remembered from the Company. King Orrik stood on the platform and addressed his citizens.

"Welcome to the Tournament. The best archer shall receive Strigi's chalice full of gold and jewels. Would the first archer please step forward?"

One of the archers approached him, and King Orrik went to sit on the makeshift throne on the edge of the stage with Prince Madoc and Lady Anissa on either side. Caelfel noticed an empty chair for Brenin. The first archer positioned himself behind a line drawn on the boards with charcoal and aimed at the first target. The crowd fell silent, holding their breath. He released his arrow, and the tournament officially began.

There were three targets every archer had to hit, each one further than the last, and they were only given one chance for every mark. Caelfel noticed that human archers took plenty of time to aim, which made the whole process pass by slowly. There were twelve other archers competing, Caelfel being the thirteenth. Huwel was the fifth archer and was well received by the cheering crowd.

As the eighth archer stepped onto the stage, Caelfel whirled around to Brenin in concern. "They are all men."

"They are," Brenin agreed uncertainly.

"Where are your women archers?"

"We don't have any," Brenin admitted with a note of guilt that suggested he felt ashamed of the fact.

"This whole festival is to commemorate a *goddess* and you have no female archers," Caelfel pointed out with a raised eyebrow.

"Then show them what you are capable of doing," Brenin said, flashing a grin.

When the twelfth archer descended the steps, it was her turn to take the platform, so she did. Her presence was met with a hushed silence, and this time, Caelfel wasn't sure if it was because she was an elf or a female. She looked out at the sea of faces before turning to King Orrik who handed her three arrows.

Caelfel took them and lowered herself into a low bow—not a curtsy—as the other archers had and raised her head to look King Orrik in the eye. "Thank you, your grace."

King Orrik offered her a thin smile. "Make them count."

Caelfel straightened and stepped to the line as she inspected her targets. They weren't very far away. Caelfel couldn't imagine why any of the archers would have any difficulty. Then Caelfel became victim to a moment of pride and vanity. She gripped her bow, which was probably taller than most of the humans below her, and decisively took twenty paces back. Her new distance put her rather close to the royal party. She glanced back to wink at Anissa before hitting her first target.

It landed dead center and was met by a roar of applause from the crowd and a peal of thunder from the gathering clouds. When both died down, King Orrik remarked, "I believe it will rain."

Her second arrow met its target at the same time as a bolt of lightning appeared on the distant horizon. The crowd was too entertained by Caelfel to be afraid of the storm.

Caelfel found herself smiling as she drew back the third arrow. A raindrop splattered against her cheek just as she released it.

But her smile disappeared before the arrow found its mark in the center of the third target. For on the horizon, Caelfel saw a pack of wolves racing for the city.

7. Tragedy

Caelfel whirled around to face the king. "You need to get everyone inside the city, immediately," she instructed severely. The Tournament spectators were still cheering wildly for her archery prowess. Their weak eyesight did not allow them a glimpse of the danger that was fast approaching. Orrik looked stunned by the authority she used to address him, and a flicker of anger flashed through his eyes. But there was no time to argue. If they did not hurry, the citizens of Umfeld would be a sitting feast for the wolves.

"What are you talking about?" Orrik demanded harshly, getting to his feet. Even standing, he still was not as tall as Caelfel.

"I am sorry for my rudeness, your grace. But I can see a pack of werewolves racing towards us as we speak. They may only appear as dark spots on the horizon to you right now. You must hurry," Caelfel spoke quickly under her breath. She did not want to cause alarm among the crowd. That would only make things worse.

To her relief, Orrik nodded at her request and went to inform the Captain of the Guard to begin herding everyone back inside Palpses immediately. Madoc rose from his seat and narrowed his eyes at the horizon.

Realizing something was amiss, Brenin was suddenly standing by her side. "What's wrong?" he asked her quietly.

The Palpses Guard were quick in their work. The citizens of Palpses streamed towards the city with confused expressions. Those who dallied were encouraged by gentle prods from the butts of the soldiers' spears.

Caelfel turned her attention back towards the horizon. "The

werewolves are coming," she answered Brenin a low voice. They were still too far away to determine if they were the same ones that had attacked her days ago, but Caelfel suspected they were.

King Orrik returned to the platform and ushered Lady Anissa and Lord Barad back to their carriage. Once they were safely on their way, he turned to Brenin. "Nice of you to show up."

Brenin's face hardened but he ignored the remark. Madoc brought their attention back to the present danger. "I still can't see them. Caelfel, how much time do you think we have before they get here?"

"I would guess a few minutes."

"How many are there?" Brenin asked.

"Right now I count seven. There may be more. The pack in the forest was much larger."

"It's not Lycaon and his pack, is it?" the king asked gruffly.

Caelfel only knew Lycaon's visage from a brief glimpse in a shared vision, and she could not tell if these wolves were his. Luckily, Brenin had an answer. "Lycaon would not charge the city in wolf-form."

"Do they appear hostile, Caelfel?" Madoc asked.

Caelfel's superior eyesight allowed her to see the thick saliva that dripped from their yellow fangs. "I would not doubt it."

The Captain of the Guard, who Brenin identified as Captain Lewod, returned to inform them that that the citizens were safely inside the city. "What are you going to do about the werewolves, my prince?" Captain Lewod asked.

Brenin glanced at his father who returned the gaze with an icy smile. "You are the Lord of Kanetalm, my son. The decision is yours," King Orrik told him.

Brenin only took a moment to consider his options. "We don't know what their purpose is yet. I want twenty soldiers here when they arrive. The rest need to guard all of Palpses's entrances. Keep citizens away from the gates. Encourage them to continue the festival. Captain Lewod, I want you to watch us from the east tower. If something goes wrong, keep them safe, no matter what happens."

"Let us hope it does not come to that," Captain Lewod replied before choosing the twenty men that would remain outside. "Will you stay out here, my prince?"

Brenin nodded fearlessly, and his bravery touched something within Caelfel.

"They are coming," she reminded them quietly.

The twenty soldiers Brenin had asked for surrounded the base of the platform. Caelfel recognized Huwel, though he was notably not a Palpses Guard. He stood closest to Brenin.

"I'll go back and make sure everyone remains calm, no matter what," King Orrik volunteered.

Caelfel whipped her head toward the king of Umfeld in surprise. "You will not confront this threat on your land?" she accused.

"Look around you," Orrik snapped. "You have the king and both his sons sitting out here as easy prey. If something happened, Umfeld would be left without a king. The throne would go to my brother Orren, and no one in Umfeld wants that."

Caelfel pursed her lips but did not question him further. It was probably best Orrik left. She did not think she would care for his diplomatic negotiating skills.

Orrik turned to leave and beckoned for Madoc to join him. "Come, Madoc."

Madoc blinked at his father. "I will not hide behind the walls of Palpses and abandon my little brother to face this danger alone."

"Brenin has things under control," Orrik said dismissively. Still Madoc did not move and a dark expression crossed Orrik's features dangerously. "Madoc. I am commanding you."

And since Orrik was king, Madoc had no choice. The alleged Prince of the Vale followed his father sullenly towards the gates. By now, the huge wolves were easily visible to everyone present.

"I can't believe they would leave you out here," Caelfel spat. "Let a foreigner and the youngest prince deal with this matter."

Brenin turned to Caelfel. "Maybe you should go with them."

Caelfel turned towards him, appalled. "I will *not* be dismissed."

"I am a prince," Brenin pointed out, though there was no real argument in his voice.

"You are not *my* prince," Caelfel sniffed. "I cannot leave you when I am bound to protect you. And even if you were not here, I would stay for Garvanna."

Brenin nodded at her certainty. She gripped her bow tightly and turned to Cyrus. "Would you happen to have my quiver?" she asked him.

Cyrus offered a knowing smile and detached the quiver hanging from his belt. Caelfel slipped it over her shoulders, taking one arrow into her hand.

She was surprised to see the werewolves slow as they neared their position. The twenty soldiers held up their heavy shields defensively as the large, black alpha stopped before them. Caelfel recognized the bright, brown eyes of the wolf that had attacked her. The thought of Garvanna filled her with a sudden rage that made her restless.

"I am Prince Brenin," Brenin addressed them loudly. "Why have you come?"

The other wolves had stopped a few paces behind their leader but their bodies trembled with suppressed growls. The alpha's entire being quivered violently until he assumed the form of a naked man. The man's hair was long with thick, matted coils and a number of talismans hung from his neck.

The werewolf man had a deep, guttural voice that matched his appearance. "My name is Tarion. My pack and I have come to discuss territory lines with you." Despite his words, the other six werewolves remained in their bestial state. Only he had transformed into human form to speak.

Brenin folded his arms. "Good, I've been waiting to have this discussion. The Pirinac Forest does not belong to you. You can't attack everyone who passes through it."

"But, my prince. You are mistaken. Just as Haradrop belongs to those domestic *pups*, the Pirinac is ours and we have a right to protect what is ours from outsiders. I grow tired of people trespassing into my home."

"You do *not* have the right to kill everyone indiscriminately. Either put a stop to it or I will," Brenin informed him in a low voice.

Tarion inclined his head and took a step toward the prince, but the soldiers quickly closed ranks. Tarion shifted his weight and glared. "Are you threatening me, *boy?*"

"Consider it a warning, Tarion. You will answer for your crimes."

"I've committed no crime. We are only defending what is ours."

"What about the girl from Sorasaen? Was she such a great threat to your territory?" Brenin demanded, voice rising.

"She was a cheeky one," Tarion said with a throaty laugh. Caelfel saw his upper lip curl over his yellow teeth.

"And the two harmless elves passing through the forest?" Brenin asked, growing angrier with Tarion's cruelty.

Tarion's head turned to lock gazes with Caelfel, and his features suggested he recognized her. Caelfel scowled back at him. "The two harmless elves proved to be quite more dangerous than you suggest. This one took down two of my brothers before I finally subdued her. Their loss cannot be stated."

"You attacked us first!" Caelfel exclaimed, trying to keep her voice from shaking.

Tarion turned back to Brenin. "And you are not wholly correct, my prince. I've had three elves strutting about my forest."

Caelfel was shocked. "Three elves?" she repeated. Her mind automatically went to Feraan. He was the only elf that would venture beyond the Honey Water borders, and for a brief moment, Caelfel allowed herself a glimmer of hope that Feraan was looking for her.

But Tarion was quick to crush that hope. "I'm afraid the third was not as fortunate as your friend there. That third one did not make it out of the forest alive."

Caelfel felt very cold, and her fingers went numb. "What did you do?" Caelfel asked in a thick voice, emphasizing each word.

Tarion smirked at her dread. "She looked very much like you but perhaps a smidge older. She wielded blue magic like a master. It might have been a shame to eat such a powerful mage."

Something ripped through Caelfel's chest, painfully tearing through her lungs and heart. Tarion's description of the elf, though not Feraan, was an accurate portrait of another elf precious to her. Caelfel thought back to the Seer's words and how she used a voice that belonged to her mother.

"You are lying," Caelfel said through clenched teeth. She did not want to believe Tarion or picture his maliciously smirking face smeared with mud and blood. Caelfel did not want to think that the blood belonged to her mother.

"I'm afraid not," Tarion replied smoothly. He removed one of the talismans from his neck and threw it to her feet. When Caelfel bent to pick it up, she immediately recognized the emerald amulet worn only by a daughter of Sal'Sumarathar. Caelfel's mother had often said that there were only seven of the emerald amulets and, despite being ostracized from her family, Sylaera Gyssedlues had been allowed to keep hers.

But Caelfel didn't understand why her mother would venture into the Pirinac Forest. She had sent a message to her only a day ago. "You killed her. You *ate* her," Caelfel restated with disgust. Caelfel experienced a new rage thrumming through her veins and heating her cheeks. Caelfel felt herself becoming dangerous.

"She had a very sweet taste," Tarion mused as if he had not committed some abhorrent crime. "Only, her temper was not so sweet."

Caelfel felt her legs tensing, preparing to charge at the werewolf as the will to kill Tarion flashed through her entire being. She glared at him murderously. "Her name was Sylaera Gyssedlues, wife to Eviat Gyssedlues and mother to only one daughter. *And I will kill you for this!*" Caelfel screeched, gripping her bow.

Before she could aim for his insignificant head, Brenin sidestepped in front of her. "Caelfel, no."

She hated Brenin in that moment as he denied Caelfel of her proper revenge. "You *cannot* tell me *no*, Brenin. He took my mother from me."

He placed his hands on her shoulders, as if he had the strength to resist her. "Tarion is only provoking you. If you attack him, it would only give him reason to attack the city."

In an uncharacteristic moment, Caelfel did not care for the fate of the city. Brenin saw this and grew worried. Elves were notorious for proving unable to control their grief.

"Remember that life debt you told me about? Isn't it sacred to you? Attacking Tarion would only get me killed." He was grasping for straws, for a rational argument to appeal to her.

She felt her rage dim fractionally. "You are assuming I would not win."

"You've lost against them before," he pointed out.

"He killed my mother, Brenin," she said through tight lips. Her throat cracked, and her eyes pricked. Her jaw hurt from clenching it so hard.

"I know, and you deserve your revenge. But now is not the time. You wouldn't be avenging your mother. You would only be getting us killed," he told her urgently.

Caelfel lowered her bow. "As you command," she whispered, irate that Brenin would humiliate her in front of their enemies.

When Brenin was certain that Caelfel would not do anything rash, he turned his attention back to the werewolves.

Tarion, amused by their dispute, rumbled a husky laugh. "Your prince is right, she-elf. It would be unwise to challenge me."

Caelfel levelled her gaze at Tarion. "My prince's only concern is that I would get your blood all over my dress."

The six other wolves snarled at her. Tarion turned his head over his shoulder. "Calm yourselves, Skolt, Gunilla." He turned back to them. "Are you threatening me, she-elf?" Tarion asked.

"Consider it a warning," Caelfel said, echoing Brenin from earlier. Tarion heaved a sigh, and the sound reverberated through his chest as a growl. "Then I would be happy to return the favor," he said, pacing back and forth, his long arms swaying as he yearned to be on all fours. He fixed his gaze back onto Brenin. "Tell your people that if they need to go around the Ruxlitta Mountains, they should go through the desert. Anyone who enters the Pirinac risks death. Or worse."

Brenin gave a single, curt nod. "I will spread the word."

Tarion gave a wolfish howl as the matted fur once more sprouted all over his body and he rejoined his brothers in animal form. They took off running for the horizon, and all the humans sighed in relief.

Caelfel angrily whipped around to Brenin. "You let him leave without retribution? You will allow him to continue terrorizing your people?"

"I cannot confront him here, Caelfel," he defended. "I don't know the extent of their strength or numbers. But believe me, they won't get away with this—"

"They already have," Caelfel cut him off, ending their conversation. She jumped from the platform and raced after Tarion's pack. Caelfel ignored Brenin's cries for her to stop and lifted her bow to aim for Tarion's head. But Tarion dodged her arrow and Caelfel only managed to nick his ear. Tarion yelped and spun around to meet her. Caelfel suddenly found herself inches from the alpha's frothing muzzle. From the corner of her eye, she saw the others continuing on without their alpha.

And though she had attacked him, giving him reason to strike her down, Tarion merely blew his hot, rank breath across her face. Caelfel wrinkled her nose and stood her ground. "I am not afraid of you."

Tarion's chest vibrated, as if he were laughing at her naivety, and then he turned and followed his pack across the plain.

The threat was gone, and Caelfel could hear the soldiers behind her dispersing to tell their king what had transpired. But she merely stood there, her chest heaving as she tried to recall the last time she had seen her mother. It had been in the desert, a brief goodbye and a promise to see each other again soon. *What a cruel lie.*

"Caelfel?" came Brenin's voice, interrupting her mind-numbing recollection. She blinked to see his face and belatedly noticed the tears flowing from the corners of her eyes. She wiped at them angrily, though she knew she was incapable of stopping them.

"I need to be alone," Caelfel told Brenin, avoiding his gaze. Her mother was dead. She needed to be alone to grieve. Births were so infrequent among her race that any elf life taken before its time was mourned deeply and forcefully. While in the throes of grief, elves were unable to control their emotions and often their actions.

Caelfel struggled to remember the last times she had cried. Then she realized that it had only been a few days ago when she lost Garvanna. Before that, she had shed tears for the lost fate of a ruined city. Both times she had expressed a wild temperament. But this would be different. This was not some city destroyed before her birth or a friend she had only known for less than a few months. This was her mother, her own blood murdered by some self-assured, bloodthirsty beast. Caelfel had never truly mourned for someone before but she knew she would be uncontrollable.

And she would not have Brenin see her this way.

"Caelfel, wait—" Brenin started, afraid of the decision he saw in her eyes.

But Caelfel did not wait. She turned and ran.

She had no concern of being followed; she was quicker than most elves and certainly faster than any human. But she found that, with sobs choking her lungs, she could not run very far. After crossing a few fields, she vaulted over a stone wall to find herself in a garden of wildflowers. Caelfel allowed herself a moment to gaze impassively at the soft petals. Most of them were blue, and the color only made her chest tighten as she remembered her mother's blue aura.

The garden belonged to an abandoned, rustic farmhouse whose broken window panes were coated with thick webs. Eying the disrepair, Caelfel felt confident that she was indeed alone. She sat by an old well that now stood dry as it guarded the wildflowers. It was there that she sat among the flowers and her newfound garden and faced east toward her homeland.

The horizon provided no view of her beloved forest, and the sounds of the festival were beyond earshot. Caelfel's only companion was the sharp whistling of the wind that rattled the cottage's broken frames and doors as the rainstorm approached.

The pain rolled through her chest like nausea, and she struggled to keep from vomiting. Caelfel wanted to believe Tarion was lying, but the amulet she so desperately clutched in her hands was real. The pain she felt was real. Mother's death was real.

And so Caelfel buried her face in her lap. She remembered her mother and she mourned to the sound of relentless thunder.

***

Caelfel kneeled over the water's edge to stare at her pudgy reflection on the mirror-like surface. Her eyebrows knitted apprehensively just as her mother's visage appeared beside her on the water.

"Jump in," Sylaera instructed.

Caelfel furiously shook her head and scrambled away from the bank. Before Caelfel could protest further, Sylaera plucked her from the ground and tossed her into the lake.

Caelfel remembered splashing and coughing as she treaded water. "I can't swim, mummy!" she gasped.

"This is Lake Rumfel. It is your namesake and it will not let you drown," Sylaera called back before jumping into the water with her.

Caelfel doubted her mother's words, but as usual, Sylaera was correct. Sylaera held onto her daughter's sides as Caelfel learned to swim. She kicked through the water slowly to propel herself forward and held her breath as she dived under.

When they were finished for the day, Sylaera summoned a small wind to dry both of them off. They walked back home, hand in hand.

"I told you that you could do it, my little fish."

***

Caelfel was as tall as Father's hip now, so she felt old enough to venture into the forest on her own. Father had left for the capital so he could not take her hiking. But Caelfel would not allow that to spoil her day. Somehow, she had managed to sneak out of the house without alerting her mother, so she ran to the Blaidd River as fast as she could before she could get caught.

She reached the river's edge, laughing from breathless excitement. She followed the river south, skipping along merrily. She stopped when the bank dropped off suddenly and she leaned over the outcropping to take a closer look.

"Be careful, youngling," warned a voice.

Caelfel snapped her head up to see a tall elf standing across the river, staring at her.

"The river's currents are very strong right now," he continued, not unkindly. Caelfel stood, puffing out her chest. "I'm not afraid. I know how to swim." The elf laughed at her pride. "What's your name, child?"

"It's Caelfel. What's yours?"

"My name is not important," he said, sounding rather sad before slipping away through the trees.

Caelfel stared after him sadly for a few minutes before turning her attention back to the rushing water below. She lowered a long stick into the water and watched as it sliced through the current, making white foam spray around it.

But then a chittering noise distracted Caelfel from her entertainment, and she looked up, thinking the elf had returned to tell her his name. "Hello? Are you there?"

The trees fell eerily silent, and Caelfel knew in her heart that something was wrong. She scrambled to her feet as an animal fell from the branch above her.

The tiny, green creature scurried to face her, and Caelfel found herself staring into the black, liquid eyes of a goblin.

Caelfel gasped as she smelled the stench of goblin-fire.

More goblins fell from the trees, and Caelfel screamed as they ambushed her. She fell, and they rolled around on the rocks as goblins clawed at her hair and face.

Then they fell off the ledge. Caelfel screamed until she hit the water.

The river did not slow their efforts. The goblins continued to mercilessly scratch her, producing streaks of blood as they ripped her clothes. Caelfel's heart hammered as she inhaled gulps of water.

Then the goblins stopped attacking, and Caelfel froze as she tried looking around but could see nothing in the murky water. She began to float upwards until she suddenly broke the surface. Relief spread through her body as she finally filled her lungs with air.

She kept floating above the river, bobbing around gently and coughing up water. She noticed a blue light that surrounded her like a bubble and when she turned around, Caelfel saw her mother standing on the bank of the river. With one hand, she kept her daughter suspended in midair and she used the other to blast away at the offending goblins until they scampered off into the forest without a glance back.

Caelfel, ignoring the shame she should have felt for disobeying, clapped wildly as her heroic mother proved victorious, using only one hand.

Sylaera fixed her daughter with a stern look, wanting to scold Caelfel for her actions. But a smile quickly won out and Sylaera bowed low to the ground several times to Caelfel's applause.

They returned home, and Caelfel told Mother about the lone elf she saw in the woods. "*He wouldn't tell me his name,*" *Caelfel pouted.*

Sylaera frowned, but she appeared more thoughtful than troubled. "*His name is Feraan, and he has the reputation as the most hated elf in the empire,*" *she said carefully.*

Caelfel scowled. "*Why?*"

"*Do not let someone else's opinion of a person spoil your own,*" *Sylaera reprimanded lightly.* "*Especially if you don't know who they are or what they've been through.*"

Caelfel nodded dutifully, cataloging this bit of wisdom for later use. "*I think he was trying to be nice. He warned me about the river currents.*"

Sylaera laughed, ruffling Caelfel's hair even though she knew that Caelfel did not *like it when she did that.* "*He should have warned you about the goblins instead. Next time, be careful and always be aware of your surroundings, my little explorer.*"

***

On her fiftieth birthday, there was a celebration held in honor of Caelfel's coming of age. Many in Sal'Sumarathar came to celebrate in the plaza, dancing and drinking. It was the first time Caelfel tasted any spirits, and Mother watched her every sip like a hawk.

As the center of attention, Caelfel often found herself spinning around with various partners until someone had stopped her. It was time to receive her presents.

Caelfel had always showed an early talent for ranged combat, so many of her gifts were tailored this way. The Council of Sal'Sumarathar presented her with an array of blades designed for throwing. Head Councilor Uthruil and his son Daerad personally gave them to her. Sir Kennyratear, an instructor at the college and dear friend of Father's, gave her a set of arrows fletched with raven feathers. Nimuath, the Headmaster of the College, gave her another set fletched with swan feathers.

"*But I don't have a bow,*" *Caelfel despaired. Then, as if to quell her fears, her parents presented her with the last gift.*

It was a bow, tall as her shoulder when strung, made of yew wood and decorated with ivy and leaf carvings. Caelfel marveled at it as she tested the weight in her hands. When she drew the string back, it felt extremely powerful.

"*Your father made it,*" *Sylaera explained.* "*And I've imbued it with magic so it will last forever.*"

Caelfel gave both of her beaming parents a grateful hug. The music continued, but Caelfel was anxious to try out her new gift. She grabbed the quiver Sir Kennyratear had given her and set off for the archery range alone.

She had tested a few shots before she realized someone had followed her.

Caelfel whirled around to see Daerad, son of the Head Councilor, standing nearby.

Caelfel was the youngest elf of Sal'Sumarathar, but Daerad was the second youngest, only forty-eight years her senior. As the two youngest, they were often expected to play together, but Daerad was too much older and preferred games that would torment her. Caelfel always avoided him when she could.

"What do you want?" she demanded.

Daerad gave a casual shrug, and then she noticed that he held one of her throwing knives. He tilted it so that the sunlight glinted off the tempered steel. "I asked Father for these for my half-century celebration. He wouldn't give them to me. He said I wasn't a warrior." Daerad took a step closer to her, and the blade suddenly looked threatening in his grasp.

Caelfel tightened her grip on her bow, feeling a new sense of empowerment she had never felt before. "I'm sorry you didn't get what you wanted." She wasn't really sorry. Daerad was too cruel to deserve anything he wanted.

His blue eyes flashed, and quick as a blink, he towered above her with the knife pressed against her cheek. "I bet you're sorry," he hissed, backing her into a tree.

The look in his eyes warned Caelfel that he was about to kiss her, and he did. Surprisingly, Caelfel found herself kissing him back until she decided she did not like the taste of his lips. She moved the bow in her hands until the arrow tip pushed against the bob in his throat. Daerad suddenly became afraid and he dropped her knife to the ground as he pulled back.

"I'm not really sorry," Caelfel told him. She nodded to the blade on the ground. "You can keep the knife, if you want."

Then, retrieving her arrows, Caelfel bravely turned her back on him and headed towards the plaza once more.

Caelfel's vision shifted. She saw herself walk away as something else tugged at her awareness. She continued to see Daerad in the archery range.

Then her mother appeared from the trees, alight with crackling blue fire. She pointed menacingly at Daerad's now cowering form.

"You will leave my daughter alone," she commanded him.

"I will!" Daerad cried desperately, recoiling as if he was in pain. "I won't touch Caelfel again."

Sylaera lowered her hand. "Good." She sighed when Daerad ran from the clearing. "Oh, my little heartbreaker."

***

The Chief of Sal'Sumarathar, Markis Rilynnzea, was a disconcerting sort of elf, resembling a snake with his slithering movements and the silver paint he wore on his face. He executed his duties with a precise ruthlessness and, as a government official with the backing of the Council, there wasn't an elf who stood up to him.

Sylaera Gyssedlues was the rare exception—

Caelfel remembered this day. She had been wrongfully arrested for a wildly imagined crime she could not have possibly committed.

— "What have you done with my daughter?" Sylaera demanded, approaching the Chief Executor.

Markis stood in front of the Hall of Court and he turned to meet Sylaera with a wide smile. "Caelfel has been placed into my custody."

"For what crime?" Caelfel realized her mother had an unusual talent for sounding angry without raising her voice.

"Lady Gyssedlues, I'm afraid I cannot reveal the details of my investigation." Caelfel remembered how Markis always sounded unapologetic when delivering unpleasant information.

Sylaera stood so close to him that she was able to jab her finger against his chest with each word. "For. What. Crime."

Markis calmly stepped back from Sylaera's prodding. "Lady Gyssedlues, need I remind you that you are no longer a Daughter of Sal'Sumarathar? Your demands have no bearing on me."

Sylaera gave a dangerous smirk. "Master Rilynnzea, you should know that my family's titles have no bearing on me. I will get what I want with or without their backing." A blue spark flew from the tip of her finger and landed on Markis's shoulder. He impatiently brushed it off.

"Are you threatening the Chief Executor?" Markis asked, tilting his head. Sylaera did not shrink from the insinuation that she was committing treason. "I'm reassuring the Chief Executor that I will stop at nothing when it comes to my daughter."

And though she was indeed threatening him, Markis looked impressed with her resolve. "Caelfel has been arrested for necromancy."

"Necromancy? That's absurd. She cannot even perform magic."

Markis narrowed his eyes. "She hasn't told you what she's done?"

"What has she done?" It was Sylaera's turn to become impatient.

"She saved the condemned. The most hated elf of the empire. Raised him from the dead."

Sylaera appeared surprised with this news. She quickly recovered. "Whatever happens, Chief Executor, you best make damn sure nothing happens to her."

"If she is found guilty, she will be taken to Yamalvon to be executed," Markis said, shrugging. "There is nothing I can do."

Sylaera's gaze was cold. "Then you better think of something, because if Caelfel dies, you will die." She moved to leave, walking down the steps of the Hall.

And for the first time since Caelfel had met him, Markis looked afraid. *"I can arrest you for saying that."*

Sylaera paused. "Try it," she dared.

And though she waited for Markis to make his move, the Chief Executor remained frozen in place. Sylaera Gyssedlues continued on her way.

***

Sylaera was marching through the forest, making her way to a house hidden from the rest of elvenkind. A healer wearing a green tunic followed her. When she reached the door, she did not bother knocking and instead flung the door open without invitation. Her rage was tangible.

"How can you sit there?" she demanded of the elf who was bent over his desk. "How can you do nothing and allow this to happen?"

The elf—Feraan, Caelfel realized—*stood up to match her anger. "What do you mean?"*

Sylaera thrust a letter into his hands. Feraan scanned through it quickly before reading it aloud.

"Dear Master Eviat and Lady Sylaera,

We regretfully report that your daughter Caelfel has been taken while in combat. She is currently under the custody of Admiral Grimault of the Umfang army. The nature of her well-being is unknown.

Honey Water's imperial army does not have the resources to reclaim her from enemy hands. Unfortunately, there is nothing we can do, as the Umfang army has departed and no longer poses a threat to elvenkind. We will be withdrawing from the border in a few days' time. You may reclaim her personal possessions once the army disbands.

We send our best regards.

Captain Sanddef—"

Feraan only paused for a moment before he rushed through the house to gather his things.

Sylaera followed him. "Well?" she demanded expectantly.

Feraan finished attending to his sword before straightening to answer her. "What would you have me do, Lady Gyssedlues?"

Sylaera did not flinch. "Find her and bring her back."

* * *

Sylaera was in a desert, standing before the high, black-stone walls of a fortress. The Cromlech Palace. A spray of arrows and missiles rained all around her and the small army that had gathered behind her. Sylaera stood at its forefront, with her hands raised, as a brilliant blue light rammed into the front gates. Within moments, Sylaera had reduced them to rubble.

* * *

Sylaera strolled through her garden peacefully, until a raven descended from the trees, a scroll tied around its leg.

"She received my letter," Caelfel realized.

But when Sylaera read the words sent to her, she looked panicked. She flew into the house to find her husband. Eviat was sitting in the front room, carving a new bow. His expression changed to match Sylaera's alarm. "What is it?"

"Garvanna has sent us a letter. Caelfel has gone missing in the Pirinac Forest. They were attacked by werewolves. I'm going to find her."

Sylaera's words left little room for argument as she briefly kissed her husband—

"No!" Caelfel cried.

The scene changed again, and Caelfel's awareness was pulled into Sylaera's head, seeing things through her eyes.

Sylaera was riding fiercely through a dark forest that Caelfel recognized at once as the Pirinac.

The sound of ringing howls and beastly snarls caused Sylaera to press her steed onward.

It wasn't until she passed a crumbling statue of the Ruxlitta goddess that the growls became dangerously close. At that moment, Sylaera caught sight of an enormous wolf bounding through the trees in front of her.

It sailed through the air to knock Sylaera off her horse. The she-elf and wolf collided, and Sylaera felt sharp leaves and underbrush scrape against her face as she fell. When she looked up, Sylaera saw her wolfish assailant already on its feet.

It panted, and hot steam curled from its open mouth. From the intelligent shine in its eyes, Sylaera knew she had found the werewolves. It waited, circling her, as Sylaera got to her feet. Her steed stood at a distance, restlessly pawing the ground in agitation.

"Where is my daughter?" Sylaera asked the werewolf.

The wolf only snapped its teeth. It would not return to its human form to

97

answer.

"*My daughter is Caelfel. She looks very much like me. I am told she passed through this forest with a friend and hasn't been found since.*"

Then the wolf howled, and Sylaera knew the bone-chilling sound was a call to its brethren.

Sylaera focused her aura, and a transparent blue blade materialized in her grip. "*Don't do something you will regret,*" *she warned it.*

"*Regret? What would we regret?*"

Sylaera whirled around to see the owner of the voice standing in human form a short distance away. He was nude and muddy, and his long, dark brown hair was matted. He wore a strange necklace full of odd talismans and pendants. Tarion.

"*I have no quarrel with the werefolk, but that might change with your answer. Tell me where my daughter is, and I will be on my way,*" *she said.*

"*You are rather brave to be giving out demands. This land is ours, and we do not care for trespassers.*"

"*I will not ask again. My daughter. Where is she?*"

"*I recall two she-elves passing through here a few days ago. They escaped. You will not be so lucky, she-elf. My family has never tasted elven meat before. If I see your daughter again, I'll be sure to send her your regards.*"

Sylaera would not be afraid, but his threats horrified her. "*Werewolves do not eat people, be it elves or humans.*"

The man before her gave a dark chuckle. "*My name is Tarion, and I am father to a new race of werewolf, a much stronger breed. We are not afraid of your elvish magic.*"

Tarion jumped, shifting into wolf form, and Sylaera saw four more wolves emerge from the shadows.

Caelfel screamed as the brilliant show of blue lights was extinguished by thick streaks of blood.

8. Plots of Revenge

Gwyndolyn was not one to express insecurity. She was the only daughter of the elvish Empress Haelyn, and as such, she never found herself wanting for anything, despite her illegitimacy. She was a powerful mage, possessing a strong aura of silver luster. She had been appointed Head Mara on the Board of Wizardry long before reaching her half-century mark. She had rooms and libraries, a fortress in the mountains. She was the Warden of the Labyrinth Cells, an underground prison that held every criminal of Honey Water. A personal band of soldiers shadowed her movements, protecting her at every moment. The best swordsman and obliterator, renowned for his victorious military campaigns as army general, served as her personal bodyguard.

And yet Gwyn did not have everything she wanted, her chief desire being her rightful title as Princess. She was only Lady Gwyndolyn Ernmas, only allowed to keep the royal family name as a courtesy of the empress. There were many that petitioned against Gwyn having a family name at all.

But this had been Gwyn's life since she had been born a century ago. She had not concerned herself with a rightful inheritance until recently when seeds of doubt started taking root in her mind. She approached her mother in private, her thoughts weighing with this new uncertainty.

"Your majesty, I would like to talk to you about your heir," Gwyndolyn began formally, addressing her mother by her formal title.

They were in Haelyn's private rooms, and the empress had her back turned to her daughter, facing an enchanted mirror that Gwyndolyn did not understand the full capabilities of. The empress rotated to face Gwyndolyn in a single, fluid motion, her burgundy silk dress rustling soundlessly. Gwyn met her mother's guarded gaze with one of her own.

Despite being mother and daughter, they shared nothing in appearance. Where the empress had flawless skin the color of rich ebony, Gwyn was pale and fair. Her own hair was long and erratic, the shade of fresh honey. Empress Haelyn's hair was dark like midnight and reached as far as her jawline. Gwyn never met or knew her father, but she imagined he had passed along her lightly shaded beauty. Mother would always refuse to speak of him or even acknowledge his existence.

After staring for a minute of painful silence, Empress Haelyn carefully avoided Gwyn's eyes. "If I cannot produce a legitimate heir, the noble families will compete for the mantle after my death."
Gwyn steeled her chest. "A legitimate heir, your majesty?"

"I would have to marry an approved suitor and bear his child," the empress explained curtly.

Then the characteristic temper Gwyndolyn had been keeping in check since she had entered the room slipped from her grasp. "You have me," Gwyndolyn said with a quiet, unrestrained indignation.

The empress did not even bat her eyelashes. "You are not a legitimate heir."

"I am your flesh and blood, born of your own womb. I am the only thing you have," Gwyn cried petulantly.

"No, you are not the only thing I have. I am the only thing *you* have." Gwyndolyn flinched, but Haelyn continued. "I have a whole empire and the subjects who dwell in it. I have the Ormr Bank and its influence at my back. I have an undisputed army that has *never* lost a battle while under my command. And lastly, I have an ungrateful daughter who has been spoiled her entire life in spite of her unique condition."

Gwyn chewed the edge of her tongue as she deliberately ignored her mother's final sentence. "If you have all that, then why do you need an approved husband? You can name me as your heir and no one would question your command."

Haelyn sighed wearily as she turned to gaze at her mirror once again. "You would not even outlive me to rise to the throne. My dear daughter, you are but a child in years and yet you already show the signs of a greyling who ages."

Gwyn swallowed to ease her dry throat as the brutal truth was shoved in her face. She was dying, would be lucky to even see her second century. "If it matters so little in the end, I could still be crowned princess."

Empress Haelyn flew into a rage. "Because it *does* matter. What if I were to die before you? Then my mother's empire would be left to *you*? You are only *half* elf. You do not even have our pointed ears."

Gwyn blinked. "It is not by my choice. You bedded a human to conceive me."

Haelyn continued as if it mattered little. "You think you will inherit my empire? You destroyed one of my cities. My beautiful city."

Gwyn gasped when her mother brought the unmentionable to light. "It wasn't my fault."

"So we found the perfect scapegoat, and still you are not satisfied by my measures to ensure your safety. Blaes has told me, Gwyndolyn. How you seek Feraan Auvrearaheal out and how you still keep those *things* underground."

"They are not *things*," Gwyn began heatedly. "They are living creatures and they help—"

"They are uncontrollable monsters that destroyed my city. You should have let Feraan destroy them like the rest. I would not let you rule over Honey Water by that fact alone. But the truth of the matter is that even if Amasel did not fall, I would still not name you as my heir. You are selfish and vindictive. You would see Honey Water burn to get what you wanted. I will never let you be my successor."

Gwyndolyn was left gaping like a fish. The fine hair on her arms began to rise, and slight trickles of electricity crackled at her fingertips and set her teeth on edge. "You are wrong. I would be a beloved empress. I have been reforming Sal'Sumarathar. The entire Gyssedlues family has been pardoned. The Chief Executor has been imprisoned. The Head Councilor is to be put on trial for misuse of authority."

Haelyn chuckled darkly. "You will bring Uthruil Killelvris to trial. You stupid, simple girl. The Killelvris family has secured *your* safety, hiding away every piece of evidence that would incriminate you on the case of Amasel. Without their help, I would have been forced to send you to the executioner. But I was weak, and my poor daughter was only twenty. So I took pity." But Empress Haelyn shook her head, unable to finish the thought. "Blaes, come here please."

Gwyndolyn's body guard appeared from nowhere when summoned. He waited patiently for his orders from the empress and would not even look Gwyndolyn in the face, the one he had been sworn to protect.

"Compose a letter to Head Councilor Uthruil. Inform him that he is pardoned from his ridiculously imagined crimes and reinstated to his position."

"Of course, your majesty." Blaes set to work transcribing the missive at her desk.

Gwyn watched with muted rage as her mother exercised this cruel use of power to undo the progress Gwyn had worked so hard to achieve. "You are robbing me of everything," Gwyn hissed icily.

"I am mending what you have broken," Haelyn clarified.

"And you are using my most treasured friend to do it," Gwyn said.

Haelyn gave a bitter laugh. "Your most treasured friend? He dedicates his life to guard you because it is what I ask. You will learn, Gwyn. Blaes?"

Blaes straightened from his work. "Yes, your majesty?"

"Tell me how many elves are standing in this room?" she asked of him.

"Two, your grace."

"And the third person in this room?"

"Not an elf, your grace."

"And is 'not an elf' fit to take the throne after me?"

"No, your grace."

"Is there anyone fit to be my successor?"

Gwyn heard Blaes swallow.

"Go on, Blaes. Tell your charge the news," Haelyn prompted.

"It is my duty to marry the empress and sire a legitimate heir through her."

Gwyndolyn's whole world began shaking, even after Haelyn dismissed Blaes from the room. "You would take him from me," Gywn said lowly.

"He was not yours to claim," Haelyn said simply.

"You knew I loved him," Gwyn said, louder this time.

"He is not yours to love. This will teach you not to be so careless with your heart."

Gwyndolyn saw her own fury in the flashing silver that tinged the periphery of her vision. When she spoke, she could taste energy dripping from her teeth like silver venom. "If everything I am displeases you so, it is only your fault for creating me. I had no choosing in it." A tendril of silver magic erupted from a clenched fist at her side.

"*You will not use your magic against me*," Empress Haelyn shrieked, her bronze aura flickering around her hands. "You will learn or you will perish, Gwyndolyn. You are not invincible. You will be put in your place."

"How dare you insult me, drag me in here to spite me. You think I am this monster, but what does it say of you if you created and birthed me. You are the one who has hurt me."

Haelyn glared. "Get out of my sight."

Gwyn squared her shoulders. "I would not want you in mine."

She couldn't stand being in the palace so Gwyn went to the only place where she had absolute power. The Labyrinth Cells.

The Labyrinth was a maze of tunnels under the elvish capital Yamalvon. There were no walled cells for the prisoners, who were condemned to wander aimlessly. No one but Gwyn knew the way out, and her precious globes ensured that no one would find out. But when Gwyn entered the Labyrinth, she did not make her normal rounds to visit every inmate. She made her way directly to her newest and favorite prisoner, the one who had begun planting those seeds of doubt in her thoughts.

She found him in his usual place, in the furthest reaches of the caverns. She arranged her face into an indifferent expression and then approached him alone. In keeping with general practice of the Labyrinth, he was not chained, but Gwyn did not worry over her own safety. She could easily handle every prisoner detained in the Labyrinth. Gwyn often felt that her personal company of soldiers that normally shadowed her every move were unnecessary since she could protect herself better than they ever could.

On her first encounter with this particular prisoner, she had explicitly explained that the guards that flanked her during the interrogations were present as a courtesy to the prisoner's safety. Gwyndolyn could easily suffer from a headache, a cataclysmic episode, putting everyone's life at risk. In truth, the soldiers were primarily tasked with the job of neutralizing her, in the event that Gwyn lost control of her powers. But that hadn't happened in over eighty years.

"You came alone this time," the prisoner noted, rising to greet her.

Gwyndolyn quirked an eyebrow at him in the dim light. She had picked up the habit of communicating with him telepathically, relishing the way it had intimidated him. *Does that frighten you?* She challenged him temptingly.

"Mostly, you intrigue me," he said, brushing off his dirty pants. An easy smile came to his lips.

She moved her head slightly, as if the cavernous room interested her more than he did. *You take a risk in flirting with me.*

"A risk I'm willing to take," he said, arms spreading wide. "For there is no greater honor."

She allowed herself a half-smile at his gracious compliments. *You are a true courtier. You belong in a royal court.*

"I have trained as a steward, my lady, but I don't believe you've paid me a visit to discuss my abilities."

On the contrary, human, *that is precisely why I have come.* Then aloud, she said, "Tell me about your other abilities, steward."

His eyes widened in feigned shock. "I have been allowed the highest honor of hearing your voice."

She became stern with him. *Answer the question.*

He settled back, leaning against the wall, and exhaled with the sound of obedient resignation. "You know of my abilities. They are much like yours, like other elves. I have an aura and with it, I can perform magic."

Did you steal this aura?

"No, I was born with it. I didn't realize auras could be stolen," he pondered with a bit of awe.

"A human with an aura is rather odd," Gwyn noted.

"Very rare but not impossible. I know of only one other human with an aura and we met very briefly, for only a few minutes."

She continued through her observations of him. *And a human sorcerer in the employ of Admiral Grimault. That sounds even stranger to me.*

The pride vanished instantly. He had turned cautious. "I have an aptitude for waiting for the right opportunity. I am very careful with everything I do."

And look at where it's landed you. She looked about the room for emphasis.

"It was not my doing. I owe it entirely to a man notorious for making rash, idiotic decisions."

You owe it entirely to yourself for choosing the company of a rash, idiotic man, she countered.

His eyebrows quivered as he examined her face. "What do you want? I was told I would be tortured here, and so far I've received no such torture aside from the trepidation of expecting it. You come every day with your smug expression, like you're trying to scare me."

I come to you every day to hear you talk, to determine your innocence or guilt.

"And what have you decided?"

"I already know the truth," she said, taking up a slow pace around the room. "I have seen your aura and everything you have done with it."

"Then why do you come?"

She paused to show him her mouth flickering in a quick smile. "I come to hear you speak because I like your voice."

He gave a silent laugh, perhaps figuring he had her seduced. Maybe he did. "The things I've said mean something to you. I told you that you were the most powerful being in existence."

Don't waste your breath with flattery. I already knew that.

He checked himself, bowing his head at the appropriate authority in her voice. "My apologies. I did not mean to offend."

She chuckled. "I have come alone today to tell you something. I want to remind you that while you've been under my care, you have received no ill treatment and especially none of this torture you were promised."

He nodded. "I haven't."

"I wanted to warn you that I am leaving Honey Water, but not for long. Whoever my replacement may be will not be as kind as I was. So I bring you an invitation. Come with me and serve a better master than your previous one."

His eyes shone as a plan developed behind them. He took no hesitation to answer her. "I will, of course, follow you, my lady."

She smiled at him faintly. "Serve me well, and in return, I will keep you safe and give you power. Perhaps this was the right opportunity you were waiting for."

"I've no doubt of that."

"I have my soldiers, but I will require you to find me an army. I will be addressed as Princess and then, when the time comes, Queen. I may only be half elf, but I am more powerful than any elf who would dare cross my path. I will reclaim Honey Water as my empire. I will right the wrongs and cleanse the corruption of my mother's reign."

He bowed his head. "I know where to get you an army. We will have to go to Umfang, though I'm sure some of the other prisoners in the Labyrinth would be eager to hail you as their rightful empress, as well."

Feeling newly empowered, she pushed her shoulders back and turned to take her leave. She stopped, before passing beyond the torch's glow, and looked at him over her shoulder. *After all this time, you never told me your name.*

His grin was sinister. "My name is Lisiek."

***

Runa awoke with a breathless start from some mostly-forgotten but terrifying nightmare. She looked around in frenzied bewilderment before realizing she was at her home, a stone, one-room cottage, every detail of which she had memorized long ago. Though it was a welcome sight, she had no memory of getting there.

She struggled to breathe and pressed a fist against the terrible pain in her chest, just as her stepmother came to her bedside.

"Oh, Runa, darling. You're awake at last," she said with a note of teary relief, her hand fluttering to Runa's brow, feeling for a fever. Runa's forehead was damp with sweat, but the fever must have passed for her stepmother Ellee did not appear concerned with Runa's condition.

The pain in her chest subsided drastically at the sight of Ellee, so Runa felt it safe enough to speak. "What happened? Where is Father?"

Ellee's face grew grim at the questions with a shade of pity for Runa. "Oh, my sweet. Do you not remember anything?"

Runa hid her frustration as she pressed her lips into a thin line and stared pointedly at her stepmother. Runa never knew her birth mother, and Ellee had filled that void in her life since she was ten. Ellee was always tender and kind, so Runa always tried tolerating her simple mind. As much as she would like to, Runa did not point out to Ellee that if she remembered anything, she would not need to ask what had happened.

Ellee flinched at her harsh gaze, as if sensing the blunt remark Runa had not spoken. "Little lamb, you went off to look for Remly on the mountain. You did not return for days. About a week later, the goat boy found you stumbling by the Cliffside. We brought you back and you were—" Her voice broke off, and her lip trembled.

"And I was what?" Runa snapped impatiently.

Ellee held her hand, as if to tether her to the earth. "My dear starlight, you came back to us muttering and stuttering awful things about your cousin and an evil sorcerer."

Runa blinked. "An evil sorcerer?" she repeated as small details slowly came back to her.

Remly was Runa's seven year old cousin. Remly's father had died of fever some years ago. Runa had taken it upon herself to teach her small cousin the ways of a warrior. They had been practicing with wooden staves, and Remly had started developing her strong swordsman's grip when her stave had flown out of her hand, landing somewhere in the trees. Remly went to retrieve it and with the muffled sound of a shriek, never returned.

Runa remembered she had charged after her cousin but beyond that, her memory was disturbingly blank. At the mention of a sorcerer, her chest began to hurt once more, and she cried out in pain, clutching the spot where her beating heart pumped. She recalled the image of a shadow hovering above her as she was tied to a table. It whispered urgent instructions to her, orders she could not defy or ignore.

"I have to go," she announced, jumping to her feet. The thin blanket fell from her bare shoulders, and the smoldering peat fire in the hearth did little to ward off the spring cold. In the village of Ruxcloke, the constant shadow thrown by the mountain's peak meant that the snow fell often and seldom melted completely.

"What do you mean, Runa? You've only just woken up. Your father is in Palpses, petitioning to Prince Brenin."

This made Runa freeze. "Father is in Palpses?"

"He's asking the prince for Kanetalm soldiers to look for Remly," Ellee explained, getting to her feet with some difficulty. Her belly had grown since the last time Runa remembered it, but she still had months to go before the baby came and joined the brood of Ellee's fat boys.

"*No!*" Runa screeched quickly. "No one should go to the mountain. You tell him that when he gets here." Runa rushed about the room, dressing in her leather armor and packing her things.

"But what about Remly, Runa? Surely you have not forgotten about her. Her mother is sick with grief."

Runa felt sadness for her cousin but could find nothing in her to express it. "Remly isn't coming back," she admitted quietly, looping her axe through her belt. "The sorcerer barely left anything recognizable."

Elle expressed her revulsion with a gasp and her short temper with the clicking of her tongue. "You're still going on about that sorcerer?"

Runa whirled around to face her stepmother. "You don't believe me? You think I would make this up?" Her fists were shaking, and though she wouldn't allow herself to cry in front of her petulant stepmother, Runa couldn't banish the image of Remly's broken and butchered body from her head.

Upon seeing Runa's reaction, Ellee softened. "Where are you going?"

Runa turned away. "Somewhere in the desert. I have to find someone."

"But *why*?" Ellee pleaded.

"I have no choice. The sorcerer commanded me, so I must obey. He forced me to be his servant." Ellee made a move to feel Runa's forehead again for a fever, but Runa caught her stepmother's wrist with a tight grip. "*Don't* touch me," she said with a thick voice and dead eyes.

By the time Runa stepped outside with her pack, a soft layer of snow covered the ground, dusting the rocky fields like goose down. It crunched under her boots with a light sound. Ellee followed her to the front gate, a hand pushing at the small of her back to support her swollen belly as she attempted once more to dissuade Runa from her appointed journey.

"You're not allowed to leave the village without your father's permission," she called, her other hand going to the fence post. She leaned against it.

Runa did not even look back. "I am not a child. I can do as I please."

A whine had entered Ellee's voice. "At least wait for Ralfric to return. He will want to see you well."

"I can't wait. I must go now." And there she left Ellee, calling Runa's name as her four trueborn sons raced down the hill towards their distressed mother.

Runa couldn't wait. The sorcerer's commands burned through her. She was supposed to find someone in a burning desert fortress.

If she waited, they might burn alive, and the sorcerer would punish Runa, even half a world away.

She passed through the stone archway that guarded the road that wound through Ruxcloke and thought of Remly. Though Runa was angry, she could not cry in her grief. The sorcerer had made sure of that.

9. Misty

By the time Caelfel roused from her stupor and once more became aware of her surroundings, the rain had settled, chilling her skin and clothes. The cold matched the numbness in her chest, and she found it to be almost soothing. She breathed carefully through her nose as she assessed the stiffness in her knees and joints, wondering how long she had been there.

When she looked up, she realized the rain had compromised the decrepit roof of the cottage. The collected water made the weak spots bow in dangerously. The webs that had lined the windows had been washed away, probably lying forsaken in the puddles of mud that seeped around the weak foundation. Caelfel straightened from her crouched position, suddenly noticing a new cloak wrapped around her shoulders. She knew its smell and didn't have to turn to identify its owner.

Caelfel felt that she should be surprised by Brenin's presence but she wasn't. "How long have we been here?" she asked him hoarsely. The overcast sky offered nothing in terms of timekeeping.

"Two days," he answered meekly. "And it has rained the entire time." Brenin turned his gaze to the ground. "I don't think you have entirely lost your magic as you believe."

Caelfel gave him a puzzled look before realizing he was referring to the bed of wildflowers. They had all wilted, turning brown in the excessive rain. "That is not magic. That is nature. Flowers die all the time."

Brenin shook his head. "You didn't see them. Flowers don't naturally die in a matter of seconds. And if I had to wager, I would say you're the cause of all the rain."

Caelfel looked at her hands. "You didn't have to come here and wait for me."

Brenin shrugged. "I wanted to."

She sighed and eased herself off the ground. Her mourning had sapped all of her energy from her limbs, so no matter how desperately she wanted, Caelfel could not seek revenge against Tarion at the moment. But the mourning visions provided a new insight, and she shared the news with Brenin. "My friend Garvanna is alive."

"How can you be so certain?" he asked.

"She had delivered a letter to my mother first, so Mother set out for the Pirinac Forest to look for me."

"Where is she?"

"I don't know. I didn't see that in my visions."

"Your visions?" Brenin repeated.

"Elves have certain methods of grieving. Death is so rare among elves that it hits us the hardest out of all the races. I saw visions of my mother up until she was killed," she explained.

"You didn't have these visions for Garvanna," Brenin pointed out.

"Perhaps because Garvanna isn't truly dead. I wish I knew where she was."

"What will you do now?" Brenin asked her.

Caelfel thought for a long moment, considering his question. Her original plans to travel to the coast had been dashed once she thought Garvanna had died. Now that her mother was certainly gone, Caelfel only saw one choice—to deliver the news of Sylaera's death and to find Garvanna's whereabouts.

"I have to return home," she answered finally, but when she looked at Brenin's face, she felt another responsibility tugging at her core. She was indebted to Brenin, and Caelfel feared something might happen to the second prince if she left without him. His disappointment only lasted a moment when Caelfel informed him, "You must go with me."

Brenin did little to conceal his excitement. "You're taking me with you to Honey Water?" Then, just as suddenly, his face darkened. "Orrik would never allow it."

"It matters little what he would allow. I am not leaving without you."

All the same, as she picked up her discarded bow, they both

111

decided to at least notify King Orrik of their intentions. The walk back to Palpses was longer than Caelfel remembered. When they passed the platform that held Strigi's Tournament, Caelfel asked, "How did you find me?" She had been under the impression that she had run far enough to not be found.

"I followed the dark cloud that hovered over you," he told her. Caelfel couldn't determine if he was being serious. She felt too exhausted from her grief to tease him back.

Even though it had been two days since the Festival of Strigi, Palpses still held remnants of its existence, most notably in the burnt shells of the used fireworks that littered the ground and the smoky odor they left behind. Though Caelfel had originally found them beautiful, she could not conjure any lingering fondness for them. Fireworks had little bearing on her while she longed to be home with Father.

An alarming thought came to her just as they stopped before the palace doors. "You said before that your father might not let me leave."

Brenin sighed, realizing the direction of her thoughts. "There is that possibility."

"I don't understand why he would want to keep me here."

"Power is the only thing that matters to him. He might think that if he has you, he has the only elf outside of Honey Water. He sees that as a badge of honor, leverage against his foes. Or a bargaining chip. Elves are magic, even if you don't have your aura, and magic is power."

"And what would make him think I would let him use my power?"

Brenin shrugged with a single shoulder, a grave expression on his face. "No one's stopped him before." Then with a great heave, he pushed both doors open.

King Orrik and Prince Madoc stood in the keep as if waiting for them. Brenin immediately turned shamefaced in their presence, avoiding their eyes. Madoc looked similarly uneasy as both brothers looked to Orrik for the king's reaction. Caelfel thought it customary to allow the king to speak first, so she remained silent, waiting for Orrik to acknowledge them. Otherwise, she would have initiated conversation so they could quickly be on their way to Sal'Sumarathar.

"I'm relieved to see you are in good health after your extensive absence," Orrik remarked eventually, addressing Brenin.

Caelfel exhaled, releasing the tension in her shoulders. "I'm returning to Honey Water, and Brenin is coming with me."

Madoc appeared alarmed, and Brenin seemed to shrink in size beside her. Caelfel wondered if she should have phrased it as a question or a request for permission. She didn't imagine King Orrik had many people telling him things they were going to do without his consent.

But if Orrik was angry, he did a good job of hiding it. He continued examining a piece of paper held between him and Madoc as if he hadn't heard her. Caelfel began tapping her boot impatiently to remind the king of her presence.

He pointed to something on the paper, as if deciding on some mysterious conundrum, and handed it over to Cyrus who stepped up immediately to take the burden from the king's hands. Finally, Orrik responded, "If my son does not have the time to visit his dying grandfather, what makes you think he can make time for your empire? He has a realm to keep, people to protect. He has a duty to uphold."

Caelfel was quick to think of an answer. "Kanetalm has a werewolf problem. The elves can help. We are fierce warriors. On my own, greatly outnumbered, I killed two of them."

Orrik laughed, and it sounded like he was choking as his lips pulled back to reveal his teeth. "You think your people will help out of the kindness of their stone cold hearts? Where have they been for the past five hundred years?"

"I was not here five hundred years ago and neither were you. Brenin could help establish foreign relations."

The king laughed again. "You want Brenin for this? Would it not be better to bring Madoc, the future king of Umfeld?" Orrik gestured toward his elder son who looked none too keen to visit elvish lands.

Caelfel raised her chin. "I will take Brenin and no one else. If you want any chance of elvish reinforcements, you should listen to me. We will return soon."

Orrik must have been greatly amused, for he laughed a third time. "Take him if you must. I will see after Kanetalm until he returns. You best be good on your word about these reinforcements, she-elf."

"Or what, you'll roll over and die like the human that you are?" Caelfel mumbled under her breath so that no one else could hear. She bobbed a quick curtsy for good favor, and King Orrik waved them away.

Brenin and Caelfel went up the stairs to pack their things. "Just you. No one else," Caelfel reminded him when they reached the top.

"I know," he said, pausing.

"Which means you won't have anyone to wait or cook for you. You will have to do everything yourself. So pack light."

"I understand." He blew a sharp breath. "I'm surprised he let us go."

"You said he wants power, so I offered him some."

"Did you mean it about the elvish reinforcements? Will they help us against Tarion?"

Caelfel frowned. "I will try, but I cannot guarantee anything."

"I will not want to be there when Father discovers that you lied to him."

She scowled. "I did not *lie* to him, and there is nothing he can do to me otherwise. Go on, get your things."

They met back up with each other at the stables, Caelfel arriving first with the meager possessions she had brought with her. She had changed out of the vividly colored dress into her normal garb. When Brenin joined her, he was giving instructions to Cyrus. Madoc trailed behind them.

"You have a way of handling him. Just make sure Father doesn't kill anyone. I don't want that on my conscience."

"Of course, my lord." Brenin parted from his steward with an uncertain nod, and to her surprise, Cyrus approached her. "What of your handmaiden?"

Caelfel blinked, belatedly remembering she had taken responsibility of Forra's life. "Look after her, Cyrus. I don't want her hurting herself."

Cyrus nodded and returned to the palace. Madoc stepped up to her then, placing his hand on Brenin's shoulder when the second prince finished saddling his horse. "Be careful, little brother," he said seriously. Then with a laugh, "Take care of your she-elf here."

Brenin's face turned red with a muttered, "I will." Then he led his horse out of the stables, leaving Caelfel alone with the Prince of the Vale.

"Your father has not come to tell him goodbye," Caelfel observed.

"My father is not sentimental enough for goodbyes. Keep him safe, Caelfel," Madoc said fixing her with a stare.

She returned his gaze. "That's why I'm taking him with me. I can only ensure his safety if I am with him."

They left for the Palpses Gates with no one accosting them in the streets except for a small girl who ran to meet them at the front gates. When Caelfel saw her bright face, she recognized Ameala who hugged her legs tightly.

"Are you leaving Kanetalm forever?" she asked tearfully, wiping her nose against Caelfel's pants.

"No," Caelfel answered, patting the girl's head. She glanced at Brenin. "I will have to bring your prince back soon."

Ameala brightened considerably with this news and she stepped back to look Caelfel in the eye. "Good. You beat my brother in the Tournament."

"Who is your brother?"

"Don't you know him? He's one of the prince's soldiers," Ameala said.

Caelfel looked to Brenin, confused. He explained, "Huwel is her brother."

This made Caelfel laugh. "I will definitely have to come back to at least see him. Perhaps one day I will even bring you with me to the Fey Forest."

Ameala grinned and skipped away, humming a tune and needing no further farewell.

Caelfel chuckled as she mounted the horse Brenin offered her, and they passed through the gates.

Caelfel had traveled enough with Garvanna to expect an endless stream of chatter to keep her mind occupied on a long journey. Brenin offered no such distraction, scowling at his hands as he focused on moving forward. When they passed Fort Wymdall, Caelfel decided it was her job to break the silence in an attempt to cheer up her sullen companion. Considering *she* had recently lost her mother, Caelfel thought it a strange arrangement.

She decided to be straightforward with her concern. "You don't appear very happy to be coming with me right now, Prince Brenin."

"Please do not call me Prince Brenin," he said gruffly.

"Why not? You are a prince; it is who you are. Nothing you do can change that. I did not choose to be Caelfel Gyssedlues. I was born Caelfel Gyssedlues."

Brenin laughed at her. She felt stung until he gave his reasoning. "I did not deny being a prince. I just ask you not to call me one. It's nice to just hear my name by itself."

"Well, *Brenin*, did you really stay by my side for two days?" she asked, having difficulty keeping the sharp note from her voice. "Because that is not what a prince does."

"Is what I did so wrong?" he asked, the roughness giving way to surprise.

She glanced at him sideways. "You had better things to do than bear witness to my grief. It's like your father said, as much as I loathe agreeing with him. You have a realm and people to take care of."

Brenin blinked and his face hardened. "I thought you needed someone to be with you, given that you had just lost your mother."

Something in Caelfel's clenched at the mention of her mother, and she brushed off the sudden rush of emotion with terseness. "I should not be so important to you, Brenin. You have werewolves attacking your people."

"But you are," Brenin argued quietly. "You are my guest."

"I am your bodyguard," she corrected gently, pretending she didn't hear his first statement.

"Is that why you're taking me with you? Because you feel a need to protect me everywhere you go?"

Caelfel fell silent. She had not anticipated that her motives would be perceived as offensive. She stared into Brenin's patient face for a long minute as she considered him. As an elf, she felt honor-bound to protect him, even if he was a human. But she had shouldered this responsibility for reasons beyond the life debt. The idea of leaving him behind, potentially exposed to Tarion's menace, actually *frightened* her. As much as she had been trying to bury her emotions in the wake of heartbreak, she was beginning to discover that Caelfel Gyssedlues could never completely mask her feelings. Her emotions were what made her Caelfel Gyssedlues, and Caelfel Gyssedlues could admit that Brenin possessed a certain amount of openness that was refreshing and welcomed when compared to the secretive nature of her first love.
Brenin was fascinated by the elves, enamored with *her*, a stunted elf without an aura. She could not deny him something he so desperately craved.

And so she grinned mischievously at him. "I believe you are the only human who can appreciate the elves for what we are, so I am taking you to see something no human has ever seen, something many elves rarely see themselves."

"What is that?" Brenin asked, instantly intrigued.

Her grin faded softly. "An elvish funeral."

"I am nervous," Brenin volunteered at length. "I don't like it when my father is left in charge."

"You don't think he is a good leader?"

"He is an excellent leader, an effective king. I simply do not agree with his methods. You may think I don't act like a prince but I do care about Kanetalm and the people left in my charge."

"I believe that. You have a kind soul, Brenin. Not many would save lost elves in the forest."

"It was the right thing to do, and you were injured, not just lost."

"I was lost in more ways than one," she muttered, more to herself than for his benefit. "And you've been relentless in making sure I do not get lost again."

"I don't understand what you mean."

"The similarities are curious, really," Caelfel went on as she realized something. "A short time ago, when it was still winter, I found an injured elf in the forest. I saved his life, so he owed me the life debt, like I told you about. He was a very powerful and cunning elf but he was still lost in another way. He was always alone, and I helped him not to be." She sighed wistfully, thinking of Feraan and all they had shared together. After she had left him in the desert fortress, Caelfel hadn't imagined she would adopt his closed-off personality herself.

"And where is he now?" Brenin asked, interrupting her thoughts.

"At home, I would imagine."

"And you decided not to stay with him?" Brenin asked warily.

"*He* made the decision to not stay with me." Caelfel was reluctant to reveal things concerning Feraan. "Garvanna and I talked a lot about it. Despite my misgivings, she came to the conclusion that if I had stayed behind, things would not have soured between us. She says I never gave it a proper chance and that I just ran off at the first opportunity. Garvanna says I require complete commitment. I don't think that's true. I don't think emotional reciprocation is *complete commitment*," Caelfel huffed, annoyed already with some past conversation. "And maybe complete commitment isn't a bad thing."

"So you loved him," Brenin realized slowly. Something in his voice sounded strained.

"I did love him, yes."

"Why did you come to Kanetalm, then?"

"Because everything reminded me of him. Feraan became molded into my identity. I couldn't turn in any direction without being Caelfel Gyssedlues, the elf who saved Feraan, but I am so much more than that."

"So. His name is Feraan?"

"Yes, of course. Keep up," Caelfel said impatiently.

"And do you still love him?" Brenin asked carefully.

"It does not matter how I feel about him now if he does not return the feeling. Or if he is incapable of saying it aloud. Emotional reciprocation. That's not too much to ask for."

"You're right. It's not," Brenin agreed.

"He could not offer what I wanted, so I saw no reason to remain with him."

Caelfel sighed, relieved her needs were finally understood or at the very least, that Brenin understood her enough to know that agreeing with her put her mind to ease. But it must have been a weary sound, for Brenin called her name.

"It is not a sin to want to be loved, Caelfel," he assured.

"I don't want to be loved. I just want to be loved in return," she explained unhelpfully.

Brenin's silence told her that he puzzled over her words. Caelfel was inwardly delighted, having never before seen herself as cryptic. She felt as though it made her seem wise and experienced, despite her young age as an elf.

The sky darkened at a rapid pace that Caelfel had not anticipated. They stopped their horses, and Caelfel observed the sinking sun as she contemplated the advantages of riding through the night.

But Brenin made the decision for them. "There's an inn a little ways down this road."

"I don't remember seeing an inn on our way to Palpses," she said suspiciously. She and Garvanna had already painstakingly learned what an inn was and its purpose. Elvish customs were different; their hospitality allowed no room for a person to turn a profit by exploiting weary travelers looking for generosity, like the humans.

"We're not going the same road as we did before. We can't, unless you want to risk meeting Tarion again in the Pirinac," Brenin pointed out.

Caelfel snapped her attention in the direction they were traveling, her mind whirring to pinpoint the route they were taking on a mental map of Ariang'ron. "Then that means we will cross the Amhsis

Desert," Caelfel said, her face turning to thunder.

"Do you know another way to the Fey Forest?" Brenin shot back with a hint of dry humor. "You should put your hood on, cover your ears for when we reach the inn."

Caelfel shot him a look. "You should put your mud on your face."

Brenin looked alarm. "Why?"

"You are their prince. You are too recognizable."

"I should think being a prince would win some favors."

"I don't want any problems. They might think I am kidnapping you. Or you might find you have enemies outside of your city," Caelfel said, thinking of the rebellion Forra mentioned. The idea of an inn sounded more dangerous to her now. Brenin did not share her fear, and so they continued down the road, Caelfel wearing her hood and Brenin with ash smeared on his face.

Soon they came across a long, two-story boarding house of paneled wood. It had a fenced stable yard and a swinging, wooden sign on a post that introduced it as Juniper Cove Tavern. A scrawny dog with matted, gray hair stood chained at the front gate and greeted visitors by barking ceaselessly. Caelfel and Brenin led their horses to the stables, discovering a stable lad sleeping in a soiled pile of hay, undisturbed by the yapping hound. Caelfel took in his dirty toes and patched-up clothes when Brenin touched her elbow.

"You shouldn't speak either," he instructed.

"Why not?" she hissed.

"Your accent is too—*different*," he explained uncertainly. Caelfel merely rolled her eyes and gestured for him to lead the way.

They entered the inn, and Caelfel wondered how the humans could see anything with their inferior eyesight because of how dark it was inside. The light of the fire crackling in the hearth hardly illuminated anything. Even so, Brenin expertly picked his way around the tables to reach the long counter that stretched across half the width of the entire building. Caelfel was careful to avoid meeting anyone's gaze but she doubted anyone would notice her, as most of the patrons were too busy with their mugs of ale and singing off-key tunes.

"I need a room with two beds," Brenin informed the innkeeper at the bar. Brenin passed the man a few coins across the table. Caelfel did not miss the thin, white scars that pitted the innkeeper's knuckles as he accepted.

"Would you like some dinner with that too?" the innkeeper asked, pocketing the money. "My wife's made potato and turnip stew."

"That doesn't sound too bad," Brenin said with a grin toward Caelfel for affirmation. She shrugged, and the innkeeper moved to retrieve them some bowls.

Brenin led them to a secluded table and sat down, his back to the rest of the room. Caelfel sat opposite of him and studied everyone else in the tavern.

She would often see pairs of men taking part in a game they loudly proclaimed as arm-wrestling. They would clasp hands with their elbows firmly planted on the table. The one who successfully pushed the other arm back on the table was declared the victor.

"We should arm-wrestle," Caelfel suggested brightly as their stew was brought to them. The innkeeper gave her an odd look before shuffling away.

Brenin laughed. "I think not. I would lose."

Caelfel blew some hair out of her face, resigned to stirring her steaming soup. She took a sip to taste and was surprised to find it favorable. She continued sipping and watching the room's activity.

A few minutes after the innkeeper brought their soup to them, the door opened again for a young woman of medium build. She looked about the tavern discreetly before speaking to the innkeeper about renting a room for the night. Caelfel couldn't help but stare at her, even as the girl lowered her hood to reveal tightly woven, brass-colored hair.

The innkeeper greeted her warmly. "What brings you here, Runa? It's been a while since we've seen you around here."

Something akin to panic crossed Runa's face at being addressed so familiarly. She whispered to the man in quiet, urgent tones. Caelfel watched more intently, recognizing her name.

The innkeeper nodded knowingly when Runa finished explaining her case to him. "Ralfric doesn't know you're here?" he guessed, Caelfel's sensitive ears picking up their words.

Caelfel gasped, recognizing Runa at last. "It's her!" she hissed to Brenin.

Brenin who had his back turned throughout the entire exchange, did not trouble himself to look around. "What are you looking at?"

"The man that came to you about the sorcerer on Crone Mountain? His daughter is over there." Caelfel made a move to stand, but a kick from Brenin kept her seated.

"And what are you going to do?" Brenin challenged in a low voice. "Confront her about the sorcerer and reveal us?"

Caelfel sank in her seat with a frown. "I might be able to help her."

Brenin braved a glance at Runa who now sat at the bar, stirring her own bowl of potatoes and turnips. "What does she need help with?" Brenin asked, turning back to Caelfel. "She looks fine to me."

"Escaping a sorcerer is no small thing," Caelfel pointed out, her hand going to the marks permanently branded to her hip.

Brenin sighed, pushing his bowl away from him. "Do what you want. I just don't think it's a good idea. She may not want your help."

Brenin's reaction to the proposal made Caelfel even less certain about approaching Runa. She decided to keep watching her from across the room. Another man stepped up to the girl, and when Runa greeted him, her cloak shifted, flashing the head of a war axe and hardened leather armor underneath. Caelfel concluded that Runa was perhaps more dangerous than she thought.

The drunken man who was brave enough to approach her would only prove this. He placed a hand on her shoulder and leaned against her. "I just want to give you a good time, *girl.*"

Runa's look of disgust at his hand and slurred speech would have been ferocious enough to drive any rational-thinking man away. Unfortunately it would seem that men were not rational in their drunkenness. "Please leave me alone." She crushed his hand in her grip and pushed him away from her.

The man shifted his weight to lean against the bar as he looked at her properly. He gave a delayed wink. "I'll just see you later tonight."

"You will do no such thing," she told him calmly.

Caelfel heard Brenin huff irritably as she continued to ignore him for Runa.

Another man called to Runa from his table. "She would rather have a real man in her bed tonight." His words were met with a round of laughter.

The innkeeper looked as though he were about to intervene on Runa's behalf, but she raised a hand to stop him, an amused smile on her face. She turned to the rest of the room. "The person who can beat me in arm-wrestling may share my bed for tonight."

Her challenge filled the room with excitement. A table was cleared for the game, and Runa moved from her seat at the bar to the table, sporting a look of utter confidence.

It seemed as though every man except Brenin and the innkeeper lined up for their chance. The first man that sat in front of her was the one who had hollered at her from the table. He rolled his sleeves past his elbows, showing the tight, brown skin over his thick arms. Runa was undaunted as she pushed up her own sleeve to produce a pale arm. Her cloak hid the rest of her arm from view.

The rest of the men that crowded around the table hooted and chanted. Runa and her first potential suitor clasped hands, someone counted, and the game began.

With a loud grunt, the man pushed all of his strength against her arm, but to his surprise, Runa did not budge. Her smile deepened as she allowed the man a few more moments to try his strength against hers. Caelfel held her breath as she watched Runa carefully.

Then, Runa gave a shrug and with a single, fluid motion, she crushed his arm back against the table.

Everyone fell silent at the show of Runa's superior strength. They stared at her with wide eyes, mouths agape with dumbfounded awe. Then, in an instant, the room erupted in cacophonous shouting, each man wanting to try his own luck. The sound was enough to prompt even Brenin to turn around.

And Runa proved victorious against each one. It would seem she would sleep alone that night. Caelfel's grin matched Runa's, and the pale girl leaned back in her chair, delighting in the attention and proper respect given to her.

Then Runa's eyes met Caelfel's gaze, and her smile immediately disappeared. Keeping her eyes on Caelfel, she stood and backed through the crowd, silently slipping away like a shadow. Caelfel blinked at the odd occurrence and felt even more compelled to seek out Runa. Brenin discouraged her however, and they retired to their assigned room for the night before the commotion in the tavern became too out of control.

The upper floor of Juniper Cove was a long hallway with doors leading to the inn's rooms. As Brenin requested, theirs had two beds, and Brenin claimed the one closest to the door when he sprawled across the mattress. Then he declared he was tired.

"I don't see how," Caelfel said with a bit of a smile. The way he lounged on the bed amused her. "You've done nothing but sit next to me for two days and ride a horse for one afternoon."

The room was small, especially compared to the queen's rooms at the Palpses palace, but this did not surprise her. There was a single window that overlooked the stable yard, and Caelfel could pick out their horses even in the growing darkness.

A stone water basin sat on the low shelf next to the window, and the innkeeper had informed them that it had been freshly filled with hot water. Brenin had to patiently explain to her that it was for bathing.

"Will you be staying up, then?" Brenin asked sluggishly, slowly nodding off to sleep.

"For a little while, I suspect."

"Don't get into trouble," he mumbled just as he drifted off into unconsciousness. Caelfel chuckled as she watched him, finding that his unique boyish charm endeared him to her. She had an urge to push some of his hair from his face, and since no one was around to witness the tender gesture, she didn't suppress it. She watched him sleep for a moment, remembering a time that felt a generation ago but was really just months before. And in the wake of the memory, she felt suddenly conflicted, so she left Brenin's bedside to return to the window.

"What would you want most in this world, Brenin?" she softly wondered aloud. Caelfel knew she should take advantage of this moment of respite to relax, but her anxiety would not allow her. She remained awake and on diligent watch, though she doubted there was any need.

Around midnight, Brenin's snores had become increasingly louder, but they did not mask the sound of the slight creak of the door opening to Caelfel's vigilant ears. She was suddenly on her feet and at the door. Without a weapon, Caelfel used her strength to snatch the unexpected visitor by the neck and pin them against the wall of the room. Her fingers tight around their airway prevented any speech.

The predatory reaction ebbed when Caelfel recognized Runa in front of her. She relaxed her grip but did not remove it. "You're Runa."

"I don't have the advantage of knowing *your* name."

"No, but you were the one to sneak into my room in the middle of the night." Caelfel scanned Runa for weapons and quickly relieved the girl of her war axe.

"You've taken my weapon now. There's nothing to fear from me," Runa pointed out.

Caelfel nodded and released her. Runa rubbed her throat. "What are you doing here?" Caelfel demanded, acutely aware that Brenin was still asleep.

"I came to ask you the same thing. What's an elf doing in the middle of Umfeld?"

"And the only time you can ask me that is in the middle of the night?" Caelfel hissed.

"I didn't want to draw attention in the tavern with everyone around."

"Is it any of your business where I decide to go?" Caelfel asked.

"No, but you don't understand. It's my master—" Then suddenly, Runa doubled over and clutched at her chest as if she was in pain.

"Your master?" Caelfel repeated, her voice gentler now. "I don't understand. Who is your master?"

Runa gasped for breath as she struggled to speak, and still Brenin did not stir at the noise. "I can't speak of it. But elves should not be leaving the Forest. That's only a sign for bad things to come."

"What do you mean?" Caelfel could not grasp the warning. "Are you talking about the sorcerer?"

Runa's pale blue eyes grew wide and her face drained of what little color it had. "How do you know about that?"

"I was in Palpses when your father came to the court. Runa, I've faced a sorcerer before. I know what it is like; I know what you've been through."

Runa's eyes searched Caelfel's for something, but then her face turned grim when they yielded no correct results. "You say you know what I've *been* through, but you don't know what I am *now* going through."

"How do you mean?"

"I am enslaved. I am a tool, a vassal to do my master's bidding. I can no longer be Runa Snowaxe. I am the Raven's Hand, only a mindless servant. My life is to fulfill his commands. I can do nothing without his permission. I speak now because he permits it. He believes you should know and warn everyone in your path about the destruction he will wreak. *I cannot even cry over my cousin's death.* Tears are a sign of weakness, and the Raven's Hand cannot be weak."

Runa's voice cracked with her grief, but as she promised, her eyes betrayed no tears. Caelfel's chest wrenched for Runa's servitude. "I am sorry—"

"Don't be sorry," Runa snapped. "Your pity can do nothing for me."

"But what does this have to do with elves leaving the Fey Forest?" Caelfel pressed, ignoring Runa's short temper. The human girl certainly had a right to it.

Runa hesitated, and her eyes gained a dead look as she consulted some deep part of her brain. "My master was told that once the elves leave their forest, it will be the beginning of the End Times."

"The End Times?" Caelfel repeated with a scoff. "I am only one elf. I don't think the rest of my people would be so eager to leave their home."

Runa shook her head, the dead-eyed look still in place. "One elf is the start of many." She closed her eyes and sighed, a grimace of recovering from excruciating pain.

And though Runa did not want it, Caelfel pitied her and wanted to reach out to the human girl. "Where are you going?"

Runa took a deep breath. "I am on my way to a distant village in the desert."

"We are headed for the desert as well. You could travel with us," Caelfel offered.

Runa looked shocked. "I must travel alone," she said uncertainly, heading for the door. "May I have my axe back?"

Caelfel handed Runa her weapon, and the girl took it without a word. Runa was almost out the door when Caelfel called out to her. "My name is Caelfel, by the way."

Runa paused over the threshold. "You should not have told me that. Now he knows who you are."

10. The Road Back

"**I** can't believe you didn't hear anything," Caelfel said, not for the first time.

Brenin sat grumpily upon his horse, not fond of early morning conversation and completely oblivious to the previous night's events surrounding Runa. "I was asleep," he pointed out flatly.

"I did not think you were such a heavy sleeper," Caelfel mused with a hint of a smile. She filled him in on everything that had happened with Runa, and Brenin responded in a series grunts.

"The Raven's Hand," he repeated eventually when he found the energy. "That sounds dangerous and mad."

"Do you think she was making it up?" Caelfel asked him.

"I think the mad part is that you just let her go. Whether she's lying about it or not, a girl who believes she's doing the dirty work of a sorcerer is not someone I'd want loose in the kingdom."

"I think she's mostly harmless, and even if she's not, she'll be in Umfang."

Brenin shrugged. "Better in Umfang than in Umfeld."

"I could take her in a fight though," Caelfel continued. "For a human, she shows impressive might, but I am still stronger than her."

"But the elves are leaving the Fey Forest. What do you think that means?" Brenin asked.

Caelfel was surprised he had been alert enough to remember that part of her narration. She shrugged as though the prophecy did not trouble her. "Fortune-telling is often an incorrect science," she dismissed, referencing one of their previous conversations. In truth, Runa's conviction had made her uneasy. She continued, "I do not expect the elves I know to leave their home, not even in your grandchild's lifetime."

Brenin laughed with some bemused, dry humor. "Ah, if only I had a grandchild." He paused, turning melancholy. "He would probably visit me, unlike I, who will never visit my grandfather."

Caelfel stopped her horse suddenly, and it took Brenin a delayed moment to follow suit. "Is that what you want right now, to visit your dying grandfather?" Caelfel asked gently.

Brenin looked surprised by her concern. "My grandfather is in Onusal, which is opposite from the direction in which we are going."

Caelfel squared her gaze with him. "My mother is dead, and nothing can change that." Caelfel's heart clenched at the blunt statement. "But your grandfather is alive, and *that* can and will change."

Brenin hesitated, and his lip trembled with the deep desire to accept Caelfel's invitation. But some reasoning deferred to their current objective. "No, the king has only permitted me to journey with you to Honey Water."

Caelfel frowned at Brenin's reluctant obedience. "He wouldn't have to know," she tried.

But Brenin was already shaking his head. "He would notice such an extended absence. I do not want to leave Kanetalm in his hands for so long."

Caelfel nodded, and they continued riding. She was impressed that Brenin would put aside his own wishes in favor for that which was best for his people. She did not think she could stand it if Brenin had based his decision solely on King Orrik's command. It made her wonder at her own loyalty to Empress Haelyn. Caelfel had never personally met the elvish empress, but the abhorrent actions of the Council of Sal'Sumarathar had given her enough reason to become a disloyal rogue of the state. As it were, Caelfel had volunteered for the imperial army to defend Honey Water's forest against the desert princeling. For most, that would undeniably settle the question of her loyalty. But Caelfel could not confirm that if Empress Haelyn were to forbid her from seeing her family, Caelfel would obey without question. Then again, what sort of empress would Haelyn be to order such a thing?

Once they skirted the mountain range, the landscape abruptly changed, and the fertile grassland gave way to a vista paved to the horizon with cracked, dusty ground and sand. Before entering the desert, they stopped at the Crossroads Village to water the horses and arrange their clothes in a manner so they would be protected from the unforgiving sun. Brenin confessed to her that he had never visited the desert. Caelfel responded with a dry chuckle and told him he hadn't been missing much.

She found herself scanning the distance for Runa or any sign of the human forces that had dragged her into the desert the last time, though she knew she would find neither. She tied her cloak sleeves at her wrists, watching Brenin do the same as he scowled at the heat. Then a tug at her elbow sent her hand flying to her dagger hilt as she turned to see who had touched her.

It was a short, brown man, and Caelfel took in the puckered scars around his face that marked him as a cutthroat. "Need a guide through Amhsis?" he offered in a thick, rolling accent. A single leather strap stretched across his bare chest, holding a large, curved blade at his back.

Caelfel glared, showing her own blade to him. "I believe we can manage on our own."

The man took in her towering stature without a word of disagreement. His dark eyes rested on her pointed ears, but to her surprise, they did not shock him. He shoved a thumb behind him to a building constructed of dried mud with only a sheet of linen to act as the door. "There are more of you in there. Good customers, buy all the horses."

Caelfel's suspicious glare faded into wide-eyed bewilderment. "More of me?" she repeated, but the man had already drifted away to watch for more oblivious travelers. Caelfel studied the building a moment, curious if elves were truly inside.

But in a sudden panic, she looked around for Brenin who was no longer next to her. The panic was short-lived, for Brenin was making a fool of himself by dunking his head in the livestock watering trough. Sheep crowded around him with bleats of protest, their thick coats dyed brown from dusty, red clay. Brenin snapped his head back, his dripping hair drenching his shoulders. The shepherd's children laughed at the sight of him, and Caelfel found herself genuinely giggling along as well. She gently pulled him up by the crook of his arm.

"Come along, my prince," she said, still laughing.

Brenin ran his hand through his wet hair, obviously in much better spirits than he had been in that morning. "Where are we going?" he asked, noticing she was not leading them back to their horses.

Caelfel did not answer him, ducking into the hut to see if her own people were truly inside. The building was a place for travelers to rest and drink. An older woman manned a counter and looked wholly uninterested with everyone who might enter her tavern, paying no mind to Caelfel and Brenin who stood awkwardly gaping at the doorway.

The elves were not hard to miss. Even seated, they towered over the barmaid and were the only patrons of her hut. There were two of them, soldiers with purple under-dressings and breastplates stamped with the Honey Dew flower petals of the Honey Water Empire. Once Brenin's eyes adjusted to the sudden dimness of the room, he was subdued into an awed silence at the sight of them.

The two elvish had not noticed their entrance. Caelfel approached her countrymen, taking a seat at their table uninvited while Brenin trailed like a shadow and sank into a chair behind her.

"Now where are you from?" Caelfel asked with a coy smile before they could start at her sudden appearance.

They took a moment to assess her and confirmed she was one of their own. Surprisingly, one knew her. "Caelfel?"

She turned to the one sitting on her right, who had been sitting with their back to the door. She tilted her head, and her smile brightened. "Winwaloe?"

Winwaloe had volunteered for the recruitment with her to face Admiral Grimault's army. They were both archers from Sal'Sumarathar, and while he had not been accepted to the college to study magic, they had applied together. But his new uniform confused her. Winwaloe's talent was for the bow; but imperial archers did not wear metal armor. They wore leather.

Noticing her questioning gaze, Winwaloe explained, "I'm not just an archer anymore. I'm a swordsman and a cavalry officer now."

Caelfel nodded and turned to his companion. "And what is your name, sir?"

He smiled. "I am Erryn, my lady." Caelfel guessed he was also a cavalry officer, judging from his matching uniform.

"What are you doing here?" she asked them.

"I'm not sure if we should say," Erryn said uncertainly, looking to his partner.

But Winwaloe was laughing. "There can be no harm in it. She's the reason we're here anyway."

"What do you mean?" Caelfel asked impatiently.

"When Grimault captured you, the army took over the Cromlech Fortress when we won you back. Now the elves use that as a base in the desert, and a base needs maintaining. Erryn here and I were promoted straight from the Volunteer Regiment.

The news stunned Caelfel. The elves were expanding, conquering. Perhaps Runa's prediction would prove true.

"But never mind us," Winwaloe said, cutting across her thoughts and leaning toward her across the table. "What are you doing here? I just remember you and that battlemage disappearing from the fortress one morning." His eyes flitted to Brenin behind her briefly.

"I've been traveling around and ran into some werewolves," she mused conspiratorially.

"Werewolves? You've been to Haradrop, then?"

"No, these are feral werewolves. Vicious, territorial." Caelfel looked down at her hands. "They killed my mother."

Winwaloe's face darkened, and Erryn hissed angrily. "Where are these werewolves?" Winwaloe asked.

"They're in the Pirinac Forest."

Winwaloe nodded at Erryn. "We should speak to our commander about *retaliation*."

Caelfel was surprised they were willing to help with her revenge. "Really?"

"Without Sylaera Gyssedlues, we would have never taken the Cromlech palace," Winwaloe told her seriously. "We will do everything we can."

"Where is it you're going now?" Erryn asked.

"Back to Sal'Sumarathar for her funeral. We can't go through the Pirinac Forest or risk being eaten by werewolves."

"You should speak to your High Executor about sending reinforcements," Erryn offered. Caelfel nodded but said nothing to the advice. She remembered Markis, Sal'Sumarathar's Chief Executor, and the frightening visage of the elf who had hunted and followed her for the better part of a month still haunted her. She did not think she would visit him soon.

Erryn lifted his chin. "Who is your companion?"

Caelfel glanced behind her to see Brenin looking as unprincely as possible while he gaped at the elves before him. Caelfel snorted. "This is Brenin." She lowered her voice, turning back to Winwaloe and Erryn. "His father is the king of Umfeld."

Their eyes widened, and they inclined their heads respectfully to the still ogling prince. Brenin appeared to take no notice of the gesture. Caelfel nudged him sharply in the ribs, and he finally shut his mouth.

"The werewolves have been giving Kanetalm problems as well. I figure Umfeld could attack the forest on one side, the elves another," Caelfel explained.

Winwaloe nodded at this plan. "As soon as we return to Cromlech, we will do everything we can."

Erryn and Winwalow followed them outside to their horses, and Winwalow caught Caelfel's elbow before she mounted her horse. "You're just going back to Sal'Sumarathar, correct? No further?"

Caelfel hesitated, her hand on her horse's saddle. "Why would I go further?" she asked carefully.

Winwaloe looked uneasy to answer. "I don't know all of the details. I've only heard whispers through the chain of command about prisoners escaping the Labyrinth in Yamalvon."

Caelfel felt everything turn cold, despite the heat of the desert sun, and her face went white with fear. "What sort of prisoners?"

Winwaloe shook his head. "I'm sorry, Caelfel. I'm not a high ranking officer so I don't know much. Just be careful when you go to Honey Water."

"I will," she promised quietly. She mounted the horse, pulled the hood over her face to protect it from the sun, and took off into the desert with Prince Brenin.

The familiar desert heat plagued her with unpleasant memories and a dizzy head, so Caelfel pushed the two of them along fast and hard to traverse the Amhsis as quickly as possible. Brenin issued no complaint, as if sensing and sharing her mad desire to be out of the desert.

When night came, they had still not completely crossed it, and Caelfel judged they had a few more hours yet before reaching the Fey Forest. Caelfel would have kept going to finish the distance, but Brenin stopped them when he nearly fell off his horse in a state of exhaustion. Caelfel could not fault him, for they had barely stopped since entering the desert, but she remained on her horse nearly twitching with anxiety.

"Why don't you get some rest?" Brenin asked, patting the ground next to him. He did not even trouble himself to retrieve his bedroll.

"I am not tired," she said but reluctantly slid off her horse to join him. Even while sitting, she looked about wildly as if they were in danger. There was no sign that they would be. They were completely alone in the desert.

"I don't see how. We've been riding all day," Brenin teased her sleepily. He yawned and tried studying her closely, his body swaying dangerously as he sat up. "Are you all right?"

She brushed off his concern. "I'll take the first watch. You go to sleep now."

Brenin needed no further convincing and he was unconscious within minutes. Caelfel walked both horses to cool them down. Her eyes remained trained on the distant blackness, ready to catch any sign of threat. She saw none, but the darkness felt as though it penetrated her skin and seeped into her blood. She saw images of a malevolent face grinning at her, and the sense of foreboding pressed against her from every side.

Admiral Grimault had been defeated, killed by her own hand, but though he had ordered her capture, Admiral Grimault's ghost was not what frightened her. His sorcerer and acting steward had been her personal warden, implementing and performing his own methods of torture on her. The scars on her hip blazed at the memory.

Lisiek had survived the siege of Cromlech and was shipped away to an undisclosed location as a prisoner of the empire. Perhaps Lisiek was one of the prisoners that had escaped the Labyrinth. Perhaps he would return to the desert to reclaim his master's fortress. Perhaps he would seek her out and finish what he started.

Caelfel sat next to Brenin's sleeping form, her leg bouncing restlessly. Her heart pounded frantically in her chest. The marks on her hip felt as if they were being burned into her flesh anew, and she scratched at them feverishly, as if she could remove the marks and memory from her skin. Her mind showed her Lisiek everywhere, in the marks of the sand, the shape of the sky. She heard his soft chuckle in the empty silence of the desert. She would jerk her head over her shoulder, expecting to see him standing there.

Caelfel got to her feet and paced around their campsite. She forced herself to take slow, even breaths. The exercise calmed her anxiety somewhat, so she returned to her seat.

But her heart continued to thud rapidly as though she were still pacing. She remained sitting, knuckles pale as she gripped her knees against her chest.

Lisiek was at her ear, whispering promises of terror. She felt his breath fluttering against her throat. Caelfel swatted at open air, sweat beading down her neck in thin trails despite the chill of the desert night.

The sharp, odiferous haze of blue magefire hung in her nose like a smothering blanket. Her magefire scars pricked more insistently at her side, escalating to shooting jabs of pain.

She couldn't breathe, her throat constricted. Her neck prickled with a sensitivity of knowing something was drawing close. But as she peered into the darkness, nothing revealed itself to her. She grew so paranoid and fearful of the vast desert that she could not breathe, and her pulse drummed feverishly in her ears.

Caelfel held herself very still and sat for as long as she dared before shaking Brenin awake.

"Brenin," she hissed, just realizing that tears were choking her throat and streaming down her cheeks. "Brenin, I'm sorry. Wake up, please."

Brenin started with a thick gasp and looked about in a frenzy for the source of his disturbance. What he found was Caelfel stammering in a series of suffocating sobs. "What is it?" he demanded in a bellow that ended in a hoarse whisper.

"We need to go," she tried explaining to him, desperately pulling him to his feet. "We need to leave the desert."

Brenin blinked at the sight of her, wild and crying, and he did not argue. He attempted a curt nod before clambering back onto his horse.

It was a difficult ride with Caelfel pressing them on as hard as she dared, Brenin struggling to keep up in his drowsy stupor. Caelfel felt an indescribable relief that he did not interrogate her behavior as she focused on putting as much desert as she could behind her.

Eventually the sands changed into coarse heathland and then mercifully into the grassy plains that tapered between the mountains, towards the pass that was the site of the rather short battle Caelfel had volunteered for before her kidnapping. Caelfel did not feel secure until they abruptly crossed the treeline border, and she stopped them there. Without a word of complaint, Brenin rolled off his horse, falling to the damp earth underfoot with a muted grunt. Then he immediately fell back to sleep, trusting that Caelfel had led him to safety. He did not remain conscious long enough to question her judgment.

Caelfel, finally able to breathe easily once more, gave a soft laugh as Brenin resumed snoring. The tears dried on her face, and her heart rate returned to normal. The forest air tasted like a balm to her lungs, and now she felt quite silly for her previous episode of fright. It had left her drained with no explanation, save for the sincere yearning that Lisiek was dead so that she may sleep soundly once again.

Before she settled down for the night, Caelfel walked among the trees, wondering why she felt so safe now when the very forest had previously betrayed her by allowing Lisiek across the border. She wondered if Runa's ruthless master of sorcery or the prison break at the Labyrinth held any relation to Lisiek. She stopped at a tree with wide limbs, recognizing it as the tree her ranger captain assigned to her and her scouting partner.

Then Caelfel remembered that the last time she had been in the forest of her home was just before Lisiek had captured her. She held her bow tightly in both hands, recalling that the sorcerer had stolen it and used its theft as a ploy to lure her out of the protective shadow of the magical forest.

And strangely, Caelfel still felt glad to be home.

Dawn came soon after they had entered the Fey Forest, but Caelfel let Brenin sleep since she had robbed him of it in the desert. He shocked her when he bolted upright to stretch his arms less than two hours after the sun began floating above the horizon.

Caelfel started in surprise. "I was going to let you sleep some more."

Despite the smudges that darkened the space beneath his eyes, Brenin grinned, heedless of his fatigue. "How can I sleep when I am in Honey Water?" he exclaimed with an excitement that did not match his usual moodiness in the mornings. "I'm probably the first human in centuries."

Caelfel managed a small smile and fondly touched his cheek as she remembered Lisiek standing in the same place they now stood. "I'm afraid you are not the first, my prince."

This did not dampen Brenin's spirits as he jumped to his feet and readied his horse. Caelfel watched him with a wary eye, holding her breath in her chest as she prepared herself to explain her strange hysteria from the previous night. She waited for Brenin's curiosity to bubble out of him in a string of difficult questions.

And though she waited and held her breath some more, Brenin

proved to be curious about other things. He whipped around to her with impossibly wide eyes, suddenly coming to a realization. "I did not know humans could even enter the forest."

Caelfel laughed at his expression and got on her horse to lead the way. "Why would you think that?"

"I thought the forest was protected by magic, he admitted. "I had heard no one could cross the border unless they were an elf."

"That's a half-truth," Caelfel said slowly. "Humans can enter the forest if they do not have malicious intentions."

But now Caelfel started to doubt the magic that purportedly protected Honey Water's borders, for she clearly recalled Lisiek entering the forest without any trace of hesitation. And he had certainly had malicious intentions.

The ride to her city of Sal'Sumarathar took most of the day, and Caelfel reveled in the familiar sights of her home. By late afternoon, they had reached the curve of the Blaidd River, which led them to the horse meadow. They broke past the trees and entered the clearing full of elvish steeds either grazing or sunbathing. The sight Caelfel was so used to made Brenin gape in bewilderment. "What is this place?" he asked, quite in astonishment.

Caelfel dismounted. "This is the horse meadow. We keep our horses here instead of the stables that you have."

"Won't they run away?" Brenin asked, sliding to the ground.

Caelfel shrugged, noting that the horses from Palpses appeared much smaller than the ones in the Fey Forest. "It's never been a problem before."

Before she could tell Brenin to stop gawping before anyone saw them, a honey-colored mare came trotting up to Caelfel with a soft, excited neigh. Caelfel smiled so big that her cheeks ached with the effort. She greeted her horse by stroking its dappled gray nose.

"This is Rowan," Caelfel introduced, stepping to the side for Brenin to see. "She's been my faithful companion since I was old enough to ride."

Brenin continued staring at the horse who towered above him. In return, Rowan curiously nuzzled at Brenin's ears to sniff him. She must have liked him, for her nuzzling became more persistent. Brenin felt obligated to pet her.

Caelfel laughed at his reluctance. "Don't look so intimidated. This is Honey Water, and everyone will be bigger than you. You're shorter than me, and I'm considered by most to be a short elf."

Brenin nodded. "I'm not intimidated," he protested. He watched Rowan imperiously herd away the two Palpses horses in the direction she wanted. While he was distracted, Caelfel made a quick scan of the meadow for another horse, black with unnatural eyes, Feraan's stallion. But when she didn't see him, she swallowed the unwanted feeling of disappointment and took Brenin into the city.

"It's all trees," he noted, craning his neck about to see their tops.

"What else do you expect in a forest?" Caelfel countered.

Then Brenin snapped his attention forward as they stepped onto the main road. He stopped. "Where are we going?" he asked, suddenly on alert as if something had spooked him.

"We are going to see my father first," she said, slowing her pace to wait for him.

Brenin's eyes darted around, taking in the pale buildings made of soft stone, the gentle babble of the center market just ahead. No one had noticed them yet, and Caelfel remembered the nearest building belonged to a family of healers called the Baeltylars.

"Am I allowed to be here?" Brenin asked, eyeing the elves in the marketplace warily.

"Of course, you passed through the border. There's no reason why you shouldn't be." Caelfel decided not to mention that she had brought home an unwanted visitor once, and the decision had nearly had her executed for treason.

But Brenin was not Feraan. Brenin was a prince of Umfeld. Brenin was kind and open, not secretive to the point of coldness. Caelfel knew the elves would take to Brenin, even if he was a human. She knew that they would at least like him better than Feraan, one of their own.

"If you don't want to stand out, you should stop staring," Caelfel suggested, hiding a giggle behind her hand.

Brenin turned his gaze to her. "I shall only stare at you then."

Caelfel gave him a sympathetic smile and reached for his hand. "There will be plenty of other things for you to stare at."

Walking through the marketplace, Caelfel recognized the jeweler, the fletcher, the armorer, the book lender, and the weaver, among others. Whenever anyone looked her way, they smiled genuinely and half-raised their hands in greeting from afar. Caelfel acknowledged each one brightly, aware of how they were all ignorant of the human trailing behind her. Hunters that flocked the edges of the market plaza met her with a warm regard they usually reserved for their comrades. She said a few more words to them but did not stop to converse; the closer they reached her street, the more anxious she was to see her house.

"You know them better than everyone else in the market?" Brenin pointed out curiously.

Caelfel shrugged. "My father was a hunter, and I was a hunter. I've hunted with them many times before. And *this*—" Caelfel said when they turned for the last time. "This is my home."

After traversing distant countries and foreign forests, the sight before her filled her with such respite that it welled up in her throat, threatening to erupt in a sob. Caelfel managed to keep it down.

Returning from Kanetalm, her home looked rather small compared to Brenin's. She didn't grow up in great palaces with elegant courts. Her home was a relatively small but tall structure with five rooms, standing against the backdrop of the thick trees of the forest. Around it was the magnificent garden, growing foods and flowers that sustained the Gyssedlues home in both cooking and alchemy. Tucked in the corner of the garden and against the house was the bathing fountain, curtained off from view for privacy.

The front door was not painted, for they did not use their home for a specialized occupation like a healer would. There was no healer in the Gyssedlues household. And now there was no longer an elf capable of performing magic. Caelfel took a sharp breath to brace herself and, still gripping Brenin's hand, went inside to bring Eviat Gyssedlues the grim news of his wife.

II. Reunion

"Father?" Caelfel called to the house that now felt too empty and too big. She released Brenin's hand in time to catch her father bursting through the back door that led to the garden. In the early evening light, the house appeared too dark, and she cringed at the thought of Father sitting in the darkness all day.

"Caelfel, darling? You're back!" Eviat exclaimed, stepping back. He held her at arm's length to look her over, and the relief he felt was tangible. Caelfel hesitated to shatter it, and embraced him with an unusual tightness when he stepped forward to hug her. She buried her face in his neck as soon as she realized she'd been shaking. It wasn't until she became aware of her father rubbing her back that Caelfel realized she'd been unsuccessful in stifling the sobs.

In the back of her mind, Caelfel was aware that Brenin was witnessing this humbling moment between her and her father. But he had seen her time of mourning. This reunion would not be any degree more humiliating.

"It's all right. We thought something had happened to you, but you're safe now." Eviat paused, realizing there was something important he was missing. "Where is your mother?"

At this, Caelfel only shuddered harder. She lifted her face to speak and struggled to keep her words even. "Mother is—*gone.*"

Eviat tensed. "Gone," he repeated in a hollow voice. "How?"

"Dead." Caelfel nearly choked on the word.

She pried herself from Father with trembling hands as she produced Sylaera's distinctive amulet from around her own neck. Eviat took it from her and held it tightly with both hands, as if it were the only thing that existed in the world. And for several long minutes, he stared at the amulet as if there was nothing else worth seeing while

138

he absorbed the terrible truth.

Caelfel bit her lip, watching her father, and waited.

He finally sighed and pressed the emerald gem against his brow. He kept it there, and Caelfel saw his hands trembling. She took the time to really look at her father. It had only been about a month since she had last seen him, but he had aged rapidly while she was gone, in spite of being an elf. The ash-gray hair was the same as she had always known it, but the weary lines on his face had deepened in her absence. The clothes he wore were not the outdoor garb he usually preferred, and Caelfel wondered apprehensively if her father, master of archery and hunting, had truly spent all of this time inside.

She remembered his accident just before she joined the Volunteer Regiment. Eviat had been summoned to take part in a hunting party and he had been injured and simultaneously poisoned. The incident nearly cost him his life, and he had not even fully healed when he had joined the rescue mission to liberate Caelfel from the desert. Caelfel speculated he would never be in peak physical condition as he was before he was poisoned.

Eviat looked up suddenly, and his eyes were red. "I don't understand how—"

Caelfel's voice was hoarse, as she recalled her own realization. "Werewolves. When she went through the Pirinac."

Father attempted saying something, but his voice cracked. The pendant in his hands began shaking more violently. "I need to—" He looked around wildly for the words to make sense of his primal needs.

Caelfel delicately stroked the side of face twice with her thumb. "I know. I'll take care of everything."

Father nodded and shut himself in the bedroom he used to share with his wife.

Caelfel hovered where she was, wanting to go to Father but knowing he needed to be alone. She sighed and turned back to Brenin. The prince had tried excusing himself as best as he could from the encounter by standing on the threshold of the open front door and looking outside with feigned interest. When Caelfel approached him, he appeared surprised by her presence, as if he had not witnessed the grief of the Gyssedlues.

"You have a lovely home," he tried lamely.

Caelfel gave him a half-smile and scrubbed at her eyes with her sleeve. "It's no palace."

"It's more beautiful than a palace."

She gave a short laugh. "I need to go arrange my mother's funeral. Will you come with me?"

Brenin glanced at the house as if the alternative, being left there with her grieving father, was the last thing he wanted. He hesitated. "Is there somewhere I can wash first?" He sniffed his own shoulder for emphasis.

Caelfel grinned, realizing that the stench of dried desert sweat clung to them both. "We have a fountain."

The idea of bathing outside in a fountain proved completely foreign to Brenin, and Caelfel struggled to give him the basic lecture on plumbing and the availability of fresh water combined with magical processing. Eventually, Brenin relented, stripped off his clothes, and left them just outside the bathing area. Caelfel set them aside and went to find him a fresh tunic and pants while he cleaned himself.

"I'll be right back," she promised him.

"And I'll have to stay here until you do," he complained lightly.

Caelfel chuckled to herself, deciding she did not want Brenin to know how much he amused her.

She didn't want to disturb her father, so Caelfel decided to borrow some clothes from someone else, particularly since Brenin refused to wear hers. Her mind initially went to Feraan, but Caelfel refused to consider that option. The thought that he might be home was enough to send her stomach vibrating with unwanted anticipation.

She decided her best course would be to visit Thoroth, the healer and friend that lived nearby. She frowned as she stepped up to his green door, the color of a healer's abode, when she remembered that Thoroth had preferred Caelfel, breaking Garvanna's heart in the process. Caelfel never shared nor returned his affection and thus had decided to never speak to him if he was so inclined to continue pursuing her. She hoped his feelings for her had cooled while she had been away.

And so Caelfel knocked.

Thoroth opened the door shortly and he stared at her in a state of shock. His appearance had not much changed with his thick eyebrows and amber hair tied back. "Caelfel? You've returned?"

"Yes," she answered shortly, determined to get straight to the point. "I have—"

"Is Garvanna with you?" he interrupted suddenly, looking about as if she would be hiding nearby.

"No, but I need—"

"Where is she?"

Caelfel forced herself to be patient by taking a slow breath. She pointed out to herself that at least Thoroth was interested in Garvanna. "I can't say," she answered him finally.

He looked stricken. "Is she hiding from me? Can you tell her—"

"Listen, Thoroth. I can't tell you where Garvanna is, because I don't know where she is. But you should know that my mother has died."

Something changed in Thoroth's expression, and his concern transferred from Garvanna to her. "Oh, Caelfel. I am so sorry."

He made a move toward her, perhaps to offer some form of physical consolation, but Caelfel couldn't help but be cold. She held out a hand to stop him. "Look, I need to borrow some clothes, just one set. I will return them as soon as I can."

Thoroth blinked when his attention was so abruptly diverted. "Who do you need clothes for?" he asked with an audible effort to not sound suspicious.

"My friend needs them."

"Friend?" he repeated skeptically.

The last time Caelfel had wanted help with an unidentified friend, it turned out to be the most hated elf of the empire, and Thoroth's help nearly cost him his life. Caelfel spoke to alleviate his fears. "His name is Brenin, and he is a prince of Umfeld."

"He's a human?" Thoroth repeated, his tone taking on a blunt prejudice.

Caelfel evened her gaze with him. "Yes, a human, and a human that saved my life."

Thoroth softened. "What happened, Caelfel?"

"A lot of things happened," Caelfel said, unable to keep the coldness from her voice. "I've no wish to speak of it at this moment. Please, will you help me, Thoroth? I'll need to see the Council about arranging my mother's funeral soon."

Thoroth nodded and led the way into his house. He took her down a narrow hallway and stopped to open a linen closet. It contained sheets and dressings, which made sense for a healer. On a shelf above these sheets were folded sets of clothes. He showed them to Caelfel and let her take her pick.

Thoroth spoke as she looked through them. "Is he more than a friend?"

"More than a friend?" Caelfel returned his question.

He offered a dry smile. "Feraan was more than a friend," Thoroth reminded her bitterly. He gave a short laugh. "I'm almost too afraid to ask."

"Why should you be afraid?" Caelfel asked coolly, keeping her eyes on the clothes before her. She longed to be away from Thoroth and back to Brenin.

"I'm afraid to know the answer," he said. Then he took a deep breath and without any trace of warmth in his voice asked, "How is Feraan?"

A rage exploded within her, but Caelfel worked to keep it contained. Only her barbed voice betrayed her. "I would not know, Thoroth. I've not seen him since I left Cromlech."

Thoroth sighed, but his relief did not penetrate Caelfel. It only made her angrier. "Goddess above," he prayed quietly with gratitude.

Caelfel whirled to him. "It does not matter what the question is, because the answer will always be the same. Whoever I choose for my friends, *I* choose. And I choose that you will remain only a friend to me. *Only* a friend. And as my friend, you are not justified to presume that you can control who my other friends are or who I choose for my lover."

Thoroth paled to a sickly sheen as the blood drained from his face at her outburst. "I have only ever cared about you," he shot back. "I have wanted your safety and well-being. I have wanted to protect you from others." His voice softened, "I have only loved you."

Caelfel never wavered. "I do not need your love."

He staggered backwards as if he'd been slapped and clutched at the closet door, his knuckles white with the strength of his grip. After a moment, he released the door and reached for her cheek. He cradled it and pleaded, "If you would only let me show you." Then he kissed her.

In the next instant, Thoroth was reeling back against the wall, cupping his cheek where the red impression of a hand was quickly becoming visible. The stinging pain in Caelfel's right hand told her she had slapped him *hard.* In a low voice, she swore, "You will not touch me again."

"Caelfel, I—"

She continued, her voice rising. "Thank you, Thoroth for allowing your own selfishness to take precedence over my mother's funeral. I'll go now and find clothes elsewhere."

She went to leave, but Thoroth quickly blocked her path. She refused to look at him when he said, "No, I'm sorry Caelfel. Go ahead and get the clothes. I—I will not touch you again."

Caelfel waited a full minute for him to move and when he did not, she slowly returned to the linen closet without another word. After a short search, she selected a chemise of ivory-colored Vinius thread, a jerkin of dark red silk, and brown pants Brenin would probably need to roll up for size. She gave Thoroth a curt word of thanks before she all but ran out the door.

Once she was free of the healer, Caelfel slowed her pace to collect herself. Thoroth had soured her mood with his petulant whining and unwanted advances. She scrubbed the taste of him from her mouth with the back of her hand, preferring the acrid taste of dried desert sweat to that of the healer's lips. She entered the garden through the gate and carefully approached the bathing area.

"Brenin?" she called tentatively.

"Do not worry, for I have not moved since you left," he called back from the other side of the curtain.

A smile came easily to her face at the sound of his voice, and she found she was quite glad to be back in his company. "I brought you some clothes," she told him, reaching out to draw back the curtain.

"Don't open it!" he yelled suddenly.

Caelfel froze. "Why not?"

"I'm not wearing anything." His exasperation made it sound as though this should be evident to Caelfel.

"But I have your clothes."

Brenin thought for a moment. "Just push them under the curtain and I will get them."

Caelfel did as he asked and waited.

Brenin waited too. "Turn around or something."

"*Why?*" she asked, half amused and half impatient.

"You're looking, and I don't want you to see me."

Caelfel nearly laughed aloud at Brenin's insecurity but stopped herself. "There's a curtain. I can't see anything."

"But *I* can see *you*."

"Because I am on the outside of it!" she nearly shouted.

Brenin paused. "You promise you can't see me?"

Caelfel strained her eyes but could see nothing past the thick, gauzy material. "I promise."

After a moment, she heard water splashing as he stepped out of the fountain. His footsteps padded lightly and stopped just in front of her. "Are you sure you can't see me? I can see you so well."

She tilted her head to him, his voice close and just beyond the fabric. "I can't see anything." She thought of deviously turning her eyes to where she imagined the rest of his body would be but trained her attention to where she thought his head was.

"You look troubled, Caelfel. Is something wrong?" he asked.

She didn't want Thoroth to occupy her mind or any of her conversations with Brenin. "Nothing other than the obvious," she lied.

"Right, the obvious. I'm sorry."

"There is nothing to apologize for." She narrowed her eyes, teasing. "Unless you have taken all the water for *my* bath."

He only laughed, and she saw the clothes on the stone tiles slide the rest of the way under the curtain. "I brought my own clothes," he pointed out. "You didn't need to bring me elvish ones."

"You're in elvish land now, my prince. It's only fitting that you should wear elvish clothes. I wore human clothes when I was in Kanetalm."

"You wore one dress and then promptly mutilated it," he said, laughing.

"Humans should not have ridiculous clothes," she defended mildly.

"I admit that I preferred the second version. Nice legs and all."

The curtain was pulled back to reveal Brenin in his new, elvish clothes. Caelfel concluded he looked rather handsome and that red was a striking color for him.

His hair was long enough to hang past his face, so before she took her bath, she tied it back in an elvish fashion. It revealed his round ears but also drew attention to the strong planes of his face and his endearingly flat eyebrows. She experimented with various styles, allowing Brenin to decide his favorite from a small looking glass she gave him. Secretly, Caelfel enjoyed the sensation of his hair running through her fingers. She saw from the reflection Brenin closed his eyes in contentment with each of her strokes and she realized he was enjoying the grooming as well. Caelfel firmly told herself there was nothing to it but knew that to be a lie.

Then Caelfel took her own bath with honey dew oil. She braided her hair when it was still wet. She almost asked Brenin to do it for her but denied herself that opportunity, unsure if Brenin would be willing or able to do it properly, unsure of her own response and desire for it. She stepped out of the bathing area and could not fail to miss the disappointment in Brenin's eyes when he saw her hair already plaited.

The sun was setting by the time they left for the town plaza, and Caelfel was unsure if a member of the Council would still be on duty or if she would have to return the next day. When they reached the Hall of Court, Caelfel saw one member still seated at the Council Table, and it was the one councilor she had hoped to avoid.

Head Councilor Uthruil was bent over piles of papers, studying them under the failing sunlight. He hadn't noticed her entrance, and Caelfel half considered turning around and leaving altogether. No one would blame her, for not much time had passed since he had ordered her execution in that very room. She approached the table anyway. Her name had been cleared of all crimes. She'd even received a political pardon. She had nothing to fear.

"Councilor?"

Uthruil looked up, a single, fluid motion of his head. "Miss Gyssedlues," he greeted, sounding pleasantly surprised, as if he had not called for her execution over a month ago. He set aside his papers to give her his full attention. "Are you here for personal matters or is this a business visit?"

"It's business, I'm afraid." He nodded for her to continue. "My mother has died, and I must arrange her funeral."

The mask of Uthruil Killelvris cracked, and his face turned hollow. "Sylaera is dead?"

Caelfel nodded. She remembered how his brother Nimuath had been fond of her mother. It was not surprising to think Uthruil was equally fond of her.

Uthruil cleared his throat, and his mask returned, all indifference now. "I am very sorry for your loss, Caelfel. If I may, how did it happen?"

Caelfel swallowed. "She was murdered by werewolves."

"Do you have her body prepared with the necessary death rites?"

She shook her head. "They left no body behind."

Uthruil took a moment to process that horrifying information. He began writing. "I'll arrange for a special priest to send her spirit away, then. When would you like the funeral to take place?"

"I'm not sure. Perhaps in a few days, once my father has come to terms with it."

"How is Eviat doing, by the way?" Uthruil asked. "I've not seen him for a while."

Caelfel sensed that there was something besides polite curiosity behind the question and she remembered how the Council arranged for the accident that should have taken her father's life. "Well," she answered curtly. "All things considered."

Uthruil set down his writing for a moment. "You should know, Caelfel, that it was not *my* doing."

Caelfel narrowed her eyes, unsure of what he meant. "Isn't it someone's doing if that someone ordered the hand that holds the dagger?"

Uthruil deliberated a moment. "I did not order the hand."

"And yet the hand is under your command. It is *your* hand. Forgive me, Councilor, if I have trouble believing you."

Uthruil sighed, resigned to the fact that he would not change Caelfel's mind. He picked up his writing again. "Would you prefer a community ceremony or a private one?"

"I don't care."

Uthruil scribbled some more. "I'll let you know when the arrangements have been made. I'll take care of everything and inform the Family."

"The Family?" Caelfel repeated.

Uthruil glanced up at her. "Don't you think your grandmother will want to know of her daughter's death?"

Caelfel felt strangely protective. "As far as I'm concerned, I have no grandmother. My father and I are Sylaera's only family."

Uthruil shrugged and pushed the papers away. "Caelfel, this doesn't have to be just business. If you would like to talk—"

"I would rather not become personal with you, Councilor."

Uthruil nodded solemnly. "Of course."

"Good evening." She turned to leave.

"Who is this with you? A human?"

Caelfel froze, glancing at Brenin who had been silent throughout the exchange. "He's my friend."

146

Uthruil gave her a weak smile. "You certainly have a penchant for making new friends."

"He's the prince of Umfeld," Caelfel said firmly, ignoring the reference to Feraan.

Uthruil turned his smile to Brenin. "Welcome to Sal'Sumarathar, prince of Umfeld."

Brenin inclined his head to Uthruil as a sign of goodwill and followed Caelfel out of the Hall of Court. "You're afraid of him," he noted when they were alone.

"I'm not afraid of him," she flared defensively.

Brenin let that subject pass. "It doesn't appear as though you are having a pleasant homecoming."

"I came home for a funeral," she sighed airily. "How pleasant is it supposed to be?"

"Right, of course," Brenin nodded grimly. "I'm sorry."

She attempted a slight smile. "*I* am sorry. I haven't been as gracious a host as you were for me. Tomorrow, I will show you around."

Brenin took her bed for the night. Eviat's door was still shut, so Caelfel let him be. Caelfel slept on the floor next to Brenin, and she lay wide awake until his snores filled the air. She thought of many things before falling asleep but not at all about Brenin's snoring.

Keeping Brenin occupied was no difficult feat. She took him through the town, introducing him as a prince of Umfeld, but making no distinction that he was officially just the second prince. Caelfel believed he was Orrik's only rightful heir and she would not be responsible for reciting misinformation. The shopkeepers and their patrons all took to Brenin well, as she had predicted. They smiled and inclined their heads at his royal title. During the morning, Caelfel saw Daerad crossing the plaza and staring at them with a touch of envy. Caelfel did nothing to hide her smugness.

They ate lunch with the hunters, and the hunters provided meat for Brenin's meal. "I think we can spare a single haunch for a prince," one said as he threw it in a separate stew.

"So you hunt animals but you don't eat meat," Brenin observed with a question in his tone.

"Most elves don't eat meat," the hunter clarified, shrugging. "I've heard of more elves in Yamalvon eating it than anyone around here. We mostly trade the animals we hunt to caravans heading towards

Umfang or to ships sailing for the Vinius Islands."

"You don't trade with Umfeld?" Brenin asked curiously.

The two other hunters looked uneasily at each other. The third one finished off his cup of honeyed wine and kept his eyes on Brenin. Caelfel didn't feel as though he were making a threatening gesture so she didn't intervene.

"The caravans go to Umfang. We can't help that." There was something else, a bit of mystery hidden in his tone.

"Why don't they go to Umfeld?" Brenin pressed, leaning forward.

The hunter carefully set his cup on a barrel before answering. "This can't get out, what I'm about to tell you."

Brenin didn't nod. He continued staring intently at the hunter who sighed in resignation.

"Maybe you know this already, since the two of you just came here. There's only one road to Umfeld now. The Pirinac's too dangerous. The trees are infested with wild wolves, bigger than elves."

"We know," Caelfel interjected. "But we went through the desert. The caravans will have to cross the Amhsis to get to either Umfeld or Umfang."

The hunter leaned back. "The wolves don't just stay in the Pirinac Forest. They roam the mountains as if they are patrolling the borders."

"We crossed the border, though," Brenin pointed out. "We didn't run into any of them in the Farpass or at the Crossroads."

"Perhaps you're one of the lucky ones, then, but I've seen too many of those damned beasts myself."

Caelfel looked up to Brenin who stared at the cup in his hands as if trying to solve a difficult problem. "They're not just wolves," he said. "They're werewolves."

"That doesn't surprise me," the hunter said. "Given how big they are. But we've never seen them in their human form."

"We have once," Caelfel said.

"What happened?"

Caelfel gave the hunter a dead stare. "He wanted to tell me that he had killed my mother."

When they finished, Caelfel took Brenin to the archery range to show him what the proper distance between archer and target should be. He laughed when she pointed this out to him, and Caelfel could not help showing off her talent as she drew her bow and fired. After a few rounds, she passed the bow to Brenin to allow him a chance.

"Huwel couldn't even draw it back," he pointed out to her as he struggled to lift it to height.

Caelfel giggled as she took it back from him. "Perhaps we should find you a child's bow." And she did after going through the practice equipment kept in a nearby chest. She handed that one to him, and it seemed to better suit his strength.

"I'm not much of an archer myself," he admitted apologetically after his three tries flew wide of their mark. He returned the bow to the chest in shame.

"Are you trained in any combat at all?" Caelfel asked, astounded. "You have a personal company of soldiers, the *Company of the Prince.* Can you even hold a sword?"

Brenin appeared wounded. "Yes, I can hold a sword," he said defensively. "Father had Madoc and I trained since we were boys. Madoc preferred the greatsword. I never tried anything beyond the longsword. Cyrus trains with me regularly to make sure I don't lose the skills." Brenin's brow furrowed as he recalled something from memory. "*A prince should always be able to defend his honor and protect his countrymen,*" he recited. "Or something like that."

Caelfel went back to the chest of practice equipment. "We should spar," she suggested. "I've not trained with a sword, so you would have that advantage."

"You would beat me," Brenin said, sounding horrified.

Caelfel bit down on a laugh and produced two wooden practice staves. "Perhaps, but Cyrus is not here to practice with you."

Brenin was shaking his head. "I won't do it. I didn't come all the way to Honey Water to embarrass myself."

Caelfel rolled her eyes in mock annoyance but complied with Brenin's wishes all the same. They strolled back to town in a lazy fashion as Caelfel considered ideas aloud. "I wonder if the theatre troupe is performing tonight."

"Theatre troupe?" Brenin repeated.

She smiled devilishly and took his hand to lead the way to Sal'Sumarathar's amphitheater.

It was a magnificent venue fashioned out of the eastern hillside. The stage was a polished stone patio, and the seats of the house were made from fallen tree trunks, smooth and glossy from a woodworker's shaping hands. When the two of them arrived, the actors of the troupe were practicing their voice amplification, and a small crowd of spectators had already appeared for the show. At Brenin's behest, Caelfel chose seats for them nearest to the stage.

Musicians crowded below the stage and made a discordant rabble as they tuned their instruments. When twilight hit, illuminating the amphitheatre in dim light, the conductor suspended his hands, and the show began.

The troupe portrayed the story of a distraught prince after the death of his father. The throne went to the prince's uncle who turned out to be the original king's murderer. The story did little to hold Brenin's attention. He was mostly interested in the show of lights the actors put on during intermission. Using their auras, they created a multitude of shapes and figures in just about every color. When they left the production, Brenin was none the wiser on the matter of elvish performance art.

A courier arrived at the Gyssedlues household later that evening just as Eviat emerged from his bedroom. Caelfel read over the missive as Father approached her. She looked up at him.

"Everything is ready for Mother's funeral," she relayed to him.

"Head Councilor Uthruil asks when you would like to have the event," the courier said.

Caelfel looked to Eviat, and his expression was one of numbness. "We can have it tomorrow evening," he decided.

The courier nodded and excused himself politely. At the reappearance of Eviat, Brenin remained at the edge of the room, waiting to be acknowledged.

It didn't take Eviat long, and he brightened considerably in the presence of Caelfel's guest. "And who do we have here?" he asked with piqued curiosity.

Of all the elves he had recently met, Brenin was visibly nervous in the face of her father, so Caelfel did the introducing for him.

"Father, this is my friend. His name is Brenin, and he's a prince of Umfeld."

"He's a human?" Eviat said. Like the other elves they met, he was not prejudiced against humans. Caelfel was surprised at the positive response Brenin elicited, particularly in comparison with Feraan.

"Brenin, this is my father Eviat Gyssedlues," she said turning to him.

"It's a pleasure to meet you," Brenin stammered. Caelfel noticed how he didn't even attempt to pronounce their surname in the standard method of address.

Eviat smiled warmly and embraced the second prince of Umfeld in a familiar hug. After a moment, Eviat stepped back. "How did the two of you meet?"

"Garvanna and I were crossing through the Pirinac Forest before we were attacked by a rather territorial pack of werewolves. The attack separated us, and I was knocked unconscious and severely injured. Brenin found me. He saved me and took me to Palpses as his guest."

Eviat gripped Brenin's shoulder. "Thank you for helping her, Brenin."

Brenin nodded, unable to form words. "I am sorry about your wife," he managed shortly.

Eviat shook his head. "You at least protected my daughter. I couldn't possibly ask more from you." He turned back to Caelfel. "Garvanna had sent us a letter, saying she had lost you. That was why your mother left, to go find you."

"She was killed by the same werewolves that attacked us. I don't know where Garvanna is."

"Her letter didn't say," Eviat said.

Brenin excused himself from the room, and Caelfel and her father watched him leave. "How strange. He was rather social around the other elves."

"He probably wants to give us privacy, given all that has happened." He gave her a sideways glance. "He seems rather fond of you."

Caelfel turned suspicious. "How can you be sure? You've only known him for a few minutes."

"For one, he is a prince of Umfeld, and he's let you drag him all this way."

"Because I asked him," she flared defensively, only realizing belatedly that it didn't help her case.

Eviat angled his gaze pointedly. "What other reason does he need?"

"He's always wanted to see the elves, and the promise of military aide for his father can be quite persuasive."

"That's for his father, though. I'm sure Brenin needed no persuasion other than your company."

Caelfel irritably shrugged off her father's observations. "Is Feraan home?" she asked, changing the subjects.

"Of course, prince or no prince, Brenin is no Feraan."

"Father, *please*," she hissed impatiently. "Brenin is human."

"Is that your only reservation?"

Caelfel rolled her eyes. "Is Feraan home?" she repeatedly firmly.

Eviat sighed, ceding the argument. "No, he left the Cromlech Palace the night you did. We all assumed he went with you."

Caelfel bit her lip, recalling their last conversation. "He didn't."

"Well, he didn't come back to Honey Water either."

Caelfel turned her gaze out the window. The green leaves of spring trees rustled with the lightest breeze, casting shadows that danced against the berry bushes and the fountain in the garden. She imagined that the garden at Feraan's house looked similar at this time of year. "Where else would he have gone?" she wondered aloud.

But Father had left the room, leaving nothing but her own imagination to answer her.

12. Dead Things

Now that Father had rejoined them from his grieving, another trip to Thoroth to pilfer clothes for Brenin would be unnecessary. Caelfel didn't look forward to when she would have the return the ones she had already borrowed. She entertained the idea of asking Eviat to do it instead.

"I don't understand what you have against him," Eviat said when she asked him the next morning.

Caelfel pressed her lips together as she deliberated about telling him what had happened the other day. "He kissed me."

"That's hardly a crime," Eviat said, but she could hear the teasing in his voice.

"Who kissed you?" Brenin suddenly asked from the doorway.

Caelfel's cheeks burned, shamefaced as she avoided his gaze. She didn't understand why she felt so embarrassed to admit this in front of Brenin. "His name is Thoroth," she told him softly.

"I do not recall that name," he remarked, joining them at the table.

"Because you haven't met him yet."

Brenin said nothing to that, and Eviat passed him a slice of bread dotted with dewberries and walnuts. Brenin muttered something akin to gratitude for the breakfast and continued scowling at his hands.

Caelfel, not understanding his surliness, forgot her embarrassment and confronted him. "Does that bother you?" she demanded sharply.

Brenin was surprised at her tone. "What?"

"Does it bother you that someone kissed me?" she asked him again. She felt a nudge from her father's foot under the table.

"Why would that bother me?" Brenin returned, his own face reddening.

Caelfel examined him a moment longer before turning away. But she glanced sideways before admitting, "Well it bothers me. You shouldn't kiss someone without their permission."

Brenin was silent a moment. "I was under the impression that romantic kisses were spontaneous."

Caelfel considered the kisses she had shared with Feraan and compared them with Thoroth's kiss. "Still, you should not have to be kissed by someone you did not want anywhere near your mouth, especially when you've made it quite clear you do not share their feelings."

"Shall I ask permission before each of my kisses?" he said, and Caelfel could hear him biting down on a laugh.

"You should." But she was smiling as well.

"That sounds awfully impractical. I think it would ruin the moment."

"Have you ever kissed anyone, Prince Brenin?"

To her dismay, Brenin didn't respond. She was afraid she had mysteriously soured his mood again and could not put it out of her mind until he amiably inquired about the funeral arrangements for later that day.

"What do I do there?" Brenin asked when Caelfel brought him some formal clothes.

She shrugged. "I've never been to an elvish funeral before. The closest things I've seen was the memorial service for the people of Amasel and another one for the fallen warriors of the Vinius Islands. What do humans do for funerals?"

"We stand around and watch their body burn," Brenin replied grimly.

Caelfel shuddered at the thought and passed him his new tunic. "I don't think it will be like that."

And it wasn't. The elves didn't burn bodies. If Sylaera's body had survived, it would have been carried away to the vaults of the Heather Tombs carved into the Baetic Mountains or so Eviat had informed her, who had witnessed his fair share of funerals in his lifetime.

When the sun began sinking to the horizon, they went to the Orchard of Silence, a grove of trees that surrounded the gates of the college of Sal'Sumarathar. When they passed the college, Brenin marveled at its great size and structure and asked Caelfel what it was.

"That's the college, where the elves study magic. I studied there for a short time before my *accident*."

Eviat, Caelfel, and Brenin arrived at the Altar of Transcendence that sat in the middle of the orchard. Two priests already stood on either side of the altar, a priest of Sal'Sumarathar and a priest of Ewyn. In the distance, Caelfel could see acolytes picking the fruit from trees, keeping their distance from Sylaera's ceremony.

Uthruil came with his son Daerad. Thoroth arrived next, and Caelfel recognized Nimuath, headmaster of the college, after him. She lost interest in the visitors after Nimuath and waited for everything to begin. Everyone was completely silent, and she tugged at her dress, the dress of crushed blue velvet Sylaera had made for her necromancy trial. Everyone wore blue in honor of Sylaera's aura.

The light of the setting sun hit the jeweled emblem on the stone altar, and the priests finally moved. The priest of Sal'Sumarathar procured a small stone from his sleeve that turned out to be a seed. He placed it in crystal vessel, and then the priest of Ewyn began singing in an ancient language Caelfel recognized as Daemona. Their auras floated about them in a thick haze of silver, and the first priest began singing as well. The crystal goblet pulsed a glowing blue with the fluctuations of a heartbeat. The acolytes in the distance paused their harvesting to watch.

In a flash of blue light, the green shoot of a plant emerged from the rim of the vessel. The priests stopped singing, and the vassal of Ewyn lightly touched one of the delicate, miniscule leaves.

In a clear voice, the priest said, "Rest easy, Sylaera Gyssedlues."

A breeze drifted through the orchard, and Caelfel imagined her mother's tree sapling sighing. Eviat approached the plant first, said a few things, and then stepped aside for Caelfel's turn.

Caelfel took Brenin with her, looked upon the small plant, and whispered, "Mother, this is Brenin." Feeling rather awkward and having nothing else to say, she joined her father.

The other visitors to the service paid their own respects and then offered their condolences to the Gyssedlues family. Caelfel gave a shuddering sigh and heard none of their words.

"So *that* is Thoroth," Brenin remarked in a whisper after the healer had passed by them.

Caelfel gave a slight, barely perceptible nod when the healer left hearing range. "That is Thoroth, the offensive elf. Look how stupidly he walks."

Brenin gave a snort that he tried to disguise with a cough when several elves turned their heads.

"He is still my friend, no matter how cross I may be with him," Caelfel said with a sigh.

"What a friend," Brenin noted darkly.

Caelfel nudged him with her elbow. "Were it not for him, I would have never met Garvanna. *She* is a true friend, honest to a fault."

"I wish I could have met her."

"Perhaps you will. We know she is alive right now. I only wonder why she has not returned to Honey Water."

Brenin turned his gaze to the tree sapling, and Caelfel watched his expression as he puzzled over its meaning.

"Do you understand it?" she asked him.

"I think you've explained it to me before. The sprout represents rebirth."

Caelfel beamed with pride at his correct explanation. "Like the forest fire. There is no true death. We are reborn from the ashes."

"Does that mean your mother's spirit is in that tree?"

Caelfel accepted the condolences from the Sal'Sumarathar Council before answering. She shrugged. "Who knows? If she is the tree, she probably isn't the same person that I knew."

The last family to approach the altar was an older she-elf shadowed by five mature daughters. Of them, Caelfel only recognized the she-elf Adar. When Caelfel had been issued her armor for the Volunteer Regiment, Adar had been the blacksmith who had taken her measurements and crafted her leather armor.

After a brief word to the sapling from each of them, the head of their party turned and marched towards Eviat and Caelfel.

"Who are they?" Brenin asked her in a low voice. But Caelfel could only shake her head to signal she did not know.

The eldest elf wore a velvet dress of dark burgundy, the only clothing at the funeral that wasn't blue, and held herself with a proud air of regality. Her platinum hair was tied back tightly, revealing the sharp height of her pointed ears. Her sea glass eyes pierced Caelfel as she waited expectantly for someone to acknowledge her.

"Well here is the heiress," she said shortly when no one did. "Eviat, aren't you going to introduce us?"

Caelfel looked at her father, puzzled.

Eviat sighed. "Caelfel, this is your grandmother, Lady Ellissara Ambrosius."

Caelfel blinked at the she-elf before her. Had she been thinking clearly, she might have guessed that Lady Ellissara was related to her. However, Caelfel was simply shocked into speechlessness by the number of emotions coursing through her. She suppressed the urge to grip Brenin for support.

Lady Ellissara gave her a thin smile. "Yes, we are the Family of Sal'Sumarathar. I had seven daughters, and Sylaera was the oldest. These are her sisters, your aunts, behind me, except for the youngest who is currently away in Elewyr and could not arrive in time."

Caelfel could still find no words to say to her grandmother.

"Speak, child," Lady Ellissara snapped. "Were you not taught manners? It would not surprise me with your common upbringing."

"It's a pleasure to meet you, Lady Ellissara," Caelfel said softly.

Ellissara smiled at that. "You may call me Grandmother, child." She brusquely turned to Eviat, her moment of warmth gone as quickly as it came. "There is to be a feast, correct?"

Eviat nodded. "Headmaster Nimuath is hosting it in the college."

"How wonderful. There is much I would like to discuss with dear Caelfel here. You won't mind if I claim her for most of the evening?"

"Of course not," Eviat said, smiling grimly. "I am sorry you could not find time in the past seventy-six years to meet her."

Ellissara ignored the remark and, tucking Caelfel's hand in the crook of her elbow, led her away towards the college. Caelfel cast Brenin a furtive glance before being helplessly towed along.

Caelfel couldn't fathom why a grandmother, who had made no previous attempt to meet her, suddenly took an interest after her mother's death. In fact, Caelfel recalled informing Head Councilor Uthruil that Lady Ellissara was not to be invited. Yet here she was, dragging Caelfel along with the self-assurance of one who always got what she wanted.

"You're not married?" Lady Ellissara asked once they had passed through the gates.

"No," Caelfel answered carefully, trying to discern the she-elf's purpose. "I am only seventy-six."

Ellissara nodded at this, as if making some mental calculation. Before entering the college, she stopped them just inside the gates and turned around to see her five daughters. "I suppose you'll want to meet your aunts. Adar is my second oldest and a blacksmith in the imperial army."

"We've met," Caelfel interrupted briefly. She turned to Adar, one of the dark haired sisters. "How is Olwen?"

"Olwen has left my service," Adar said quietly. "He's in another apprenticeship at the Cromlech Palace."

Ellissara continued as if she hadn't been interrupted, turning to her only daughter with red copper hair. "My next oldest is Eleanir, the apothecary of the family."

"Please, mother." Eleanir held her hand out for Caelfel and smiled. "It's Elaine."

Caelfel recognized the name Elaine and gladly shook her aunt's hand for saving her father's life.

Ellissara moved to the first of her golden haired daughters, and Caelfel easily detected the resemblance to her mother. "This is Guinerva and her interests mostly revolve around politics. She's usually in Yamalvon or the Vinius Islands for diplomatic meetings."

Guinerva offered neither hand nor acknowledgment, so Ellissara quickly moved on.

"Morwen is training for temple work," Ellissara said in a tone that suggested she didn't approve of this line of work at all.

Morwen, another dark haired beauty, turned her sullen expression to her mother. "I'm an acolyte, Mother. It means I'm going to be a priestess."

Ellissara waved her hand impatiently, having no time for Morwen, and turned to the last daughter present. She did not smile, but her voice was evident of her pride. "Liavyn is my starlet, an artist. She sings and performs, mostly for audiences in Yamalvon and Elewyr. She also writes, paints, and plays music."

Liavyn, another daughter with hair as yellow as honey, approached Caelfel with a skip and extended her hand before sweeping into a low bow. "It is most wonderful to meet you, dearest niece." Liavyn rose from her curtsy. "Our youngest sister regrets being unable to make it."

"What is her name?" Caelfel asked curiously.

Ellissara answered for Liavyn. "It's Ruefel." She paused, laughing quietly at some private joke. "She wants to be a sailor."

Caelfel hesitated, unable to see her amusement, but she saw her aunts giving the slightest shake of their heads to not press the matter. So Caelfel remained silent about the aunt whom she was probably named after.

Ellissara took her elbow again and began leading them all inside. "What about you, Caelfel? What is your vocation?"

Caelfel was reluctant to answer, wondering if her skills would only be laughable to her grandmother. "I am a ranger, trained in archery and hunting."

Ellissara nodded approvingly. "You are a warrior, then, just like your mother. That is a marketable talent after all."

There was a unanimous groan from all five of Ellissara's daughters, but one sharp look from their mother silenced them all.

"I'm sorry. Marketable?" Caelfel repeated apprehensively.

"My dear, whatever conflicts I had with your mother remain with your mother. You are still my granddaughter. My *only* one, I might add." Ellissara looked back at her daughters pointedly, as if intending her last remark to be directed toward them.

"Then why haven't I met you before?" Caelfel asked bluntly.

The question silenced the Ambrosius Family. As they passed through the entrance hall of the college, the Eye of Ewyn hummed quietly on its pedestal. She had wanted to be the one to explain the story concerning the Eye of Ewyn to Brenin, but she suppressed the urge to look around for him. She trusted him to be in good hands with her father.

But even the enormous white gemstone with its soft humming was louder than Ellissara, and Caelfel wondered if she had offended her grandmother with her question. Then she decided she did not particularly mind if she had.

Minutes passed, and Ellissara finally answered. "That was totally your mother's doing." And then she would explain no more on the matter.

The classroom Caelfel had originally studied in was fashioned as the banquet hall for Sylaera's funeral feast. Caelfel remembered it well, as one wall, comprised of only stone columns, left the room exposed to the elements. As night began to descend, Caelfel could see firefaeries twinkling throughout the garden. Without pause, Ellissara led her family to the head table and took her seat, placing Caelfel in the chair to her right. Before Caelfel had a chance to look around for Brenin or her father, Eleanir took the seat on her other side.

The other seats in the great hall were filled, and Nimuath stood to welcome them all to the funerary feast. Having already lost interest, Caelfel turned to her aunt. "Shall I call you Aunt Eleanir?" she asked, unsuccessfully masking the bitterness in her voice.

Her aunt smiled wanly. "Just Elaine, please."

"That doesn't sound very elvish," Caelfel remarked coldly.

"It isn't," Elaine agreed.

Before Caelfel could interrogate her further, Ellissara reclaimed Caelfel's attention. "You're not married?" her grandmother asked again, as if to assure herself of the fact.

"I'm not," Caelfel confirmed for her.

"No betrothed? No lover?"

Caelfel sighed, and it was a rueful sound. "I have nothing of the sort."

"I do remember something of those necromancy charges, that could be a dampener," Ellissara mused as the first course of food was served.

"I was cleared of those charges," Caelfel pointed out defensively.

Ellissara nodded. "Of course, dear. And you were crowned Beauty of Spring with political pardon. Your name is certainly out there. It can easily make one desirable." Ellissara began filling her plate with honey dew berries and rosemary bread.

Caelfel watched her as she pieced everything together. "My name is out where? *Wait!* You knew I was crowned at the Spring Festival?"

Ellissara's gaze turned sharp. "Lower your voice. I was there at the Spring Festival myself."

"But you didn't speak to me?" Caelfel pressed.

Ellissara blinked impassively. "We are speaking now, dear."

Before Caelfel could angrily lash out at her grandmother, Nimuath appeared to fill their silver goblets with red wine. Elaine deliberately piled Caelfel's plate with food, but Caelfel touched neither plate nor goblet. She focused on keeping her rage in check and her breathing even. She wondered how her mother would want her to deal with Ellissara.

"She certainly has Sylaera's temper," Liavyn chimed in a few seats down. "It's almost like our sister's ghost is among us." Only Nimuath and Guinerva chuckled at the joke before the headmaster slipped away.

"Can I ask why you disowned my mother?" Caelfel asked slowly.

To her surprise, although Ellissara had previously seemed to avoid the conversation, she didn't shy away from the topic now. "It's all rather simple. Sylaera and I disagreed over politics."

"Politics?" Caelfel repeated skeptically.

"Aside from being a battlemage, Sylaera had duties as my oldest daughter. She accompanied me to Yamalvon for every legal hearing. At first she had no interest in legal proceedings. Then she began to develop an opinion, a rather vocal one."

"What opinion was that?"

"Humans," Ellissara sniffed. "She wanted to establish diplomatic relations with humans, Umfeld in particular. Imagine the thought. She even went so far as to argue in favor of interracial marriage. When she started lobbying to restore Lady Fawnrial to her original seat in the High Council, I had had enough."

Caelfel's fingers shook as she clenched them into fists. She thought of Brenin and didn't interrupt, waiting for Ellissara to continue.

"I went to her and said she was an embarrassment to the Family. Then she said the Family was an embarrassment to her." Ellissara scoffed and took a sip of her wine.

For a time, Caelfel could hear nothing but the blood pounding in her ears. She vaguely registered Ellissara prattling on about how Sylaera's estrangement ended up being for nothing when the empress herself partook in such a blasphemous relationship and named her bastard as her own. Caelfel thought of the scorn her grandmother would have for Brenin, and she had a difficult time suppressing the urge to rake Ellissara's face with her fingernails.

Elaine cut across her deep silence. "Caelfel, dearest, eat something. You've not touched your plate."

But Caelfel rounded on her instead. "Why do you want to be called Elaine?"

Elaine turned away from her and did not answer. Caelfel seethed at the irony of Sylaera being disowned while Eleanir publicly preferred a human name for herself.

"What do you want with me?" Caelfel asked Ellissara in a hard voice.

"What do you mean?" Ellissara asked, setting down her goblet.

"Why would it take my mother's death for you to finally meet me?"

"As I said, that was entirely your mother's doing. When you were born, I attempted to see you, but Sylaera slammed the door in my face after telling me I had no granddaughter." Ellissara gave another scoff, as if the memory was utterly ridiculous to her.

"And now?" Caelfel pressed, jaw clenched.

"I told you that Sylaera was my eldest and therefore my heir. Even though she broke away from the Family, the line of inheritance still extends to you, darling. *You* are my heir, even before Adar."

"What does that mean?" Caelfel asked warily.

"It means that upon my death, you will inherit the Ambrosius lands, titles, and wealth. My seat in the High Council. I only want to ensure you are prepared for such a responsibility and that any husband you marry will not shame you or the Ambrosius name."

Caelfel sighed, realizing Ellissara's intent. "You're trying to marry me off."

"You are quite an eligible bachelorette. There is no reason we should not find you a good husband," Ellissara argued. "After I revoked her birthright, even your mother married well, for a commoner."

"What if I don't want to marry?"

"How else do you expect to have children?" Ellissara shot back. "I will not have any illegitimate bastards claiming the Family's name." Caelfel leaned back in her chair and deigned not to say anything more to her grandmother. She could suffer through one evening and then leave to take Brenin home.

"There is one matter I must put to rest right now, if you hope to have any husband with at least a marginal ranking. I was at the Spring Festival. I saw the dance and heard the talk about you. I must know at once if any impropriety occurred between you and Feraan Auvrearaheal."

Caelfel broke her silence quicker than she thought she would. "Feraan?" she repeated. "I don't see how that is any of your business," she said indignantly.

Ellissara's eyes turned to daggers. "It is entirely my business. An open relation with him would be political suicide. I won't have it. If something did happen, then it's in the past. Nothing can be done if it's not brought to light, as long as you promise me you will pursue him no longer."

Caelfel titled her head back and closed her eyes. Despite having only met Lady Ellissara, Caelfel was not surprised that her close-minded grandmother had strong feelings against an elf she knew only through rumors. She recalled Feraan's indifferent face as he had last turned away from her. "That is the only thing I can guarantee you," she said at length.

Ellissara patted her hand in an uncharacteristically maternal gesture. "Family sticks together."

Caelfel thought it a strange adage for someone who abandoned their eldest daughter.

Ellissara continued on to list off potential suitors, but Caelfel didn't pay attention until someone approached their table.

"Caelfel?"

She opened her eyes to see her scouting partner from the Volunteer Regiment standing in front of her, and it was a welcome sight. "Galath!" She couldn't imagine that he had traveled from Rasaen just for her mother's funeral.

He gave her a sheepish smile. "It feels like ages since I saw you last. I wanted to tell you how sorry I am about your mother, but I don't think you recognized me at her service."

"I'm sorry, Galath—"

But he shook his head. "I am sure your mind was understandably elsewhere." He paused. "May I talk to you?" The way he eyed Ellissara made it evident he would rather do so alone. "When you have a moment."

Caelfel stood without a glance towards her grandmother for permission. "Of course."

Galath wandered outside, and Ellissara held her back by the wrist to whisper, "Now *he* is an eligible bachelor, son of Lord Lanslak."

"He hates his father," Caelfel hissed back.

Ellissara ignored her. "Part of the Rasaen Family and he's around your age. I would most certainly approve of the match."

"Do you even care how my mother, your *daughter*, died?" Then with a louder voice, "Does it even bother you that she was ripped apart and then eaten by werewolves?"

The room fell into a terrifying silence when Caelfel challenged the Lady Ellissara. Then, conversation in the hall picked back up in a more rapid pace, as if making a point not to eavesdrop.

Ellissara did not waver. "Do not test your limits too early," she warned in a low voice before releasing Caelfel's wrist. "Sentimental creature," she scoffed.

Caelfel left to find Galath without looking back. But instead of lingering in the crowded room, she opted for the deafening silence of the entrance hall of the college, broken only by the humming of

Ewyn's Eye. She knew Galath wasn't in there but she currently preferred her own company as she pressed her back against the near wall, shoulders shaking. She hid her face behind her hands.

The door opened a moment later to allow another person through. Caelfel angrily rubbed her face, irritated that someone had interrupted her momentary peace. When she saw it was Brenin, the tightness in her chest subsided. The sight of him removed a defensive barricade within herself, and she struggled to keep herself composed.

"Brenin, I—" But she had no words to explain her state or the relief he had brought with him.

But Brenin was clever for a human. "Sad about your mom? Insufferable relative that doesn't understand your grief?" he accurately guessed. After all, his own past mirrored her situation.

She nodded with the tiniest of laughs, and he gave an encouraging smile in return.

They stood a short distance apart, as if suspended in time. Then clever Brenin held his arms out in invitation. She gratefully accepted his embrace and sobbed against his neck.

They separated after a minute, and Caelfel wiped at her eyes. Brenin coughed and stepped away from her to look at the Eye of Ewyn. "What is this?" he asked conversationally.

It was sufficient for a distraction. "Father hasn't told you?"

"He said you would want to tell me yourself."

Caelfel suppressed a smile at the thought of her insightful father. "It's called the Eye of Ewyn and it's basically a magical gemstone that stores and harnesses energy. There are two of them, and the other one is in Yamalvon, the capital. When I applied to study here at the college, it tested the strength of my magical capabilities." Brenin continued staring at it curiously. "You should touch it," Caelfel suggested.

"What would happen?" Brenin asked, intrigued and alarmed. Caelfel shrugged. "Probably nothing since you are human."

"Don't say it like it's a bad thing," Brenin muttered. He held his hands out, palms facing the gemstone and hesitated before touching its surface.

For a moment, nothing happened. Then a red haze flickered around Brenin's body and his eyes glazed over like blood red orbs. He didn't move, and Caelfel was afraid.

"Brenin?" She reached out to touch his shoulder, and her fingers were met with an electrical shock. Green light flooded her vision, and

Caelfel was thrown across the room.

Blinking, she sat up, rubbing her head, and saw Brenin returned to normal and inches away from her face. "Are you all right?" he asked, voice high-pitched with fear.

She stood. "I'm fine. What happened? Did you see something, like visions?"

"Visions?" Brenin repeated.

"When I first touched the Eye, it showed me visions," Caelfel explained. She rushed to the white stone and touched it again, only nothing happened. Disappointed, her hand fell back to her side. For a brief moment, she had hoped that the shock coupled with the green light meant the return of her own aura.

But she scrutinized Brenin over, remembering his rather visible red aura. "Did you see anything?" she repeated firmly.

"I saw—" But Brenin stopped himself. "I don't remember."

Caelfel narrowed her eyes at him, suspicious for the first time in their time together that he was lying to her.

"What was that red light?" Brenin asked, changing the subject. Caelfel looked back at the stone. "I think it means you have a red aura."

"Caelfel?"

They were interrupted by her Aunt Elaine who had suddenly appeared at the door. Brenin turned his gaze to the ground as if he had been caught doing something wrong. Caelfel tried hiding her impatience with her aunt's interruption.

"Elaine, this is Brenin. He's the—"

"Yes, he's the prince of Umfeld," Elaine interrupted softly. She approached them with a smile. "I am more familiar with humans that you might think, Caelfel."

"When he touched the stone, it was like he had a red aura. Does he? I didn't know humans could have auras."

Elaine looked Brenin over carefully. She touched his brow, and Caelfel felt jealously protective of him. Her aunt began to explain, "Humans have auras, but usually it's not like how elves have auras. Some humans can perform magic with them."

"Can I?" Brenin asked hopefully.

Elaine offered a small smile. "I am afraid not, Prince Brenin." She turned to Caelfel. "Will you take a walk with me?"

Caelfel glanced at Brenin, and sensing her refusal, Elaine pointed out, "Your friend Galath is waiting for you."

Caelfel frowned and reluctantly followed Elaine outside.

The garden was dark, save for the blinking firefaeries, and at first, Elaine said nothing. She walked among the plants and flowers, running her fingers through the plush leaves of bushes.

"You wanted to know why I call myself Elaine," she began slowly.

Caelfel folded her arms across her chest and waited.

Elaine turned to face her. "I believe you should choose Galath but not for the same reasons as my mother."

This direction surprised Caelfel. "What do you mean? What does Galath have to do with your name?"

"I went to Umfang once. I met a human, fell in love. His name was Tristram. As you might expect after speaking with Ellissara, I was disowned for my actions."

Elaine sighed at the painful memory and her eyes fluttered close.

"Tristram couldn't pronounce my name—Eleanir. He said there were too many syllables for such a short name." Elaine laughed as she reminisced. "So he chose a name for me that he could pronounce."

Caelfel was reminded of one of her first conversations with Brenin. "Elaine is better than cow field," Caelfel mumbled with a small chuckle.

Elaine laughed again. "Is that what he calls you? Your human, the prince?"

"His name is Brenin, and he's not my human." Caelfel paused. "He only mispronounced my name once. He can say it correctly now."

"Caelfel, I've heard how you laugh with him—"

"What of it?" Caelfel asked sharply, face reddening. "What does Brenin have to do with Galath or your Tristram? If you were disowned like my mother, why are you here now?"

Elaine sighed, her face suddenly drawn with ancient lines, and continued her tale. "I married Tristram, and he was my husband for two short years before he became ill."

Caelfel waited patiently, her body suddenly tense when the only end to Elaine's married life became painfully obvious.

"I'm a healer and an alchemist. I know just about every plant and its use. I tried everything but I couldn't save him."

"You mustn't blame yourself," Caelfel said gently.

Elaine looked at her sternly. "But I do. I made the decision to love a human, knowing the only outcome. Whether it had been two years or twenty, death would have come quickly for him while I would live on."

Caelfel swallowed. "I am sorry about your husband."

"I don't want your sympathy, Caelfel. I only want you to listen to me. I do not hold the prejudices my mother does. I have seen how you are with Brenin, and though you may deny it as much as you wish, it is the same way Tristram and I were with each other. When I tell you that Galath is the better choice, I do not say it out of spite. Brenin will die while Galath will not."

Caelfel couldn't bring herself to look at her aunt. "What are you suggesting I do?"

Elaine stepped closer and held both of Caelfel's hands. "I am pleading you to end your relationship with the human."

"You don't think I should even give it a try?" Caelfel managed through her tight throat. Prior to hearing Elaine's story, she hadn't even considered trying anything with Brenin but Caelfel couldn't help but turn defensive at her aunt's words.

Elaine shook her head. "It's been over two hundred years since Tristram died, and I still prefer the name Elaine. Two years was not enough. It is not worth breaking your heart."

Caelfel pulled her hands out of Elaine's grasp and turned away. "I'm going to find Galath."

Elaine nodded and left her alone in the college gardens.

She felt like sobbing again but pushed the feeling down her throat, straightened her shoulders, and went to find Galath.

She had known Galath for a brief period of time, and in that span, they had become fast friends. But no matter how close they might be, Caelfel could not see him in the light Elaine suggested. Caelfel tried for a brief moment but quickly abandoned the exercise when her stomach turned sickeningly. Galath was a friend and only a friend.

She didn't allow herself to think of Brenin in such a light, for fear Elaine may be right about her feelings.

"I tried staying in the new desert outpost like Winwaloe and Fódla," Galath explained as they walked. "But the desert was too hot for me."

"I understand completely. The desert is absolutely horrendous."

"What adventures have you been busy with? You left one day without saying anything, and your father has told me you've just returned to Honey Water."

"Remember when I said I wanted to see the humans? My friend and I were doing just that, before we were attacked by werewolves."

Galath scowled. "Werewolves?" he repeated. "I thought it was only your mother. I did not realize they attacked you too."

"Yes," Caelfel said, nodding. "If not for Prince Brenin, I would be dead."

Galath remained silent for a while. "I am very sorry about your mother, Caelfel."

Her muscles tensed as she expected Galath to reach out and touch her as Thoroth had. But her scouting partner was smarter and knew when to keep his distance.

"You are out of sorts, Caelfel," he observed when she said nothing.

"I just lost my mother," Caelfel said derisively, tired of pointing out that fact.

"I know, but it's more than that. I know what it's like to lose your mother. I understand what it feels like."

Caelfel gaped at him. "Your mother?"

Galath turned away, and the veins in his neck popped out. Eventually he explained, "When I returned home from the desert, it had already happened. She had been found in the river, undoubtedly by her own hand. I don't know what drove her to it."

Something sharp stuck in Caelfel's throat, making it difficult to swallow, and she was at an utter loss on how to respond. "It's not your fault."

Galath shook his head, and when he spoke, his voice was strained. "I just wanted to tell you. You remember how I spoke of her the night before you were abducted? She was the most important thing to me. I would never have volunteered if it could have prevented her decision. But this funeral isn't for my grief. It's for yours." He released a shaky sigh.

"It's not your fault," Caelfel repeated. Galath said nothing as he sat on one of the benches and stared with stony eyes at the air in front of him. As a gesture of comfort, Caelfel wrapped her arms around Galath's shoulders. At first, his rigid shoulders did not move, but then with another sigh, his body relaxed against hers. They stayed this way without speaking for several long minutes.

"You're scarred by something, Caelfel," Galath insisted, changing the subject. "I can tell. It's like I said. You are out of sorts."

"Me?" Caelfel asked, unsure if he truly thought she was more traumatized than him. "Scarred by what?"

Galath shrugged. "I don't know what happened when you were abducted, nothing short of unspeakable, I'm sure. But you need to let go of those demons and move on. They're dead, dead things."

Caelfel's chest was tight. "Lisiek's not dead," she said quietly.

"He's in the Labyrinth, waiting for execution. If he's not dead now, he soon will be."

Caelfel held her breath, and decided to not breathe life into the rumor of the Labyrinth's escaped convicts.

13. Infiltration

For the remainder of the evening, Caelfel's involvement at the feast was minimal. By the time Caelfel slipped back into her seat beside Ellissara, Elaine was once again seated at her right. Once seated, Caelfel did little to acknowledge her surroundings or attempt to maintain a public appearance. She resisted the urge to look around for Brenin and settled into her chair, overwhelmed by a new numbness, Galath's and Elaine's words repeating in her head.

Around midnight, Eviat appeared before them to reclaim Caelfel. "I've come to take her home," he said by way of explanation for his presence, which was clearly unwelcome. "I am sure she is exhausted by this evening's events."

Ellissara's face looked as though she had swallowed something sour, but she smiled in spite of it. She faced Caelfel. "We will have to talk later, darling," she said sweetly, patting Caelfel's hand.

Caelfel nodded. "Good evening, Lady Ellissara."

And this time, Lady Ellissara didn't insist Caelfel call her grandmother.

"What will you do now?" Eviat asked on the walk home.

Caelfel sighed, feeling her weariness tug at her joints. "Now I will go home and sleep." She looked around, just realizing that the two of them were alone. "Where is Brenin?"

"He said he was tired, so I took him back to the house. Then I came back for you."

She forgot her exhaustion, suddenly on alert. "Is he all right?"

"He's fine," Father assured her. "Only tired. What do you think of your mother's family?"

"I don't consider them as my mother's family, or mine."

"You would inherit quite a bit," Eviat pointed out. "Titles, land, wealth."

"I don't care about any of that. Why have you never told me about them?"

"Your mother wanted to wait until you reached your century year before she introduced you to them."

"You could have still told me about them," Caelfel said.

"Sylaera didn't regard them as family, especially Ellissara. She didn't want to raise you on the hope that they were as loving as we were to you. She had hoped one of your aunts would reach out to meet you once you were born; she would have allowed that. But when none of them came to see you, she gave up hope in calling them family as well."

"Who is my grandfather, Lady Ellissara's husband?"

"He was a greyling from Amasel and died before I even met your mother. Your mother told me his name but I can't even remember it right now."

"What about your family?" Caelfel asked.

Eviat tensed beside her, but his voice didn't change. "My parents are dead."

"But you have a brother," Caelfel pressed.

"Travin is no brother of mine."

"But he is still my blood, and I would rather not be blindsided like I was with Ellissara."

Eviat sighed. "Travin lives in Umfang with his wife," he volunteered reluctantly. "I don't expect him to make any sort of reappearance in my life or yours."

But Eviat was wrong. When they reached home, Brenin had stayed up to show them a message delivered by a courier. Father read it first and then gave a low curse before tossing it to the floor. Caelfel picked it up when he left the room and read it to Brenin with a hint of a smile.

"*Dearest brother and niece,*

I am sorry for the loss of your wife and mother. Though we have had our differences, I would never wish such pain upon you. Enclosed are some dessert treats, caramelized nuts you will not find in Honey Water. Pay us a visit soon, for it is times like these that we ought to put our quarrels aside, and I am willing to forgive

the past even if you are not. I should love to meet dearest Caelfel. Please consider my request; Umfang is lovely in the summer.
  Camilla sends her love.
  T. Copperlyre—"

"Copperlyre?" Caelfel repeated as she searched the envelope for the promised candy. She passed some over to Brenin. "Why is his name not Gyssedlues?" Caelfel asked.

Eviat appeared in the doorway and frowned when he saw them eating his brother's treats. "He adopted the name when he left Honey Water," he said flatly.

"Why don't you go to Umfang and see Uncle Travin?" Caelfel asked, amused with her father's rare temper.

"Don't call him that."

"You should visit him," Caelfel pressed, moreso to tease her father. "He's willing to make peace."

"He cannot even stop himself from offending me in his letter."

Caelfel chewed on the nuts, pondering. "How has he offended you?"

Eviat picked up the letter and pointed to a line. *"Camilla sends her love."*

"How is that offensive?"

"Camilla is his wife," Eviat insisted urgently.

"You would write similar things about Mother."

Eviat sighed, passing a hand over his face, impatient that Caelfel did not understand. "Camilla is a vampire."

Caelfel remembered Feraan telling her this some time ago, so it did not come as quite the shock Eviat expected. "What of it? Mother was disowned from her family for fighting for the right of human-elf relationships."

"It's different. Vampires aren't the same as humans. Camilla is physically incapable of crossing the Honey Water border. Why do you think they live in Umfang?"

Caelfel stared at him dumbly. "Because she is a vampire?"

"Because she is dangerous."

"She must not be that dangerous if Uncle Travin is still alive and well after all this time."

"You don't understand," Eviat sighed. "He is not well. Vampires prey upon everyone, even their spouse. A vampire doesn't recognize the bond of marriage."

Caelfel shrugged. "All the same, it was Travin's decision to marry her."

"Just as it is my decision to not visit him. I would not have anyone I love around a vampire." And with that, Eviat stormed to his bedroom.

Caelfel frowned. She had not intended to argue with her father on the eve of her mother's funeral. She glanced at Brenin who was picking the caramel bits from his teeth.

Brenin shrugged. "I don't really speak to any of my uncles."

Caelfel laughed and swiped at his nose. The movement nearly caused Brenin to lose his balance and fall out of the chair. Caelfel jumped and held him by the elbows before he could fall. It was reason enough for them to follow Eviat's suit and go to bed.

The next morning, Caelfel sat across from Brenin, their heads bent together.

"What will you do about the army you promised my father?" Brenin asked.

Caelfel frowned. The obvious answer would be to speak to the Chief Executor but the last thing she wanted to do was see Markis Rilynnzea. She thought back to her conversation with Winwaloe, hoping he would prove successful on his promise to supply reinforcements. Caelfel told Brenin this plan.

The prince looked dubious. "A desert outpost? Surely it would be better to arrange something with the army here."

"You will need to see Markis Rilynnzea, then," Eviat said as he entered the room, voicing the one solution Caelfel had been hoping to avoid.

"I would rather not," she began uneasily.

"Who is Markis?" Brenin asked.

"He's Sal'Sumarathar's Chief Executor," Eviat briefly explained to Brenin. "If you went to the Cromlech outpost first, they would need permission from the imperial army. With Sal'Sumarathar's militia, you will only need to go to the High Executor, but I'm not sure why you would want to go about starting a war."

"Starting a war or defending Kanetalm?" Caelfel shot back. "Tarion will not stop with human or elf. He proved that with mother."

"You would start a whole war over revenge?" Eviat asked skeptically. "Your mother wouldn't want that, not for her sake."

"One pack of werewolves would not be war," Caelfel reasoned. "It would be pest control."

"You should not be promising the king of Umfeld an army you cannot supply."

"You should not be eavesdropping on conversations that do not concern you," Caelfel told him irritably.

"Caelfel, you are not an ambassador or a diplomat. You do not have this power."

Caelfel fumed, annoyed that Father would humiliate her in such a way before Brenin. "I can ask the Council to grant me the militia. Since Tarion attacked an elf, he's made a declaration of war against the elves."

Eviat wasn't convinced. "Do you think the Council will do that?"

"They should," she asserted, electing to remain optimistic.

She was wrong. When she brought her request before the Council, Uthruil cited some new bylaws that adhered elves to a new, stricter code of isolation. Empress Haelyn wanted it placed into effect immediately in order to secure the borders.

"For what purpose?" Caelfel demanded of the Head Councilor.

Uthruil shifted his weight as he replied shortly. "Miss Gyssedlues, I understand you have recently suffered through a tragic event, but that does not privy you to information regarding internal affairs."

"They killed my mother. I have a right to my revenge."

"Perhaps a week ago you did. However, the empire will be shifting its concerns away from petty revenge now. Empress Haelyn's current focus is on national security."

"If Empress Haelyn wants national security, she needs to protect her people from werewolves. Otherwise she fails as an empress. The Fey Forest connects to the Pirinac Forest. They are as much a threat to us as to Kanetalm."

Uthruil leveled his gaze with her. "Watch your words, youngling. You might unwittingly commit treason, *again*." He cleared his throat. "The Pirinac Forest is not the concern of Honey Water. I would personally recommend petitioning to your Umfeld friends to secure their own lands."

"What if Tarion attacks Honey Water?" Caelfel asked, just as two militia guards stepped up to escort her away.

Uthruil waved his hand to them. "Honey Water has bigger problems than a pack of rabid dogs."

Caelfel let the guards escort her out of the Hall of Court as she considered the councilor's words. She wondered if some other danger outside Honey Water's borders had Uthruil and Empress Haelyn suddenly tightening security.

***

Lisiek, I do not care much for this desert.

"I do not either, but some discomforts are necessary, my lady," he told her apologetically.

Gwyn held a hand up to shade her eyes from the sun. The Cromlech outpost stood on a plateau in the distance like a dark speck against the sky. Behind her was a collection of soldiers and escaped convicts that had proved faithful to her cause.

What shall we do, Lisiek?

He turned his horse to face her. "Any army would be seen for miles around. But you're the expert on elvish outposts. What do you recommend?"

Gwyn recalled some distant figure from her memory. The fortress was comprised of the remnants of the Volunteer Regiment, a scant number compared to her own outfit of soldiers. The defensive walls had been badly damaged when it was taken by the empire. However, she had no doubt the fortress had already received word about the escaped prisoners and the runaway royal bastard by now.

"Send a messenger. Tell them we will accept their surrender," she decided aloud.

"And if they do not surrender?" Lisiek inquired.

Gwyn's mouth curled into a ruthless smile. "Take them by force."

***

It was not where Runa was supposed to go. Cromlech Fortress stood as a guardian on the very edge of the vast Amhsis desert, but something deep inside her commanded her to stop. The purple flag that flew from its tower was not of Umfang. It was the color of the elves.

The elves are leaving the forest.

Turning her head to the east, she saw another purple flag fluttering in the distance above a roving army, but this standard showed five black diamonds splashed across the familiar purple field. Runa wasn't sure what it meant, but the more she stared at the advancing army, the more she realized the army in the east was heading for the Cromlech Fortress.

Runa squinted. *What do I do?*

The Hand of the Raven stood indecisively between these two forces. She stared longer at the approaching company until she could just make out two distinct figures at its head. She had seen neither of them before, but the face of the black-haired man stirred something within her.

Warn the fortress. Fight with them, came the command.

"And then?" Runa demanded angrily of the voice inside her head.

But there was no response, so she ran for Cromlech.

***

Caelfel returned with her promise unfulfilled. "I am sorry, Brenin," she said with her head hanging.

If Brenin was upset, he did not show it. "It will not be the first time my father is disappointed." His tone suggested he was excited by the idea of disappointing King Orrik. He placed the rest of his clothes in a satchel, already deciding to wear his new elvish garb back to Umfeld. He had been speechless when Eviat told him he could keep it.

And then Eviat appeared at the doorway, looking forlorn. "Are you sure you need to leave so soon?"

Caelfel straightened and crossed the room to embrace her father. "Brenin needs to return home. I'll be back soon," she added.

An unspoken question hung in the air, wondering what Caelfel would do after Brenin was back in Palpses. Caelfel wasn't entirely sure herself but whatever happened, she knew she needed to find Garvanna.

"Are you ready?" Caelfel asked Brenin when he had his things packed.

Brenin took one last sweeping gaze of the room before nodding reluctantly.

Caelfel offered him a smile. "Don't look like that. You're more than welcome to return any time."

Eviat's smile for Brenin supported the invitation, and he walked with them all the way to the meadow, keeping up an amiable chatter as if to prove that he did not dread the moment when he would be left alone again. Before Caelfel mounted her steed from Palpses, Eviat gently restrained her by the elbow. "Whatever you do, just write to me. Keep me informed."

She gently rubbed his cheek with her thumb. "I won't be away for long," she whispered.

He pressed her hand against his face, giving it a warm squeeze. "I'll remember that."

Eviat gave her a parting kiss on her brow before stepping back to give her room. Brenin, who had been studiously toying with his reins, glanced up. Caelfel smiled at him when she was ready.

Brenin gave a nod to her father. "It's been a pleasure, Master Eviat."

"And you as well, Prince Brenin," Eviat bid.

And then, with the pounding of hoof beats, Eviat and the meadow disappeared behind a thicket of the trees.

They had barely let the shadows of Sal'Sumarathar when Brenin, looking suddenly determined, interrupted the silence of their ride.

"Caelfel, I must ask you something," he began stoutly when their horses had slowed to an easy pace.

"Hmm?" Her mind had been elsewhere—the whereabouts of Garvanna, her promise to King Orrik, the escaped prisoners of the Labyrinth, the next time she would see her father again—anywhere but the present.

"What will you do once we arrive at Palpses?" There was an uncertain tremor to his voice that Caelfel did not understand, as if he would be afraid of her answer.

She sighed. "I do not think I will go to the coast anymore. I know Garvanna is alive. I need to find her."

"Where will you look?" Brenin asked curiously, and Caelfel easily detected that it was a brief distraction from whatever was on his mind.

"It's too dangerous to search the Pirinac again. I believe that the Morrígna sisters had delivered a letter to my mother from her. Perhaps they will know. If not, I will start asking the people in your cities if they came across a tall, angry she-elf."

"Angry?" Brenin repeated.

Caelfel gave a laugh. "Garvanna has a bit of a temper," she explained.

They were silent once more for the span of a minute. Brenin asked her, "What about after you find your friend?"

Caelfel blinked and struggled to formulate her reply. "I do not yet know."

"You are always welcome in Palpses," he told her.

"I thank you for your hospitality," she said awkwardly.

But Brenin drilled forward to voice his thoughts. "In fact, I would be delighted if you chose to stay in Kanetalm for any extended time."

Caelfel, believing she understood the source of his turmoil, leaned across her horse and reached out to touch his hand. "I will not soon forget you, Brenin."

But when he looked back at her, there was a deeper conflict brewing in his dark eyes. The comforting smile she had for him vanished as soon as she saw the intensity of his features. "I don't want you to ever forget me," he managed in a dauntless voice.

"Brenin," she said quietly, at a complete loss for how to respond.

He continued. "*Guh-sid-did-luss.* Is that how you say your name?"

The corner of her mouth twitched into a minute smile of empathetic humor. "Gyssedlues," she corrected. "Almost. There's only three syllables, and you're stuttering the second one."

Something in his face changed, and he looked away before she could identify it. "You know that I have always held a fascination with elves. When I met you, I thought you were perfect and beautiful. When I met other elves, I knew they weren't the same. No one is the same as you."

He stopped his horse and turned to face her. Caelfel's fingers went cold at his compliments, but she stopped her horse too.

"And Caelfel Gyssedlues," he said, tongue rolling perfectly between the second and third syllables. "I know I love you."

"Oh, Brenin," she breathed. The words of her aunt's warning caused her skin to prickle with gooseflesh. Her stomach sank, and suddenly her heart clenched with a new coldness as something changed in her countenance. She laughed in his face. "What do you know about loving an elf?"

Brenin's face broke as if Caelfel had injured him. "Caelfel—"

But she would hear none of his pleas, give him no chance to appeal to her empathy. She could not afford to allow herself a moment of mutual affection. She became cruel. "You don't love me. You only idolize me," she accused sharply.

Brenin blinked several times, and with each consecutive blink, his eyes grew more distant. "Why are you saying these things?" he asked in a hoarse whisper.

It all but broke the cruel mask; she was incapable of maliciously hurting Brenin. She might have been elated with his confession, had it not been for Elaine's forewarning.

"Brenin—"

Caelfel was interrupted by a sudden flash of fangs, and abruptly Brenin disappeared from her line of sight. Caelfel snapped her head around to see Brenin sprawling on the ground, thick red gashes stretching down his face. A large wolf growled a few feet beyond Brenin, and Caelfel knew it was a werewolf from Tarion's pack.

Caelfel's mind raced. *How could a werewolf be in the Fey Forest?* But she drove everything to the back of her mind as Brenin's safety became a priority when the wolf began to move towards the wounded prince. She turned in her saddle and grabbed her bow. She leveled an arrow between the wolf's eyes. "Leave him," she warned.

The wolf trained its dark eyes on her and though deep growls shook its body, it made no move for the prince. Brenin began backing away.

But wolves moved in packs, and before Caelfel had time to react, a second wolf knocked her to the forest floor as the others of the pack closed in on them.

Her back flared with pain, and the skin felt like it was burning. She pushed herself up to look around. Her vision flickered for a moment, and then she saw her bow in front of her. Caelfel grabbed it and nocked an arrow. She rolled over in time to fend off a werewolf just as it loomed over her.

She scrambled to her feet and spun around to search for Brenin. She saw him leaning against a tree some distance away. Just behind him, she noticed Tarion's pack begin to tighten their circle. She yelled at him to run, but Brenin remained where he was, staring at her numbly.

The werewolves pressed closer to them, and Caelfel twisted her body around to raise her bow against the nearest threats. They communicated amongst each other in a series of snarls, and Caelfel feared what they were planning and began to suspect that she and Brenin might not survive this encounter.

One wolf broke the circle and bounded toward them. Caelfel raised her bow and her arrow flew to nick its side. The wolf didn't stop, colliding with Caelfel and shoving her to the ground. It kept her pinned there with its massive claws and she struggled to push herself free. She drew her feet up and, using all her strength, kicked the creature off of her. It howled in pain as it crashed against the nearby trees. Caelfel was on her feet in time to see the other wolves in the pack swarm around Brenin.

Without hesitation, she loosed three arrows into the crowd. Two wolves went down. Three wolves turned to chase after her. She raised another three arrows in defense.

But beyond the three wolves, Caelfel saw the largest, black wolf, presumably Tarion, pick Brenin up by the boot with his teeth. The prince hung limply from Tarion's mouth.

Caelfel lowered her bow in horror. She raced past the three wolves to chase after Tarion. As soon as he saw her, he bolted through the trees.

Caelfel heard herself screaming Brenin's name, and the wind caused her hair to whip about her face erratically. She focused solely on Tarion's bushy, black tail and drove herself forward.

Noticing her pursuit, the wolves following Tarion left their retreat to divert her. Caelfel didn't pause. She used her speed to vault through the air and landed on the back of a wolf.

They tumbled and rolled, and Caelfel anchored herself to the wolf by tightening her legs around its neck. The wolf became frenzied, emitting strangled howls as she restricted his breathing.

Her arms wrapped around its underbelly as they crashed through the trees. She felt her head thrashing against rocks and surfaced roots.

Finally they came to a halt when the wolf stopped moving altogether. She untangled herself from its body in time to have another wolf ram her against a tree. She pushed back, gripping its snout, but soon more wolves joined the first. With their combined strength, they threw her back against the tree.

Her head gave a sickening crack against the bark, the last thing she heard before falling to the ground.

The last thing she saw was Tarion standing victorious in the distance with Brenin as his prize.

***

The Cromlech Fortress would not withstand an attack. This was evident to Runa as soon as she crested the plateau and saw its state.

The entire eastern wall had been reduced to crumbling debris. Runa stared at the rubble with a crushing sense of defeat, knowing tactically that this new elvish outpost would not last.

"State your business," an elf guard demanded nearby.

Her eyes flitted to his impassive face. There were stone masons and laborers all around working to reconstruct the decimated wall. She knew their efforts were wasted. "I bring news of an approaching army," she told the sentry.

The elf looked to his companion who gave a curt nod. The original guard turned to her. "Follow me."

They stepped over the black stones of what once was the outer wall, and he led the way inside the fortress. Runa was shocked to see that the number of soldiers stationed at the outpost did not appear promising either.

The central castle was dark inside even with the aid of burning torches affixed at frequent intervals on the walls. To Runa's relief, the temperature inside was considerably cooler than outside, and she imagined that the elves didn't care for the desert heat either. A glassy, black throne sat on the opposite end of the entrance hall. But no one sat in it. Instead, a tall elf with a long, blond braid stood by its side. His back was towards her, and Runa could not see his face.

"Captain Sanddef," her guard greeted. "This human girl brings news of an approaching army."

"An approaching army?" Captain Sanddef repeated, turning around.

He was taller than the other elves and he took a moment to gauge Runa. She returned his calculating gaze unwaveringly.

"An army of what?" he asked.

"I believe they are elves," she said. "They are coming from the east."

Sanddef arched an eyebrow. He turned his head fractionally to show off his pointed ears. "You might want to take a moment to realize that we are elves as well."

Runa glared. "*You* might want to take a moment to realize that there is an army coming to attack you, whether you are an elf or not."

Sanddef folded his arms. "What did their banner look like?" he asked, still not convinced. "They are more than likely reinforcements."

"Black diamonds on a purple field."

Sanddef's mocking demeanor changed to one of complete shock, and Runa knew he recognized the banner from her description. And it wasn't the one flown by reinforcements. "What's your name?" he asked.

"R—" Runa had been about to tell him her name, but a sharp pain in her head made her revise herself. "Raven," she told him instead.

"Did you see their numbers?"

She frowned. "More than what you have here."

Sanddef began pacing the great hall. Runa and her guard watched him warily.

"Is there any word from the empire?" Sanddef asked.

Her guard shook his head.

"This fortress isn't defensible," Runa told him angrily, feeling her fingernails dig into the skin of her palm. "If you can't hold them at bay on the edge of the plateau, the only thing you can do is put everyone inside this tower."

Sanddef rounded on her. "Do not preach to me, girl. I have been a part of military strategies for over seven hundred years."

Runa did not flinch. "Then you know you have only a limited amount of choices to make, *captain*."

Sanddef narrowed his gaze. "Who are you? Why have you come to tell us this?"

"You already know my name," Runa told him evenly. "I saw the army marching in this direction and came to warn you."

Sanddef turned to someone else. "Should they be arriving so soon? Have our scouts reported anything?"

Another elf stepped forward. "There is indeed the army as the human girl indicated. A lone rider has gone ahead and will arrive here at Cromlech shortly."

Sanddef nodded at this report. "Probably to discuss terms."

Runa burst to life at Sanddef's remark. "And to look for weaknesses in your fortress! You should meet him at the bottom of your plateau so he will not see the state of your eastern wall."

Sanddef spun around to confront her. "Who are you to give me orders? How do we know you're not a spy yourself?"

"If I was a spy, why would I be trying to help you?"

"A clever ruse, for a human." Sanddef's mouth tightened into a thin line as he scowled at her. He proceeded to ignore her and called to the elf that had delivered the scouting report. "Find Fódla. Tell her to get the archers into position." The soldier nodded and left the room.

Runa became angry. "What position could they be in? You have *no* east wall."

Sanddef glanced at her and then turned to her guard. "Erryn, you will relieve this woman of her weapon and then escort her to a prison cell."

"I have come to *help* you! I am not your prisoner!" she yelled as the elf took her axe.

"I will not have you pose as a threat to my outpost," Sanddef countered smoothly.

"Your entire outpost will be killed!" she shouted as Erryn dragged her away. She knew better than to resist the strength of elves.

"Better to be killed than thought a traitor," Sanddef swore in a low voice.

***

The overwhelming odor of fire and smoke brought Caelfel back to consciousness. She blinked, seeing blurry bits of white ash drifting to the ground like deceptive snowflakes. She felt a dull, persistent pain in her back, and her head throbbed.

Caelfel sat up, struggling to remember everything that had happened, and though most of the fires had been extinguished by this point, she could identify them by their smell.

They were goblin fires.

Based on the resulting aftermath, this goblin attack had been more ferocious than any Caelfel had ever witnessed and she wondered if they had anything to do with the appearance of Tarion and the other werewolves. She wondered how she had remained alive. "*Caelfel.*"

It was her father, and she felt a small wave of relief upon seeing him. There were other elves in the distance battling with the last of the goblin fires. Thoroth was with Eviat, and the two of them raced toward her.

Her head felt too heavy to support herself so she rested it against a tree as Thoroth set to work on healing her back. Caelfel didn't protest and sighed at the cool touch of his magic. "What happened?" she asked.

Eviat, looking teary at finding her alive, rubbed at his nose before responding. "We were hoping you could tell us that."

"Goblins didn't do this to you," Thoroth observed grimly as he inspected her injuries.

She shook her head. "There were werewolves. Tarion was here." She gasped, looking to her father with pleading eyes. "Where is Brenin?"

Eviat said nothing, and she could easily guess what had happened to the prince of Umfeld.

Her throat constricted, fearing the worst. "Did you find anything left of his body?" Her voice cracked.

Eviat shook his head. "There is no sign of Brenin. Your horses, though. They are not a pretty sight. They're just half-eaten carcasses. We think Brenin was taken, not killed. We thought they had taken you as well."

"Taken? Why would they take Brenin?" But neither Father nor Thoroth had an answer for her.

She sighed wearily and closed her eyes, thinking of her last, unpleasant conversation with Brenin. A few minutes later, Thoroth finished his healing, and the two of them helped Caelfel to her feet as another elf with gray eyes approached them calmly.

He looked to Thoroth first. "Is she well?"

"I've healed everything," Thoroth confirmed.

The gray-eyed elf looked to her then. "I would like to speak with you, Miss Gyssedlues. Not here, of course. We will bring you back to Sal'Sumarathar."

Caelfel stared dumbly at his placid appearance. "Who are you?"

He gave a small, courteous smile. "My name is Rindur Faalingar. I am Sal'Sumarathar's new Chief Executor."

14. Lady for a Master

"I thought Markis was the Chief Executor," Caelfel said carefully.

They were back in Sal'Sumarathar. Rindur Faalingar had taken her to a room in the Hall of Court with a stone desk. Caelfel easily assumed it was the office of the High Executor, appearing mostly unused.

Rindur studied her with his cool, gray eyes. "Markis Rilynnzea is currently imprisoned at Yamalvon pending trial for high treason. I have been assigned this position since his arrest."

"High treason?"

Rindur levelled his gaze. "You were victim to many of his crimes and bore witness to his gross abuse of power, Miss Gyssedlues."

Caelfel nodded. "I was. I didn't think anyone would restrain him."

Rindur smiled weakly. "About this attack—"

"How did the werewolves enter Honey Water? I thought there was magic around the forest," Caelfel interrupted.

"This is what I wanted to discuss with you. It appears that the goblins living underground have formed an alliance with this pack of werewolves. The goblins granted them safe passage underground. That is how the wolves bypassed the wards of the Fey Forest."

"The goblins helped them?"

"As it turns out, the underground colonies of goblins are vastly more complex than we initially thought. I am aware that you were ferrying a prince of Umfeld when you were attacked."

"I was. He was kidnapped."

"There was no evidence of his body in the forest, so I can't help but agree with you. However I would strongly urge against pursuing them through the tunnels."

"Why? I can't just abandon him."

"Miss Gyssedlues, as we speak, the Board of the Wizardry is working to contain the goblins. If you entered the tunnels at this time, you would have a likely chance of being ambushed, either by goblins or elf mages. The tunnels lead directly to the Pirinac Forest. Braving them on your own, even if you managed to avoid the ambushes, would ensure your own demise against the werewolves."

"What if I wasn't alone? You could send the militia or even the mages with me."

Rindur shook his head. "We will not confront the werewolves," he told her in a decisively calm tone.

Caelfel was shocked. "But they attacked me—"

"They trespassed upon our lands, yes, but left you generally unharmed."

"They took Brenin—"

"A human prince is no concern of Honey Water, Miss Gyssedlues. After all, he is only human." A polite smile curved his lips. "As much as I would love to help your plight, Miss Gyssedlues, a Chief Executor does not take personal liberties. If you remember, that's what got the last Chief Executor imprisoned for high treason."

Caelfel grit her teeth, having difficulty in not biting her tongue. "Given his faults, at least the previous Chief Executor braved the desert for my sake when the elves attacked the Cromlech fortress.

Unmoved, Rindur leaned closer toward Caelfel. "And as you might notice, the previous Chief Executor is in the Labyrinth, no matter how valiant his actions might have been."

Her sharp fingernails began clawing into the heels of her palms, breaking the skin. "I made a promise," she nearly growled in frustration.

Rindur nodded, as if this was not news to him. "I have heard of your exchange with the king of Umfeld. Perhaps you should not have taken personal liberties and appointed yourself as ambassador to Umfeld," he told her. In a low voice, he added, "I don't understand your distress anyway. The prince is only human."

Caelfel sighed, unable to meet Rindur's gaze. She thought of Brenin in Tarion's clutches, and the idea tore at her stomach. "Brenin is more than just a human," she relented.

***

The fortress walls shook with unimaginable force. Runa could feel the vibrations through the metal grates of her cell, locked without much effort by her reluctant elvish guard who lingered in the dark dungeons for a moment before hurrying away to the surface level. Runa hadn't even been granted the privilege of torchlight, so no matter what the catacombs of Cromlech held, Runa was blind to it all.

The floor made wet sounds when she stepped through the pitted indentations of the stone flags, which she thought strange since they were in the desert. When she ran her hand along the low ceiling, Runa felt water droplets coating her fingertips and estimated that there was some sort of well or reservoir overhead. Her search yielded little else, so she pressed her back against the bars, suppressing the overwhelming sense of defeat.

"What do I do?" she asked desperately of the nothing that surrounded her.

To her surprise, the ever-silent voice in her head spoke like a puppeteer giving instructions. *You wait*, it told her firmly.

And so Runa waited on the advice of a voice in her head, unsure it actually quite existed. Her waiting did not last long. Not even a day had passed when the rumbling and the vibrations ceased, the attack over. Within an hour, after the outcome of the battle had been decided, a visitor had probed their way to the dungeons with an orb of red light hovering inches away from their face.

"Is there anyone down here?" asked the male, tall like an elf but indefinably different than the elf that had originally escorted her down there.

Runa opened her mouth to speak when the voice inside her head hissed at her sharply. *Answer him.*

"There is someone down here," she answered cautiously.

The elf—for she could certainly make out his pointed ears now—turned his head in the direction of her voice, and the orb turned with him. His features appeared gaunt in the pulsing red light as he looked her over with unreadable eyes. "Just one?" he said, though Runa wasn't sure if he was directly asking her.

To prove this point, Runa slowly moved her gaze about the otherwise empty dungeon to demonstrate her singularity.

Her visitor grinned at her unspoken wit. He brought a large key to the rusted lock, and her cell door swung open with a screeching creak. He motioned for her to go through.

But a suspicious anxiety that tightened her chest kept her in place. "Aren't you curious as to why I'm down here?" she asked him.

His grin suddenly appeared malevolent. "The lady will decide for herself."

Since Captain Sanddef had been the commanding officer, Runa easily determined the first elves did not prove victorious. And hearing no other alternative from the commanding voice inside her head, Runa accompanied the elf with a lady for a master out of the Cromlech dungeons.

The doors of the main castle had been blasted open, and Runa wondered if Captain Sanddef had followed her advice in holing up inside the palace. In the end, it mattered little to the rows of Cromlech prisoners bound and sitting on the floor. Runa did not see Captain Sanddef among them but she could recognize Erryn from a distance.

Then a strong magnetic-like force pulled her attention to a woman, presumably also an elf, sitting on the throne that Captain Sanddef had pointedly avoided. Her elvish escort brought them before her.

Runa felt familiar fluctuations of power rolling over the imperious woman in crashing waves. It made pain erupt behind her eyes as she was reminded of her own master, but she steeled her expression and met the gaze of this intimidating woman unwaveringly.

She smiled warmly at Runa and her tone was inviting. "I am Princess Gwyndolyn Ernmas of the Honey Water Empire. What do we call you?"

Runa's head throbbed, deciding Gwyndolyn's form of address must be the result of warring over the elvish throne, which explained their variation of the elvish banner. Having no cause to offend her, Runa was about to speak when movement behind Gwyndolyn's shoulder drew her attention away to someone else.

It was a man with human ears of tall and lean build. He was pale like the mountainfolk with long black hair braided in the style of an old warrior. But his unlined face suggested youth while his cruel eyes suggested an unstable demeanor.

She took a long moment of silence to examine this man, and he spoke, "Princess Gwyndolyn has asked you a question."

At the sound of his smooth voice, the pain in her head disappeared entirely. Her lips moved of their own accord as she stared solely at him. "I am the Raven."

Her words startled this man, and he had no response for her. Gwyndolyn, on the other hand, trilled a delighted laugh. "Your name is Raven? Is that what you meant?'

Runa returned her attention to the princess and suffered a smile for her benefit. "Excuse me. That is precisely what I meant."

***

She traveled alone and on foot across the treeline border and through the Amhsis. She carried little in the way of physical possessions but made sure to pack her blade among her weaponry. An immense shame weighed on her shoulders. She was alone without the military aid of her people and she was making her way to seek help from a king who might do anything in the face of such disappointing news.

The werewolves did not attack a second time, and Caelfel could only imagine what else occupied their time. She pushed the thought entirely from her mind to prevent herself from flying into a blind rage. She clenched her jaw for so long that an ache persisted in her face, and by the time she reached Umfeld, the pain had spread to her neck. She did not stop at inns as she had before with Brenin. She continued walking, sometimes running. The horses they had brought from Palpses had been devoured by Tarion and his pack, and she did not want to risk riding Rowan though this perilous environment. She was completely alone.

She followed the roads, hoping they would eventually lead her to Palpses. The landscape looked like nothing she had seen when she had first been traveling with Brenin. The countryside and rocky moors stood out as entirely unfamiliar to her. There was no distinguishing landmarks to guide her path, save for the irregular farms that dotted the hillsides. She stopped to sleep very little and ate even less.

After her third day of wandering Kanetalm, Caelfel in her impatience to find Brenin felt compelled to demand directions from a thin farmer coaxing his cow along a trail. He appeared frightened by her sudden and towering presence but he kindly assured her that if she crossed the nearby river and continued south, she would find the capital within the day. Caelfel stared dejectedly at the bovine creature, recalling nostalgically Brenin's first pronunciation of her name. But she pushed the sentiment furthest from her mind, curtly thanked the man, and followed his directions so she could report her failures to King Orrik.

The afternoon brought the sight of the Palpses's walls. Of all the concerns that had plagued her thoughts, being allowed in the city of Palpses had been the least of her worries. As it turned out, an elf without a princely escort did not have as much influence as she might have thought. The city watch stood guarding the closed gates with a resolute stubbornness.

"I am here to speak to King Orrik," she informed them.

Only one guard afforded her the courtesy of a glance. "Palpses is no place for dirty beggars."

Caelfel glanced at herself for a brief inspection. She had not realized how much of a vagrant she looked. The sands of the desert and the mud of the moors did little to enhance her appearance. "I am *not* a beggar," she told the guard firmly. She hesitated, casting around for an authority that might help her. "I am Lady Caelfel Gyssedlues of Honey Water and the Champion of Strigi's Tournament. I have come to speak to King Orrik about military aid from the elves."

An eyebrow was raised at her ragged appearance. "The king holds court in the mornings before noon. You may return then."

Caelfel felt her fury brimming. "I can't even enter the city?"

"The city is closed due to rampant werewolf attacks," the guard informed her in a rather bored voice that did not indicate any sort of fear in regards to Tarion and the others.

But another guard turned his head to look in her direction. "Aren't you the one that left with Prince Brenin?"

At the mention of their prince, all the nearby guards stationed at the gate turned toward her, their hands on their swords and their spears.

Caelfel glared at their suspicious faces. "I bring news of that as well. I just need to see King Orrik or even Prince Madoc. Bring me Cyrus if you have to!" she cried desperately.

They all stared at her in accusing silence before the first guard spoke. "Someone bring Captain Lewod."

When the Captain of the Guard finally made his appearance, it had started raining. Before Caelfel had a chance to plead her case, one of the guards informed Captain Lewod of the situation.

Lewod, a middle-aged man with thin hair, rubbed at his pock-marked cheek. "Do you not recognize her?" he asked his city watch irritably. "She's the guest of the prince."

Caelfel felt a sigh of relief escaping her lips when one of the guards pointed out, "She returns without the prince."

Captain Lewod's left eye twitched as he assessed the observation. "It is not for you to decide. She should have been brought before the king immediately. Come on, Lady Elf."

And Caelfel did not hesitate. She followed him inside the city as he took her up the winding path leading her to the palace.

Captain Lewod instructed her to wait inside the main keep. As he left to retrieve the king, Caelfel worked on composing herself as she prepared to deliver unsavory news to the most powerful man in Umfeld, away from the protective shadow of her elvish forest. Her stomach twisted with anxiety.

Madoc had entered the keep first, his face alight with eagerness to see her, but that eagerness quickly dimmed, realizing something was amiss when he noticed her grave face and absent brother. "Where is Brenin?"

She had no time to answer him as the King of Umfeld marched commandingly into the keep. He kept his shoulders rigid and his face ultimately blank. Caelfel would not have feared him as a man, but as a king with a country at his command, she knew when to keep her reservations.

"What is your report?" the king asked simply in a tone that suggested he was not moved by her appearance.

Caelfel did not break her gaze. "I have been unsuccessful with my promise, and your son has been kidnapped."

King Orrik's features were unchanged. Madoc was horrified. "Kidnapped by whom?"

Caelfel turned to him. "Tarion, the werewolf."

Madoc's face darkened with the news, but King Orrik remained unimpressed. "Why have you returned to Palpses?"

At this, Caelfel was confused. "How do you mean?"

"As you belong to a race infamous for unreliable warriors, it does not surprise me to learn you have failed in your promise to supply military force. To learn you have lost my second son does little to shock me as well. But your presence here can only be an assurance of conspiracy."

Caelfel scowled, puzzling over what King Orrik meant. Madoc looked similarly confused. "Brenin is my friend—"

"You have a fine way of protecting your friends, Lady Elf. Did you come here simply to give me bad news? Would you rather I forged a new alliance with a single elf and forgave you for the loss of my second heir? You will receive no pity here. Your presence is only a confirmation of your treachery."

"Treachery?" Caelfel repeated indignantly. "I have only come to help."

"You were the one to anger the werewolves in the Pirinac. You have quarrel with them. You were the one to lose the Prince of Kanetalm. I have seen no help from you." He waved his hand at her, a dismissive gesture. "I would recommend that you leave."

The air in the keep was suddenly charged with animosity brewing from the king and his subjects. The rage Caelfel had been keeping in check threatened to boil over. She methodically clenched her jaw to exert some small measure of control of herself. "What will you do for Brenin?"

King Orrik barked a humorlessly laugh. "There is nothing that can be done for Brenin."

"You will not help him?" Caelfel demanded angrily. Even Madoc appeared appalled by the news.

"What can I do for him?" King Orrik challenged her. "If he has been taken by the werewolves, he is likely dead. If not, then he will be dead soon since I have not received any letter of ransom."

"You can take your army to the Pirinac and save him!" Caelfel exclaimed desperately.

King Orrik gave a careless shrug and looked to Madoc. "He is only my second son." He turned his attention back to her. "I believe you have overstayed your welcome here, Lady Elf."

Caelfel glared at him and did not waver. "I believe that you are a tyrant that never loved his son." Her eyes flitted in Madoc's direction. "Perhaps your only son," she added in a low voice.

"Your opinions of my sovereignty matter little to me. You should leave Palpses before I have you hanged as a traitor and an enemy of the state."

Caelfel, having the sense to avoid her own execution, watched mutely as King Orrik turned to leave the room. So it was not her voice that challenged the authority of his retreating back. It was Prince Madoc, perhaps the only person that would dare do so.

"You would let Brenin die?" Madoc demanded.

"He should have never left Kanetalm in the first place," King Orrik countered without turning.

"I will not abandon my brother. I will go to the Pirinac and rescue him," Madoc decided.

King Orrik slowly turned, arching an eyebrow. A hint of amusement glinted in his face. "You are defying me, your king?" he asked, intrigued rather than angry.

Madoc straightened. "I am saving my brother."

"You would risk inheriting the throne for that spineless coward?" King Orrik asked.

"Brenin is not a coward," Madoc defended evenly.

King Orrik stepped closer to Madoc and tilted his son's chin with a thick finger. "You will face a pack of werewolves on your own?"

"I will bring the Company of the Prince. Protecting Brenin is their job."

King Orrik's demeaning laugh came once again. "You may go on your little adventure but don't expect me to approve it. You will need a blessing from Voten if you wish to use the Umfeld army without the king's consent, which includes the Company of the Prince."

Madoc grimaced as Orrik laughed himself out of the keep. He hovered where he was before turning his stony gaze to Caelfel. "Let's go."

He touched her elbow as they sped out of the palace. "What is a blessing from Voten? What does that mean?" she asked in a low undertone as they trekked down the path into the city of Palpses.

Before Madoc could answer her, a desperate voice crying Caelfel's name came from behind them. Caelfel stopped to see Brenin's faithful steward Cyrus racing toward her. His face was the very essence of panic.

"Cyrus? What is the matter?" she asked him as he approached, breathless from running.

"I am sorry. I have failed you," Cyrus said in between pants.

As comforted by the idea that she hadn't been the only failure, Caelfel was puzzled over the steward's meaning. "What are you talking about?"

"It's Forra. They've arrested her. She's walking to the scaffold at this moment."

Caelfel's brow knotted. "Scaffold?" she repeated.

Cyrus became exasperated. "She's to be hanged—*executed*. Do you understand?"

"For what purpose?" Caelfel asked. "Where is she?"

"I had her followed, as you asked, but she's done nothing wrong. King Orrik ordered her to be executed as a traitor without trial. They've built the scaffold in the marketplace."

Caelfel glanced at Madoc's perplexed expression. As much as she desired to retrieve his brother from Tarion, Brenin would have to wait for the moment.

They all ran, Caelfel the fastest, to the gathering crowd that swarmed the marketplace. It was not the excited, cheery rabble of Strigi's Festival. This was a scene of an agitated mob, screaming for justice. Caelfel stopped at the fringe, her eyes darting around for Forra. Cyrus and Madoc joined her shortly.

"What will you do?" Madoc hissed. "If you try to stop it, you will be arrested and put to the same fate."

"Can't you do anything as a prince?" Caelfel asked him.

"I can't pardon an execution my own father has ordered. What does she matter anyway?"

Caelfel snapped her head to him with a steely gaze. Madoc visibly shrank back from the severity of her glare. "She matters. I am responsible for her."

"Like you were responsible for Brenin?" Madoc muttered under his breath.

Caelfel ignored him and looked to Cyrus. "Do you have any ideas?"

His grave face alone suggested nothing in the field of ideas. "If you do something, we will need to escape the city immediately."

Caelfel nodded appreciatively, already knowing this obvious bit of information. She stared intently at the scaffold and the crowd surrounding it. The gallows towered over the scaffold with a single rope noose swaying in the breeze. Forra had already climbed the wooden steps and stood, shivering in her shift in the light rain.

Thinking quickly, Caelfel pushed her way through the crowd.

***

Gwyndolyn watched the Raven girl with a keen interest. Lisiek had described her as a mountain girl, and the mountain girl kept her peace and held her tongue, watching the events around her serenely. But soon, Gwyndolyn found that she could not devote her entire attention to the mountain girl.

"Captain Sanddef," Gwyndolyn addressed the elf aloud. Her spirit orbs floated around the room, preventing everyone except her to use magic. Captain Sanddef stared at the three orbs apprehensively.

Lisiek stepped toward him. "The princess is speaking to you."

At this, Captain Sanddef turned his head to acknowledge them. "She is no princess of mine."

Gwyn offered him a wan smile and ignored the slight. "Captain Sanddef, I want you to compose a letter for me."

Sanddef looked wary. "What sort of letter?"

"It is to be addressed to my mother, the Empress Haelyn. You will inform her of my arrival here and your support of her abdication of the throne."

"Why would I write such a letter?" Sanddef asked quietly, calmly.

Gwyn's gaze turned severe upon him. "You *will* write the letter, one way or another."

Sanddef scoffed, and it was the sound of an elf who had comfortably decided he had nothing else to lose. "We had received word some time ago already of your betrayal to the empire. We are not ignorant of these criminals you've released. You are not the princess. You are not the heir. You will never be our empress."

The room was silent, awaiting anxiously for Gwyndolyn's reaction. She knew they all feared her, as they should. She wanted to be perceived as a kind, merciful leader but not one that would stand for such an open challenge to her authority. She took a deep breath. "For all of your military experience, Sanddef Pyrd, you know very little in the ways of war. The strongest, the victors—the ones that win— they make the rules. They become the rulers."

Sanddef didn't break his gaze. "You haven't won anything."

Gwyndolyn sighed. "I can only perceive your insubordination as treason." She turned her head. "What is the punishment for disloyalty?"

Lisiek spoke up. "Hanging, I believe."

The elf that had accompanied her from the Labyrinth and had retrieved Raven from the catacombs interjected. "Actually, the elvish death sentence for treason is a beheading."

Gwyndolyn's mouth twitched into a fraction of a smile for him. "What is your name, soldier?"

He gave her a generous smile and a low bow. "Markis Rilynnzea, my princess. I was the High Executor of Sal'Sumarathar before the Labyrinth."

Gwyn nodded, returning her attention to Sanddef. "I suppose we will have to behead this traitor."

Immediately, Markis and Lisiek moved toward Captain Sanddef, but Gwyn, being as flighty as she was gave a shrill laugh and changed her mind.

"Wait!" she called. "I've changed my mind. Markis, take him to the catacombs instead."

Markis gave a humble bow at the waist. "Of course, my lady."

"What's on your mind?" Lisiek asked when Markis had disappeared with the prisoner from the hall.

"I'm thinking that Captain Sanddef is of more use to me alive than dead," she muttered.

"Lady Gwyndolyn?" asked one of the captives from the floor.

Lisiek bristled beside her. "She is Princess Gwyndolyn," he corrected roughly.

Gwyn raised her hand to him. "It's all right, Lisiek. Transitions take time." She stood from her seat and approached the elves huddled on the floor, her eyes trained on the one that had addressed her. His pale hair was tied in a short braid that reached the nape of his neck, and his blue eyes met hers unwaveringly.

"What is your name?"

"Winwaloe," he answered without hesitation.

She pointed to his hair. "You are wearing a commander's braid. What are you commander of?"

"I'm just a cavalry officer, my lady."

She gave a single nod. "And what did you want to tell me, Officer Winwaloe?"

"I wanted to ask what the plan is for the rest of us."

She smiled at him. "That has yet to be decided, Officer Winwaloe. There are far too many of you to put in cells like your Captain Sanddef. Everyone will remain here for now until I've met with my advisors." She turned to all of them. "If any of you have any further concerns, you will direct them to Markis Rilynnzea for the time being. Now, Lisiek. A more pressing matter."

She turned again until she was facing Raven. "What to do with the human girl?"

Raven hardly reacted. She showed no fear or uncertainty at her fate, and Gwyn felt that that was odd.

"Raven, why were you a prisoner of Cromlech?" Gwyn asked her.

Raven lifted her chin as she answered. "I was only a visitor offering advice to Captain Sanddef. He did not want to heed my advice and imprisoned me on accusations of being a spy."

"What sort of advice were you offering?"

"I saw an army approaching Cromlech. I assume it was yours. I was suggesting defensive tactics and strategies. My guess is that my military intelligence hurt Captain Sanddef's pride."

Gwyndolyn laughed at that. "How old are you girl?"

"Twenty years."

Gwyn laughed again. "You are only a child in our eyes. Imagine Captain Sanddef's affront of being counseled by a child."

"And see what his pride did for him," Raven said, looking about the room placidly. "Princess Gwyndolyn, I have committed no crime against you and if you have no reason to detain me, I must leave."

"You want to leave?" Gwyn asked.

"I had not intended to stay at the fortress and I have my own mission to complete. You are not my master and therefore have no reason to keep me."

Gwyn's amusement vanished as she looked up and down this insignificant girl who felt she had the ability to speak so frank to her. Sensing the tension, Lisiek stepped beside her.

"What is your command, my princess?" he asked in a low, seductive voice. When she turned her head to look at him, she saw his dark eyes meeting hers intently. For a moment she forgot to breathe, and the irritation Raven had incited within her vanished. "Where is Markis?" she asked.

As if on cue, Markis reappeared in the hall. "Here, my lady."

Gwyndolyn tore her gaze from Lisiek. "This girl wishes to leave. You will escort her out of Cromlech."

"I would like my weapon returned to me," Raven interrupted.

Gwyn turned to the girl with the wild locks of brass and honey hair that resembled nothing like a raven. "Your weapon?" she repeated.

"A double-sided axe. It was confiscated upon my confinement."

"Markis, find the girl's axe. Escort her out of the fortress and kindly inform her that if she does anything to cross me, I will gladly kill her."

Markis gave a delighted smile. "It would be my pleasure."

15. Reformation

The angry chanting and the atmosphere of the forming mob made Caelfel's blood boil. Her temper flared, reflecting the crowd's, and Caelfel knew theirs would not be easily quelled. She shoved her way through people, weaving through any open gaps she could find. Their words were ringing in her rings.

"*Hang her! Hang her!*"

"*Traitor! Traitor!*"

She made her way to the side of the scaffold and started climbing the steps when two Kanetalm guards barred her path. "Step back, my lady," one of them told her firmly.

Caelfel's eyes assessed the humans before her, and she had no doubt that her strength would best theirs. But a show of strength would not help Forra who now stepped forward to have the noose secured around her neck, much to the cheering of the crowd of witnesses.

"Can't I see her first?" Caelfel asked, keeping her voice light and pleading.

The guards did not answer her or even acknowledge she had said anything. Caelfel looked desperately at the furious mob that were fueling the speed of the executioner's hand. Caelfel called out to them instead.

"Where is her trial?" she demanded of them. But her words were lost in the sea of chanting. Caelfel screamed her question at them. "*Where is her trial?*"

A few individuals paused their rioting to look her way. That was all Caelfel needed. She would not quell their tempers, only redirect it.

"Where is her trial? This girl has done nothing. She has done *nothing. Where is her trial?"*

More people began looking her way.

Caelfel continued, gaining confidence. "Do not be angry at her for doing nothing! Where is the trial to prove her sedition?"

"She is a traitor!" someone yelled back at her.

"By whose word? She is a traitor because King Orrik says she is one? So she is to be executed without trial? What if King Orrik thought you were traitor?" Caelfel challenged. "Where would your trial be?"

"You're just an elf. You don't understand our ways!" someone else shot back, but they sounded uncertain.

Half of Caelfel's mouth lifted into a triumphant smirk. "I understand that in Honey Water we are tried before we are executed, even for treason."

The chanting changed as the eyes of the mob turned to the hillside palace. *"Where is her trial? Where is her trial?"*

The turn of events was a suitable distraction as the citizens of Palpses turned their anger to King Orrik and began marching up the hill path. The guards, stunned by this transformation, all but forgot the execution of Forra as they shifted their attention to restrain the crowd that now threatened their king. Caelfel seized her chance and raced up to the platform to cut Forra free. Only two guards noticed what she was doing and they only called out to her for a moment before their duty claimed them to the protection of the king.

Caelfel pulled her own hooded cloak over Forra as she hissed in her ear, "Hurry."

Forra did not hesitate as Caelfel steered them toward the waiting Madoc and Cyrus. The two men blinked at her, stunned she had just accomplished the feat so quickly. Madoc might have even been impressed if he did not turn his concerned gaze toward the angry crowd making their way to his father.

"I don't know if I can agree with your choice," he said. "You've just endangered the King of Umfeld who happens to be my father."

Caelfel glanced at Madoc who looked nothing like the King of Umfeld. "Make your choice, then. Your brother or your father?" She did not think it would be a particularly difficult choice, and as expected, it was simple for him to make. He threw one last, parting glance at the palace before following Caelfel out of the city.

The guards standing watch by the city proved as no obstacle for them with the presence of Prince Madoc who thanked them for their service before rushing the four of them down the path. The road was quiet after the shouting mob, and the sky was darkening. Caelfel longed for the speed of another horse, but it seemed that fate would not be so kind to her again after her failure to protect Brenin.

"What is a blessing from Voten, and how do we get one?" Caelfel asked when the hillside of Palpses drifted out of sight.

"A blessing from Voten?" Cyrus repeated in shock.

Madoc, having remained silent since they had departed Palpses, continued to say nothing, and his distant eyes only hardened his face. Caelfel set about explaining the latest events to Cyrus.

"Brenin was kidnapped by Tarion while we were in Honey Water," Caelfel began uneasily. She took a shaky breath. "King Orrik said that, in order to use the Company of the Prince to go after him, we would need a blessing from Voten."

Cyrus nodded in comprehension. "Only divine intervention can overrule the commands of a king."

Caelfel recalled Brenin detailing to her the patron gods. Voten was the center of the pantheon, a Bringer of Justice or something to that effect. "How do you get a blessing?" Caelfel repeated.

"Depending on how you view the concept," Madoc suddenly interrupted. "You ask for it." His tone was bitter.

"*How?*" Caelfel repeated impatiently. "Do you go to a temple?"

The bitterness was still clear in Madoc's short laugh. "If you believe in the use of that. Do you think a priest would be stupid enough to publicly disagree with the king?"

Forra, who had kept her silence since her narrow escape from execution, spoke up. "There is a way around that," she said matter-of-factly, pulling Caelfel's cloak tighter around her shoulders.

Cyrus and Madoc looked at her in confusion.

Forra sighed. "You don't need a priest or an acolyte to speak with the gods. If you really believe in the necessity of priests, then you're more backwards than I thought."

"How do you mean?" Madoc demanded.

"If Miss Caelfel needs a blessing from Voten, she should just go ask him for one herself."

Caelfel exchanged puzzled expressions with Cyrus and Madoc. She had never heard of personally visiting a god.

But when Madoc spoke, it was apparent that the notion wasn't quite so alien to the rest of them. "It's blasphemy. She's not a human. Voten wouldn't even see her. He'd probably kill her on the spot."

Forra chortled. "I doubt that. Just because they are gods does not mean you should fear them."

"What in the name of Ewyn are you talking about?" Caelfel asked, nearly shouting in frustration. "How can you speak to a god?"

Forra fixed her with a serious stare. "Because he lives in Umfeld, in a cave on Matron Mountain."

***

Gwyndolyn formed a council with Lisiek, Markis, and, at Lisiek's recommendation, another she-elf called Dagwen, and they all sat in a small, dark chamber Lisiek had identified as the war room. Gwyndolyn remained standing, facing them before starting to pace the room slowly.

"You all came from the Labyrinth, and I was its warden. You will each take turns and tell me the crimes you committed that led to your incarceration."

Markis leaned back in his seat with a hint of a smirk. "You should know my crimes, princess. You were the one to have me incarcerated."

Gwyn returned his smirk with a hint of her own. "Just state your crimes, please."

"Abusive exertion and misuse of executive power. Treason and murder," Markis listed off, sighing.

Gwyndolyn turned to Dagwen. "And you?"

The she-elf's hair framed her face in long sheets of lustrous black. She twirled a knife through her fingers with expert manipulation. "Assassination," she answered in a laconic alto voice.

Gwyndolyn nodded and looked to Lisiek.

The human sorcerer gave a long sigh, looking so out of place compared to the elves in the room. "Kidnapping and torture, war crimes against the fey."

Dagwen narrowed her eyes at Lisiek. Noticing her sudden uneasiness, Gwyn addressed her. "Does something trouble you, assassin?"

Dagwen stopped spinning her stiletto and threw it to the table, the blade embedding in the polished wood of the tabletop, hilt sticking up. "Not at all, princess. Let's get started."

Gwyndolyn pulled out the head chair and, dragging it across the floor with a loud scrape, set it apart from the rest of the table. She made a show of making herself comfortable in it, settling on a position that draped her legs over the arm. She kept her gaze on a recruitment list in her hands and opted to speak using her mind. *Since everyone that has joined my venture across the desert was a prisoner of the Labyrinth, you might understand why this might be considered as an unwise decision.*

She watched from the corner of her eye for their reactions. Lisiek, used to this form of communication, remained unchanged. Markis gave minimal reaction while Dagwen started visibly before quickly smoothing over her features.

I have chosen the three of you because, while your crimes might have been heinous in nature, they were initiated with some measure of loyalty, whether it was to a master, a system of justice, or a profitable contract. I can offer each of these to you, if you can ensure your loyalty to me.

"And you are confident that criminals will prove loyal to you?" Dagwen challenged in her alto voice.

I was your warden and theirs. I never maltreated you.

Dagwen gave a euphonious chuckle. "If criminals cared about treatment, they would not be criminals," she countered.

Gwyn gave a small smile, silently wondering at Lisiek's recommendation for the council. *I understand that. So I will give you criminals something you do care about, and if that does not suit you, I will simply kill you.*

Dagwen remained silent at that, but Gwyndolyn felt that she had not managed to appropriately frighten the assassin. Gwyn leaned back, tipping her chin toward the ceiling, and released a bored sigh. Aloud she said, "I am sure you all understand the necessity for a council. Even a powerful princess such as myself does not have the means to communicate with the rest of my army and followers. You are also here to counsel me, but I want it understood that nothing happens without my command. Oh, talking is so exhausting—" *We also need to decide what to do with the prisoners.*

"Prisoners?" Dagwen repeated.

Yes, they would be the ones littering the main hall of the palace, Gwyn replied scathingly.

"Sorry, my princess. There seems to be a bit of interference with your telepathic communication." Dagwen did nothing to cover her chuckling.

A single throb of pain flared throughout Gwyn's head as she

became annoyed. She took a deep breath to calm herself before responding. "I apologize, Dagwen. I did not account for thick heads in my audience."

Markis laughed at that. Dagwen scowled and abandoned the catty exchanged.

"They should each be given an option," Lisiek interjected, refocusing the conversation. "It seems such a waste to kill them all. They should be allowed an opportunity to swear their loyalty, prove their usefulness."

"And if they refuse?" Gwyn asked.

"Then there is only one option left for them," Lisiek answered simply.

"They are still Honey Water citizens," Dagwen pointed out indignantly.

"If they do not swear loyalty, they have forfeited their rights as citizens," Lisiek replied calmly.

Gwyndolyn looked to Markis. "What is your say in all this?"

He gestured widely with his hands. "Your commands are my priority."

"That's not an opinion," Gwyndolyn pointed out flatly.

Markis looked evenly between Lisiek and Dagwen. "Transitions in power are a difficult time for everyone. If they refuse, imprison them for however long. Pick one to execute, maybe even Captain Sanddef, to make an example of disloyalty. It might move the rest of them."

"That sounds fair," Gwyndolyn mused. "I have not yet decided Captain Sanddef's fate. Would anyone like to share their ideas?"

Lisiek said, "I believe Master Rilynnzea has the best solution. He is uncooperative and unwilling to aid our cause. Allowing him to live, even now is an undeserved kindness."

"Captain Sanddef is a venerated military official," Dagwen cut across sharply. "And he deserves more than the casual dismissal by a mere human and our half-elf princess."

Gwyn's jaw clenched with the insult. Lisiek rose immediately to her defense. "You will not speak in such a way to our princess," he said hotly.

"I will speak my mind as the princess asked. It is no fault of mine if she has no wish to hear it."

"Noble words from a cutthroat assassin," Gwyn observed in a low voice. "Dagwen, what alternative can you conjure for our Captain Sanddef?"

"You yourself stated that Sanddef was more useful to you alive than dead," Dagwen pointed out.

"He has outlived that usefulness if he will not cooperate," Lisiek said.

"It would not be difficult to loosen his tongue or persuade his hand, given the correct incentive," Dagwen replied.

"And I am sure you are uniquely gifted in that area, Dagwen," Gwyn quipped.

The she-elf smirked unabashedly. "I am."

"Then that is your task, and if you fail to persuade him, you will be held accountable."

"Even if he will not cooperate, he can be used in our favor upon our return to Honey Water."

"Upon our return?" Gwyn repeated.

"I presume your majesty intends to return to Honey Water to rightfully claim your throne. If all else fails, Captain Sanddef may be our hostage—leverage."

Gwyn swung her feet over the chair, sitting upright. *Very well. Dagwen will see to Sanddef. Markis, you will see to the prisoners until they are given their ultimatum. Keep them fed. I don't want them ill-treated. You are all dismissed.*

Dagwen rose and swept out of the war room without hesitation. Markis paused long enough to offer her a curt but respectable bow. Lisiek hung back in the absence of the others.

"Lisiek, I'd like to speak with you," she called softly.

He was at her side instantly. "What is it, my princess?"

She leaned her head back. *I do not care much for Dagwen. I struggle with seeing her in the light you suggested.*

"She is strong and possesses a unique but beneficial skill set. Her personality is not so favorable, but I am sure she will prove herself a valuable asset. Besides, it is good for a ruler to have differing opinions in their council."

You are so confident with her abilities yet she does not like you or your ideas.

"It does not trouble me. She will commit to our cause."

She does not seem faithful to our cause, only to those against us, like Sanddef.

Gwyndolyn fell silent, pushing the unpleasantness of Dagwen from her mind. All the while, Lisiek stood faithfully next to her, never flinching, waiting patiently for either her command or to be dismissed. His position reminded her strongly of Blaes, and her throat tightened at the comparison.

"Princess?" Lisiek asked, sensing her distress.

I will require a body guard, she told him banishing all thoughts of Blaes.

"I will be happy to fill the position," he immediately offered.

She glanced at him from the peripheral of her vision, thinking of how he was weak as a human. *You are already my steward.*

"I was both to Admiral Grimault, the desert princeling."

And look how he ended up. Would you be able to hold your own against an elf? I think not.

She waited for Lisiek to be offended, but he did not show it. He held very still and conceded to her point. "Did you have someone in mind?"

Her thoughts flickered to a strange place. She imagined the elf that had defeated Lisiek in battle but she knew not the location or the loyalties of Feraan Auvrearaheal. She turned to Lisiek with an intense expression. "I do not trust anyone," she confided aloud.

He appeared struck by the intensity of her gaze. "They have traveled from Yamalvon to Cromlech and have taken this fortress for you."

Lisiek, my army is only a number of criminals that were under my charge, and we have enjoyed one small, chance victory. I will need to gain followers and soldiers that respect me. I need a people who love me, not fear me because I lead an army of thieves and murderers. No one will take my claim seriously. Her thoughts became muddled in a moment of uncertainty and insecurity.

Lisiek became brave and ran two impertinent fingers through her hair. "Your claim is a serious as any. Your army is a band of liberated citizens that had been incarcerated unjustly. You became their savior. You are their voice. Who else if no one will listen to them? And who better than such a powerful enchantress, their proper and true princess?"

With her spirit orbs absent from the war room, Lisiek could successfully summon his aura and he brought it forth to draw out her silver one. He plucked at her shoulder, as if picking at a loose thread. When activated, Gwyndolyn's aura illuminated every dark corner in the war room with brilliant silver light.

"And you are the most powerful," he swore in a thick, irresistible voice.

***

"But how can a god live in Umfeld?" Caelfel persisted.

Their journey to Matron Mountain proceeded on foot, Madoc taking the lead and Caelfel following closely at his heels. The patience Madoc used to answer her endless questions was quickly wearing thin. "Where else would they live?" he challenged. "How else would we know they exist?"

Caelfel frowned and turned her dissatisfied expression forward. "That does not mean they are gods. That just means they are a different creature entirely."

"What makes a god in your eyes?" Madoc asked with a hint of amusement.

"Gods—*our* goddess—is a creation story. She does not live in Honey Water or anywhere else in Ariang'ron. Her children founded the cities and became the ancestors of all elves."

"So your goddess created the elves. What of the humans? Were we born of rocks?"

"Your heads are as dense as rocks," Caelfel grumbled irritably.

Madoc laughed at that. "Is it so difficult for an elf with her longevity to believe that our creator is still alive after all this time?"

"And your other gods? Voten is your creator, so what purpose do they serve?" Caelfel asked shortly.

"They are the facets of humanity," Madoc answered simply. "Together they make up what it means to be a human."

"So where do they live?" Caelfel argued.

Madoc had no answer to that, so Caelfel turned to the two trailing behind them. Caelfel had already forfeited her cloak to Forra who had nothing but her shift, and the girl had secured it around her waist with Madoc's belt. Even in her humbled, disheveled state, Forra would not allow herself to look ashamed. She held her head high, arms crossed with apathetic disinterest.

"Tell me about Matron Mountain," Caelfel asked her.

Despite the confrontation from their first meeting, Forra no longer harbored contempt for Caelfel. She plunged into an amiable description of the mountain without hesitation.

"It is part of a mountain range called Marsda's Mantle. The mountain range runs down the length of Kanetlam, and the three highest peaks stand a great height from the rest." Forra pointed ahead to the horizon, and Caelfel turned her head to look. The three peaks guarded the skyline ominously in the distance. Caelfel gauged that they still had some ways to go.

"Which one is Matron Mountain?" Caelfel asked Forra.

"Matron is the one in the middle. It's the tallest. The other two are called Maid Mountain and Crone Mountain."

Caelfel remembered Ralfric from Brenin's court calling Crone Mountain his home. "And Marsda is your goddess?"

"That's right. She is the wife of Voten. The mountains are named for the stages of a woman's life."

"And *she* does not live on her mantle?" Caelfel asked, unable to fully mask her derision as she glanced back at Forra.

The girl shrugged. "Perhaps she does."

"And you are sure Voten lives on this mountain?" Caelfel asked all of them in general. She was becoming impatient, and the distance ahead felt like a considerable waste of time to her.

"If we were not sure, we would not be walking this far," Madoc responded.

Caelfel looked at him once more, unable to fathom his conviction. She noticed for the first time he wore a greatsword on his back. She reasoned with herself that her concern for Brenin was what made her overlook such an obvious detail. "I do not understand the point of going this far. Why not go straight to Fort Wymdall? You are their prince. They will listen to you."

"It would seem, Lady Elf, that men listen to their king before their prince. Not even news of Brenin's abduction would move them if King Orrik's command was to stay put."

"He might not even be alive to give that command," Caelfel mused, thinking of the angry mob, her last sight of Palpses.

"If you're referring to that riot you unleashed in the plaza, I must say that I do not approve of your actions," Madoc said tautly.

"I have done nothing wrong. They were going to execute an innocent person."

"That does not justify provoking public outrage."

"They should be outraged," Caelfel said, her voice rising. "The king was going to execute a woman without even a fair trial. A king does not have the right to be a tyrant. His purpose is to look after his people, not abuse them. Brenin would understand that."

"Brenin would also understand that there are consequences to every decision. You ignited a fire bent on a justice fueled by rage. Imagine the destruction. They would destroy anything in their path. They would fight the guards, and the guards would fight back. A soldier would not hesitate to kill someone that attacked him, particularly when the safety of the king was at stake. You must understand that, Caelfel. You probably killed more people than you saved."

Caelfel said nothing and frowned. Madoc's words were not illogical, but she hated to think he was right. She did not want to be responsible for the death of anyone, particularly Brenin's people. The guilt she had for Brenin's capture increased in light of bringing harm to the people he had looked after.

She slowed her pace, hanging back from Madoc. Forra caught up to her, matching her steps with Caelfel's. Caelfel didn't acknowledge her presence, but Forra spoke to her anyway.

"I know we have disagreed," she began. "But, for what it's worth, I think you were in the right for what you did in Palpses, and I'm not just saying that because it saved my neck. Before in the palace, you said a rebellion was not worth the lives it would take. You might have started one in the plaza, but that's not a bad thing. You know how King Orrik is. He does not care for his people."

"I hope you realize, Forra, that the words you speak now are what probably ordered your execution in the first place," Caelfel pointed out with the hint of a grim smile.

Forra squared her shoulders. "I do not regret them. I do not want to live in a place where I should be afraid to speak my thoughts, particularly if our Master Prince here would not be afraid to say the same thing just because he is the king's bastard."

"I am not a bastard," Madoc corrected, though he did not sound angry.

Forra grinned mischievously. "I should hope not, for you would be thrown in with our lot."

When they reached the base of the mountain the next day, they came across a small shack. Cyrus declared that it was probably abandoned, but Madoc knocked on the door anyway. They waited anxiously, the humans with growling bellies that Caelfel found quite annoying with her sensitive ears. Forra had slept poorly that night, a fact which she mentioned repeatedly the following morning. Cyrus usually remained silent, and Madoc had occasionally risen to buffer Forra's constant comments when Caelfel's temper nearly reached its mark.

An elderly woman finally answered the door. She blinked at her visitors with wide, milky orbs, her face sunken with countless creases.

"Excuse me, mistress," Prince Madoc said. "Do you have any food to spare?"

The woman looked between them all, as if not hearing Madoc's request.

Her eyes fell upon Caelfel last. "You want to see Voten, the Judge of Souls." She turned back to Madoc. "He is in a good mood today. You will not want to eat if you climb the mountain."

She ushered them all into her shack, which was surprisingly warm compared to the sharp winds blowing outside. Forra instantly huddled next to the wood stove.

"How did you know we're going to see Voten?" Madoc asked carefully as the woman began rifling through cupboards.

She gave a dry cackle. "There are no villages on Matron Mountain. The only thing is Voten's cave. That's the only reason why anyone comes through here."

"Why can't we eat, then?" Madoc pressed.

"When you climb the mountain, the height will make you sick. You can drink water instead and chew on these." She shoved several large leaves into Madoc's hands. "Those are white sugar leaves from Umfang. They will help against the sickness."

"What if we just want to stay here?" Forra asked shrilly. "Will you feed us then?"

The woman laughed at her. "What a spoiled girl."

Forra shrugged, unconcerned. "I have no business with Voten."

"We will still need to eat. I will you pay you any amount you desire if you feed us, before or after," Madoc offered the woman.

She waved him away. "You have nothing I want. Go on, chew your leaves before you see him. I will take care of your companion." The old crone proceeded to hobble into another room of the shack, muttering inaudibly to herself.

"Are you sure we can trust her?" Caelfel asked Madoc in a low voice, questioning the woman's sanity.

"She hasn't given us reason not to, unlike your charge," he pointed out, nodding toward Forra. He turned to Brenin's steward.

"Cyrus, stay here with Forra in case something happens. Caelfel and I will climb the mountain path ourselves."

"And if you don't return?" Cyrus asked solemnly.

Madoc grimaced. "Be sure to take care of yourself."

"Is there a strong likelihood of us not returning?" Caelfel asked suspiciously, wondering if she should be alarmed.

"Why do you think no one else lives on the mountain?" Madoc asked. "The path to Voten's cave is dangerous in itself, and there's no telling what we will encounter once we arrive."

"And if we die here, who will help Brenin?" Caelfel demanded, her temper flaring. The shack rattled with a strong gust of wind.

"We don't have a choice," Madoc hissed. She might have heard his teeth chattering.

"Of course we have a choice. We go to the Pirinac and get him ourselves."

"And then what?" Madoc was almost yelling, but his voice was still muffled by the howling wind. "Shall we get kidnapped like him? Torn to bits and eaten, like your mother? You might have noticed that we're outnumbered here. Attacking Tarion and his pack on our own is a stupid idea."

Caelfel felt her fingernails clawing into the heels of her palms at the mention of Sylaera. "Are you calling my mother stupid?" she shrieked back at him. "My mother was a powerful battlemage and a fierce warrior, unlike anyone else—"

Madoc's face hardened in defense, and in that moment, he looked exactly like Feraan. She forgot her argument, almost mistaking Madoc for him. "I am not insulting your mother," he said. "But I am calling you stupid if you make the same mistake she did. One elf, on her own, killed. Two elves, separated and fatally injured. An elf and a prince against them? Well look at where we are now."

"You think it's about numbers? Caelfel scoffed. "A war is not won by strength of numbers alone."

"And it's not won by irrational she-elves either," he deadpanned.

His comment was enough to shut her up, and she fumed silently. She turned her back to him and waited by the door. "Tell me when you are ready to leave," she muttered through clenched teeth.

There was a minute of bitter silence between them, as they stood deaf to the violent wind outside. As if to make peace, Madoc addressed her in a softer voice. "Caelfel—"

"No," she cut him off in a thick voice. She just realized her cheeks were wet with tears, and she pressed her forehead against the wooden door, determined not to be seen like that. "You are right."

Madoc sighed. "Do not think I don't care about Brenin. I love him too, and I will do anything to get my brother back. That is our goal and why we're here."

Caelfel released a shaky sigh. "I know."

16. Divine Intervention

The path to Voten's cave was cut into the mountainside to form natural, stone steps. The steps were steep and icy, making it a perilous journey to the peak for Madoc and Caelfel. Shortly after leaving the base, the air became thick with swirling snow. It did not feel like spring to Caelfel as she buried herself deeper into the fur robe provided by the old woman who revealed her name as Lutselle.

Caelfel was faster than Madoc, but unlike other humans, he did a fair job of keeping close to her. His speed only made her even more suspicious of his elvish paternity. At one point, Caelfel misjudged her next step, and her weight crumbled the eroding stone away. She caught herself before she could fall, but Madoc had instantly raced to her aid. He would have been there in time if she had required his help.

The leaves Lutselle gave them made her head buzz with energy, and the higher they climbed, the more the effects helped her to focus on their task at hand. The change in the thinning air was tangible and made her ears hurt. She struggled to breathe, like a fish partially out of water.

"Are you sure this will work?" Caelfel shouted with some difficulty over the blizzard.

"What do you mean?" Madoc struggled to shout back.

"When we reach the end of this path, will there even be a god there? Or are we wasting our time?"

"People have visited him before and continue to visit him. I do not think this is a waste of time."

It took them two days to reach the peak of Matron Mountain.

The pain of their hunger only dimmed in comparison to the cold. Caelfel actually thought she might miss the desert.

The path had levelled off at the peak, and they trudged through knee deep snow that caked onto their pants and soaked through to their skin. The pelting snow made everything dark, and Caelfel slowed her pace to not lose Madoc as she tried avoiding hidden snow drifts.

"Are we close now?" Caelfel asked him.

Madoc lifted his hand and pointed in the distance. "There."

Caelfel squinted, seeing the enormous cave entrance looming like a gaping maw in the side of the mountain. Caelfel took another step when the sound of a screeching bird made her hesitate. A crow landed smoothly on the snow bank in front of her. Its wings shifted, increasing in size, until the crow had transformed into a girl with short black hair and ice-blue eyes. Caelfel remembered her name, though she had never spoken to her. This was Macha.

"What are you doing here?" Macha demanded of them. The werebird was nude in her human form, though unaffected by the freezing temperature.

"We want to see Voten," Madoc answered.

Macha kept her eyes trained on Caelfel. "Not you. Her."

"I'm here for the same thing," Caelfel answered in a hard voice.

"And what business do you have with Voten?" Macha asked venomously, stepping closer to them.

"What business do you have to stop me?" Caelfel countered.

"You are an elf. Voten is not your god."

"That does not mean I cannot see him. What authority do you have to determine people's fates?"

Macha folded her arms, doing little to rein in her hostility. "I control no one's fate. Why do you say that?"

Caelfel stormed up to her, numb hands shaking into fists. "Do you not recognize me? Do you so easily forget a face when you visit Honey Water?"

Macha's eyes widened in brief recognition. "I don't know you."

"But you know Feraan. You came to warn him about the desert army." Caelfel was shrieking from rage now. "You could have warned *me*, since I was there and the one the army was after."

Macha's hostility turned to submission. "I didn't know it was you."

"*Didn't know?*" Caelfel repeated hysterically. In a moment of anger, she shoved Macha to the ground, faintly registering Madoc attempting to restrain her. "You looked me in the eye and smiled just before you flew off, and you *didn't know?* Do you have any idea of the things that the princeling and his sorcerer did to me?"

"I can't imagine," Macha pleaded. "I am sorry I did not do enough to help you."

"You're sorry? You should see the scar they left on me," Caelfel screamed, her mind filled with nothing but anger and revenge. "Maybe I should leave one on you too."

The wind and the blizzard stopped suddenly. Snowflakes hung suspended in midair as if time had stopped. Everything was quiet, and when Caelfel looked at the cave entrance, she saw two sapphire lights, glinting in its darkness like great eyes as tall as the tallest tree.

A great mountainous voice spoke with the power to shake the air around them. "To threaten my daughter is either bravery or foolishness."

Every muscle in Caelfel's body tensed painfully as she looked upon the shadowed form of Voten. She thought with some chagrin of a wonderful impression she had made on Voten by threatening someone he named as his daughter. She forced her rigid muscles to straighten and stepped away from Macha. Madoc mirrored her steps nervously as they drew closer to the cave entrance.

"I hope I am one and not the other," Caelfel carefully answered. Macha remained where she was in the snow, watching the exchange silently.

There was a dry choking sound that took Caelfel a moment to identify as a laugh. "What a witty one you are, daughter of Sea Foam."

The address confused her. "Daughter of Sea Foam?" she repeated.

"You cannot deceive me. Even buried in your furs, I can see you are no creation of mine. What an insult you have made, attacking one of my own right in front of me before you come to ask me your favor."

Madoc cursed beside her, and Caelfel's face burned with indignation. She had the impression Voten had the personality of an ancient, self-righteous king. But as a god, she supposed he had a right to be this way. But the fact that she had so quickly spoiled his opinion of her only infuriated Caelfel even more. "I meant no offense by my actions. I was only settling some prior dispute I believe was owed to me."

Voten was silent for a long minute, never stepping out his cave. Then finally, "Macha, what do you say about this?"

Macha was immediately on her feet and next to them. "Father Voten, I have indeed committed an unintentional wrong to this elf by remaining indifferent to her plight." There werebird paused. "I believe you should grant her wish as penance for my inaction."

Caelfel's anger vanished, and she looked at Macha with astonishment. She didn't have the words to voice her gratitude, but Madoc was busy fervently thanking her in Caelfel's stead.

Voten hummed a moaning sigh that sounded like the collapse of a great tree. "Very well. I have never had a visitor from the Honey Forest before. What is your desire, sapling?"

The range of monikers he had for Caelfel made her head spin. "I wish to save Prince Brenin of Kanetalm."

"Brenin of Kanetalm." Voten took another long minute to consider. "You have misplaced the Prince of the Vale."

Caelfel remembered Brenin naming the successor to the throne of Umfeld as the Prince of the Vale, which everyone believed was Madoc, the eldest brother. Upon meeting Madoc, Caelfel had harbored suspicions that he wasn't the first or trueborn son of King Orrik.

"No, I'm the Prince of the Vale," Madoc interrupted. "We're looking for my brother, the prince of Kanetalm."

Voten laughed again, and Caelfel thought it a terrible sound. "You are no prince," he told Madoc. "Now that I look at you, you are very much like the she-elf."

Madoc struggled to grasp his meaning. "But my father is King Orrik."

"Your father was no king, and your mother was a liar. Now, what's this about misplacing the Prince of the Vale?"

"We didn't misplace him," Caelfel answered before Madoc could argue his paternity again. "He was stolen from us by the werewolves in the Pirinac."

"Stolen, because you misplaced him in the jaws of the wolves." Voten laughed again at his own joke. "So you need to challenge the werewolves. To hunt them down, you will need a werewolf hunter."

"We need permission to use the army, the Company of the Prince," Caelfel tried correcting respectfully.

"An army helps too. And while you're at it, who knows werewolves better than other werewolves?"

"I don't understand," Caelfel said, keeping her patience in check.

"Take the Horn of Command, get your army. Find your werewolf hunter and visit the city of werewolves. Reclaim the Prince of the Vale."

After delivering his instructions, the blue eyes of Voten began winking out of existence. The swirling blizzard began picking up speed once more, and time felt like it began moving again. At the front of Voten's cave, a blue light flashed, leaving behind the dull shine of a metallic object in its wake. When Caelfel picked it up, she saw it was a bronze horn fashioned in an ornate curve with a leather strap to be worn over the shoulder.

"What does this mean?" Caelfel asked, looking to Madoc. Macha had already disappeared into the winter storm in her raven form.

"It means," Madoc said, his face like granite. "We got what we came for."

Madoc said nothing the entire journey down Matron Mountain, and Caelfel wondered if his silence stemmed from a simmering anger of being denied his royal birthright by a divine entity. When they neared Lutselle's shack, he suddenly took Caelfel by the shoulders and spoke with an earnest frenzy.

"I am not a prince," he said in a low voice, as if admitting the truth would be the very act of treason. "I am not King Orrik's son."

Caelfel shook her head, having nothing else to say. She wasn't sure what would help him.

"Then who is my father? And my mother for that matter?" he asked in a wild voice.

Caelfel placed a calculating hand on Madoc's pleading one. She didn't have all the answers for him, but she had no doubt now that Feraan was his true father. Despite whatever empathy she felt for him in this world-shattering moment, her present objective was rescuing Brenin. She needed everyone to focus on that task. "I have no doubt Queen Fronia was your mother. Orrik would not keep an adopted son as his successor otherwise. That means Brenin is still your brother, and your brother needs us right now."

Madoc nodded, and having a mission to focus on helped him recover from his frenzy. "I don't understand why my mother would lie to me, though."

Caelfel thought of King Orrik's vanity and easily imagined Queen Fronia's motives. "She would only do it to protect you."

217

When they entered Lutselle's shack, Madoc kept very close to her after that, and Caelfel wondered if he understood that he shared elvish blood.

Caelfel did the job of repeating Voten's instructions and showed everyone the Horn of Command. In the firelight, the bronze shone brilliantly, its surface flawless from any blemish.

"So we have it then, our token," Cyrus said. "We just take this to Fort Wymdall to get not only the Company, but the whole army."

"Not quite," Caelfel said. "Voten said we should do the other things too. But I don't understand them. Where are we supposed to find a werewolf hunter? What is the city of werewolves?"

"The city of werewolves is easy," Cyrus interrupted. "He means Haradrop. It's an old fortress where the Dirus Clan lives, a pack of werewolves."

"How do we know they're not helping Tarion?" Caelfel asked suspiciously.

"They're not like that. They're only mercenaries. Lycaon and his family keep to themselves but they've never hurt anyone like Tarion has."

"Lycaon?" Caelfel repeated. It was a name familiar to her. She remembered Feraan, speaking fondly of him and the wolves in Haradrop. She remembered Brenin similarly mentioning him. That was enough for Caelfel to trust them. "He can help us against Tarion as well. That just leaves the issue of the werewolf hunter."

They paused, considering the dilemma. Caelfel's heart sank, hoping Voten's riddle would be understood by his human subjects. "There's been only one known werewolf hunter," Madoc eventually volunteered. "And he's been dead for centuries."

Caelfel sighed, also remembering this from her time with Feraan. "You mean Saint Hubertus."

They all nodded grimly.

"But Voten had to have meant something by a werewolf hunter. Does Saint Hubertus have any descendants?"

Cyrus shrugged. "It's hard to say. It was assumed his children were all killed in the same battle that killed him. He might have killed them too, being half-werewolf. He might have had some illegitimate children otherwise."

"And how would we find that out?" Caelfel urged.

"Assuming no one else has done research on the subject, which I find unlikely, your best chance would be to visit Sorasaen. That's where he lived and where the Temple of Saint Hubertus stands. It's close to Haradrop too."

Caelfel was getting excited by the forming plan when Madoc interjected. "We'll have to split up. Fort Wymdall is in the opposite direction from Haradrop. One of us should get the army and meet everyone else at Haradrop."

"You should do it," Caelfel said. "They see you as their prince," she explained carefully.

But the look in Madoc's eyes told her he was unwilling to deceive the people of Umfeld further. "I can't," he said quietly. They had said nothing of his parentage to the others in the shack.

No one put up an argument, and Cyrus volunteered. "I'll do it. The men there know me already. It would be best for someone they're familiar with to approach them with the Horn of Command."

"So it's decided," Caelfel said, nodding. "Cyrus will get the army and everyone else will go to Sorasaen, then we will all meet up at Haradrop." They all nodded their heads in agreement.

Forra, who had never joined the discussion, remained in the corner by the woodstove and finally spoke up. "You're forgetting one important detail."

"Please enlighten us," Madoc said in an impatient tone.

Forra sighed. "You are going to such great lengths to save Prince Brenin, but has it not occurred to any of you that Tarion has already killed him? Your efforts will probably be for nothing."

"If Tarion wanted Brenin dead, he would have killed him when he attacked us in Honey Water," Caelfel said through clenched teeth.

"You said you blacked out. For all you know, he could have."

"The militia didn't find his body," Caelfel defended.

"People make mistakes, elves can too I am sure. Better yet, Tarion might have eaten him whole, leaving behind no evidence. Or he might have killed him in Umfeld."

Madoc intervened before Caelfel could jump Forra like she almost had Macha. "Brenin's too valuable as a hostage. Tarion wouldn't have entered Honey Water just to kill him. He must have a plan."

"That's what I'm trying to say," Forra said. "Do you think whatever plan they might have involves keeping Brenin safely in the Pirinac for us to march in and rescue him?"

"Do you think they would go to such measures to kidnap him

only to kill him?" Madoc asked in disbelief.

"All of you are too close to Brenin to think logically. What did he want with Prince Brenin in the first place? My first guess would be to ransom him back to his father. King Orrik will more than likely refuse, because the King is not a man to take risks against his pride. What then? What will fate have in store for Brenin?"

"You're saying that my brother is probably dead?"

"I'm saying his abduction was no accident, and werewolves are notoriously infamous for their short tempers. You need to prepare yourself for anything."

Caelfel shook her head. "I refuse to believe it. Brenin is alive. And I'm going to save him."

***

Brenin rarely stayed conscious for long. A deep-seated terror and disgust of his captors and their forest remained as his constant companions. He tried escaping to some deep recess of his mind, but they always made sure he was awake when shoving some bloody mess into his mouth for sustenance. He had vomited it up the first time only to have it forced down his throat again. He wasn't even sure what exactly they were feeding him, only that they rarely bothered to pick the bones from it.

"A dead hostage is a useless one," Tarion had said to him.

So being a hostage was the only thing that kept him alive.

They didn't tie him up. There was no need to when they all could run faster than him anyway and chew his leg off for good measure. Brenin kept his head down, never speaking. He kept his whole body limp, and it slumped forward, face to the ground, between his legs. He clasped his hands tightly behind his neck.

In an attempt to block out the pervasive smell of cloying blood and rotten flesh, he tried to fill his thoughts with better, lighter things. It was difficult, especially when his leg began to give off a putrid smell from the puncture wound of Tarion's fangs.

He thought of his mother and her sweet manner. Her face had mostly ebbed from his memory over time. And the perfect memories he had of her did little to comfort him.

He thought of his brother with his loud voice, boasting or jesting. Brenin had little in the way of pleasant memories with Madoc, just an overall contentment with his brother's company.

He thought of his steward's unwavering loyalty. The wise counsel of Cyrus had never failed him, and he was always a dependable teacher and mentor.

The voices of the Company of the Prince had brought much enjoyment, and he faintly recalled their competitions and friendly brawls.

But most of all, Brenin's thoughts centered on Caelfel. From the first moment he had seen her, Caelfel's beauty struck him. Her kindness and strong morality were the perfect complements to her own quiet passion. Caelfel was both justice and mercy. And she was so beautiful. He had no doubt of his love for her.

But in the dark moments, when he forced the bile down his throat and bit back cries of pain when his leg troubled him, he chiefly remembered her blunt rejection of him. The stony eyes that had never belonged to her before were a stark memory that did little to soothe his soul.

But he had reminded himself that there was a brief moment before Tarion's attack that she had changed. Her face had cleared, as if it had all been a front. And then she had protected him with an unbridled ferocity. His reasoning told him it was because she returned his feelings. His insecurity made him uncertain and clouded his thoughts in the darkest moments of his captivity.

A strong kick pushed him to his back, revealing Tarion hovering above him.

Tarion rarely came to speak to him on his own. Skolt was usually the one to relay messages to him. Brenin took a quick breath to brace himself. His mind went to the feeling of Caelfel's hand over his, the floral scent of her white gold hair after she had bathed.

"Your father has responded to my message," Tarion began.

Caelfel accepted his embrace and sobbed against his neck. It was not a happy memory but one where she made the decision to be close to him.

"Despite my reliable source, King Orrik's official documents do not list you as the Prince of the Vale."

"I told you I wasn't," Brenin managed in a hoarse voice.

"As a result," Tarion continued. "You mean very little to him. A title holds a heavy weight, but only if people believe it."

Brenin replayed the moment in his mind when he professed his love to Caelfel.

"Do you hear me? Your own father doesn't even want you."

Caelfel gave him a hard look. "You don't know how to love an elf."

"He doesn't negotiate," Brenin said after a fit of coughing. He tasted blood. He always tasted blood.

"He wouldn't accept my ransom, so not only are you useless to him, but you are useless to me. But no need to worry quite yet. I have another interested buyer." Tarion made a move to walk away but stopped himself. "Would you like to know what his letter said?"

Brenin said nothing, imagining Caelfel's deft fingers pushing his hair behind his ears, braiding it with gentle movements.

Tarion shrugged. "I'll read it for you then. 'We will not negotiate with the likes of you, particularly over so insignificant of a prize.' Not very verbose, your father."

And Brenin didn't want to, but he imagined Caelfel dancing with a handsome elf that looked undeniably like his brother.

***

"Do you think he is alive?" Caelfel asked Madoc solemnly.

Cyrus had already parted for Fort Wymdall with the Horn of Command while they started on the road for Sorasaen with Forra trailing behind them. The girl had volunteered to accompany Cyrus, but Caelfel was immediately against it. She would feel better if Forra was where Caelfel could keep an eye on her. Forra did not argue with Caelfel.

"I do not think Voten would trouble himself to send us on this journey if it was doomed from the start."

"Do you think Voten could know if Brenin was dead?"

"He knew I was not the true Prince of the Vale," Madoc said with a shrug. "He said I was like you. What could that mean?"

Caelfel held her breath and shrugged one shoulder. "I think it means your father was an elf. Honestly, I have no doubt of it," she admitted.

"An elf?" Madoc repeated, breathless. "I'm an elf?"

"Only half, at most," Caelfel stipulated. "Your ears aren't even pointed."

"You knew?" he asked. He didn't sound angry, which surprised her.

"I suspected," she revealed slowly, gauging his reaction. "But I wasn't certain until after our meeting with Voten. Forgive me for not saying anything. I wanted to be sure."

"You know who my father is?" His tone took a note of accusation.

Caelfel chose her next words carefully. "You look similar to someone I know. I have a good idea as to who your father is."

"Tell me, then," Madoc said, stunned.

Caelfel frowned, chewing her bottom lip. "I don't want to unless I am absolutely sure. I might be mistaken."

Madoc rolled his eyes. "I did not take you for someone so careful with their actions," he said with irritation.

Caelfel didn't respond. If she was being honest with herself, she did not want Feraan to be Madoc's father. Saying it would be like making it true, and it was a truth too painful, one that felt too much like a betrayal from him.

When they stopped for the night, they camped some distance from the road, downwind from a rocky hillside. Forra assumed responsibility and set to work building a fire before the last of the sun's rays escaped them.

"How far until Sorasaen?" Caelfel asked, settling down on a rock damp from melted snow.

"We should reach it by tomorrow. Cyrus should be at Fort Wymdall tomorrow morning, supposing he had no trouble on the road."

Caelfel's chest tightened in panic as she imagined the slight steward being overtaken by burly bandits. "Do you think it's safe to let him go on his own with the Horn of Command?"

"He'll be fine," Madoc said with a noncommittal shrug.

Caelfel watched him carefully. She would have pressed the possibility of losing such an integral item more, but Madoc's utterly forlorn expression discouraged her. She couldn't imagine how he felt, raised as a prince his entire life only to have it taken away in a humbling moment before his god. She pitied him.

"Tell me about Saffir," Caelfel said in an attempt to improve his mood.

Half of Madoc's mouth lifted into a smile. "What's there to tell? She's beautiful and kind, not the awful things Father—*King* Orrik likes to say about her." He scowled. "She had already returned to Atalon before you came back to Palpses."

"Do you think she'll worry about you, now that you've gone?"

"I imagine. There's no telling what Orrik has said of my absence.

Not that it matters," he sighed. "I don't know how I'm going to tell him. He'd just as soon execute me and Brenin for our mother's infidelity."

"He wouldn't, at least not both of you. Orrik is all pride and vanity. He wouldn't want his brother Orren taking the throne after him. He'd rather it be his son. He probably would keep it all a secret to save his reputation."

Madoc shook his head. "He would not let a slight like this go unpunished. He might even go after Saffir because of me." Caelfel watched something in his eyes tighten. "I'll have to make sure she is safe before I tell him."

"You don't have to tell him," Caelfel suggested.

"I can't take my brother's birthright from him by claiming to be something that I'm not." His face turned inexorably sad. "She will probably want nothing to do with me now," he said, passing a hand over his face.

"You shouldn't make such assumptions," Caelfel began softly.

"She's the daughter of the Officer of Trade, the highest ranking official in Atalon. She's not born a princess but she lives like one. I can't offer that any more. Her father would settle for nothing but a prince."

Caelfel hardened and she turned to snap at Madoc. "If she really loved you, it should not matter to her if you are prince or peasant."

"But I was a prince. Now I am nobody, hopelessly in love with a princess."

Caelfel flew to her feet in a temper. "And I am nobody. A she-elf nobody. But a prince managed to fall in love with me. I'm sorry, Madoc, but I've no patience for your moping. Saffir isn't being held captive by werewolves right now."

Madoc blinked up at her with wide eyes. "What do you mean? What did Brenin do?"

Caelfel found herself furiously blinking back tears as she thought of her last conversation with him. "It is none of your concern," she snapped at him before retreating to the far end of their campsite.

17. Hunter

Fódla did not care for the self-assured princess who claimed to be their rightful emperor but Fódla *did* care about her own general well-being. When given the chance, she immediately took the vow, swearing her allegiance to Princess Gwyndolyn. Winwaloe appeared reluctant to follow suit but did after catching Fódla's sharp look. Most of the other prisoners chose similarly with only a handful remaining obstinately loyal to Sanddef's plight.

Even after taking the oath, their weapons were not returned to them, and they were always chaperoned by either Markis or Dagwen. But this did not really bother Fódla. She would work her way through the ranks as she had before.

"What are you doing?" Winwaloe asked, terrified. "This is treason."

They whispered to each other in the darkness of their shared quarters. "Surviving," Fódla retorted. "Whether or not Gwyn's cause is just is irrelevant. She has the power to kill you or reward you, and I'm not risking my life for an empire that can't be bothered to rescue me."

Winwaloe nodded but he didn't look convinced.

Fódla sighed. "Self-preservation. It's why I was going to be Sanddef's first lieutenant and you were just a cavalry officer."

"If the imperial army does come to take down Gwyn, they won't want to make a traitor first lieutenant of anything."

"That's supposing that the imperial army even troubles themselves with the effort. I won't worry about being first lieutenant if I'm one of Gwyn's army generals."

"Some army you'd be commanding," Winwaloe scoffed.

"Convicts and captured volunteers."

"You're missing the point, Winwaloe. How many of us didn't swear fealty to Gwyn even after our oaths with the empire? Only five out of almost a hundred. Elves are not fickle with their loyalty. We're smart with our own survival. We sense a change coming, and Princess Gwynfolyn is spearheading it."

"If this is us being smart, I don't see the elves surviving for very long," Winwaloe muttered.

Fódla gave a noise of disgust and rolled over in her bunk. "You'll see, Winwaloe."

One day, Fódla was on patrol with Dagwen as they roamed the outer wall. Fódla still hadn't been allowed her weapon, a black bow that Dagwen kept strung on her back. Fódla eyed it enviously but uttered not a single complaint, thinking her compliance would win her bow back sooner.

They stood guard at the northwest tower, looking over the vast sea of sand. It looked as red as her hair from their height. Most days, the desert stood still without disturbance. But from the southwest, Fódla saw a bird heading north. She narrowed her eyes, recognizing it.

"Do you see that?" Fódla asked, turning to Dagwen.

The other she-elf squinted in the direction Fódla pointed. "It's a crow."

Fódla nodded. "It's probably a messenger bird. You should shoot it down."

Dagwen arched a black eyebrow, unconvinced. "A crow?"

"How often do you see a crow in the desert?" Fódla countered.

Dagwen shrugged, showing no concern for a messenger flying through the desert.

"There are these couriers. They are werebirds. They've visited the outpost before. What if they're delivering a letter about Princess Gwyndolyn's presence here? You can't be too careful. You have to shoot it down."

Without a word, Dagwen took the bow and aimed for the bird. After a moment, she lowered the weapon. "The sun is too bright," she said dismissively.

Annoyed, Fódla ripped her bow from Dagwen's hands. She took three seconds to aim before releasing the arrow and forfeiting her bow back to Dagwen.

They watched as the arrow sailed through the air. It hit the raven's wing, and the bird began to careen wildly towards the ground.

"Doesn't look like a werebird," Dagwen noted indifferently.

But when the crow reached the ground, its entire form began to shift and grow until it had assumed the shape of a human. For once, Dagwen didn't appear bored as she stared at it in shock before yelling to Markis to retrieve the body.

Fódla was present in Gwyndolyn's receiving chamber when the werebird, still alive, was brought in for questioning. The girl with short black hair and golden eyes was completely naked, so Markis had taken the liberty of giving her a blanket to cover herself. Her right arm was injured, streaked in blood rivulets, where the arrow had pierced her wing.

Princess Gwyndolyn asked the girl to sit down on a cushion for her own comfort. The girl quietly thanked her but kept her eyes to the ground, awaiting interrogation.

"What is your name?" Gwyn began simply.

"Anann. Anann Morrígna."

"And what are you doing flying through the desert, Anann?"

"I did not mean to cause alarm. I was delivering a message. My sister and I are couriers. We deliver them faster than anyone else in Ariang'ron because we can fly."

"And who are you delivering a message to?"

"To the Chancellor of Umfang."

"What did this message say?"

"It's—well, it's a more of a business proposition. I don't have much liberty to discuss the contents of the letter, but—" Here, Anann unfastened a scroll from her leg and tossed it carelessly to the ground. "I can't stop you from reading it."

Lisiek, the human steward, picked it up from the floor, eyeing Anann warily, and began to read the scroll aloud.

"*To Master Chancellor—*

I have in my possession the Prince of the Vale, the heir and next king of Umfeld. I am willing to make an economical exchange for him. I desire only free reign of my lands while you may have the future of Umfeld in your hands.

Reply promptly.

Tarion, Lord of the Pirinac."

A smirk came to Gwyn's face, and Fódla saw an idea forming in her head. "Who is this Lord Tarion?"

"He is the alpha of a pack of werewolves, currently residing in the Pirinac Forest."

"Is the Chancellor of Umfang expecting this letter?"

Anann shook her head. "No, but Tarion is quite keen on selling the prince."

Gwyn rose from her seat and approached the girl. "Well, I am quite keen on purchasing him. Would you deliver that to Tarion for me?"

"I cannot fly, my lady," Anann said, looking to her injured arm.

Gwyn waved her concern away. "No need to worry about that." And with one touch from Gwyn, the blood disappeared, and Anann's wound healed. Anann rotated her arm in a series of tests, satisfied with her mobility. She nodded to Gwyndolyn.

"Lisiek, write a letter." She waited until Lisiek was ready to write and then Gwyn recited. "*To Tarion—*

I am not the Chancellor of Umfang. Instead, I am the princess of Honey Water and its rightful emperor. I will gladly give you your lands and more in exchange for the prince and certain combat services. We can arrange a meeting at a place and time of your choosing. Bring the prince with you. Anann will attest to my integrity.

Signed,
Princess Gwyndolyn of Ernmas
Emperor of Honey Water.'"

Gwyn turned back around to Anann. "And of course, you will be compensated for your services."

Anann nodded eagerly, shaking the blanket from her shoulders. "I'll expect payment when I return with his reply."

Gwyn smiled at her. "Of course."

After Anann had set off with her new letter, Lisiek asked Gwyn, "What do you have in mind, my princess?"

"I see myself having control over an army of werewolves and Umfeld in a single move." At last, Gwyndolyn turned to Fódla. "And I have you to thank for this."

Fódla inclined her head respectfully. "I recognized her as a werebird. I wanted to make sure she wasn't delivering intelligence about our position."

"That was very insightful of you. Your name is Danann, correct?"

Fódla nodded. "Yes, Fódla Danann."

"Thank you, Fódla Danann. I will not forget your service.

Dagwen, please return Fódla's weapon to her."

And Fódla did little to hide her smug expression as she earned her bow back.

***

Sorasaen was a village unlike Palpses. It had a single paved road running through its center with everything built around it. The temple sat in the center, its spire towering above the other buildings. The three of them entered the temple and were greeted by its keeper, a hunched man named Ólff. His eyes were bloodshot, but Caelfel didn't think they normally looked like this.

"How can I serve you today?" Ólff asked in a pleasant, mousy voice.

Madoc went straight to the point. "We were wanting to research Saint Hubertus, particularly if had any descendants."

Ólff bobbed his head in consideration and ushered them into the sanctuary. "It is commonly known that the children Saint Hubertus conceived with Refurinn perished in the same battle that claimed his life."

"Did he have any other children?" Caelfel asked, her eyes trailing the dark walls of the building. She felt that their morose surroundings were not conducive to a place of reverence or worship. Perhaps this was merely a human trait of religion.

Ólff lifted his finger. "That is a widely debated topic. It is thought that Hubertus was unfaithful to his wife Refurinn, and as revenge, she turned herself and their children into werewolves, igniting the battle that killed them all."

Caelfel tilted her head thoughtfully. "I had heard Refurinn was already a werewolf, not that she turned into one."

Ólff offered her a weak smile. "Are you a scholar on the subject of werewolves and Hubertus?"

"I read a book once," Caelfel admitted sheepishly.

Ólff nodded. "Might I ask the reason behind your interest of the subject?"

Madoc continued to be straightforward. "Voten told us that we needed a werewolf hunter. We didn't know where else to turn."

"I don't know of any descendants, but have you spoken with Nym?" Ólff suggested quietly. He looked down at his hands and gripped a nearby bannister tightly.

"I'm sorry, Nym?" Caelfel repeated.

"It's short for Nymaaria. She owns the blacksmith shop next door. She's also an effective mercenary who has some experience in werewolf hunting."

"Nymaaria?" Caelfel repeated. The name sounded elvish but it was not one she was familiar with.

"She's elvish like you, but her ears are pointed differently."

"Where can we find her?" Caelfel asked.

Ólff shrugged. "I've been looking for her myself. The apprentice at her forge just says she left town. He wouldn't tell me anything else. You can try to get more information from him. Let me know if you are successful." He turned away from them then, shuffling away as if oblivious to his surroundings.

"Master Ólff, is everything all right?" Caelfel asked him.

Ólff hesitated. With his back still turned to them, he said, "If you're going to hunt werewolves, make sure you kill every last one of them. Even the bastards in Haradrop." His voice trembled with tears and a quiet rage.

"Did something happen?" Caelfel asked tentatively.

"Forgive me for my grief. My daughter Reuthe was taken by werewolves," he said in a thick voice.

Caelfel wondered if the wolves in Haradrop were responsible as Ólff seemed to think. She stepped closer to him. "I am sorry for your loss. Don't worry. They took my mother. I won't let them get away with it," she promised him. Ólff could only whisper his thanks before Caelfel rejoined Madoc and Forra.

"I'm going to ask about this Nym girl," Madoc said. "Maybe I can loosen a few tongues as prince."

Caelfel nodded. "I think I want to look around here some more. We'll meet back up later."

"What do you want me to do?" Forra asked.

"You can go with Madoc," Caelfel decided.

They nodded and split up. At her request, Ólff showed her the old library hidden away in the attic of the temple. The room was warm to the point of suffocating. A look around told Caelfel it was rarely visited.

"Do you know if the rumors of Hubertus's affair are true?" Caelfel asked Ólff as she scanned the room. She ventured across the weak, wooden planks of the floor. Ólff stayed at the door.

"One name came up twice in historical record. Fawnrial."

"Fawnrial?" Caelfel repeated, startled. The name was eerily familiar. "That sounds elvish."

"I agree," was all Ólff said.

Caelfel took a turn past a bookshelf to see an enormous painting of Saint Hubertus hanging from the wall. Caelfel froze and gaped at it. She struggled to make words or to process the striking familiarity of the portrait in front of her.

"Are you all right?" Ólff asked when she had not moved.

"This painting, Ólff, is it a true likeness of Saint Hubertus?" Caelfel asked, starting to feel light-headed.

"It's hard to say. Saint Hubertus lived over five hundred years ago. But every account says it's a true painting. It was painted just before his thirtieth birthday. Why do you ask?"

Caelfel didn't answer. She only stared at the painted figure that looked exactly like Feraan.

Caelfel fell into an obliterating silence as she numbly followed Ólff back to the sanctuary. He inquired after her well-being when she still retained the expression of utter shock. Caelfel only shook her head, unable to speak just yet.

Lady Ellissara had made mention of a she-elf named Fawnrial who lost her noble status for fornicating with a human. Caelfel wondered if she was Feraan's mother and after a moment she realized she had no doubt. Saint Hubertus was Feraan's father. Feraan was half-human and descended from a werewolf hunter.

Despite this revelation, she had no idea where Feraan was. It mattered little, for Madoc undeniable shared the likeness of Hubertus as well. That was Madoc's grandfather, making him also a descendent of a werewolf hunter. So Caelfel could only sit and wait for Madoc to return.

"I couldn't find anything out about Nym," he said, entering the temple some time later and taking a seat next to Caelfel. "All I could find out is that she left some weeks ago on a business contract. Her apprentice wouldn't say much else. He didn't even know when she would return."

"It doesn't matter," Caelfel said quietly. She didn't meet his gaze. "We already have a werewolf hunter."

"Who?" Madoc asked, surprised.

Caelfel turned her head to give him a meaningful look. "You."

"You mean—I *can't* be. Hubertus lived over a five hundred years ago. I'm not that old. He can't be my father."

"No, not your father. Your grandfather."

"Saint Hubertus is my grandfather?" Madoc repeated slowly. Caelfel nodded. "But I know nothing about hunting werewolves," he pointed out.

"That doesn't matter. It's in your blood. You can't fail."

Madoc released a deep breath. "I'm glad there aren't any high expectations of me."

"You won't be alone. You'll have the Company and the King's army. Maybe the werewolves in Haradrop. And you'll have me."

Madoc nodded, feeling more reassured by this. "So, who is my father?" he asked her cautiously.

Caelfel sighed, expecting this. She had no doubt now, and it was only fair if Madoc knew. "His name is Feraan Auvrearaheal, and he lives just outside the city of Sal'Sumarathar in Honey Water. Feraan is five hundred and thirty-six years old. He has a mother named Fawnrial and an evil witch of a sister called Luewyn. He is trained in stealth and tracking and is also a master of forging and magic. He's known by two other names, commonly as the Wandering Elf because he is one of the few elves that frequently leaves the Fey Forest. More recently, he's been known as the most hated elf of the elvish empire."

"That's a dark title to earn."

"He didn't earn it. He saved the elvish people from this mysterious, terrifying magic. In return, he was framed for mass murder and the destruction of a city. He is not bad. He is a very good elf."

"How can he just abandon me and my mother?"

"I don't think he would have if he knew about you. Feraan rarely stays in one place, always wandering. I don't know where he is right now. He wasn't in Honey Water when I went with Brenin."

"You seem to know a lot about him," Madoc observed.

Caelfel didn't blink. "I suppose I would know more about him than anyone else." And she left it at that.

"Well now that we came here for nothing," Forra stated blandly from behind them. "Shall we go to Haradrop now or shall we wait for Cyrus to come along with the army?"

"I believe that we should reach Haradrop first," Madoc decided. "Approaching the fortress with an army might be taken offensively."

Haradrop was another day's walk from Sorasaen and it stood

guard closer to the Pirinac. Caelfel eyed the woods apprehensively, as if Tarion and his pack were hidden just beyond the darkness of the trees.

"How do we know they won't eat us?" Forra asked.

"They won't," Madoc asserted. "They're not feral. Brenin would visit them regularly. They have never hurt anyone."

"That priest seems to think they're responsible for his daughter," Forra pressed.

"I doubt it. People are prejudiced against them for being werewolves. And he's not a priest. He's a temple keeper," Madoc corrected. He turned to Caelfel. "How can you be so sure about my grandfather?"

"Not enough for you to be the grandson of a god?" Forra teased with a light giggle, who had by now picked up on Madoc's true bloodlines.

"He can't be a god," Caelfel argued irritably. "Saint Hubertus was a man that lived centuries ago, immortalized by his massacre and martyrdom. Ólff had a portrait of him in the attic. The likeness was unmistakable," she explained with a relinquishing sigh.

In the late afternoon, Forra dragged behind the length of their long shadows, leaving Madoc and Caelfel relatively alone. He cleared his throat and began a conversation that obviously weighed heavily on his mind. "Caelfel, after Matron Mountain, I must admit, I know very little of you."

"How do you mean?"

"I knew you were brave when you challenged my fa—*King* Orrik. You were kind, especially to Brenin. You bravely confronted Tarion. But you are also angry. When I think of elves, I do not think of them as angry creatures, but upon your return to Honey Water, you possess a rage far more vengeful than Donar's fiery wrath."

She didn't understand the divine reference but continued as though she had. "Do I not have good reason for my rage? My mother was taken from me, as was my prince."

"Your prince?" Madoc repeated.

Caelfel said nothing in response, feeling her face burn from the slip.

"Aside from all that," Madoc continued, ignoring the awkward pause. "You attacked the werebird."

"I pushed her to the ground," Caelfel stipulated quietly. "I didn't *attack* her."

"If I hadn't been there to try to restrain you or if Voten hadn't interrupted, I'm afraid of what you might have done."

"I would not have hurt her," Caelfel asserted. Now, as the walls of Haradrop loomed closer in the crisp air and with a clear mind, Caelfel would never intentionally harm Macha, even if the events she spurred were irreversible to Caelfel's psyche. But in the moment of heated rage, as before, Caelfel could not ascertain what she would be capable of.

"Can you just tell me *why*?" Madoc pleaded with an air of exasperation.

Caelfel pressed her lip into a thin line and drilled her attention ahead of her at the fortress that was rapidly approaching. "Do you want to see it?"

"See what?" Madoc asked.

"My scar," she said through gritted teeth. "I mentioned my scar before. Macha had visited Honey Water, supposedly to offer a warning to your father about a desert army approaching the Fey Forest. The army was after me. Macha knew it, Feraan knew it. They did *nothing*." Her voice had become a hiss, so she cleared her throat before continuing. "The army belonged to this desert prince, Admiral Grimault, and his sorcerer tricked me into leaving the forest, where I was captured. They took me across the desert where they beat me, tortured me, and anything else they wanted." She was growling now, and her palms were shaking.

Madoc softened at this, turning sympathetic. "Caelfel, I had no idea—"

"*It doesn't matter now*," Caelfel spat, blinking back furious tears. "It happened. Nothing can change it now. I know Macha wasn't responsible. She didn't raise a hand against me. But if she had done something other than *smirk* at me with that smug expression, then perhaps I wouldn't have endured it." She stopped walking to raise her shirt up and twist her body around, showing him the ugly brown scar branded there.

Madoc's expression was one of horror. "Not to be insensitive, but what does it say?"

Caelfel roughly pushed her shirt down and continued onward. "It says 'Feraan,' your father's name, as a general reminder of why I was even out in that damned desert."

"Do you blame him?" he asked quietly.

Caelfel gave a derisive laugh. It was an innocent question, one that, oddly enough, no one had bothered asking her, not even herself. She gave it some thought. "At first, I didn't think to blame him. After all, he did ride through the desert, alone, to save me. But the longer I think on it, the more I do." And she left it at that, preferring not to think about anything concerning Feraan. She had only blamed him for breaking her heart, but perhaps he was responsible for far more than that.

Madoc was never given a chance to respond, as they were halted in their steps by a female archer who had an arrow pointed directly at them.

"*Stop!*" the woman called harshly in a thick voice. Caelfel, an experienced archer herself, could determine she was aiming for Madoc first. "What business do you have in Haradrop?" she demanded.

She was dirty, face streaked with dirt and ash, and her dark auburn hair was wild and matted. For clothing, she wore a spare amount of leather. Caelfel took in her rough, brutish appearance and assumed she might have been a werewolf herself. She struggled not to gape at the women's ferocious presence and allowed Madoc to do the diplomatic talking.

"We need to speak to Lycaon," Madoc called back calmly.

"Who does? For what purpose?" the woman pressed, reaffirming her grip on the bow. Forra, who had finally ambled up next to them froze at the sight of the threatening woman.

"They're going to kill us," she whispered to Caelfel, terrified.

"They won't. Hush," Caelfel whispered back.

"Don't you recognize your own prince?" Madoc attempted with a small smile.

The woman did not lower her weapon. "I recognize Prince Brenin as my prince—"

But she was cut off mid-sentence as the heavy wooden doors began to creak open, swinging outwardly. Alarmed, the archeress turned her attention back to the inside of the fort. "No, Geri—*stop her.*"

But *her*, whoever she was, would not be stopped. The doors continued opening, and a sharp voice greeted them before its owner came into view. "Prince Brenin or prince whoever, it's about *time* someone showed up—"

The voice was unmistakable, though she wore her hair differently now, tied up high on her head, revealing the height of her pointed ears. The critical gaze of her bright eyes and the proud cheekbones were the same, as was her dignified gait. She had barely a moment to register Haradrop's visitors before Caelfel rushed her without any regard to the previous tension with the archeress.

"*Garvanna!*"

Garvanna blinked in surprise, having no time to respond to Caelfel who flung her arms around her neck and buried her face against her friend. Garvanna gently patted her on the back a few times before surrendering into Caelfel's embrace entirely. And though Caelfel barely managed to breathe in a series of teary gasps, everything finally felt right in the world, even if just for that singular moment.

***

Brenin wasn't aware of anything other than the cold mud that blanketed his face, where they last left him. He didn't bother moving, barely registering the movements of the werewolves around him. His thoughts were numb, like his damp cheek pressed against the earth.

The voice of Skolt, Tarion's second in command, hovered at the edge of his perception. Brenin barely made out his words, "Tarion's found a buyer."

There was a pause, where Brenin supposed he expected a response. Brenin gave him none.

"The Chancellor missed his chance," Skolt continued. "We've got a princess now. She's to meet us at the Crossroads within three days. Who knows what'll happen to you after that." He let out a guttural chuckle.

Brenin kept his silence, which annoyed Skolt and elicited a hard kick to the ribs.

"Did you hear me?" Skolt growled.

Brenin coughed out a short, "*yes*," tasting blood.

***

What do you think, Lisiek? Gwyndolyn leaned against the open window looking to the east. The Fey Forest was not visible from the Cromlech Palace, but Gwyn imagined the green forest against the distant horizon. She imagined Empress Haelyn about to retire for the evening, perhaps settling in her private chamber with her new husband

236

General Blaes, if they were married by now. The Rite of Consummation crossed through her memory, a ceremonial ritual performed to ensure the fertility of the royal couple. She felt her fingernails digging into her skin as she tensed at the thought.

Lisiek approached her silently, hands clasped behind his back. "Think of what, my princess?"

This Prince of the Vale. Bargaining with werewolves. Am I being foolish? Can werewolves be tamed?

"Anyone can be controlled. Werewolves can be tamed. They and the prince will prove a great asset. You are not being foolish."

Gwyn was not satisfied with his answer. It bore the hollow sounds of a courtier who had been trained his whole life in entertaining and agreeing with powerful nobles. *I do not believe you, Lisiek.*

His face was suddenly before her, eyes burning with fierce earnestness. "Have I given you reason not to believe me?" he asked.

Gwyn watched him evenly, stifling a growing desire in her core. Blaes was all but forgotten now. *No, but I need more than blind support.*

"With the Prince of the Vale, you will effectively control the whole of Umfeld, once King Orrik expires. Getting rid of King Orrik will be no trouble. You have the werewolves. If Tarion betrays you, our force is strong enough to put him down. The volunteer recruits have all but transformed their loyalty and proven their effectiveness. And if Tarion doesn't betray you, he will only add to your strength for your return to Honey Water."

I did not intend to dominate the whole of Ariang'ron. Perhaps I am reaching for too much. I am not one for greed or power.

"It is not greed to make use of the opportunities handed to you. It is the mark of a great leader. You are already powerful. It only makes sense you should be afforded such chances." To emphasize his point, he ran the tip of two fiery fingers down the back of her arm. The touch sent warm quivers reverberating through her chest. She betrayed none of these mounting feelings.

Instead, she nodded. *Round everyone up. We leave in the morning.*

18. Newfound Alliance

Caelfel thought it strange, almost comical, how Garvanna had nestled herself among the werewolves after all this time. As soon as they had embraced, the tension between the werewolves of Haradrop and Caelfel's party vanished. When they had stepped back, Caelfel and the others were invited inside where Garvanna instantly dove into an explanation of her whereabouts since their separation.

As Garvanna told it, after Caelfel had been knocked unconscious by Tarion, Garvanna had enchanted a temporary magical ward around Caelfel before drawing off the werewolf pack and rerouting them to the other side of the forest, effectively saving Caelfel's life. Because she was maintaining the wards around Caelfel, Garvanna couldn't use any magic to defend herself and merely ran as fast as she could for as long she could. She didn't think she would have stopped running, except she had crossed the path of another werewolf pack, the Dirus Clan of Haradrop.

They had intervened on Garvanna's behalf, pushing Tarion's pack deeper into the forest. By the time Garvanna had returned for Caelfel, she had already disappeared—picked up by Brenin and the Company of the Prince, Caelfel explained. After that, Garvanna went to Haradrop with her new companions, although very reluctantly, and was told she would have to wait for Prince Brenin and his Company to make his rounds to Haradrop before she could find out anything for certain. During the time she had waited for Prince Brenin, the Morrígna sisters stopped briefly in Haradrop before reaching Palpses. Garvanna had utilized their services, sending a letter to Caelfel's mother that explained their situation. It was Garvanna's letter that sent Sylaera riding furiously out into the Pirinac to find her daughter, just as Caelfel had suspected from her vision. And since then, Garvanna had waited, rather impatiently, for the arrival of Sylaera, Prince Brenin, or even Caelfel.

Likewise, Caelfel narrated her own adventure, starting when she was found by Prince Brenin and the Company. She told her how she was taken to Palpses where she met the king of Umfeld and the Morrígna sisters and sent her own letter to Sylaera, only to be told at the Festival of Strigi how Tarion had willfully killed her mother in an altercation.

Here, Caelfel had paused, swallowing past the dryness in her throat.

She explained how she had returned home then for Sylaera's funeral, with Prince Brenin in tow, when she met her grandmother Lady Ellissara. Only, on their way back to Umfeld, Tarion had attacked them in Honey Water, capturing Prince Brenin. Caelfel then explained her current mission of getting the prince back, going so far as Matron Mountain for Voten's blessing.

They were inside the walls of Haradrop by now. The two she-elves were oblivious to the crowd forming around them as they caught up with each other. Caelfel watched Garvanna's penetrating eyes flick occasionally to Madoc, and it took a moment for Caelfel to understand why. Garvanna would immediately have spotted Madoc's uncanny resemblance to Feraan, and Garvanna all but hated Feraan. So Caelfel skimmed over the details involving Madoc's paternity and Saint Hubertus for now.

"You're looking for Prince Brenin," Garvanna repeated. "So who is this?" she asked, gesturing to Caelfel's two companions.

Caelfel turned. "This is Madoc, Prince of the Vale and Brenin's older brother. And this is Forra."

Garvanna arched an eyebrow. "Just Forra? No special title or anything?" Caelfel genuinely couldn't tell if Garvanna was being critical or sarcastic.

All the same, Forra swept into a low, gracious bow. "I am Forra of Kierm, a city in Umfang."

"I didn't know you were from Umfang," Caelfel noted quietly.

Forra straightened and gave her a wink. "You never asked," she sighed wistfully.

Caelfel returned her attention to Garvanna, just noticing the two humans behind her. "And who are your companions?"

Garvanna glanced at the ones behind her. For Caelfel and Garvanna, they carried a strong scent of wet pine and dusky fur, unmistakably werewolf. Caelfel had trouble keeping her face neutral and she wondered how Garvanna could tolerate the smell. "This is Aeliria," she said, indicating the archeress that had first confronted them. She turned to the man behind her. "And this is Geri. They're part of the Dirus Clan."

Caelfel tilted her head, puzzling over Garvanna's softened tone, so she looked to Geri who was as tall as Garvanna and twice as thick. His hair and stubble were dark brown, and the pallor of his skin made the scars and grime on his face that much more visible. His eyes were gray and he had a strong nose that dominated most of his face. Caelfel didn't find him particularly attractive.

Caelfel nodded at them all the same. "Pleased to meet you. I'm Caelfel."

"I'm afraid we already know your name," Geri said in a thick, rolling accent that sounded like he was trying to spit from the back of his throat. "Garvanna has not let up about you since she came here."

Aeliria avoided the pleasantries. "You came here for our help?" she said, refocusing their conversation.

"It was Voten's suggestion, really," Madoc said. "We have to fight Tarion."

Aeliria nodded. "We have some experience in that regard. Come in, we should speak to Lycaon."

"Lycaon is here?" Caelfel repeated. She knew this to be true, since he had been mentioned several times already. But she wondered if it was the same Lycaon that went into battle with Feraan over eighty years ago.

"Of course," Aeliria said. "He is our alpha."

The hall inside Haradrop's tower was dark with few windows and torches to guide their path inside. But Garvanna followed Aeliria inside without hesitation, so Caelfel could trust there were no surprise pitfalls or other dangers. Soon the narrow entry hall opened to a wide room with long benches crossing the room, very much like a dining hall. The far end of the room was a raised stone platform that held a humble seat covered with furs, reminiscent of a throne.

An older man stood just below this platform, with his back turned to them. Caelfel could see his long, silver-gray hair and the muscles on his sleeveless arms. He spoke to another man, much taller than anyone else in the room with the same face and hair as Geri, only his hair was longer. Upon their approach, the two men fell silent and turned to greet their guests.

"Lycaon, Freki. This is Forra, Prince Madoc, and Caelfel. They have come for our help," Aeliria introduced.

The older man, Lycaon, directed a quizzical look between them all. "A prince has arrived on my doorstep, accompanied by the famous Caelfel we've been hearing so much about recently. The pleasure is all mine." Despite being the alpha, Lycaon offered them a respectable bow.

Madoc stepped forward. "Master Lycaon, we need your help."

Lycaon held up his hand. "Please, just call me Lycaon."

They explained the situation regarding Brenin and Tarion in brief detail that skimmed over the specifics of the encounter with Voten. Lycaon nodded, not seeming surprised by all of this. He asked minimal questions, listening patiently until their tale ended with a request for his clan's help.

"First, I want it known that we have no affiliation with Tarion's actions. I don't condone it. Werewolves had a bad enough reputation before he started recruiting, and now he's making sure to drive it into the ground."

"Recruiting?" Madoc repeated, picking up on Lycaon's word choice.

The alpha nodded. "We've been watching Tarion's movements for some time, ever since he began settling in the Pirinac Forest. He was quick to draw territory lines and is very determined to claim the forest as his. He brought probably two wolves with him, and then he started travelling, picking up some rogue werewolves we didn't even know existed. I've never been one for openly recruiting anyone to our pack, but I try to make it known that any and all werefolk are welcome here. I suspected he even changed some of his followers.

"Our contact with him has been minimal. We've been given no reason to directly confront him until he attacked someone in Sorasaen about a month ago. Fortunately, Freki happened to be there. After that incident, we started patrolling the borders of the forest. There were scattered reports of other werewolf attacks, but they were too far away for us to reach them. Then, while on patrol, we ran into your friend Garvanna."

"So you know all that he is capable of?" Caelfel asked. "Does that mean you will help us?"

Lycaon inclined his head. "I will help in any way I can. But we need to go over details and what you plan to do exactly."

"We have the army on their way. They are supposed to meet us here in a few days. That includes the Company of the Prince and the king's army, since we have the Horn of Command."

Lycaon nodded at this information. "That's very wise. Combining the king's army with werewolves." Caelfel detected a new hardness to his voice and wondered if Lycaon was being sarcastic. He continued. "I want it known that my family are not to be maltreated, Prince Madoc."

Madoc nodded. "Of course, I will not allow that. I know my brother always tried his best to be good and fair to you. I will do the same."

Aeliria was about to show them to their rooms when Lycaon interrupted one last time. "That reminds me," he said. "We need to sort out one thing."

Although Lycaon was undeniably compassionate in his manner and speech, these new words brought about a new tension in the room. Caelfel waited anxiously to hear what he had to say.

"Since we're going off into battle with you now, we should make something clear. As noble as your pursuit of Prince Brenin is, you must understand he is not our main objective. At the very least, not our only objective. Whatever happens to Brenin, Tarion needs to be put down."

A range of conflicted emotions flickered across Madoc's face. "I agree," he said with a curt nod.

But something in Caelfel inflamed. She had felt assured enough to step back and allow Madoc to take over the battle planning and the diplomacy with Lycaon, but she could not allow her entire, *original* purpose be forgotten in a new alliance. And as the two of them nodded, easily forgetting the plight of Brenin, Caelfel could not allow Brenin to escape their memory. She took a step past Madoc, facing Lycaon herself. The werewolves tensed tangibly as their alpha was approached by a potential threat.

"Brenin will not be forgotten in all this," she swore in a low voice. "I don't care about your reasons, but he is *my* reason." Everyone watched her carefully, but Caelfel kept her eyes on Lycaon.

His face eventually broke out into an easy smile. "Of course,

Caelfel. Prince Brenin will not be forgotten."

Caelfel narrowed her eyes but relented for now. If Garvanna, of all people, trusted these wolves, Caelfel had no reason not to.

"It will interest you to know," Lycaon said, stepping away from Caelfel and facing the rest of them. "That we intercepted one of their messages."

Their eyes widened at this shocking news. "What did it say?" Madoc asked.

"Follow me," Lycaon said, turning.

He led them to an underground dungeon where the stone walls were damp and the packed dirt floor was slick and inclined deeper into the earth. They stopped before a heavy wooden door, illuminated by a single torch with a single open slot at eye level, too small for anything to pass through.

"What is this?" Madoc demanded. "What message are you talking about?"

Lycaon peeked into the room before stepping out of the way. "More of a courier than a message. Take a look for yourself."

Madoc went first, squinting through the darkness. After a moment's examination, he stepped back. "I don't understand."

Caelfel pushed her way to the door and peered through the slot. Though the room was dark, her eyesight allowed her a better glimpse into the cell than a human. She clearly made out the female body sagging against the wall. When she moved, the short hair shifted past her face, and when she blinked, Caelfel could distinctly make out the golden eyes.

"Why do you have her locked up down here?" Caelfel demanded.

"She's a werebird," Lycaon simply explained.

"I already know that," Caelfel snapped.

"If we put her anywhere else, she would just simply fly away."

There was a chilling cackle from the other side of the door. "Like I could fly in this state. This is the *second* time I've been shot down this week."

Caelfel turned back to Lycaon. "You people are werewolves. You should know better than anyone not to incarcerate someone just for being werefolk."

"It's not that," Lycaon said, shaking his head. "Garvanna and Aeliria have seen her flying back and forth from the Pirinac and toward the desert. We fear Tarion is looking to Umfang's army."

"*What?*" Caelfel spat. "Whatever *he's* doing, she's just a messenger."

Lycaon looked at her evenly. "She swallowed whatever letter she was carrying, and she refuses to speak to us."

"Damn right," Anann yelled from the other room. "Especially not after the way you've treated me."

"She doesn't deserve this," Caelfel insisted.

"Don't be naïve," Lycaon said in a hard voice. "Tarion is planning something, and she knows what it is. We've offered to have Garvanna heal her and then release her, but she's refused. The only thing I can do is keep her here, even if I can only delay Tarion. You're welcome to try to get her to talk."

The others began leaving the dungeon, and Caelfel turned back to the door and stared at it for a long moment before speaking. "I'm sorry for what they've done to you. It's wrong, but isn't there anything I can do for you? Just tell them what the letter says, *please.*"

Anann hesitated before speaking in a low, heady voice. "There is nothing you can give me."

"It's the only way they will release you," she pressed.

"*Nothing!*" Anann shrieked in a shrill voice.

Caelfel sighed in defeat and followed the others out of Haradrop's dungeon.

At surface level, Caelfel was properly introduced to Freki, who happened to be the twin brother of Geri. Despite his hulking appearance, Freki's rumbling voice was soft and unusually kind. He kept his pace even with hers as Aeliria showed them their rooms.

"I don't agree with imprisoning the raven girl," he told her. It was impossible for his voice to be quiet. "I'm sorry. I tried arguing with Lycaon, but he didn't listen to me."

Caelfel offered him a small smile. "I appreciate that Freki." He said nothing more, and then Caelfel was pulled away by Garvanna to their room.

When they were alone, Garvanna set her on the bed. She gave Caelfel a stern look. "Now, you have to fill me in on everything. Who is this Prince Brenin?"

"You should know who he is if you've been waiting on him to come to Haradrop," Caelfel pointed out.

"Because he's the prince. After we were separated, they—Geri, Lycaon, and the others—wouldn't let me go back for you. They said

I would be crossing into Tarion's territory and that your only hope was if the Company of the Prince had reached you in time. So I waited for Prince Brenin." She paused. "Even if he is a prince, it doesn't explain your dogged determination to save him. I've never seen you like that with anyone else. Well, maybe except—" But Garvanna clamped her mouth shut before finishing the statement.

But Caelfel reacted indifferently to the reference to Feraan, which was perhaps the wrong thing to do because Garvanna tilted her head curiously.

"So you're completely over Feraan, then? You must really like this prince." Her mouth twitched into the hint of a smirk.

"No," Caelfel defended hastily, but she felt her own face grow red as she denied it. "Brenin was taken when I was supposed to keep him safe. I owe him a life debt."

Garvanna looked unconvinced. "You're supposed to call him *Prince* Brenin, even if you're an elf," she corrected.

Caelfel scowled. "He's never corrected me before. He even told me he didn't like being called that."

"Why do you think that is?" Garvanna asked, tapping her chin in mock puzzlement.

Caelfel gave a disgusted sigh as she relented. "He said that he loved me." She immediately braced herself for Garvanna's disapproval.

But instead, Garvanna looked pleased as she shared a mischievous smile. "A prince is a nice catch. What did you say back?"

At this, Caelfel couldn't look Garvanna in the face. "I said awful things."

Garvanna gave a defeated sigh. "Oh, Caelfel. Was it because of *him*?" She didn't have to elaborate that *him* meant Feraan.

"No," Caelfel mumbled, burying her face in her hands. With Garvanna, Caelfel felt how hard she had been pushing herself to get Brenin back. She was exhausted.

Garvanna would have pressed Caelfel further, but she probably sensed Caelfel's enervation.

Caelfel sighed and decided to turn the subject back to Garvanna. "How is it living with the werewolves?"

Garvanna's body stiffened. "Fine," she answered curtly. "They could improve their manners."

"I'm surprised you've stayed here that long," Caelfel continued.

Garvanna fixed him with a stare. "Bad manners does not mean they make bad company."

Caelfel laughed at her. "Why are you being so secretive? It is obvious you are over Thoroth now."

"Thoroth? I hadn't even thought of him," Garvanna said, her voice growing louder in a moment of self-conscious uncertainty.

"I wouldn't expect you to think of him when you've been so busy with Geri."

It had been a gamble. After all, she had only seen Garvanna interact with him once. But her friend's reaction told it all. *"Geri?"* she repeated in a hiss, her face flushing. "What makes you say that?"

"Garvanna, you can tell me," Caelfel pleaded, scooting closer to take her hands.

Garvanna's blush burned more fiercely. "There is nothing to tell. Nothing has happened."

Caelfel gave her a sympathetic smile, wondering if Geri did not share her attraction. Caelfel would have to investigate later.

Garvanna plowed into another topic. "What's his name—Madoc? Brenin's brother? He looks an awful like Feraan." Her voice sounded suspicious.

"We just discovered Madoc is only Brenin's half-brother. As it turns out, Feraan is his father, which means Madoc isn't really a prince."

Garvanna's eyes widened. "His father? I didn't know Feraan had children."

"I don't think he knows it either." Caelfel's chest tightened uncomfortably and her stomach turned at the thought of Feraan fathering Madoc. "Let's talk about something else."

"What about the other girl with you—Forra? Why is she with you?"

"I saved her from execution. She has been very vocal about her dislike of the king."

"Then why did you save her?" Garvanna asked.

Caelfel's expression hardened. "Because the king is wrong, and she is right. King Orrik wouldn't even save his own son."

Garvanna scowled. "Terrible king or terrible father?"

But Caelfel had no answer for that.

They dragged another cot into Garvanna's room, which, with its lack of windows and cold stone walls and floor, had all the warmth and comfort of a prison cell. Garvanna took the cot, and Caelfel the bed with its scratchy straw mattress. As she tossed and turned beneath the dusty cover, she decided Geri must have a fantastic personality or some other remarkable quality for Garvanna to stay and sleep on this uncomfortable bed for so long.

In the morning, Garvanna had prepared a stone basin of lukewarm water and explained, "They take baths differently in Umfeld."

Caelfel gave a sardonic smile. "I've discovered that."

As Caelfel cleaned herself, Garvanna fetched her some fresh clothes that smelled of pine but were clean, although a bit scratchy. They were made out of wool and fit better than the dress Brenin had commissioned for her, and they provided warmth in the drafty halls of the stone fortress. Then Garvanna took Caelfel to the kitchens for a small breakfast of boiled cabbage and rye bread. Caelfel didn't touch her cabbage, as it had been stewed with bits of sausage which had left a lingering taste. Garvanna explained that werewolves preferred meat, but Caelfel had already deduced that much from general human diet.

They were shortly joined by Geri and Aeliria who took seats next to Garvanna and thus claimed most of her attention. Caelfel was left alone to push cabbage leaves around her pewter plate when Madoc entered the refectory. She waved him down after he took a plate of bread and greasy sausage, and he crossed the room to join them. When Madoc took a seat across Caelfel, she noticed the dark smudges beneath his eyes.

"Sleep well?" she asked.

Madoc frowned, eyes flickering to the others next to them, and gave a subtle shake of his head. He similarly began to pick at his sausage.

Forra arrived last, examining the room in a sweeping gaze before decisively taking her seat between Aeliria and Madoc. She didn't retrieve a plate of food like everyone else.

"You're not eating?" Aeliria observed.

"I rarely eat in the mornings," Forra dismissed with a demure smirk.

Caelfel watched the exchange silently, arching a suspicious eyebrow. She had seen firsthand Forra consuming food at an alarming rate, no matter the time of day.

"Where is Freki?" Garvanna asked, breaking the cadence of her conversation with Geri.

"He's with Reuthe," Geri answered, as if the answer did not interest him. "Where else?"

Caelfel brightened at the name. "Reuthe? She's here?"

Geri and Aeliria looked at Caelfel sharply. "Do you know her?" Geri asked.

Caelfel frowned, annoyed that they turned so suspicious of her. "I know her father. Where is she?"

"I'm not sure if that's a good idea—" Aeliria began, but Geri waved her off, rising.

"I'll show you. You might be able to help her."

"Her father said werewolves took her away," Caelfel said thickly, becoming suspicious herself.

Geri's expression softened. "That's only part of the truth."

Caelfel almost feared that they had stuck Reuthe in some remote cell like Anann. Geri didn't take her to the underground dungeons, but the quarters they kept Reuthe in were not any livelier. Everything was made of stone. Every room was drafty. Caelfel didn't remember seeing a single window since she had entered the fortress. She wondered if this was a general preference of werewolves but couldn't understand how anyone could stand such dark surroundings.

Geri explained that Reuthe had mindlessly entered the Pirinac Forest one day and immediately came across Tarion stealing her family chickens. She confronted him, and he attacked her. Freki happened to be in Sorasaen at the time and rushed to the site of wolf-howling. Tarion had left her alive.

"But?" Caelfel pressed, when Geri's story hung awkwardly in the air.

"He had turned her," Geri said simply.

Caelfel puzzled over the statement for a moment, but then the realization suddenly crashed. Tarion had turned Reuthe into a werewolf.

"So then?" Caelfel asked impatiently.

They stopped before a wooden door, molded from dampness. Caelfel wrinkled her nose at the smell. Geri continued in a low voice. "We had to take her here. Werewolves that are turned are different than werewolves that are born. They respond differently to the change. It disrupts the stability in their bodies. They can't control it. It's like an infection. It burns in them, all the time. They become angry easily, because they *are* angry, every minute of every day. It takes a process of coping. Without a certain degree of training, it can kill them. Or they can become rabid and kill everyone close to them."

Caelfel found some deep part of herself quivering at the unnerving information. "How long has it been since she turned?"

"Almost a month now, maybe not quite. She hasn't hit her first full moon yet, which is tomorrow night. That can be a dangerous time," Geri explained. He offered Caelfel a brief, genuine smile. "She's not dangerous right now."

Caelfel squared her shoulders. "I'm not afraid."

Geri turned away. "Good, because if you were, you are definitely in the wrong place." He pushed the door open, eliciting a loud creak.

Once again, no window adorned the room. Freki had brought a torch with him to visit Reuthe and it rested in the scone against the wall, casting flickering shadows across him and a girl huddled in the corner next to him. Caelfel blink, her vision adjusting to the constant darkness of Haradrop. She saw Reuthe wearing dirty wool clothes with a startling bloodstain on the right shoulder. The dirt and darkness were a stark contrast to her snow-white hair.

She had her knees drawn up to her face, and when she squinted against the light of the hall, she did not look afraid as Caelfel had expected. Her expression denoted weariness. Freki smiled at Caelfel's presence and started to introduce them.

"Reuthe?" Caelfel asked before Freki could speak.

Reuthe's eyes twitched in recognition. She was not suspicious like the others, merely curious. "How do you know my name?" Even her voice wavered with fatigue. Then she shrugged. "I suppose the others told you about me."

"I met your father in Sorasaen," Caelfel explained softly, unsure of what else to say. "He is quite worried about you."

Reuthe was on her feet and stepping towards Caelfel. Her sudden movements made Freki and Geri nervous, as if they thought this tired girl was a volatile force. Caelfel was not afraid. She was the only one that noticed the tears brimming in Reuthe's eyes. "You spoke with him? He is safe?" she pleaded desperately.

Caelfel nodded. "He is safe, only worried."

Reuthe breathed a sigh of relief and flung her arms around Caelfel's neck, grateful for the news. "I was so worried Tarion would go after him," she whispered.

"It's okay," Caelfel reassured the sobbing girl, patting her back. "I'm going to kill Tarion."

Reuthe's grip tightened around Caelfel. "And I'm going to help you," she swore in a whisper. When Reuthe recovered, she stepped back and rubbed at her eyes, smiling.

Caelfel didn't think she looked like a newly changed werewolf struggling to handle her new body. "What are you doing in here?"

"I was told to practice meditating. It would help the changes," she said softly, as if ashamed of admitting her lycanthropy.

"You should come outside," Caelfel suggested with a smile. "It's much brighter out there."

Geri was uneasy with the idea. "Is that a good idea?" he asked, looking to his brother.

Freki shrugged, appearing to like the idea himself. "It'll be better than sitting in here."

Caelfel joyfully led them all outside, stopping briefly to retrieve Madoc and Garvanna from the refectory. The others were content to follow. "Isn't this much better?" Caelfel asked, throwing open the doors to the fortress yard. The morning was crisp and invigorating. She turned to Madoc. "Shouldn't Cyrus be here with the others today?"

Madoc nodded. "Excluding any delays."

Caelfel frowned, hoping with every tendon of her body that Cyrus and the Company had not been delayed. She looked at the collection of mismatched tents inside Haradrop's walls and their inhabitants milling about their chores. Aeliria automatically disconnected from the group to stand guard at the gate's turret, and Forra followed her. Freki took Reuthe for a walk around the walls, and Geri watched them leave apprehensively.

"How many werewolves does Tarion have?" Caelfel asked.

"We've counted ten. It's possible he has fifteen or even more," Geri asked, tearing his attention away from Reuthe and his brother.

"Do you think he has more than twenty?" Caelfel asked.

"I doubt he would have more than fifty," Geri stipulated.

"How many werewolves do you have here?" Madoc asked.

"Eight. Lycaon, Aeliria, Dorth, Jalmar, Wurnsen, Benka, Freki, and myself. There's also Pippi, the werebear."

"What about Reuthe?" Caelfel asked.

Geri blinked. "Nine werewolves, eight of whom can fight."

"Reuthe wants to fight," she told him.

"That's not happening. Reuthe is young, inexperienced, and can't control the change. She'd be of no use to anyone," Geri said stubbornly.

Caelfel rolled her eyes and turned to Madoc. "How large is the Company of the Prince?"

Madoc shrugged. "In Onusal, my Company was two hundred men strong. I'm not sure of Brenin's Company. I would guess anywhere from seventy-five to a hundred men."

"What about the king's army?" Caelfel asked.

"It's hard to say. I don't look at recruitment lists. There's no telling how many of them would follow Cyrus here."

Caelfel thoughtfully chewed on her bottom lip. "Eight werewolves, a werebear, two elves, a werewolf hunter, and an army of at least seventy-five men could take on a pack of twenty werewolves, right?" Caelfel asked.

Madoc and Geri did not look so convinced. Before they could voice their qualms, Lycaon appeared from the tower. "Speaking of this army," he said, approaching them. "We need to discuss their accommodations. If it's not too rude as a host for me to ask, they will need to camp outside Haradrop's walls. We simply don't have the room for an army, not to mention the frayed tempers." When Caelfel gave him a curious look, he explained, "Not many are very receptive to werefolk, particularly if werewolves are causing the trouble in the first place."

"I'm sure that won't be a problem," Caelfel said. She anxiously turned her attention to Aeliria's position at the gate, willing for the army to be marching in the distance. After a moment of staring, she felt Madoc's hand on her shoulder.

"They will come," he assured.

Caelfel struggled to find words that matched or refuted his confidence, so she merely nodded.

***

The Empress Haelyn pinched the bridge of her nose. She had never anticipated that her headache of a daughter would turn out like this, a dangerous traitor that threatened to usurp her throne. Haelyn reflected on their last conversation, wishing she could have altered her words. She had not wanted to hurt her daughter or spur her to this sort of action. But she needed to be firm with her, and as the Council of Elders carefully watched her, Haelyn knew there would be no peaceful outcome with Gwyn. Either her daughter would die or Haelyn herself would.

"Your grace?" Blaes said gently, recalling her attention to their meeting.

She sighed, lowering her hand. "Yes, I know. Gwyn's army has captured the Cromlech outpost and now they're moving."

There was a scoff from Elder Nisseria. "If you call that an army," she muttered.

Haelyn did not have the patience to deal with attitudes of superiority. "Whether or not you feel Gwyn's army is a valid force is irrelevant. Gwyn is powerful enough on her own to be considered as two armies. Plus she has her orbs with her. Whether or not her followers are trained military combatants is of no significance. Gwyndolyn is formidable enough on her own." Haelyn steadied herself. "Do we know where she is headed?"

"It's too early to tell. As far as we can determine, she has not left the desert," Blaes said calmly. "There are also no reports concerning Captain Sanddef and the Volunteer Regiment."

Haelyn's eyebrow twitched. "Is he dead?"

"There is no indication of an execution. We believe that he is still alive, and our source assures us of this," said Elder Ghaenfal, the new imperial general to replace Blaes. Haelyn liked him; she trusted his judgment. But her opinion of him didn't lessen her irritation.

"Are they prisoners? Or have they joined her cause as well?" she snapped.

No one had a straight answer for her. "We do not know anything about their status, Empress," Ghaenfal said apologetically. "Our source has not told us as much."

"Have you finished the interrogations with her guard?" Haelyn asked.

"Yes, we have," Ghaenfal answered. "Our efforts yielded no new information on Gwyndolyn, other than she seems to have been influenced by a certain prisoner in the Labyrinth."

"A prisoner that I am sure is with her now, to barter for his freedom," Haelyn said, clenching her jaw. "So what is our plan?"

The Council of Elders was not a governing body with legislative power like the Senate or High Council. They served as a panel of advisors for Haelyn, handpicked by the Empress for their centuries' worth of experience and wisdom. Unless they held positions of responsibilities outside the Council, like General Ghaenfal and Nisseria, ultimately their opinions mattered very little in the way of actually determining national policy. But in these meetings, Haelyn valued their input, though at this moment, it appeared they had none.

"Our recommendation is to maintain the code of isolation," Elder Nisseria decided.

"Elves have always maintained isolation," Haelyn noted bitterly.

"And has it ever failed us?" Nisseria challenged.

"Have we ever had a threat like Gwyndolyn prowling outside Honey Water? We know she will eventually attack us."

"It's possible that she intends on forming foreign allies," General Ghaenfal suggested.

"Yes," Blaes agreed. "If she wants any hope of challenging us, she'll need to build her own army."

"You're forgetting how powerful she really is," Haelyn said despairingly.

"But her power is not infinite. If she used that much power at once, it would kill her," Blaes ventured quietly. "She would be hesitant to use her power and employ it mostly as a demonstration of authority."

Haelyn nodded, conceding to this argument. "Whatever happens, the Vinius Islands cannot hear of her crusade. There are so many rebels there, that if Gwyn even decided that she needed a naval force, they would support her to the end. We cannot afford to lose the Vinius Islands"

The others murmured in agreement.

"We should continue to keep this matter quiet. I don't want the Senate or the Lesser Councils hearing of her movements. Am I understood, general?"

Ghaenfal nodded. "Of course, your grace."

"For now, we shall watch her closely, strengthen the army. Fortify our defenses. I want a strong naval presence too, just in case she wanders too far out of the desert. She's smart enough to know Vinia would be a good ally. In the meantime, we should do our best to tame the Islands. This includes tax reductions, a smaller militia presence, charity and community events. More public services. I will make a few appearances myself. We can put an emphasis on cultural heritage, make dragon-themed festivals. Turrelia, I hope you are taking notes of this."

Her assistant Turrelia bobbed a curtsy as she continued scribbling away. "We could promote your new marriage," she suggested with unbridled excitement. Haelyn nodded at the idea.

"Your grace," Ghaenfal interjected. "If you want a strong naval presence, how are we to maintain a smaller militia presence in the Islands?"

"Vinius is not our only place with sea access. You can build the navy in Elewyr," she answered.

"How will you inform the Senate?" Nisseria asked.

"I will keep the Senate informed on a situational basis. As far as they're concerned, we're only dealing with a few escaped convicts. They've taken it upon themselves to commission bounty hunters to specifically find the criminals of their region. We can recruit the bounty hunters, if needed, for our services. Otherwise, there's no use in alarming the general public," Haelyn explained.

"You don't think the general public needs to know?" Elder Fawnrial asked skeptically.

Elder Fawnrial used to be a member of the Senate but lost her position centuries ago, disgraced from her interracial companionship. Haelyn had then appointed her as an advisor, having always valued her typically unbiased opinion. She had a keen intellect and perspective that could sometimes be considered as otherworldly as it was useful. Haelyn looked at her old friend with a steady gaze. "It does not concern the general public."

"Yet," Fawnrial stipulated.

"Yet," Empress Haelyn agreed.

Blaes cleared his throat, a sign he was preparing to announce an unpopular idea. "Your grace might want to consider enlisting the help of foreign entities."

As to be expected, silence took hold of the room. In Nisseria, it was accompanied with wave of condescending rage. "We do not need the help of humans or other lesser beings," she spat angrily.

"Calm yourself, Nisseria," came Fawnrial's soothing voice.

"I will not," Nisseria hissed. "If we do not want to become extinct, we will need keep all affairs domestic." She turned towards Fawnrial in a vengeful wrath. "Not every elf is a promiscuous slut like you."

Haelyn knew that Nisseria's prejudice against humans stemmed from the death of her father. When the elves had last allied themselves with humans a thousand years ago in the Reign of Firescales, a lot of elves had died. It perpetuated the code of isolation and a general distrust of anything mortal.

Fawnrial serenely ignored the slight. "You might find that Gwyn can win this war with the aid of humans."

"*Please*," Haelyn pleaded. "Do not give validity to her cause by calling it a war. This is nothing more than an insurrection."

Fawnrial inclined her head. "Certainly, your majesty."

When no one offered anything else in the way of helpful information, Haelyn adjourned the meeting, asking Ghaenfal to return later that evening in order to review battle plans. Soon, she was left alone with Blaes, her new husband.

In light of the events surrounding Gwyndolyn, Haelyn had been forced to keep the wedding a simple, private affair. But the cities celebrated the union for days, holding contests and feasts to observe its sanctity. It was supposed to be a wondrous affair after all; the empress finally had a legitimate marriage to produce legitimate heirs.

Haelyn looked at her husband with the weariness and strain Gwyn had placed upon her since her insurgence. Blaes quietly took her hand. "I know," he said. "There's nothing you could have done."

"I don't believe that," Haelyn admitted quietly.

"Then what will you believe?" Blaes asked patiently.

"That my daughter is willfully unstable and makes her own decisions."

"You already know that to be true," Blaes pointed out. "You would not say it otherwise."

Empress Haelyn only frowned as she considered the very real possibility of going to war against her own daughter.

19. Preliminary

It was around midday when Aeliria announced the army approaching from the southwest. Caelfel ran to greet them, abruptly interrupting her conversation with Garvanna to do so. Madoc followed close at her heels. She didn't stop until she had opened the gate and saw the men marching their way. Caelfel was stunned speechless for a moment by their numbers.

"That should be enough to take on Tarion," Madoc said, voicing her thoughts.

With Cyrus leading the way, the Company of the Prince had certainly arrived. Caelfel recognized Huwel among the faces as well as a few others. They were joined by another force, an army of men wearing silver-plated armor that glinted in the afternoon sun. The King's Men.

"And if it's not, then Tarion simply cannot be stopped," Caelfel commented. She felt a surge of pride expanding her chest as she watched the soldiers drawing closer.

"You'll have to stop them before they come to the gate," Aeliria called down to them.

Caelfel tilted her head up. "Why?"

"Lycaon says they're not staying inside the fortress. I don't want any disagreements outside of our door when there are so many of them."

"Of *them?*" Caelfel repeated. "They're people, just like you. We're fighting on the same side."

Aeliria fidgeted, as if uncomfortable with Caelfel's words. "All the same. They need to be told."

With Madoc following her, Caelfel ran to meet Cyrus and noticed he proudly wore the Horn of Command with the leather strap over his shoulder. He waved her down when he noticed her running. "Caelfel! Prince Madoc!"

She imagined Madoc cringing at the title as she remembered Madoc hadn't told Cyrus of his parentage just yet. She pushed those thoughts from her mind as she reached Cyrus breathlessly. "You got the Company," she noted.

Cyrus stopped, and the rows of soldiers followed suit. Cyrus was beaming. "The Company *and* the army." He paused for emphasis, quite proud of himself. "*And* the werewolf hunter."

Caelfel hesitated at this. "Werewolf hunter?" she repeated.

"But first—you remember Huwel and Edilon. And here is Melker, Turre, and Lovas." Cyrus gestured to the first line of men directly behind him. Caelfel acknowledged them with a smile. She remembered them all but was preoccupied by something else Cyrus had said.

"What do you mean the werewolf hunter?" Caelfel pressed.

Cyrus looked behind him, motioning for someone from the throng of men to come forward. "She was at Fort Wymdall. You might know her; she's an elf."

But as the she-elf stepped forward, Caelfel immediately knew that she did not know her. The thick locks of black hair and dusky olive skin were foreign to Caelfel. Even her pointed ears were tilted in an unfamiliar manner. Despite this, Caelfel still thought she could guess her name.

"Her name is Nymaaria," Cyrus introduced.

"Just Nym," the she-elf corrected in husky voice before quickly adding, "please."

Caelfel looked Nym over, trying not to be critical. Her left leg just below the knee had been replaced with a metallic instrument of silver luster. Her eyes were dark brown, and she wore loose, earthy colored clothes. She carried a single sack on her back with a silver shield, and her neck was adorned with silver jewelry.

"I've heard of you," Caelfel said, holding out her hand. "My name is Caelfel."

"Pleasure," Nym said brusquely.

"Are you from Honey Water?"

"No," Nym answered simply, refusing to elaborate.

"The Vinius Islands, perhaps?" Caelfel pressed, keeping her impatience in check.

Nym's head tilted as she shrugged. "I've never been there. I've lived in Sorasaen my entire life."

"Are you even a wood elf?" Caelfel pressed.

"Caelfel," Cyrus interjected. "I don't mean to interrupt, but perhaps you can have this conversation another time. Were you able to recruit Lycaon and the others from Haradrop?"

Madoc answered, "Yes, the other werewolves are willing to help us."

"Only, Lycaon says there isn't enough room to keep the army. He says you'll have to camp outside the walls of Haradrop," Caelfel supplied. Something in her chest tensed as she waited for their reaction.

But the others seemed to prefer this arrangement. They nodded to each other easily. "That suits us well enough," Huwel said.

Caelfel breathed a sigh of relief. "Have everyone set up camp. We'll discuss our battle plans later."

Cyrus nodded at this and turned to give the orders to the rest of the men as Caelfel and Madoc turned back to Haradrop. They were silent, and Caelfel pondered over Nymaaria and her mysterious origins. When Aeliria had opened the gates for them, Caelfel immediately searched for Garvanna to tell her.

"A werewolf hunter?" Garvanna repeated. "With one leg? How does an elf live in Sorasaen her entire life and earn that title?"

Caelfel had no answers for her, and Garvanna provided little suggestions.

"You don't think she would try to kill the werewolves in Haradrop?" Garvanna asked suddenly, sounding panicked.

Caelfel hadn't considered this predicament. "I doubt it. She knows why we're here and who we're after." Garvanna's frown remained dubious, so Caelfel added, "I'll talk to her myself about it later."

Garvanna nodded. "We should decide roles before meeting the army."

"What do you mean?" Caelfel asked.

Garvanna looked around uneasily. "I expect a power struggle. Geri and the others, they've been mostly self-sufficient here in Haradrop. They won't want some other military official commanding them. We need someone to bridge the two groups. Werewolves and humans."

Caelfel nodded, her eyes scanning the happenings of Haradrop. She saw Madoc in the distance sharpening his greatsword with a grim expression. She had seen him carry his sword on his back since they left Palpses, but luckily, he hadn't had to use it. Caelfel though Madoc could be the mediator between humans and werewolves, so she offered that idea to Garvanna.

Frowning, Garvanna said, "I think it should be you."

Caelfel turned to her friend, shocked. "*Me?*"

Garvanna fixed Caelfel with an unflinching gaze. "You have connections to both. The Umfeld army trusts you. Lycaon trusts you. But most importantly, Prince Brenin trusted you, and they all trusted him. I think it's what he would have wanted. And that's most important right now."

Caelfel's surroundings paled around her as she thought of the daunting task. "I can't command armies into battle," she said breathlessly.

"Why not?" Garvanna snapped. "You are a warrior, and they all look up to you. That's all that matters."

"You don't think it matters that I could lead them all to their death?" Caelfel asked, her stomach suddenly turning with anxiety.

"Get ahold of yourself," Garvanna hissed. Then more warmly, "I'm not saying you're a seasoned war veteran or that you don't make stupid decisions sometimes, *but*—" Garvanna paused here for emphasis. "But you care about people, no matter who they are. In the end, you'll do what's best for them."

"Madoc's capable of doing the same thing," Caelfel countered lamely, watching him from the distance as he continued tending to his sword.

"Maybe you're right," Garvanna mused, following Caelfel's gaze. "But when things get going, tempers are going to rise. Madoc will look after the interest of his own people. Madoc is biased."

"And I'm not?" Caelfel asked shrewdly.

Garvanna shrugged a single shoulder. "Madoc is moreso. After all, who made the decision to rescue Forra? From what you told me, it wasn't Madoc."

Caelfel supposed she should have felt proud that Garvanna held so much conviction and faith in her abilities. But the pit in Caelfel's center gnawed at her with a hollow insecurity. "You are quite confident in me," Caelfel noted. "I don't think you've ever been this supportive of me."

Garvanna chuckled and playfully nudged Caelfel with her elbow. "I hope this isn't too sentimental of me to say, but I think of you as my own sister."

"Sister?" Caelfel repeated, distracted by the idea.

Garvanna hesitated. "I don't think *friend* adequately describes our relationship. I feel as close to you as I did with any of my sisters. I'd want nothing more from you than to make sure you're safe. It's why I stayed in Haradrop for so long. It was the only way I knew to find you."

"Sisters," Caelfel repeated again, her mind furiously working at the idea.

Garvanna detected Caelfel's distracted thoughts. "Caelfel?"

But Caelfel barely heard her. She took off running inside Haradrop. Garvanna followed her without question. Some of the wolves gave them odd looks, particularly when they headed in the direction of the underground dungeons, but Caelfel ignored them. She had an idea and peered into Anann's cell once she reached it. The werebird didn't look like she had moved.

"Anann?" Caelfel whispered into the darkness.

She heard chains brush against stone and saw the shadow of Anann's face shifting.

Caelfel looked back to Garvanna who waited silently behind her. "Can you give us some light?"

In that instant, Garvanna produced an orb of golden light, and it illuminated the dungeons in soft beams. Anann was blinking at them malevolently from her cell.

"Nothing's changed," Anann said shortly. "I'm not going to tell you anything."

"Yes, because you said we didn't have anything you wanted. I think you're wrong. I think I do have something you would like, some information."

This piqued Anann's interest. "I doubt it, but I'm listening."

"I know where your sister is," Caelfel said excitedly, pressing her face against the cold bars of the door.

Anann waited a full heartbeat before giving a short laugh. "I know where Badb is too, someplace on her way to Umfang."

"Not Badb. Macha. I know where Macha is."

Another heartbeat passed when Anann was suddenly on her feet, chains rattling as she approached the door. Caelfel saw the dried blood on her injured arm. "You're lying!" she screeched.

Caelfel shook her head. "This is no lie. I give you my word."

"Then where is she?" Anann demanded.

Garvanna intervened, pushing her way past Caelfel. "First, tell us the message you were delivering."

Anann calculated the situation before her. "And in exchange, you'll tell me where my sister is, heal me, and release me, correct? All of those things?"

Caelfel nodded. "Yes, all of those things."

"How many of you are out there?"

"It's just Garvanna and me. Garvanna will be able to heal you."

"Lycaon is the one with the keys," she pointed out.

"We'll make sure you're released—"

"Then tell me where Macha is. You can let me out after I've told you the message, but I don't have any other bargaining ability outside of that."

Caelfel sighed, stealing a disapproving glance from Garvanna. "She's on Matron Mountain, at Voten's Cave."

"Matron Mountain?" Anann repeated. "What is she doing there?"

"It doesn't matter," Garvanna said harshly. "What did the letter say?"

Anann examined the two of them for a minute before finally relinquishing the information. "Tarion has been corresponding with an army in the desert. They were going to meet up at the Crossroads Village, where Tarion was going to trade the Prince of the Vale in exchange for reinforcements, legitimizing his claim over the land."

Caelfel remembered the Crossroads Village. She and Brenin had passed through there on their way back to Honey Water. Winwaloe had been there.

"An army in the desert?" Garvanna asked. "What army?" She looked to Caelfel in confusion.

But Caelfel's stomach plummeted, and something tightened in her chest. She found herself unable to breathe as she processed what Anann was saying. She forced a question out through her thick throat. "Have they made the trade yet?"

Anann shook her head. "Not yet. It was arranged for the day after tomorrow. I suspect Tarion will be leaving in the morning, if not tonight."

Caelfel turned to Garvanna, feeling desperate and wild in her panic. "We need to tell them."

"What about me?" Anann demanded shrilly.

"We'll go speak to Lycaon and get the keys. We'll come back," Caelfel called back, already running out of the underground prison.

They found him outside, drilling the other werewolves on manners and strategy. When she reached him, Caelfel didn't wait to inform him of her new discovery, breathless from exhilaration.

"Tarion's meeting an army from Umfang," Caelfel said all at once.

Garvanna had finally caught up to them.

Lycaon's bushy eyebrows knotted. "How do you know this?"

"Anann the werebird told us. She revealed the contents of her letter."

Lycaon tensed, and Geri was suddenly at his side. "Where is she now?" Lycaon demanded.

"She's still in her cell. We promised to set her free," Caelfel reminded.

"And you trust her word on that?" he asked.

"Yes," Caelfel answered severely.

Lycaon gave a single, curt nod. He and Geri took off for Haradrop's dungeons.

Caelfel called him back. "Lycaon, if Tarion is meeting this army tomorrow, his pack might leave tonight."

They shared a gaze of understanding before rushing off to investigate Anann's claims. To Caelfel's surprise, when they reached the dungeon, Lycaon unlocked Anann's door. "Garvanna, heal her, please."

Garvanna nodded and proceeded inside the room silently. Garvanna's aura activated as she worked her magic over Anann. The soft glow of it bathed the room in golden light, highlighting Anann's stark pallor. When Garvanna had finished healing her, she summoned an orb of yellow light to continue illuminating the room.

Lycaon kept the door open as he questioned Anann. "Who is leading this army?"

Anann stretched her newly recovered arm. "It was an elvish army, led by humans. Princess Gwyndolyn and her steward."

"Gwyndolyn?" Caelfel repeated. Garvanna shook her head, arching a puzzled eyebrow. "You don't remember? She helped clear my and Thoroth's name. She was at the Spring Festival."

A flicker of recognition brightened Garvanna's features. "What is she doing with an army from Umfang?"

"I *just* said," Anann interrupted impatiently. "It's not an army from Umfang. It's an army of elves. They were at the Cromlech Fortress."

"Cromlech?" Caelfel sagged against the wall, groping for support. "Why are they coming here?"

"I already told you. They're after the Prince of the Vale."

"But *why* are they after Brenin?"

Anann shrugged. "I didn't think to ask."

"It doesn't matter," Lycaon said in a voice ending the discussion. "Elves are coming to Umfeld with the intent to kidnap the prince."

"They don't represent Honey Water or us," Caelfel quickly defended. But she thought of Winwaloe and Fódla and wondered what had happened with them and Gwyndolyn.

"It matters little. We will have to meet Tarion before he trades the prince. Then we will have to meet this other army. Caelfel, you'll need to get Madoc and speak to the king's army. See when they can be ready. We will have to attack tonight."

Caelfel started to leave when Lycaon called her back.

"Best not to tell them the army from Umfang is one of elves, for your sake, Caelfel, and Garvanna's."

"I understand," Caelfel said gravely before going to find Madoc.

***

He had successfully infiltrated the Cromlech Fortress just as the inhabitants were preparing to leave. He went unnoticed as he explored the cavernous rooms of the palace, until at last he came upon the abandoned west wing.

This was his third time in Cromlech but his first time in the west wing. Each visit had offered no small degree of unpleasantness, each visit requiring some death or another. The dark magic humming within the walls of the west wing promised a visit like the others.

The source of this magic sat forgotten in the corner of a cold bedchamber. He picked up the enchanted hood, once belonging to a servant of the Blind Seer, and donned it, pulling it over his head and completely concealing his recognizable features.

Then, he left the west wing and headed for Umfeld, disguised as a member of Gwyndolyn's army.

***

Madoc, having finished sharpening his sword, remained sitting where Caelfel had last seen him. His eyes were glazed over as if in some numb stupor. His face cleared when Caelfel updated him on the current status of things.

"Why would an army from Umfang want my brother?" he asked.

Caelfel shook her head, not bothering to point out it was Brenin's association with princedom and not his status as Madoc's brother that made him valuable.

Madoc released a weary sigh. "Let's go find Cyrus."

Outside Haradrop, a Commander's tent had already been erected. The flaps were open, allowing Caelfel to see Cyrus and another man inside. Caelfel entered without invitation.

"Cyrus—" she began before being immediately cut off.

"Caelfel, this is Commander Joen of the King's Army," Cyrus introduced hastily, to get the formalities out of the way.

Caelfel turned to the second man and inclined her head slightly in an acknowledged courtesy. He wore the metal plated armor like the other soldiers of the King's Army. An angled strut decorated his helmet.

"Commander Joen, this is Caelfel, the one responsible for bringing us together."

Commander Joen offered no similar sign of mutual respect. His expression remained unimpressed, and Caelfel wondered if he'd prefer not to be there. Her eyes flitted to Madoc beside her who ducked his head and did not introduce himself as a prince of Umfeld.

"Do you bring us news, Caelfel?" Cyrus prompted when no one said anything.

"Tycaon wants to know when the army can be ready to mobilize. We need to attack Tarion tonight."

"I did not realize," Commander Joen said in a monotone voice. "That a werewolf made decisions for everyone."

His arrogance made Caelfel's temper flare, and she struggled to keep it in check as she addressed the commander. "We've received new intelligence. Tarion intends to take Prince Brenin and trade him to an army from Umfang."

"An Umfang army?" Commander Joen. His interest sounded minimally piqued. "Does Umfang intend to start a war with Umfeld?"

"I don't think this is part of Umfang's army," Caelfel said delicately, choosing her words with care. "It sounds like an independent army from the desert that only wants to legitimize their power with the prince."

Commander Joen analyzed her, and though he did not look convinced by her story, he nodded. "Very well. Where is this meeting supposed to take place?"

"The trade is supposed to be made at the Crossroads Village," Caelfel answered, relieved Joen did not put up further argument.

"It seems that the most appropriate course of action would be for the Company to meet Tarion at the Pirinac, while the King's Men will go to the Crossroads Village and meet that army there," Commander Joen decided. He buckled his sword on his belt and began making his way out of the commanding tent.

"Wait—*no*! Lycaon says we should meet Tarion before they make the trade," Caelfel said, blocking his path.

"Werewolves do not command the King's Army. I do," Commander Joen said shortly.

Caelfel clenched her jaw in frustration. "But Tarion is the one that has Brenin. We have to save Brenin."

"There are bigger things at play than *Prince* Brenin," Commander Joen said. "Rescuing Brenin will mean nothing if there is an army at our border, especially if they do not get what they came for." He sidestepped Caelfel and ducked outside. Caelfel relentlessly followed him.

"We won't be able to defeat Tarion on our own," Caelfel shouted at his back. "If you go to meet that army, it will mean nothing if Tarion gives them Prince Brenin anyway."

"I do not take orders from some she-elf girl," Commander Joen said over his shoulder. Caelfel stopped, and he disappeared in the sea of tents.

She angrily turned to Madoc. "*Do something!*" she shrieked desperately. "Don't you want to save your brother?"

"What am I supposed to do?" Madoc asked. Caelfel noticed at once that any sort of fire or fight in Madoc had left him completely. He did not feel her wild desperation. Madoc had been replaced by a shell.

"You are their prince. He will listen to your command."

Madoc's jaw clenched tautly, and he appeared angry. "I am not their prince," was his muted conviction.

"They still believe you are," Caelfel pointed out.

But Madoc was shaking his head. "I will not continue to lie to them. Besides, Commander Joen has a point. If the army from Umfang comes before we or Tarion can meet them, who knows what they are capable of? The King's Army can be there to at least absorb the brunt of their force."

"This is all depending upon if Haradrop and the Company can defeat Tarion on our own, supposing you're even willing to fight against them," Caelfel spat maliciously.

Cyrus had joined them outside when Madoc turned to her incredulously. "Caelfel, don't say that," Madoc pleaded quietly. Perhaps if he had been more assertive in his request, Caelfel would have complied and left the argument at that. But he had been reduced to that of whimpering infant, and Caelfel would tolerate it no longer. "You can continue to moan and feel sorry for yourself but you'll be no use to us the way you are when we meet Tarion in battle. At least some of us still care for Brenin's safety."

Cyrus appeared nervous at their confrontation, and Madoc's face turned thunderous in mere seconds. "I am not the one that lost him to Tarion in the first place."

This only angered Caelfel more, and her ice-like gaze met Madoc's evenly. "Go with Commander Joen, then. See how it will help Brenin. I don't need your help."

And with that, she ran back to Haradrop to report the news to the others.

To her irritation, Lycaon was not as against Commander Joen's plan as she might have liked. He even agreed with it. When Cyrus and Commander Joen entered Haradrop to discuss the plan, they cemented their strategies into reality. Already, over half the men Cyrus had brought from Fort Wymdall were preparing to leave for the

Crossroads Village that night. Meanwhile, the werewolves of Haradrop and the Company of the Prince were preparing themselves for the battle that would take place at dusk.

Cyrus suggested that the Haradrop werewolves wear something to distinguish themselves from Tarion's pack. Lycaon agreed and told them everyone from Haradrop would be wearing something red, like scarves. While these negotiations were taking place, Caelfel scowled in the corner where Garvanna joined her.

"You should not be so angry. We will be taking Brenin back, *tonight*."

"Maybe," Caelfel said shortly.

Garvanna gave a noise of disgust. "Typical youngling behavior. Pouting because you don't get your way. What is wrong with you?"

Caelfel sighed and admitted a weakness she could not reveal to anyone but Garvanna. "I don't want to take chances. I don't want Brenin to die, especially if it's my fault."

"It's not your fault," Garvanna said in a softer tone. "Were it not for you, these armies wouldn't be here to fight for him. We'll get him back," she promised.

Then Caelfel heard Cyrus's voice among the babble the others. "I think Nymaaria should come with us," he said. "Since werewolves are her specialty."

"How many times do I have to ask," Nym said, entering the room half an hour late. "Just call me Nym."

Lycaon tensed in her presence. "Who is this?"

Nym approached their conference table. "The name's Nym, master smith and expert werewolf hunter." She leaned across the table toward Lycaon, and though he looked as if he wanted to, he didn't draw back. "It's a pleasure to meet you, alpha."

Lycaon's eyes went to the metal instrument that replaced her left leg. "What happened there?" he asked crudely.

Caelfel felt her mouth gaping at Lycaon's rudeness, but Nym only smirked, tilting her head. "It's the reason why I became a werewolf hunter. Can I ask, as an alpha, do you find yourself exhibiting symptoms of an allergy to silver like the others in your pack?"

Lycaon scoffed. "Planning to kill me later?" he asked.

"Not at the moment. I've never gone against an alpha. The information might help against Tarion. Besides, I don't kill werewolves unless they've given me good reason." She withdrew from the table and elected to lean against the back wall.

Madoc finally weighed in on the conversation. "Since werewolves display a weakness to silver, the soldiers should be equipped with silver instruments," he proposed.

"Too expensive and time consuming," Commander Joen dismissed. "Not to mention, offensive to our Haradrop hosts. Just advise them on the advantage, should any of them possess some silver."

"So," Lycaon said, clearing his throat. "We will attack Tarion in the Pirinac Forest. You don't think we should wait until after they've left the forest?"

Commander Joen shook his head. "You will attack them in their nest. It will take them by surprise, hopefully scatter them in confusion."

"They will smell us once we cross their territory lines. Werewolves are rather particular about that," Lycaon pointed out.

"Pray that the wind blows in your favor. Can't risk them leaving the forest with the prince, they could scatter anywhere. Once you've secured Prince Brenin and eliminated Tarion, you will make your way to rejoin us at the Crossroads Village. Am I clear?"

"Of course, commander," Lycaon said curtly.

"We will hold off the Umfang army until you arrive. Hopefully the prince will be in a condition to negotiate, draw up some treaty lines, at least until the king arrives."

Caelfel felt an outburst forming in her chest at the mention of the king, but with a nudge from Garvanna, she remained silent.

The meeting ended then, with Commander Joen and Lycaon instantly parting ways to prepare their armies. With them gone, Caelfel approached Nym who smiled at her. "You have questions," she easily surmised.

"You're not a wood elf, are you?" Caelfel began, repeating her query from earlier.

Nym gave a casual shrug. "I don't think so."

"You've lived in Umfeld your entire life? Who are you parents?" Garvanna asked, joining Caelfel.

"I never knew my mother. My father was Vulcaan of Sorasaen. A human blacksmith," Nym explained.

"Your real father?" Caelfel asked, wondering if Nym could be half human.

Again a casual shrug. "The only one I've known. He never told me otherwise."

"How old are you?" Garvanna asked.

"About a thousand."

This deeply surprised Caelfel. She imagined a she-elf living among humans for a thousand years would have garnered much more of reputation. That, and she looked nothing like the greylings from back home. "You don't look like a greyling," Caelfel said. Garvanna gave her an accusing look, and Caelfel wondered if that was rude.

"Greyling?" Nym repeated, puzzled. "I have never heard that word."

Before Caelfel could blunder into a conversation that was unintentionally offensive, Garvanna suggested, "You should meet the others, so they do not become so suspicious of you."

The other werewolves were enjoying a quick meal in the refectory. When Caelfel and her companions found them, they had pushed their plates aside and were engaging in games of arm-wrestling. Caelfel watched Freki taking on his brother Geri and then promptly triumphing over him. Reuthe sat by his elbow, cheering him on. Caelfel found herself smiling at the scene.

"Your friends are loud," Nym observed.

"This is their favorite pastime, in human form," Garvanna explained. By then, Aeliria, Freki, Geri, and Forra had noticed them standing at the doorway and beckoned them over. Quick introductions were made for Cyrus and Nym. Only Aeliria and Geri narrowed their eyes suspiciously at the werewolf hunter who still wore her silver shield on her back.

"Never expected to have the werewolf hunter sitting at our table," Geri remarked, as Nym took a seat with Caelfel and Garvanna.

"I never expected to be granted the opportunity to grace your table with my presence. Don't worry, I'll be on my best behavior," Nym said with a sly wink.

"Caelfel," Garvanna said suddenly. "You should arm-wrestle Freki."

Caelfel looked uneasily at the hulking girth of the werewolf beside her. "I think I'd rather train with Nym," she said, thinking she needed some experience before facing Tarion.

"You'll have plenty of time to kill werewolves tonight," Garvanna said. "Arm-wrestle Freki, now. I've beaten them all in arm-wrestling except Freki. They don't believe me that you're stronger than me."

Geri laughed. "She is smaller than you. How can she be stronger?" he asked.

Garvanna smirked. "You should learn a few things of elvish superiority. Come Caelfel, show them."

Caelfel reluctantly clasped Freki's hand, not understanding their fascination in the sport. Freki smiled at her, confident in his own strength.

"Ready?" he asked in his deep, rumbling voice.

"Are you?" Caelfel countered, feeling herself become poised.

Geri counted them down to three, and Caelfel braced herself. She felt Freki's push everything against her arm, but she didn't budge. A few minutes passed without movement from either of them as everyone loudly encouraged them. Caelfel knew she was stronger than Freki, but he still put forth a valiant effort.

Then Caelfel pushed against Freki's hand, and slammed his arm back against the table, much to the cheering of Garvanna and Reuthe. Geri didn't accept the outcome.

"How can that be?" he asked.

"Because," Garvanna said grinning, clapping Caelfel on the back. "She is a daughter of Sal'Sumarathar, a direct descendent of Ewyn. She is stronger than most elves."

Caelfel turned her stunned gaze to Garvanna, wondering how she knew that when they were interrupted by Lycaon's entrance in the refectory. "Why are you all still sitting around?" he asked, a slight edge of teasing in his voice. "We should be leaving right now."

Immediately everyone was on their feet and filing out of the room. Lycaon placed a hand on Caelfel's shoulder, and she watched as everyone left them alone.

"Nym, you can stay too."

Intrigued, Nym fell back to join the two of them. When the three of them were completely alone, Lycaon went to the hearth and began throwing sand on it to extinguish the embers. Caelfel approached him. "What is it?"

"We're attacking Tarion tonight," he said gravely. His voice had the weariness that reminded her of the smoky voice of her own father.

"That's what we want, isn't it?" Caelfel asked tentatively.

"Of course," Lycaon said, facing her. "But you need to be prepared."

Caelfel gave him a quizzical expression. From the corner of her eye, she saw Nym reclining on one of the wooden benches. "I don't see why I'm still here," she said in a bored voice.

"Because as a werewolf hunter, you might find this information beneficial. It's about the change of a werewolf."

Lycaon didn't break his gaze with Caelfel. Nym straightened as she paid close attention.

"There are two types of werewolves. Those that are born were, and there are those who are infected with the change. When you meet a werewolf, it is typically one who was born that way. I was born a werewolf, as were Geri, Freki, Aeliria. Benka, Dorth, and Jalmer too. Wurnsen and Reuthe are the only ones here that weren't born as a werewolf.

"The transformations are controlled. The person decides when to become wolf and when to become human. The only exception is when they are turned."

"Turned?" Caelfel repeated.

"Infected with the beastblood, by another werewolf," Lycaon clarified. "When someone is changed, they will immediately experience the change in that moment. It'll last for however long their energy can sustain them, usually a night. Changed werewolves usually experience another involuntary change on their first full moon, that is, if they survive that long and haven't been able to control it. Reuthe has had great support. She seems to really have a handle over her new abilities. Wurnsen wasn't like that when he came to us. He was more affected by the beastblood. We managed to find him before his first full moon, and he's made great progress since then."

"Why are you telling me this?" Caelfel asked distantly.

"I am preparing you," he repeated. "When a person is changed, it is traumatic. You need to know that when you search for Brenin."

"What are you suggesting?" Caelfel hissed with clenched teeth.

"It is hardly an illogical outcome. Look at what Tarion did to Reuthe, just for walking ten feet in the forest. If Tarion feels cornered in our attack, he might resort to desperate actions."

"I won't let it happen," Caelfel swore in a thick voice.

Lycaon looked as if he wanted to argue, but stoic, calculating Nym stepped up to him with a question of her own. "What happens when a person is first changed? They can't control it, but what do they *do?*"

Caelfel turned her back with every intention of leaving the room, but something tethered her in place. She needed to hear Lycaon's answer.

It came shortly. "He would become a mindless beast in that change, with nothing but bloodlust on the mind. He could not be reasoned with but would have every intention to kill you."

20. First Assault

Caelfel prepared herself. Her hair was tied in a braid close to her scalp, and she dressed herself in the same leather armor she wore in the Desert Conflict when she had been kidnapped by Admiral Grimault's army. She took her bow and a quiver of arrows Geri gave her, but she thought her primary weapon would be the slightly curved shortsword she had brought with her from Honey Water and added to her belt.

Forra wasn't a warrior, but although Geri suggested she stay behind in the Company's camp, she had insisted on accompanying them, at least as far as the forest. Cyrus hadn't been trained as a warrior either, but he was determined to save his prince. He assured Caelfel that he did have experience in swordplay, as he was the one that taught Brenin what he knew.

The werewolves didn't travel with weapons or armor. Rather, they wore minimal clothing, including the red scarves Lycaon instructed all of them to tie around their necks. They led the way to the Pirinac and the Company of the Prince marched behind them.

Geri had put up some resistance to Reuthe going with them, but Lycaon had silenced his arguments, leaving it to Reuthe to make the decision. And Reuthe's choice was ultimately to join them. She walked beside Freki, their hands clasped in what Caelfel decided was an endearing manner. But then Caelfel's stomach twisted with jealousy and she quickly looked away.

Before reaching the trees, Lycaon stopped their convoy. "There are nine werewolves. You should choose nine of your best people to ride us."

"Ride you?" Caelfel asked, assuming that riding a werewolf would be considered rude or a form of enslavement.

Lycaon nodded, though none of the other werewolves appeared fond of the idea. "Werewolves are faster than humans. We'll reach them before you do on foot."

"Nine werewolves against twenty or so?" Caelfel asked, her previous certainty draining.

"Those with horses can follow us in," he said, but not many of the Company had brought horses. "Then half of the Company can follow after us in the forest. The other half should wait just outside the trees, in case any of them try to escape."

Caelfel didn't like this plan. But they chose werewolf mounts anyway. Madoc would go with Lycaon and Garvanna with Geri. Caelfel decided Cyrus would have Freki, thinking that would make him the safest. But when Cyrus elected to remain with the other members of the Company, Nym was selected for Freki's companion. Huwel was paired with Aeliria, Edilon with Wurnsen, Turre with Benka. Then, Lovas went with Dorth and Melker with Jalmer. No one would ride Pippi, the werebear. Pippi was tall and graced with long, soft curves. Lycaon thought it would be safest if Pippi didn't have a rider. Werebears were more unpredictable.

This left Caelfel with Reuthe, which she preferred. She shuddered at the thought of riding Geri, and did not see Garvanna's attraction for him. Caelfel thought him arrogant and absorbed. Reuthe was a refreshing personality after dealing with his constant arguments.

"Just remember we are not horses," Lycaon growled to the rest of them. "You can pull on our hair, or should I say *tug*. Don't pull too hard. If you fall off, we'll do our best to go back or save you, but keep in mind, the objective is to reach Tarion. Once we take out the alpha, the rest of pack shouldn't have much desire to fight back. But Tarion will be well guarded and ferocious on his own. When we reach the den, dismounting is your choice. Remember that the wolves will be faster and stronger than you."

A soft chuckle came from Nym's direction. "I'd like to see that."

Lycaon bristled at her words but otherwise ignored them. "Considering the likelihood of being bitten, you will want to distance yourself from everyone as quickly as possible. Any questions?"

Nym raised a hand. "How long after a bite does the change take place?"

The humans of the Company expressed a ripple of distaste at the question.

"It varies," Lycaon answered uncomfortably. "A few minutes or more. Nothing over an hour. It depends on how fast the infection spreads."

The Company issued a few more restless whispers that were silenced by Madoc.

Lycaon continued. "The wind is in our favor right now. They won't detect us approaching. We'll go in silently. If the wind changes, we will charge. Once they know we're there, Garvanna can provide some light, for those of you that have trouble seeing in the dark."

"So basically, if you're a human," Aeliria translated with a smirk. The werewolves laughed at that. Caelfel allowed herself a small snicker, given that she had no problem seeing at night either.

Lycaon nodded. "I think we're ready. Now, don't be afraid. This will only take a moment."

All the werewolves of Haradrop and Pippi took a step back. They carefully removed the clothes they had worn up to that point and placed them in an organized pile next to an old stump that marked the beginning of a path into the forest. They spread out, allowing themselves a liberal amount of space, and dropped to their knees.

The change occurred in a span of a few seconds. Caelfel blinked as their shoulders broadened with a sound identical to the snapping of wood. Hair sprouted over their bodies, and Caelfel was suddenly staring at a pack of wolves that towered over her. The wolf that was Freki was the largest. Pippi at the end was an enormous black bear.

Reuthe's fur was the same color of her human hair, and in the dark, her snow white coat would easily be visible. This didn't concern Caelfel as much as it should have as she gazed upon the beautiful she-wolf with amazement. Reuthe trotted up to her, panting with excitement, and Caelfel reached out to stroke the coarse fur.

Lycaon snapped a short growl that sounded as if he was trying to hurry them, so Caelfel climbed onto the back of Reuthe. She felt the muscles quivering with excitement beneath the skin. When Caelfel tore her gaze away from Reuthe, she saw that the others had similarly mounted. Even though the humans harbored a general mistrust of werewolves, Nym was the one looking the most uneasy with the situation, her metal leg draped awkwardly over Freki.

Then Lycaon, with Madoc on his back, led the charge into the Pirinac Forest. Reuthe bounded closely after him, and the others followed.

Even in the blackness of the night, Caelfel could distinctly make out the evergreens rushing past. The werewolves ran silently, expertly dodging trees and underbrush. She saw Garvanna close to her right, lowering her body to make it parallel with Geri's. She looked fierce and battle-worthy. Further down, Caelfel saw Nym gripping the hilt of her scimitar, her silver shield glinting in the moonlight on her back. Aeliria with her blood-red fur ran next to them with Pippi huffing at the end.

They ran for what felt like an hour. A sudden sickening fear gripped Caelfel's chest as she thought that Tarion might have already left for the Crossroads. But the wolves pressed on, perhaps by some ethereal scent Caelfel couldn't detect. They must have been certain that Tarion's pack and Brenin were still in the Pirinac.

Her heart pounded painfully in her ears. Caelfel founded it difficult to breathe as she drilled her eyes into the darkness, looking for any sign of Tarion or his pack.

Suddenly Reuthe snapped a short bark. They all hesitated at the sound but no one slowed. Then Caelfel saw a pair further down their line collide with something.

Lycaon's pack immediately stopped to assess what had just happened. Caelfel saw Edilon off his wolf and bleeding at his temple. Wurnsen was caught in a struggle with another werewolf. Deadly snarls emitted from their entanglement.

"We have to keep going," Madoc decided. Edilon nodded silently, unsheathing his sword. Before Caelfel could make out which wolf was Wurnsen, Reuthe had carried them away from the scene.

Caelfel knew the futility of lingering, but she was horrified to imagine leaving Edilon behind.

"They will know that we're here?" Garvanna called to them.

Lycaon shook his head, pressing forward. It was then that Caelfel heard a bear moaning through the forest. When she looked up, Pippi was no longer loping at the end of their line. Nobody stopped this time. Caelfel's heartrate surged as they continued sailing past the trees.

Lycaon and Madoc crashed into another werewolf. Geri howled as they pulled away to help. Reuthe fearlessly pounded forward. They crested the ridge that Lycaon had said indicated their territory line, and Reuthe came to a halt. She lifted her head and let loose a bone-chilling high-pitched howl that was met by rumbling growls that came from ahead. The others of the Haradop pack joined in to create a cacophonous reverberation. When Reuthe had finished, she plunged into Tarion's den.

***

Brenin's time with Tarion's pack didn't afford him complete fluency in the guttural, animalistic language of werewolves. But when the shrill howl echoed into Tarion's camp, Brenin knew it belonged to a wolf outside his pack. Everyone around him froze at the sound, and he saw the skin of their backs and the tips of their fingers quivering. Most of them shifted into wolf-form. Skolt appeared by his side. To his surprise, Tarion marched towards him with quick, agitated strides in his human form.

There was a look in his turbulent, stormy eyes that made him appear even more dangerous. Brenin was still not tied up because, in his severely weakened state, he was unable to run away. He did his best to scurry away from the approaching alpha but he only managed to stumble back a few feet before falling to the ground again.

When Tarion reached him, he gripped Brenin by the shoulder and slammed him against the tree. Brenin was afraid but he refused to show it, meeting Tarion's gaze with his own cold one. It made Tarion give a derisive scoff.

"Do you think you're brave?" Tarion sneered.

He dug his fingers deeper in Brenin's shoulder until blood began seeping out onto his fingertips. Brenin grimaced, swallowing back a groan of pain.

Tarion wasn't impressed with his display of tolerance. "Skolt, hold him for me."

Skolt did was he was told, bracing Brenin against the tree.

Tarion swayed, his face closer and closer to Brenin's. "I bet you're feeling smug, right now. Thinking someone's about to come save you? No one's coming for you."

Tarion stepped back, pacing in agitated circles. He changed into the lumbering black wolf and suddenly leapt back toward them. Brenin squeezed his eyes shut, turning his face away and expecting the worse.

A pain erupted in his injured shoulder. First it was sharp, and then it felt like fire. Brenin could do nothing to stifle the cry that came to his lips. He fell to the ground, clutching at his wound.

Human Tarion was above him again, dark stains outlining his mouth and dripping down his neck in thick streaks. Brenin pressed his hand into the open flesh of his shoulder, but it did nothing for the pain that sent flames licking around his arm. When he looked at it, he saw no trace of fire.

"I want you to think of everything you hold dear," Tarion said, kneeling above him.

Brenin strained against the fiery pain. His jaw clenched, and veins throbbed at his neck. His vision blurred with his stinging eyes, and his leg kicked out unwillingly. His writhing only smeared fresh mud on his clothes and face. His only thought was to ignore Tarion's words, to recede into the oblivion of his mind.

"Your sniveling father, your pathetic brother—no. How about your precious she-elf? You like her, don't you? You like her a lot."

Brenin's stomach lurched with a new sickness, and he did his best to swallow past the nausea.

His reaction must have been answer enough for Tarion. "Think about her. You will destroy her—*tonight*. She's out there, right now. You're going to rip her heart out and tear her to shreds with your own teeth. You won't stop. You *can't* stop. The anger will become your soul. It will destroy her, you, and everything else around you."

The scene Tarion described played out before his eyes. All Brenin could see was red, and as the fire consumed him, the red became a vision of Caelfel's blood.

"*No!*"

Brenin's scream reverberated in his own skull.

***

"*No!*"

Caelfel heard the cry resonate through the trees. It stirred something in her chest, and she did not need to identify the voice to know who it belonged to.

278

"That was Brenin!" she shouted over the ripping snarls of other werewolves. "We have to find him, Reuthe!" She didn't want to think of what elicited his scream.

She thought she saw Reuthe's wolfish head nodding in comprehension, but before they could press forward to the source of the scream, a massive force collided with them. Caelfel was sent tumbling across the forest floor. When she picked herself up, she saw Reuthe snapping at another black werewolf.

Caelfel ran towards it, pulling out her bow and nocking an arrow. It landed in its haunch just as it was about to dive toward Reuthe. Another two wolves joined the confrontation, rushing towards Reuthe, the white wolf. She tumbled through the trees with both.

Caelfel watched helplessly, as the wolf she had injured began stalking Reuthe. She shouldered her bow and drew her sword, holding it horizontally in front of her face. She was just about to attack it when a silver disc intervened.

It was Nym's shield, and once it made contact with the wolf's face, it shifted its form into silver bindings that wrapped around the wolf's snout. The wolf howled in pain and thrashed about in the dirt just as Nym appeared from the trees, Freki trailing close behind.

"Go!" Nym commanded, baring her scimitar as she jumped on top of the wolf. "I've got him."
Caelfel gave a single, appreciative nod before taking off for Reuthe.

Her snowy fur had been stained red and brown in various places. She had been cornered against a tree, and she snapped at the two offensive wolves trapping her. Reuthe made a decision to tackle one, and Caelfel ran up in time to jump the other. She gripped the knots in his spine, and the wolf flailed about.

As she held on, Caelfel sank her blade through the right side of his chest. It gave out a last piteous howl before lifelessly collapsing to the ground.

When Caelfel had gotten to her feet again, she noticed Reuthe walking towards her, blood staining her lips and a dead werewolf in her tracks.

Caelfel nodded to Reuthe and mounted her once again. They plunged deeper into Tarion's camp.

Gripping Reuthe's back with only her legs, Caelfel took out her bow and shot at more wolves as they ran past. She aimed for three of them that had swarmed Garvanna, but by the time that Reuthe had doubled back to help her, Geri had rejoined Garvanna's side, and they stood victoriously above their kills. It was in that moment that Caelfel saw Garvanna tenderly reaching for Geri's neck as she sent a blast of golden light shooting up into the sky to illuminate the forest.

Caelfel waved at them as Reuthe headed for Tarion again.

They were stopped by another wolf that crashed against Reuthe's side. When Caelfel heard her whimpering in pain, she pulled her leg from where it was wedged between them and jumped off. She went running after the wolf as it sent Reuthe to the ground with another swipe. It was preparing to rush her again when Caelfel interceded, jumping in front of it to block its path.

As it charged her, Caelfel shoved her bow into its open mouth. The bow began to glow blue as its teeth gnashed against the enchanted wood, and Caelfel slit its throat with her blade. She freed her bow from the dead wolf's jaw and briefly looked it over. She was satisfied that the strong teeth had left no marks on the surface.

She turned back to Reuthe and saw that the she-wolf was shaking on the ground, a liberal amount of blood marking the fur of her front right leg. Caelfel crouched over her. "Reuthe?"

Reuthe emitted a low growl, and Caelfel turned just in time to see another wolf bounding toward their position. Caelfel was on her feet, sword drawn, when Madoc appeared to intercept the oncoming wolf. He managed to fend it off with a few strikes of his greatsword.

Caelfel stared at him dumbly. She was struck by his undeniable similarity to his father, and it was easy for Caelfel to imagine that it was Feraan standing before her, protecting her.

But in a moment of distraction—when Madoc reassured his grip on the double crossguard—the wolf took its chance and lunged.

"*Madoc!*" Caelfel shrieked, running for him.

Madoc fell to the ground and, in a frantic attempt to block the wolf's attack, he gripped the hilt of his sword with one hand and the blade with the other. The scene was so similar to that of Feraan at the Cromlech Palace that Caelfel could not breathe until she charged the wolf, slicing her sword across its neck, and turned to see that Madoc was safe and definitely *not* Feraan.

He dropped his sword, and she slammed her own blade into its sheath. "Watch yourself next time," she snapped, going over to help him to his feet.

Madoc nodded and looked at the deep cut on his palm. He tore off part of his shirt to staunch the bleeding. Caelfel helped him wrap the fabric tightly around his hand.

"Have you found Brenin yet?" he asked.

Caelfel kept her gaze on his hand and did not answer.

When his wound had been sufficiently bound, Caelfel turned her attention to Reuthe. She still wasn't getting to her feet, and Caelfel became concerned. Reuthe emitted a single, high-pitched whine. She nudged Caelfel's hand away whenever Caelfel tried to look her over.

It was then that a huge wolf bounded toward them. Caelfel drew her bow and was about to shoot when she noticed the red scarf it wore. Freki.

Nym was no longer with him, and Freki rushed to Reuthe's side without a second glance at either Caelfel or Madoc.

"I'm sorry," Caelfel said tearfully to them.

However, she didn't have time to wait for their response, and she took off running in the direction she thought Brenin's voice had come from. Madoc followed closely behind her.

"*Brenin!*" she shrieked.

Her call was answered by a hostile werewolf. Caelfel paused, but Madoc went after it as it blocked their path.

"Caelfel, *go*," he yelled.

A conflict swelled in her chest. She did not want to leave Madoc alone, but it was Brenin's best chance. It was Brenin's *only* chance.

"I'll find him," she vowed, taking off again.

Her path led her skidding into a small ravine. The stream that had formed it was reduced to trail of sucking mud. She looked around desperately, Garvanna's light proving weaker in this part of the forest. She began to notice the soreness in her leg and in the back of her neck.

"*Brenin!*"

"NO!" came the response, definitely closer. She followed the sound further down the ravine. She broke through a small opening in the trees where she saw Tarion in human form, blood dripping from his mouth. Behind him was another werewolf in human form. On the ground was Brenin thrashing in agony. Caelfel found herself gaping as she watched him.

She turned her vindictive gaze to Tarion. "What did you do?" she asked in a deadly voice.

"What will *you* do now?" Tarion responded as he began to pace. "Rescue your prince? Avenge your mother? Doesn't matter what you decide. You're too late."

"I don't understand *why* you're doing this," Caelfel said thickly. "What will you accomplish?"

"So you're trying to reason with me now?" Tarion asked, unimpressed. "You won't understand. You can never understand. You're not wolfblood. You are insignificant to me." He sighed. "And as much as I'd like to leave you with your precious prince, I haven't the patience to tolerate you. Skolt, finish her."

Brenin made a strangling sound as he tossed about. Skolt stepped over him, shifting into his wolf form mid-stride.

Caelfel crouched, once again drawing her sword. Her eyes darted between Skolt and Tarion.

A flash of silver sprung from the trees, and Nym followed it. Her silver disc latched onto Skolt's face. He howled and rounded on her.

"This is for my leg, Skolt," she told him tersely before lashing out with her scimitar. "I promise to make it painful."

Skolt recoiled, and Nym went tumbling with the large werewolf further down the ravine.

Her voice carried over his growls. "Just remember that alphas are stronger than the other ones."

At this, Caelfel fixed her gaze on Tarion who began choking out dry laughs.

"So it's down to the two of us," he said. "You didn't fare so well against me last time."

"I might surprise you this time."

Tarion jumped, turning into a wolf as he soared through the air, and crashed down on top of Caelfel.

As Caelfel's head slammed into trees and rocks, she understood what Nym meant about the alpha being the strongest. She felt Tarion's claws tearing into her sides, and his strength knocked the breath out of her.

They continued tossing around, and Caelfel was reminded of the panther she had fought off in the desert. Tarion was stronger, fiercer, with nothing but murder and blood on his mind. Caelfel matched his strength with her own, and they both struggled to top the other.

Tarion snarled, and Caelfel felt his claws raking down her face. Caelfel screamed and in turn, she used her strength to shove the hilt of her blade against his diaphragm.

In the same moment, they collided with a boulder. Tarion flew over it, and Caelfel scrambled to get to her feet, climbing on top of it.

Tarion was recovering some distance away, and Caelfel aimed two arrows at him. They pierced the skin of his ears.

Caelfel released another arrow, and it was a clean shot through the shoulder. It barely slowed him down.

As he continued running toward her, she started forming an idea. Caelfel unstrung her bow and planted her feet, holding the bow in front of her. When Tarion made contact with her, she wedged it upright into his open mouth, preventing him from biting or chewing. Deep growls ripped from his throat, and his hot breath burned across her face.

The more he gnashed his teeth, the brighter blue Caelfel's bow glowed as it heated up in her hands. Every shove against Tarion's thrashing head produced a new surge of energy that charged beneath her fingertips. She twisted its angle and gave it a last, solid push, and her bow flared with blue auric power. It sent Tarion flying back through the trees with the smell of singed fur following him.

She was panting and she strung her bow to aim for Tarion again, reaching for a handful of arrows from her belt quiver.

Then she charged Tarion herself, circling around and firing each arrow in rapid succession. Two landed in his shoulders. Three in his chest. Their trails left blue smoke hovering in the air.

Tarion howled in pain and fell to the ground.

Caelfel approached him cautiously with more arrows drawn. His body lay on the ground. His only movement was the heaving of his flanks as he struggled to breathe. As she neared, she saw the hot blood streaming out of his chest wounds in great spurts. There was a moan, and his body began shaking until he was in human form again. He watched her carefully.

"I've never met an archer who had the strength to pierce my wolf hide."

She returned his gaze and said nothing as she watched him coldly.

"Perhaps you should have shot me the first time we met. Then your mother would be alive and your prince would still be *princely*."

She kneeled over him, fingers wrapping around the arrow centered over his heart. "Perhaps," she agreed.

"But you're not a werewolf hunter," Tarion whispered weakly. His chin lifted in preparation for his death. "Where is your werewolf hunter, she-elf?"

Caelfel paused. "She is busy killing Skolt at the moment."

Tarion gave a violent shake of his head. "Not her. And not the fake prince romping through the forest right now. The one who abandoned you. Where is he?"

With Caelfel's final thrust of the arrow, Tarion's shuddering stopped, and his lifeless eyes gazed back at her, his unanswered question still reflected in them.

Caelfel found herself gasping at Tarion's insight, and she wondered what he knew of Feraan Auvrearheal.

Pushing Feraan from her mind, she stepped away from his corpse and ran to search for Brenin.

He had moved from the ravine where she had initially found him. She looked around, seeing tracks where Brenin had dragged himself through the mud. Caelfel went to follow them, when Nym appeared from that direction.

"Where is he?" Caelfel demanded.

Nym seemed distant and uneasy to answer the question. "You killed Tarion? The other werewolves have grown quiet. We should find the others."

"*Where is Brenin?*" Caelfel repeated shrilly.

"You should leave," she suggested quietly.

"I'm not leaving him!" Caelfel insisted stubbornly. "Not after all this."

Nym's eyes flashed angrily. "Well, you remember what Lycaon said. I'm not staying for it."

Without another argument, Nym ran past Caelfel to meet up with the others. Caelfel looked down Brenin's trail apprehensively. She took a breath to steady herself and went after him.

He had managed to drag himself only a short distance, taking refuge behind a tree. Mud covered his skin and clothes so that he was hardly recognizable. He was curled up in a fetal position, squeezing his temples together as if his head was in pain. Caelfel immediately went to him.

"Brenin?"

His violent tremors stopped at the sound of her voice. He looked up to see if it was her, and his face changed as he desperately tried to crawl away. Her presence confirmed some deep-seated fear, and it reflected across his features.

"No! *No!* You have to go! You have to leave me!" he demanded, shrieking.

She held her hands up in a gesture of peace, not fully understanding him. "I'm not leaving you," she told him gently.

His wails became frantic when she told him that. His pleading screams for her to stay away were practically unintelligible.

"I don't understand," Caelfel said, becoming distraught herself.

"I'm *changing*," he said.

It was then that Caelfel noticed the gaping wound on his shoulder that still oozed blood. There was no question to what caused it, and she felt her blood run cold at its sight.

Her conviction only cemented. "I'm *not* leaving you," she told him firmly.

Something in Brenin snapped and made terrible ripping noises. He was suddenly on his feet, inches away from her face. And growing taller.

"*I will kill you,*" he warned.

This only strengthened her resolve. "I just killed an alpha. I think I can handle the pup."

21. Aftermath

Garvanna waited outside the Pirinac with Lycaon, Geri, and the others. The attack had ended shortly after midnight, when all the wolves in Tarion's pack had mysteriously stopped fighting. Lycaon had said it was because their alpha had been killed, and he decided to round up the survivors as prisoners. They surrendered without quarrel, and Geri went to do a head count of everyone.

Garvanna had looked around the initial battle scene for Caelfel but saw no sign of her. Freki was carrying an injured Reuthe who said that Caelfel had disappeared with Madoc.

Eventually, Garvanna found Madoc limping through the trees. She healed his leg but ignored his other, minor injuries, saving her energy to heal the others' wounds.

"Do you know where Caelfel is?" she asked him once he could walk properly.

"She was going after Tarion when we were separated," was all he knew.

Garvanna scanned the trees, deciding Caelfel must have been the one to kill him, since no one else had reported seeing the alpha.

Nymaaria appeared last. A cursory glance told Garvanna that she wasn't injured, though she was probably capable of magic and able to heal her own wounds. Garvanna ran to meet her.

"Nymaaria!"

She gave a petulant sigh. "How many times—"

"Have you seen Caelfel?"

Nym hesitated. "Yeah, I've seen her, but we need to talk to

Lycaon before I say anything."

Lycaon was going over the death toll with Geri. One werewolf from Haradrop had been killed, and Garvanna heard Geri whisper Jalmer's name reverently. Two men from the Company had fallen, someone named Melker and another named Lovas. Pippi was still missing.

"Caelfel is still missing too," Garvanna interjected. "We need to talk to you, Lycaon."

Lycaon stepped away from Geri, and Nymaaria led them to a secluded area away from everyone else. Nymaaria didn't keep them waiting. "Prince Brenin has been changed."

Lycaon sighed wearily. "I knew this would happen."

"Wait. You mean changed into a werewolf?" Garvanna asked.

Nym nodded. "Tarion did it as soon as he knew we were here. Caelfel took Tarion on by herself. She's the one that killed him."

"Where is she now?" Garvanna demanded.

Nymaaria looked anxiously over her shoulder at the forest. "She wouldn't listen to me. She wanted to stay with him."

Garvanna felt as though she had missed something crucial about the werewolf change. "What does that mean? Should we find them?"

"No," Lycaon said quickly. "Caelfel knew the risks. The only thing we can do for them is wait. If we stumble on them, it'll only make things worse."

"How long do we wait?" Garvanna asked.

Lycaon considered her question for a moment. "We'll give them until morning," he decided.

***

Brenin's body felt stiff and exhausted. When he pried his eyes open, the chilled morning light blinded him with an abrupt rudeness. He shifted uncomfortably on the cold earth, and then Brenin realized he was nude. He sat up to look at his surroundings, aware of a persistent itch behind his ear.

He was alone at the edge of a small lake into which the ravine emptied. Dawn reflected across the water's surface with a metallic brightness. It was a scene that was peaceful. Almost.

Then Brenin saw the pile of ripped clothes at his feet. He thought they belonged to him but he struggled to remember what had put them there. When he picked up the purple shirt with the shredded side and ominous amount of bloodstains, the memories of that night began returning to him.

He was a werewolf now. And Caelfel—

Caelfel.

He was holding her bloodied shirt.

He remembered changing into the furious beast. He remembered Caelfel being there. And he remembered the scene Tarion had predicted for him, a scene that involved Caelfel's brutal death at his own hand.

He didn't remember hurting her. But then again, he didn't remember anything after the change.

And here was her bloody shirt in a pool of bloody clothes.

"*No!*"

It felt as if a deep chasm had opened in him, threatening to swallow not only him but all of his surroundings.

"*No!*"

Brenin's shrieks shattered the peaceful silence of the morning as he desperately denied the evidence before him. His grief turned his face red, and veins in his neck stood out in sharp relief.

"No! No! *No!*"

"Brenin!"

It was a magical sound, obliterating all of his suffering. His tight chest relaxed, and his hot cheeks cooled when he saw her standing next to him. She wore a white undershirt that billowed in the light breeze. Her angelic presence had a calming effect on Brenin, and his breathing settled.

"Caelfel?" he panted, turning to face her.

"Are you all right? Are you in pain?" she asked, stepping closer to him.

Brenin silently stared at her miraculous figure. He had never expected to see her again, and words failed to describe what he was feeling.

"Brenin?" she said, crouching next to him.

His relief, his pain, and a tumult of other feelings left Brenin stunned. The only thing he could do was wrap his arms around her waist and nestle his face against her neck. He was afraid that this was the wrong thing to do. He was terrified that Caelfel would pull away.

But she stroked his hair. She stroked his bare back. She whispered soft words promising him safety, security, warmth. And Brenin trembled in her embrace.

After a while, when his shaking had subsided, Caelfel withdrew her arms. "We should find the others. It's not over yet."

***

Caelfel and Brenin walked through the Pirinac Forest with little conversation. She didn't need to ask about his captivity under Tarion. She understood being abducted well enough that it would be futile to ask about the traumatic things he had endured. And she wasn't yet prepared to revisit their last conversation that had taken place in Honey Water, so Caelfel settled on debriefing him on the situation with the Umfang army. Brenin made little comment.

Evidence of the night's skirmish was visible in the bowed and splintered trees and the numerous tracks in the mud, but no bodies had been left behind, leaving Caelfel to suspect that they had already been collected by the others.

When they neared the edge of the forest, Brenin stopped them. "I can't walk out like this," he said sheepishly.

Caelfel politely averted her gaze, realizing he was still nude. Her tattered clothes hadn't fit him, and her armor needed mending. "Wait here," she decided. "I will bring you something."

Brenin nodded uneasily and sank against a tree. She ran out to the camp of the Company.

Garvanna assailed her first, having apparently waited all night for her return. "Is Brenin with you?" she asked after a quick hug when she had ascertained that Caelfel had sustained no serious injury.

Caelfel nodded. "Yes, but he needs some clothes."

"I'll get Cyrus, then," Garvanna suggested.

"No, wait," Caelfel said quickly. "Get Lycaon instead."

Garvanna didn't question the decision and hurried away, Caelfel trailing close behind.

Lycaon asked no questions, but Caelfel felt he already knew what had happened. He had suspected as much before the battle. Caelfel went alone to give Brenin the borrowed set of wool clothes.

When he put them on, Caelfel realized Brenin was taller than her now, even when he slouched. She suspected it had something to do with him being a werewolf, and a part of her longed for her old, unscathed Brenin.

Then she felt guilty for thinking that way. This was her Brenin now, and there was nothing he could do about it. So what if he was a werewolf; he was still Brenin.

"We don't have to tell anyone," Brenin said suddenly. "About last night."

"They'll find out soon enough," she said gently.

Brenin's face became stormy. "I don't want anyone to know," he snapped angrily.

Caelfel blinked, deciding to not admit that Lycaon and Nym already knew. "All right. I won't tell anyone."

This seemed to assuage him, so they continued to the camp.

If Caelfel's first entrance went unnoticed, her reappearance with Brenin could hardly be kept a secret. When everyone recognized their prince emerging from the forest, they all swarmed to meet him. Several individuals attempted to separate Caelfel from Brenin, but she refused to be removed from his side.

"Prince Brenin!" Cyrus called, appearing from the throng.

Brenin suffered a small smile at the appearance of his steward. "I am happy to see you, Cyrus."

"Brother?"

Caelfel heard Madoc's booming voice above the others, and the sea of people parted to allow the one they thought to be the eldest prince through. Madoc was grinning at his little brother as he stepped up to him. He held his arms wide, prepared to embrace Brenin, but he faltered once he was within arm's reach. His arms fell to his sides.

The situation suddenly turned tense as the two brothers faced each other, and everyone fell silent. At first, Caelfel thought it might be the result of Madoc's recent revelation concerning the identity of his real father. But then, the longer she watched them, the more she understood.

Madoc had always been taller than his brother. Only now, Brenin stood taller. It was an undeniable phenomena, leaving no question about it. Brenin was different, and it made Madoc slowly back away from his brother. Caelfel watched Madoc in horror.

"Glad to see that you are well," Madoc said uneasily. "You probably need some rest. I'll leave you alone now."

Watching his brother leave seemed to trouble Brenin, and he did not respond to Madoc. Caelfel took initiative and, grabbing Brenin's elbow, she steered him away from the gawping crowd. Cyrus loyally followed them, recommending that Prince Brenin take his tent for the moment. Brenin rumbled a coarse word of thanks, and once they had herded Brenin into the tent, Caelfel was relieved to have Brenin out of public sight. She didn't like people gaping at him.

"Shall I bring you anything, my lord?" Cyrus asked. "The Company might be ready to leave soon, but I'm sure I could find you some food? Some water?"

"I don't need anything, Cyrus," Brenin said roughly. "Just let me know when we're ready to depart."

Cyrus bowed and respectfully excused himself.

Brenin lay down on the cot and released an irritated sigh. "My own brother wouldn't even touch me." His eyes flitted to Caelfel. "That's why we can't tell anyone. He knew, so he wouldn't even touch me."

"Brenin, Madoc's been going through a difficult time," Caelfel said softly, wondering if she should tell him about Madoc's paternity.

An expression of hurt flashed across Brenin's face. "Why are you defending him? Do you think, because I'm a werewolf now, that I should be avoided? Or worse?"

"No, Brenin," Caelfel said quickly. "Of course not. You're still Brenin. That hasn't changed." She hesitated. "Aren't you concerned about the change? Do you want to talk to Lycaon? He can help—"

"Don't patronize me," Brenin said angrily. "I told you that I don't want to tell anyone. I meant that."

Caelfel took a deep breath, her chest clenching because she didn't know how to soothe Brenin's new temper. She crossed the room and knelt by his bedside. She reached for Brenin's hand, and he didn't resist when she held it. "Brenin, I am glad you are here and safe. You've no idea how hard I have worked to get you back, ever since you were taken from me in Honey Water."

This changed his mood entirely. He leaned closer and reached for the sensitive spot behind her ear, pushing some of her hair back. "Really?" he asked, his voice thick and heavy.

And even though he was different with a new temper and darker voice, Caelfel nodded in earnest. "Truly."

His touch was different from Feraan's. It was not fiery, but warm. Feraan was uncontained strength and passion. Brenin was tempered metal, strength in the precision of fervent steel. Fevered and tamed. Focused and raw. It was all Brenin.

He might have wanted to kiss her, and though that wouldn't have been bad, Caelfel disengaged herself before the idea could take shape in his mind. "Garvanna is here," she said suddenly. "She was in Haradrop the entire time. You should meet her."

Brenin appeared disappointed at the sudden subject change. "I am glad you found your friend," he said stiffly.

Caelfel was sad to discourage him, but she realized, as she edged towards the tent door, that nothing really changed whether Brenin was werewolf or not. She had made him safe, and that was all she could do. If anything, she had satisfied her debt. She cringed at this line of thinking, believing it made her sound much like Feraan. "I need to find her. I'll be back later, before we leave for the Crossroads Village," she promised.

Brenin's disappointment turned darker, a self-piteous gloom. "Very well, then. I suppose you've spent enough time with me. Time for you to move to more important matters. I didn't think I was even deserving of these few minutes."

Caelfel's throat tightened helplessly as she ducked outside.

She pushed all thoughts of Brenin aside as she searched for Garvanna. She found her speaking with Lycaon on the Haradrop side of the camp. They fell silent when Caelfel neared.

"You've rescued Prince Brenin," Lycaon noted.

"Yes. He's resting at the moment," she said carefully.

Nym appeared by Lycaon's elbow then. She folded her arms and gazed at Caelfel critically. "So you're alive," she observed. "I've already told them about Brenin's disease."

"It's not a disease, Nymaaria," Lycaon sighed.

"It spreads and acts like an infection," Nym stated. "I see little difference."

Lycaon opened the flap to his tent. "Let's talk."

When all four of them were inside, Nym made herself comfortable in one of Lycaon's chairs, and Caelfel began. "He doesn't want anyone to know he's a werewolf. He doesn't even want me telling you. He doesn't want to talk to you or anyone else."

Lycaon stroked his silver beard. "That's going to be difficult when he tries to get a handle on his new abilities, especially on his first full moon. Do you find that he's already exhibiting an uncharacteristic temper? Is he irrationally angry at things?"

"I haven't been with him that long," Caelfel said. "But it does feel that way."

"If he doesn't want to seek help from us, then it is important for you to be there for him. He will push people away, but companionship will be the best thing for him now. It'll help him control his temper, and hopefully he'll turn out more mild, like Reuthe. Reuthe could even talk to him."

Caelfel gave a noncommittal shrug to the idea.

"Either way, we need to leave for the Crossroads Village now. They were trading for the prince. He will need to make an appearance. Do you think he's well enough to travel?"

Caelfel nodded.

"You don't think he's a threat?" Nym asked sharply. "You were so quick to warn us of the threat of a newborn werewolf. Well now you've got one. And a prince at that. You had that other girl practically *locked* in her room. But a prince? No, he's free to roam around, and you want to give him anything he desires."

Lycaon watched Caelfel carefully as he responded to Nym. "Prince Brenin is not a threat. He's in good hands. People will watch him."

Nym scowled, leaning back in her chair. "How can people *watch* him if they do not even know what he is?"

Caelfel squared her shoulders. "Do you doubt that I can look after him?" Nym's casual dismissal of Caelfel's abilities infuriated her.

"Even the most seasoned elf could lose a limb to a new werewolf. A lesson not easily forgotten."

"I never claimed—" Caelfel began hotly, her cheeks flaring as Nym made her feel humiliated.

"No, of course not. You're too demure for that. But you certainly walk around with all that moral pride and justice hanging from your shoulder," Nym sneered condescendingly. *"Caelfel can do no wrong."*

Caelfel's shoulders tensed, and her fingernails dug into her palms. "What can Nymaaria do, then? The she-elf without a family, who belongs nowhere? No purpose except the petty revenge against a single werewolf? What will you do now that you have had your revenge?"

Nym's chair clattered to the ground as she flew at Caelfel in a rage. "You should watch your tongue, *youngling*," she hissed, shoving a finger in Caelfel's face. For a brief moment, a white light flared around Nym's entire body. Caelfel assumed it was her aura.

But Caelfel didn't care about that. She didn't care if she didn't have an aura anymore to combat Nym's. A protective rage burned in her mind, and in a singular deft movement, she held her sword to Nym's throat.

"Where were you last night?" Caelfel growled. "When you ran away in fear? Did you care about how much of a danger he was then? Did you care about him at all? Or were you so concerned with yourself, you didn't even trouble yourself to think about that?"

Nym's anger became calculating as she assessed the blade held to her throat. Her retaliation was quick. She reached for Caelfel's wrist, attempting to disarm her.

Caelfel spun around to avoid Nym, snapping her arm back and brought her sword around to meet with Nym's drawn scimitar. They made a metallic scrape upon contact.

Nym's mouth flickered into a grimacing smile. It was only then that Caelfel noticed Nym's silver shield had dissolved into a blade held precariously close to her left kidney. "I don't think I've ever met an opponent who has the potential to be my equal in skill. Meet me again in a few centuries."

Lycaon intervened on Caelfel's behalf. "Perhaps you underestimate Caelfel," he suggested.

"Perhaps," Nym agreed. She backed away slowly, sheathing her weapons. "Fine," she said smoothly, sinking to her seat in a fluid movement. "Then I expect you will take responsibility for Prince Brenin, and *everything* he does."

Caelfel retracted her shortsword. "I will."

Garvanna had watched their heated exchange nervously. When it looked as though no blood would be shed, Garvanna spoke up. "Caelfel, can I ask how you even survived last night with Brenin?"

Lycaon chimed in. "Yes, I am eager to know that as well."

Caelfel kept her gaze on Nym as she felt her chest rise and fall. "I ran. All night."

"You ran?" Garvanna repeated.

"I ran to distract him from everything else. Sometimes I would tackle him. Anything to keep him from hurting somebody, until he collapsed from exhaustion."

Something about her answer was so compelling, it made the others stare at her in awe. She absently scratched her arm in discomfort.

"Madoc saw him," she continued, skimming over the particular details of her arduous night with Brenin. "When we came back into camp, Madoc was about to hug him. But then, Madoc stopped. He walked away, and it upset Brenin."

This bit of news troubled Lycaon. "That's not good for Prince Brenin. Why would Madoc do that?"

"I thought at first it was just Madoc and how he's been acting lately. Detached, despondent. You know, since he's not the Prince of the Vale? King Orrik isn't his father."

Lycaon was not surprised. Garvanna had already discerned as much from her previous conversations with Caelfel. Nym arched an eyebrow in surprise. None of them said anything.

"But, I realized that wasn't it. I think Madoc knows about Brenin being a werewolf," Caelfel admitted.

"How would he know?" Lycaon asked. "Unless someone told him or if he saw Brenin change?"

"I *think*," Caelfel struggled to explain her theory. "Before Brenin was kidnapped by Tarion, Madoc was always the taller brother. Now, Brenin is taller."

Caelfel had hoped that this would be a common trait of newly changed werewolves, and that Lycaon would have some explanation for it. But the alpha only looked perplexed. "Brenin is taller since his change?"

Caelfel nodded. "Taller than me now. I thought it might be because of his werewolf change."

"That's an interesting idea, but it's never happened with Wurnsen or Reuthe."

Nym played with the blade of her knife, flicking it between each of her fingers. "Maybe it's an alpha trait," she suggested, keeping her eyes locked on her knife.

"I've never heard of a werewolf immediately becoming an alpha upon being changed," Lycaon said with a scoff.

Nym gave a casual shrug. "Why not? He is *Prince of the Vale*, after all. It's in his blood to be noble. Royal. Whatever you want to call it."

The thought made Lycaon apprehensive. "If that's true, we don't want to announce it to everyone. Not that Brenin is an incapable leader, but we have to watch the prisoners from Tarion's pack. They completely dissolved when their alpha was destroyed. I assumed they would join my pack after that. I don't know what would happen if they made Brenin their alpha."

Caelfel narrowed her eyes suspiciously at Lycaon. Brenin was born a prince, the Prince of the Vale in his own right. She knew he would be a remarkable leader. But now she felt Lycaon felt jealously about sharing his alpha werewolf power. She didn't put up an argument for Brenin's case, though, thinking that perhaps she should just focus on helping him through his first month as a werewolf.

"We should leave for the Crossroads soon," she said. "I'm sure Commander Joen and *Princess* Gwyndolyn will be waiting for us."

Lycaon nodded. "I think you should all help break camp. We need to head out within the hour."

Garvanna and Nym left the tent, but Lycaon held Caelfel back by her elbow.

"He needs to know that he shouldn't be ashamed of being a werewolf," he told her.

Caelfel said. "I know—"

"I realize there's a stigma and that people are prejudice. But he is the prince. He'll be king someday. He has the power to help stop people from being so prejudice."

"I know," Caelfel repeated.

"He'll need you now, Caelfel. More than ever. He trusts you," Lycaon pressed.

Caelfel sighed impatiently. "I'm not stupid, no matter what Nym says."

"Well, don't forget it," Lycaon said dubiously, finally releasing her.

When Caelfel left Lycaon's tent, she searched for Madoc next to reprimand him for his behavior. It took a while to navigate the chaotic camp as everyone ran around to pack things up, but she eventually found him leaning against a cart, sulking. When he noticed her glaring at him, he avoided meeting her gaze. "I know," he said roughly, hoping that that would be enough to brush off her anger.

"Why did you just walk away from him like that?" she demanded in a hiss. "After all he's been through, he really needed you. And you just walked away from your own brother."

Madoc sighed. "I don't really feel like he's my brother," he admitted quietly.

This took Caelfel by surprise. "What? How can you say that? Of course he's your brother."

"No, all of our lives we were built up as brothers. That's only half true. And then when I saw him again, he was too different. He's a werewolf now, right? There's just nothing there anymore."

"How can you be so selfish?" Caelfel said harshly. "He is still your brother. Your fathers may be different, but the love you have for him is real. The memories of your childhood with each other are real. You really can't just throw all that away because you've decided to wallow in your self-pity."

"He's a werewolf," Madoc persisted gruffly. "He's not Brenin anymore."

"Is Lycaon not a person?" Caelfel countered. There was a loud rushing in her ears, and without realizing it, she began to shout. "Are Geri, Freki, Reuthe, Aeliria not people as well? Your brother is still the same. The only difference is that he needs people that love him. He needs you."

Madoc said nothing and continued to scowl at the ground.

Caelfel grew helplessly frustrated. "Does all that work, going to Matron Mountain and Haradrop, mean nothing to you now? You stood up to King Orrik and faced your own god. Does that mean *nothing*?"

Madoc shrugged himself off the cart and began to walk away.

Caelfel yelled after him, "What would your mother say about this?"

Madoc stopped briefly and looked over his shoulder. "I must be like my father then. Doesn't he abandon everyone?"

Caelfel was left gaping as Madoc retreated from her.

It took the Company and Lycaon's pack the rest of the day to reach the Crossroads Village. It was well after dark when they rejoined Commander Joen and the King's Army. Only, they didn't get as far as the Crossroads. Commander Joen had been forced to camp so far outside the village that its lights were just specks on the horizon. The Umfang Army had already arrived.

Caelfel and Geri met up with Commander Joen and Lycaon in the Commanding Tent, and he informed them that no attack had been made yet, no demands given. They were waiting.

"Have you secured the prince?" he asked.

"Yes," Caelfel answered sheepishly. "He is resting at the moment." She was ashamed to admit that she had mostly avoided him during the journey to the Crossroads.

"Tarion is dead?" Joen reaffirmed. "What losses did you sustain?"

"Two men from the Company," Geri answered. "One werewolf

from Haradrop. Pippi is still missing, but we have a number of prisoners from Tarion's pack."

"If possible, I'd rather not use them for this skirmish," Joen said. "We can't guarantee their loyalty as of yet."

Lycaon nodded. "How long has the army been at the Crossroads?"

Commander Joen shrugged. "I would guess that they got there less than a day before we arrived."

"And they haven't sent a messenger?"

Joen crossed his arms. "No. They haven't shown any violence or made any preparations to attack."

"Should we send a messenger to them?" Caelfel asked.

"We will if we haven't heard anything from them come morning," Joen decided. "Whenever Prince Brenin is well again, I will need to meet with him. Tell his steward for me."

They left the tent, and everyone headed to their own for the night. Brenin's tent was close to Joen's Commanding Tent, and Caelfel eyed it as she passed. She should have gone in to check on him, but Caelfel hurried past it. She was exhausted and couldn't remember the last time she had slept. If they were going to be facing Gwyndolyn's army tomorrow, she needed to rest. She wasn't sure if she could handle Brenin's new aggression at the moment.

Thoughts of Brenin soon left her head, for when she collapsed onto her cot, Caelfel instantly fell unconscious.

22. Gwyndolyn's Champion

Someone was shouting.

Caelfel's eyes flew open, and she shot straight up in her cot. Blinking, she tried to figure out what was happening. Weak daylight filtered through her tent, and Caelfel guessed it must have been near dawn. She ran outside without her shoes to see the commotion.

A crowd of soldiers surrounded an individual approaching the Commanding Tent. The soldiers were loud and shouting obscene things at the person who was flanked by two guards. Caelfel then picked up on the general meaning of the shouting. It was a messenger from the Umfang army. He was guarded by Geri and Huwel, who did not appear pleased in escorting him.

When Caelfel pushed her way closer to get a better look, she recognized the messenger's face. "Winwaloe?"

Her voice was drowned out by the countless angry ones around her, but the elf could hear his name. His eyes landed on her, and he looked relieved to see her. He mouthed her name in response.

Caelfel hurried to meet them at the Commanding Tent where Commander Joen and Lycaon were waiting. Commander Joen eyed her bare feet with a scornful eye but said nothing. Geri and Huwel deposited Winwaloe and then left the tent to stand guard outside.

"I bring a message from the Lady—*Princess* Gwyndolyn," Winwaloe began nervously.

"Who is this princess?" Commander Joen asked shortly.

"She is the rightful ruler of the Honey Water Empire."

Commander Joen eyed Caelfel suspiciously at that. "Elves, eh?" he asked.

"She does not represent Honey Water," Caelfel said icily.

"What does the princess want?" Lycaon asked.

"She demands that your army stand down. And she wants what is owed to her. She was promised the Prince of the Vale."

"The Prince of the Vale?" Commander Joen asked.

"Yes, Prince Brenin, son of King Orrik," Winwaloe clarified.

Caelfel watched Joen carefully, wondering where Madoc was. Joen wouldn't know that Brenin was the true Prince of the Vale.

Commander Joen's mouth flickered. "She wants Prince Brenin," he repeated.

"She warns that if you refuse her claim, you and everyone else in this camp will not live long enough to regret your decision."

Caelfel recalled the few times she had met Gwyndolyn, remembering how she had possessed a uniquely powerful aura. Gwyn had even claimed her power could level an entire city.

"She is threatening us?" Joen asked.

Winwaloe continued. "Princess Gwyndolyn also recognizes that surrendering your prince is no easy feat. She has agreed that, instead of going to battle, she would be satisfied by a combat of champions."

"How generous!" Joen barked. "Combat by champions."

"I can excuse myself from the room while you decide on your response," Winwaloe suggested.

Commander Joen nodded, and Winwaloe left the tent.

Joen looked at the ground as if struggling with a decision. "What do you know of this Princess Gwyndolyn if you are truly on our side, she-elf? I am not sure what to think now that I know we are facing an army of elves."

"Gwyndolyn is powerful on her own. She's related to the Empress Haelyn, and she must feel as though she deserves the throne. I can't think of what has provoked her to build an army in Umfang."

"She wants the Prince of the Vale, perhaps to solidify her own power, and she thinks Brenin is the Prince of the Vale." Joen tapped his chin. "We might go ahead and deliver Prince Brenin to her."

"No!" Caelfel said quickly. But she was not merely defending Brenin's title. "We just risked everything getting him back. At least three people died. Do you not respect your own prince?"

"Do you think Gwyndolyn is powerful enough to kill us all, as she promised?" Joen asked.

Caelfel looked away, unwilling to admit the answer.

"Then what other alternative do we have?" Joen asked.

"Our champion could fight their champion."

"And who would be our champion?" Joen asked. "Who would take on this Gwyndolyn, so powerful on her own?"

As the three humans shared anxious expressions, the answer became increasingly obvious to Caelfel.

Caelfel was already stronger than any human. She was stronger than Freki, the strongest werewolf in Lycaon's pack. She had already defeated Tarion and she seemed to be the only one willing to fight for Brenin's freedom.

"I can do it. I will fight their champion."

Lycaon was about to argue, but Joen silenced him. Ultimately, it was up to the commander. He looked Caelfel over carefully.

"I can agree to that," Joen finally decided. "But you will have to be the one to tell Brenin. I saw him this morning, and I can't stand to go into his tent. It smells."

Caelfel made a move to leave when Joen added, "Don't let me catch you speaking to the messenger. Don't give me a reason to suspect you of treachery."

Caelfel sighed, and when she saw Winwaloe waiting outside, she cast him a furtive glance before walking away.

She went to Brenin's tent first, not noticing the smell Joen had complained about. Brenin was lying awake on his feather bed, a luxury afforded to him due to his status as prince. He scowled at the ceiling of his tent with some dark expression plastered on his face. The sight of him made Caelfel regret not visiting him more.

"Did you sleep well?" she asked him tentatively.

His eyes didn't leave the ceiling. "No." After his blunt response, the darkness of his face faltered, and he looked at her with a trembling innocence. "Did you? You must have been exhausted."

Caelfel ignored the question about herself, uncomfortable with allowing the conversation to become too intimate. "A messenger arrived from the Umfang army."

As Brenin sighed, his expression darkened. "Shall I guess? Some princess still demands to have me. At least I am wanted somewhere."

The comment stung. "She offered to settle the matter in a combat of champions." Caelfel paused. "I'm going to be your champion."

Brenin was stunned. "You are going to be my champion?" he asked, sitting up on his mattress. "Why?"

"Because I would be the best. I will not let anyone take you."
"I do not understand your devotion. One moment you are willing to die for me. The next, it's like I don't exist. What is even the point for you?"

Caelfel watched him calmly. "I'm not asking for your permission. I'm informing you of my decision."

"Of course," he said. "When will your duel be?"

Caelfel shrugged. "I am not sure yet."

Brenin refocused his attention to his tent ceiling. "Will you see me before you leave?" he asked.

Caelfel didn't answer him, and thus leaving much unsaid, she departed his tent.

***

"You can't do this."

It was some hours after dawn, with the sun shining brilliantly warm on their backs. Caelfel was trying to have her armor repaired by the Company's blacksmith, and Garvanna was doing her best to dissuade Caelfel from her course.

Caelfel frowned, shoulders tensing with frustration, but she still would not turn to face her friend. "What alternative do I have?"

Garvanna considered the question for a brief moment. "I can fight their champion instead."

Caelfel scowled at the adjustable clasp she was attempting to reattach. "How would that be any better?"

"Because I can at least perform magic."

"Is that supposed to insult me?" Caelfel hissed. "Does that mean your magic would best my training as a warrior?"

"No, of course not," Garvanna said impatiently. "But you're facing an army of elves, elves capable of magic. And what if you faced Gwyndolyn on your own?"

"She wouldn't be her own champion. She's too proud for that. I'm the best champion we have. I'm stronger than you, than any of the werewolves. I know what to expect from an elf warrior, even from one that casts spells. I am the most qualified and the most prepared."

But as she said this, the leather strap on her chest plate snapped under the strain of the clasp. Caelfel threw the whole thing to the ground in exasperation.

Garvanna raised an eyebrow. "The most prepared?" she asked with a hint of dry humor.

Caelfel rubbed at her face, trying to find some solution. She didn't think she could face the other champion without armor. "Why don't you do something useful and use your magic to repair it?"

Garvanna shook her head. "I never trained in blacksmithing."

"I have," volunteered a new voice. Caelfel looked up to see Nym approaching them. She carried a wrapped package in her hands. "You can wear my armor. We're about the same size."

She handed Caelfel the parcel. Caelfel removed the sackcloth to reveal the polished metal beneath. A mere glance told her of its expert craftsmanship. Caelfel looked back to Nym. "You're helping me?"

Nym shrugged. "I don't agree with keeping secrets about the prince being a werewolf, but that doesn't mean I think he should be bartered off like some farm animal. And believe it or not, I don't want to see you fail." She paused, looking down at her metal armor. "My father trained me in blacksmithing when I was a girl."

"Who was your father?" Caelfel asked curiously.

Nym's posture suddenly became guarded. "He was a human from Sorasaen, not that it matters. Take care of that. I don't wear it often, because I don't like it when it's scratched."

***

Winwaloe delivered the news to Gwyndolyn later that morning. "They have decided on combat by champion and have already selected their champion."

Gwyn smiled. "Then I will have to select mine."

She looked around at the Crossroads Village and at her loyal army that had followed her there from across the desert.

"Who would like to be my champion?" she asked them, amplifying her voice with magic.

There was suddenly a loud clamor of voices, all volunteering to fight for her honor. First Lisiek, then Markis. Fódla pleaded in earnest, among others. Gwyn silenced Lisiek, for he was her steward. She denied Markis and Fódla, thinking their talents were best served elsewhere.

"Your opponent could be human or werewolf," Gwyn warned them, but this only spurred the volunteering on louder.

Then a voice rose above the others and silenced them. "I will go."

Everyone turned and parted to let this newcomer pass. When he stepped into Gwyndolyn's sight, she found herself grinning. Lisiek on the other hand, shrank back.

"I had not realized you were with us," Gwyn said, feeling herself grow giddy.

He said nothing but bowed from the waist. "I will be your champion."

Gwyndolyn turned to Lisiek. "What do you think? Is he a worthy enough champion?"

Lisiek clutched at his chest, as if scratching the memory of an old wound. "He's dispensable enough."

**

"You shouldn't take your bow," Garvanna said.

"I'm best with my bow," Caelfel argued.

Garvanna pointed out, "You'll be in close combat."

"I can use my bow in close combat," Caelfel muttered.

The duel was planned to take place in the afternoon. Caelfel was ready but she paced through the camp in a state of nervous anxiety. "I hope you're taking this seriously. You could be killed," Garvanna persisted as she followed her around.

Caelfel rolled her eyes. "I'm well aware. There have been many times I could have been killed. Let's hope my luck continues to hold out."

They passed through the section of the camp where the Company of the Prince had set up their tents. A sparring circle had been set up in the middle of their training grounds. A crowd of men began forming around the circle, and Caelfel stopped to watch. She was surprised to see Prince Brenin up and about and sparring with Cyrus.

"Oh look," Garvanna said sweetly, noticing Caelfel's gaze. "It's your fair prince in the distance."

Caelfel nudged Garvanna in the ribs. "Shut up."

"I don't get you, Caelfel. You went through hell to save him, and now you're just ignoring him."

Caelfel sighed, watching Brenin flex his arms as he gripped the practice sword. Her thoughts and gaze were lost in the deftness of his movements. "It's complicated."

"Only because you're making it complicated. You could go down there and cheer for him."

Caelfel said nothing and continued admiring him from a distance. The longer she watched him, the more she noticed how his newly developed abilities gave him remarkable strength, which he used against Cyrus. The steward struggled to fend off Brenin's powerful strikes. With every attack, Cyrus continued to fall back against Brenin's might, and everyone seemed oblivious to it.

Caelfel ran to the sparring circle, easily wedging her way through the men. When she reached Brenin, she yanked Cyrus back while simultaneously parrying Brenin's next blow with her sword.

Brenin was shocked to suddenly see her standing there in Cyrus's stead. "What's this?" he asked, lowering his practice sword. The soldiers of the Company fell silent in their cheering.

"You were going to kill him," Caelfel reprimanded. "If you're going to use all of your strength in a fight, use it against someone who can handle it." She paused, waiting. "Come on, fight me."

She saw his jaw clench, and his eyes flashed dangerously. "I'm not going to fight you."

"Why not?" Caelfel demanded, straightening her stance. "You are so full of anger. You need to release it."

Brenin gave a dark chuckle. "How can I not be angry when you told me yourself that I would never know anything about loving you?"

Caelfel was mortified that Brenin would bring that up in front of everyone. But she did not hate Brenin for it. She felt ashamed of herself.

Her tone was gentle. "How can you know anything of love when you are so full of hate and anger?"

Brenin looked stunned by her words. Everyone waited with bated breath for his reaction. His face betrayed no expression, but he turned and hurled his wooden sword towards the edge of the ring, where it splintered against a fence post. Then he stormed out of the practice ring, shoulders tense and fists clenching. Caelfel watched him go with a mixture of guilt and longing.

Caelfel avoided everyone after that. She found an agitated solace when she was alone in her tent, rocking away the nervous flips in her stomach. The source of her anxiety was not the upcoming duel against an unknown foe but rather, it was Brenin. And after a few minutes of rocking she went to look for him.

When she found him, she was glad to see he was not sulking in his tent, but he was alone sitting in the now abandoned practice ring. As she cautiously approached him, she wondered what had made him return here.

"I thought you would have been gone by now," he noted when she sat next to him.

"Not quite yet," she said. "I think we should talk before I leave."

"Now you want to talk to me?" he asked bitterly, picking at the dirt on his shoes.

She reached out to touch him. "Please, Brenin."

He sighed. "What would you like to talk about?"

"First," she began with a shaky breath. "I'm sorry. I'm sorry that I've been abandoning you."

She paused, having difficulty forcing her next words out past the lump in her throat. Brenin prompted her, "But?"

"*But.* I am honored to fight in this duel for you, but if I happen to survive it, I won't be coming back here." The words tasted sour in her mouth, especially after she had promised to Lycaon that she would look after Brenin during his first month as a werewolf.

Brenin was startled by this news. "You're leaving?"

She removed her hand from his arm. "Not right away. But I do not intend to see you again."

She held her breath, body tensed as she waited for his response.

His voice sounded strangled. "May I ask why?"

She looked to the ground. "I think you know why."

"Because of what I said back in Honey Water? Why is that so awful?"

"It's not awful," she said quickly. "But it's not going to work."

Brenin jumped to his feet and began pacing circles around her. "Please explain to me why you are so determined to resist this."

"It's difficult—" she began before he cut her off.

"Can I at least know how you feel about me?" he pleaded. He stopped pacing and crouched slightly until his eyes were level with hers. His eyes burned with that raw, earnest passion, almost shaking Caelfel's resolve. Almost.

"I can't admit those feelings to you or myself."

"*Why?*" Brenin pressed.

"Because if I do, then you, as a human, will die—it doesn't matter when—and I will still be here. I don't want that future. I don't want to love you and then live the rest of my life alone and heartbroken. I've told you before how easily elves succumb to grief. I don't want that."

Brenin blinked, shocked with that answer. "Is that it?"

Caelfel nodded solemnly.

"Is that the only reason?"

She nodded again. "I am sorry I cannot be there for you."

Brenin stepped back slowly as he considered her words. "I wish you wouldn't fight for me," he admitted quietly. "I'm capable of fighting my own battles."

Caelfel said nothing. Anything he said would not change her decision to fight against Gwyndolyn's champion.

"I hope you are victorious in the duel. And know that—" He paused. "Know that my feelings for you have not changed. And I am capable of emotional reciprocation."

"I don't want you to watch the fight," Caelfel said suddenly, her throat tightening.

"You cannot stop me from watching, just as I cannot stop you from fighting."

He walked away then, calmly this time, and when Caelfel was alone, she wept silently into her hands.

When it was time, Commander Joen escorted Caelfel to the edge of the camp. She wore Nym's armor and had forgone her bow as Garvanna had suggested. She had her own sword with her and Nym's helmet in her hands. Nym had even used magic to adjust the shape of the armor to fit Caelfel's body better.

Garvanna followed closely behind her, fastidiously tying up her hair. Lycaon and the others waited to bid her good luck by the last tent in the camp. She noticed Madoc was not among those waiting to see her off. Cyrus was there with Huwel and the others, including Brenin. Caelfel graced him with a brief glance before concentrating on Joen's words.

"We didn't tell the messenger who we would send as our champion. So they're probably expecting a weak human. So keep your ears covered and use that to your advantage."

Caelfel nodded, handing the helmet to Garvanna who carefully slid it over Caelfel's head. Nym never had a chance to ensure the helmet fit like the rest of the armor.

"If you win, you'll want to get back to us as soon as you can in case they don't keep to the terms of combat."

"And if I lose?" Caelfel asked, trying to adjust to the loss of her peripheral vision as she peered through the slits in the visor of her helmet.

"I don't think you'll be alive to worry about that," Joen said wryly.

Caelfel turned to Garvanna. "If I'm killed, don't let them give away Brenin."

Garvanna gave her a hard look. "Don't get killed."

In the distance, Caelfel could see the forces of Gwyndolyn's army gathering on the far side of the strip of land designated as the battle zone. She thought she saw one figure stepping out from the rest, clad in armor. She eyed the figure warily until Brenin's voice interrupted her thoughts.

"I would like a moment alone with my champion."

Everyone fell silent at Brenin's request. Commander Joen had no choice but to bow and say, "Of course, your majesty."

He edged away to give them privacy, and the others followed suit. Caelfel shot Garvanna a pleading look. Garvanna dutifully replied, "I cannot refused the orders of a prince." Then she too left them alone.

Caelfel found she couldn't look Brenin in the eye so she kept her attention on the dust at her feet.

"Don't worry. I just want to talk," Brenin said after a painfully awkward moment of silence.

"What is it you would like to say, my prince?" Caelfel asked carefully

"I don't think you should fight."

"I've already made my decision," Caelfel said stubbornly. "I'm going to protect you."

"But this isn't even for me. They want the Prince of the Vale. Madoc is the Prince of the Vale. It's like you're fighting and risking your life for Madoc."

Caelfel looked up at Brenin and decided to give him the truth. "*You* are the Prince of the Vale."

"No, I told you that the Prince of the Vale is the heir, the firstborn—"

Caelfel's gaze was severe. "You are the heir. You are King Orrik's first and only son."

Brenin gaped at this, and Caelfel was afraid he wouldn't believe her. "Madoc is not my brother?"

"Madoc is your brother. He is just not Orrik's son," Caelfel said firmly.

Brenin continued gaping. "Why didn't you tell me before?"

Caelfel was relieved and pleased that Brenin did not question the integrity of her information, only the timing of its revelation. She gave him a warm smile and touched his cheek. "You're going to make a great king."

And with that, she turned to meet Gwyndolyn's champion.

The steps she took were long and agonizing. As Caelfel neared her opponent, she realized how much of a disadvantage she really had. Aside from her lack of magic, Caelfel was also exhausted. The past week had been exceedingly strenuous and demanding as she relentlessly searched for Brenin and then won him back from Tarion's clutches. In the past few days, she had only the single night's sleep, and it had done little to restore her. For the first time, Caelfel was afraid she had made a mistake in volunteering to be Brenin's champion.

Whoever her opponent might have been, he wore a hood in addition to his helmet, further masking his identity. It troubled Caelfel to think she did not know who she was fighting. Gwyndolyn's army comprised of Honey Water elves, and she hated to think she would be trying to kill someone she knew, like Winwaloe or Erryn.

They stopped when they stood a few paces apart, and for a long, indiscernible moment, nothing happened. He watched her just as she watched him, studying each other in that breadth of a moment. He stood slightly taller than her, and his armor was metal and bore the sigil of the Honey Water Empire, only a large black mark defaced the symbolic Honey Dew plant, perhaps a symbol of Gwyndolyn's campaign. Her eyes traced the weak spots in the armor where her arrows could have easily pierced his flesh.

Caelfel wondered if she should bow, but then the blast of a horn penetrated the still air around them. Her enemy drew his sword.

She unsheathed her own, and deciding upon an attrition tactic, deflected each of his strikes with evasive movements. She did not exert her strength to strike back, but kept her ground with each of his blows.

She used her metal bracers to block, his blade glancing off her armor harmlessly. She kept her sword in front, aiming for the area around his neck, making it difficult for him to approach.

Bouncing on the balls of his feet, he sprung back to reassess her. Caelfel slowly waved her sword in front of her threateningly.

Something about the movement caught his eye, and he paused to examine her closely. She used the moment to charge him, and her sword banged against his shoulder.

He twisted, using her own thrust to swing her off of him. Caelfel continued running to keep her momentum, making a wide arch to circle back for him.

But by the time she turned around, he had disappeared. Her diminished visibility from her visor made her lose sight of him. She slowed her pace, looking for him.

She saw him a moment too late. He had chased after her, and the flat edge of his sword crashed into the side of her head. She fell heavily to the ground.

Before she could orient herself, he had straddled her, and he thrust the long side of his blade toward her neck. She caught it with both of her hands.

She struggled to keep his blade away from her. When her senses returned to her after his assault, Caelfel could hear loud roaring from her side of the field. She heard screams meant to encourage her. But their words were lost when she felt a thick wetness dripping down the side of her face. Her left eye blinked rapidly at the irritant.

Instead of pushing back against his sword, she shifted her weight and diverted his strength to the side. His sword twisted out of his grip and tumbled to the ground some distance away.

When he made a move to reach for it, Caelfel then rolled the two of them through the dirt further away from his sword, until she was the one sitting on top of him. She had dropped her sword when she fell, but her eyes scanned their surroundings for it. Just when she saw it sitting next to his, her rival grabbed her shoulders and slammed her to the ground. When he was free, he took off running for his sword.

Caelfel scrambled to her feet and did the same. She was faster than him but only just. They reached their swords at the exact same moment.

Without allowing him a moment to think, she charged at him. He automatically lifted his blade, expecting a high guard attack. But she

310

ducked to the ground and swung at his legs, successfully knocking him on his back again. She was suddenly towering over his prone body. She kicked his sword out of his hand and it clattered a few feet away.

She had intended to hold the tip of her blade to his throat and demand his surrender. But he grabbed the end of her blade. In an instant, black smoke curled around her weapon, and it became unbearably hot to hold. Crying out in pain, she dropped it just before his aura reduced it to a wave of cinders.

Stunned, Caelfel stumbled back a few steps, her heart hammering in terror that she was now defenseless and weaponless against a magic user.

He slowly, menacingly got to his feet. Caelfel retreated a few more steps, watching apprehensively for his next move.

He brought his hands together, and another orb of energy materialized between them. He drew back his hand with its nimbus of magic and prepared to hurl it at her. Caelfel desperately wanted to close her eyes against the oncoming attack. But they stayed open despite her wishes.

She watched as the ball of energy spun towards her at an alarming speed. She had no time to dodge it. She braced herself for impact.

But Caelfel was not touched by her opponent's magical missile. As it hurtled towards her, it bounced off an invisible shield that seemed to surround her. Caelfel glanced at her chest plate, remembering the crescent moon pendant she was wearing. Feraan had enchanted it to make sure Caelfel was protected from magical attacks. She breathed a sigh of relief.

Her opponent tilted his head quizzically as his magic dissipated into nothingness. He attempted to throw another wave of magic at her.

This time Caelfel did not flinch, and as expected, the result was the same.

Infuriated, he stalked toward Caelfel, summoning a black blade into his grip. She watched as his aura fused the blade together into a corporeal weapon. With little else to do, she ran to meet him, hoping her necklace would be enough to disarm him.

It wasn't. As soon as she made contact with his new blade, the air between them exploded. Caelfel was thrown back into the air. She heard the deep, belated *boom* only after she crashed to the earth.

Her face suddenly met with a splash of cold, and Caelfel realized it was because her helmet had fallen off. She remembered Nym never had a chance to adjust its size like the rest of her armor.

The impact had left her sore, and her hair had fallen loose from Garvanna's ties. She struggled to sit up, limbs shaking painfully.

When she managed to lift herself up, she saw Gwyndolyn's champion standing over her with his sword pointed directly at her throat.

She was panting heavily, knowing these were probably her last breaths. She waited for the inevitable killing blow. In that final moment, her thoughts went to Brenin. His dusty brown hair. His bright eyes. The pine scent of his clothes. The warmth of his hands. Flashes of memories and encounters.

But that final, decisive strike never came. Instead, the other champion lowered his sword from its threatening position. Then he pushed back the hood and took off his helmet. Caelfel gasped when she recognized his face.

"Caelfel?" he said in breathless surprise.

Then it was her turn to be astonished. *"Feraan?"*

23. Rediscovery

A wave of emotions swept through her. Feraan hadn't much changed since their last meeting, his black hair the same style, the perpetual expression of suspicion identical as before, but Caelfel felt much had changed between them, much left unsaid. But Feraan was presently not focused on such familiarities.

"You need to surrender," he said quickly. "I'm not going to kill you over this."

Caelfel frowned. "*You* surrender. I'm not going to lose this, not even to you. *I was willing to die for this.*"

Feraan glanced over his shoulder toward Gwyndolyn's army, his expression conflicted. But he quickly made his decision, and apparently deciding Caelfel was worth it, he shoved the tip of his blade into the earth before theatrically sinking to the ground on one knee. "Fine, you win. I surrender."

His action was met with an enraged howl from Gwyndolyn's army. Caelfel eyed them nervously. "Now what?"

Feraan rose to his feet. "Now you promise me immunity and take me back to your camp. We obviously have a lot to talk about."

The magical explosion had left Caelfel in a crumpled state, and she required help from Feraan to get back on her feet. Caelfel imagined that the sight of them must have been a laughable scene. Here was Feraan, the defeated opponent, supporting most of her weight as she, the supposed victor, limped back to Umfeld's camp. At one point, she felt his gaze upon her, and when she looked up, he did nothing to hide the guilt from his features.

"I'm sorry. I can heal you once we get there," was all he said. Caelfel then realized that the left side of her face was coated in a thin layer of drying blood.

The incensed roars of Gwyndolyn's camp became deafening. The sound of chanting and the pounding of metal was unmistakable. Caelfel found herself constantly glancing over her shoulder to make sure they weren't being charged.

Commander Joen and Cyrus were there to meet them, and Caelfel saw others running towards them. "Who is this?" Commander Joen asked calmly.

Caelfel slumped on a crate in a state of utter exhaustion as Feraan hovered over her. "This is Feraan Auvrearaheal. He surrendered."

"Lucky for us," Joen muttered. "He'll need to be watched, guards with him at all times. Cyrus, will you find some? Speak to Lukas."

Cyrus inclined his head and made a move to leave.

Caelfel quickly called out to him. "Can you get Brenin as well? Feraan will need immunity."

Cyrus stopped only to nod to her before disappearing behind the sea of tents.

Feraan crouched in front of her and began the slow process of healing her injuries. Caelfel felt the warmth of his aura bloom across her hip and the side of her face, where her largest wounds were. He kept his hands there, placing them in a position where it looked as though he was fondly holding onto her.

"If you're defecting from Princess Gwyndolyn's army, you will do well to answer all of our questions," Joen interrupted.

Feraan kept his eyes on Caelfel as he answered. "I will be happy to supply you with any information later."

Joen seemed impatient, but Feraan's answer must have satisfied him, because he backed a few paces away to give them more room.

"What were you doing with Gwyndolyn?" Caelfel asked Feraan.

Feraan shrugged one shoulder. "It's a long story," he dismissed. "What are you doing here? Being their champion of all things?"

"It's a long story," Caelfel countered coolly, but she smiled in spite of herself.

The reunion was postponed when Garvanna appeared and dutifully began assailing them both. "What is the meaning of this?" she demanded in a shrill voice. "I don't even know where to begin." She stuttered for a moment, trying to formulate her anger. She settled for glaring at Feraan. "Get out of the way, imp. I will heal her."

"Garvanna, I see you haven't lost your charm," Feraan greeted with a chuckle.

"I said *move*," Garvanna hissed.

When she looked as though she was about to kick Feraan, Caelfel intervened. "Stop it. Leave him alone."

As Garvanna fumed silently, Caelfel could hear Geri asking quietly, "Who is this?"

Garvanna gave a curt scoff. "To put it simply, Caelfel and Feraan have an *intimate* history with each other," she said loudly.

To Caelfel's embarrassment, it was at that moment that Brenin appeared among the group that surrounded her. She knew he had heard Garvanna's words, judging from his dark expression that only darkened when he saw how Feraan held her. The jealousy in his face was undeniable.

And though it was not good for her, she pushed Feraan away. "I've had enough."

When his hands lost contact, her body instantly turned cold without the touch of his aura. The stark contrast made her exhaustion even more prevalent. She sighed, burying her face in her hands to rub away the image of Brenin's hurt expression.

"Caelfel, that's not enough," Feraan said, sounding quite close to her face. "You're still injured."

Caelfel only shook her head, rolling her head around in her hands, unable to share or return the intensity in his gaze. She felt that things between them should have been much changed, but his body language did not suggest that. "I am *fine*," she said through gritted teeth.

In actuality, the opposite held true, and Caelfel felt her body swaying, teetering on the edge of consciousness. She pushed herself, though. She needed to be awake for this.

"They're sending messengers," Nym's voice pointed out.

Caelfel lifted her face and strained her eyes towards the horizon. There were indeed two individuals on horseback, but judging from the official banner the second one supported, Caelfel suspected that they were not mere messengers.

"Let's reconvene in the Commanding Tent," Commander Joen suggested. "Geri, you and the other werewolves will escort them to us when they arrive."

Caelfel looked around and saw the only werewolves with them at the moment were Geri and Aeliria. "Where's Freki and Lycaon?" Caelfel asked.

Garvanna glanced down at Caelfel and gently squeezed her shoulder. Garvanna sent healing magic with her touch, and it helped Caelfel to think more clearly. "Lycaon is resting in his tent. Freki's with Reuthe. Don't worry—Reuthe is better. She just needs to rest. You probably do too."

"Not yet," Caelfel sighed, getting to her feet.

Commander Joen was about to lead them all back to the Commanding Tent when he saw Brenin standing among them. The commander bowed his head. "Your highness?"

Brenin took a moment to assess them all with dark, penetrating eyes. He nodded. "To the Commanding Tent, then. I'd like some answers."

Garvanna's hand shifted to Caelfel's elbow as they walked to the tent. Caelfel was grateful for Garvanna's healing, though she was not nearly as skilled at it as Feraan. "Perhaps you should wash your face," Garvanna whispered in her ear. Caelfel only waved her off, not possessing the patience to stop and clean herself, though the blood on her face *was* uncomfortable and probably disconcerting for the others to see.

Cyrus joined them at the tent with Huwel and Turre flanking him, presumably Feraan's guards. When they were inside, Joen was about to take the head seat when he paused and gestured for Brenin to take it. Brenin sat in it without hesitation, and Caelfel resisted the urge to flinch from his stormy gaze.

Cyrus took his place behind Brenin, Joen paced off to the side, and Feraan stood before the Prince of the Vale to await his verdict. Caelfel, Garvanna, and Nym were next to Feraan, and the two guards, Huwel and Turre, flanked the entrance of the tent. The room was tense.

"What is your name?" Brenin began formally.

"It's Feraan."

Brenin's face tightened, and Caelfel knew he recognized Feraan's name from one of their conversations. "So, Feraan, you're wanting immunity?" Brenin asked.

"Yes, that would be appreciated," Feraan said.

"Tell me why I should give you that."

"Because I did not kill your champion, despite the opportunity presented to me."

Brenin looked unforgiving, and Caelfel was about to speak in Feraan's defense when Brenin responded. "And why did you decide to spare her life if you were out there to kill her? Why defect from the purpose for which you so nobly volunteered?"

"You should know that I was not so dedicated to Princess Gwyndolyn's cause—" Feraan began.

"Just dedicated enough to kill someone you didn't know? It was fortunate her helmet slipped off." Brenin interrupted.

Caelfel saw Feraan's jaw strain at the accurate observation. "I did not know it was Caelfel," he admitted quietly.

Brenin leaned back in his seat. "So you know and like Caelfel well enough to risk the wrath of your princess?"

Caelfel's stomach writhed at the direction of Brenin's interrogation, but she didn't know how to stop it.

Feraan was a bit more eloquent in response. "I do not recognize Gwyndolyn as our princess." He paused. "Caelfel and I live in the same town of Sal'Sumarathar. We're friends."

Brenin took the liberty of considering Feraan's answer for a long minute. "If you do not recognize Gwyndolyn as your princess, then why were you fighting for her?"

Feraan sighed and resolved to reveal that part of his cryptic undertaking. "It was a reconnaissance mission. I was infiltrating her ranks and volunteered as her champion to gain her trust."

"For what purpose?"

Feraan returned Brenin's hard gaze evenly. "To take her down."

Brenin scoffed at that. "And Caelfel is worth more to you than that assignment?"

Caelfel shot Brenin a pleading gaze to keep her out of this discussion. "Brenin—"

But Feraan was undeterred. "I value her life more than Gwyndolyn's, yes," Feraan admitted. Then he leaned across the table to whisper to the prince. "Something tells me that you would agree to that."

Brenin said nothing for a long time. He analyzed Feraan calmly, and Caelfel desperately wanted to say something to break the tension. Words failed her.

Then Aeliria's piercing shout interrupted them. *"It's the Princess Gwyndolyn."*

Caelfel could hear the flurry of action from outside as everyone scrambled to adjust themselves to the approach of a princess. Brenin released an irritable sigh and turned to his guards. "Turre, Huwel escort Master Feraan from here. Make sure he's not seen by the princess. He's allowed to roam as he pleases, just make sure he doesn't leave camp."

The soldiers from the Company left with Feraan between them. Caelfel was relieved they did not bind his hands.

"Cyrus, would you please delay the princess for a few minutes?" Brenin asked. Cyrus nodded and hurried out of the tent. Brenin continued. "The rest of you should leave. Except, Caelfel. Would you be kind enough to stay a moment?"

Garvanna, Nym, and Commander Joen were the last ones to exit at the prince's request. And Caelfel was left alone with him. She felt torn between a desire to avoid him and a desire to comfort him.

"Brenin—"

"Can you tell me why he looks like my brother?" Brenin asked in a thick voice.

Caelfel faltered but answered him truthfully. "It is my belief that he is Madoc's father."

"But how can that be?" Brenin sounded as though the question was meant more for himself as he struggled to grasp with this new truth.

Caelfel swallowed, feeling dizzy after Garvanna had stopped healing her. "You said yourself how your mother fell in love with an elf before her marriage to your father. The elf that could make a black sword with his magic. Feraan has a black aura, looks almost identical to Madoc, and he's the only elf called the Wandering Elf, meaning he's the only elf to regularly leave Honey Water."

"Before you," Brenin stipulated.

Caelfel's chest tightened. "Before me," she agreed.

Brenin's eyes darted to his hands as he methodically squeezed a small chain he had wrapped around his fingers. "I think you talked about him before, on our way to Honey Water."

Caelfel's body became unbearably stiff as she remembered the conversation he referenced. "I did."

Then Brenin's eyes met hers. "I think you're wrong about him," he told her severely. "I think he *is* capable of emotional reciprocation. He just lacks the capacity to commit to something, to be loyal." Brenin gave a grim chuckle. "Maybe that's just an elf thing."

Caelfel's shoulders straightened. "And you determined all of this in a single conversation with him?"

"I determined this from my time with you," Brenin shot back. But then he softened. "I'm sorry. I do not mean to be so harsh to you."

Caelfel exhaled. "It is the werewolf blood in you. It makes you more susceptible to anger."

"I am happy to see that you are alive—" Brenin started.

Cyrus entered the tent in a rather frazzled state. He quickly bowed to Brenin. "Many apologies, my lord. The princess is quite insistent on an audience with you immediately."

Brenin glanced at Caelfel, and she was shocked to think he was seeking her permission.

"It is not polite to keep a princess waiting," she managed.

Brenin nodded and gestured to Cyrus. "Bring her in."

Princess Gwyndolyn entered the tent with a dramatic flourish, and Caelfel was reminded of how she had felt nervous in her presence in their previous encounters. Gwyn was accompanied by another she-elf with black hair who lingered in the corner of the room, out of the way of everyone else.

"Prince Brenin," Gwyndolyn said in a breathless tone, taking a seat in front of him. "What an honor."

"And Princess Gwyndolyn?" Brenin returned evenly. "To what do I owe the pleasure?"

"I won't waste your time," she said brusquely. "You might have noticed that our champion surrendered to yours."

"I did happen to notice," Brenin agreed. "Which leads me to ask, why are you here? Unless you do not plan to follow the rules of combat by champion?"

Gwyndolyn held her hands up compliantly. "You have no need to worry. However, I would like to point out the unfair circumstances. Your champion was close to death and defeat, and yet, mine mysteriously forfeited the fight."

Brenin shrugged. "It is not my fault that you chose a faithless champion. So, unfortunately for you, I, the Prince of the Vale, will not be going with you."

"Of course," Gwyn said tersely. "I only wanted to ascertain your safety. I had received intelligence that you were Tarion's captive. What happened to him?"

"I killed him," Caelfel told her suddenly.

Gwyn spared her a brief glance, and if she remembered Caelfel, Gwyn did not show it. She kept her attention on Brenin. "That is comforting to know," Gwyn said. "You should know, Prince Brenin, my interest with Tarion was only for your sake."

"My sake?" Brenin repeated with a scoff. "What did you intend to do with me once you had traded with Tarion?"

Gwyndolyn leaned forward, and her voice took on a smoky, seductive edge. "I would have liberated you."

Brenin pressed his lips together in thought. "I am already free. Why would you send a champion to continue fighting for me?"

"I wasn't sure of that. I can see it is true now, of course, that you have been restored to command."

"Well, I am safe. So you should have no further business here," Brenin said, about to get up.

"Not quite," Gwyn said quietly. Her whisper was an ominous sound that stilled Brenin's movements and made Caelfel edge closer to the prince for his own protection.

"Please continue, my lady," Brenin said.

"Once I had secured you in my possession, I would have hoped my kindness would have been repaid. Since that has not happened, and I am here negotiating terms instead, I hope that my *mercy* might be equally repaid."

"Your mercy?" Brenin repeated.

"I don't need an army," Gwyn said, repositioning herself on the chair. "I can defeat just about anything on my own, including everyone in this room."

She paused to let her threat fully permeate the atmosphere.

"But yet, an army *has* gathered around me, if that is any indication of what I am capable of," she said with a growing smirk.

"How would you like your mercy to be repaid?" Brenin asked carefully.

"I'm glad we're speaking the same language," Gwyn said airily. "I would only ask a favor for a favor. I am holding my own campaign, against Empress Haelyn, my mother."

"For what reason?" Brenin asked.

"I think the particulars are irrelevant," Gwyn said. "But my mother is wrong. She is a tyrant who keeps her people blind to the issues of the empire. She does not care about her people. She blackmails officials to keep her secrets. Her interest is only in preserving an antiquated method of ruling."

"So you would like our assistance in your campaign?" Brenin guessed.

"I believe having Umfeld as an ally would tilt everything in my favor."

"Humans are not elves," Brenin said. "We are not as strong or fast as you. We are prone to illnesses and we do not have magic. The people of Umfeld would struggle with this alliance. The elves have always stayed in their forest."

"If I am successful in my campaign against Haelyn, the elves of Honey Water would prove to be a valuable ally," Gwyn said, cutting across his objections. "I would be a monarch willing to share our resources with the people of Umfeld."

Brenin rubbed his lips together, considering this enticing proposition. "As tempting as that sounds, this is not my decision to make. That power lies only with the King of Umfeld, my father Orrik."

"What would it take to convince King Orrik?" Gwyndolyn asked. "Would an alliance with the elves not be appealing enough to him?"

"It might be," Brenin said uncertainly. "King Orrik takes an interest only in things that are for his advancement."

Caelfel wasn't sure where she stood on Gwyndolyn's campaign. On one hand, it felt wrong to betray the empire that was her home. On the other, it was Gwyndolyn that had once saved her from a wrongful execution ordered by the empire.

Gwyndolyn touched her hair, pulling at the strands around her ears. "What about a royal marriage? Would that be enough to cement our alliance and assure your father of our allegiance?"

"A royal marriage?" Brenin asked.

"I don't know if you are aware, Prince Brenin, but I am an eligible bachelorette," Gwyndolyn said. She eyed Caelfel and the other she-elf in the room. "But perhaps we should discuss this alone. Dagwen, would you mind?"

Without a word, Dagwen exited the tent. Brenin looked to Caelfel and arched a meaningful eyebrow. He didn't say anything, but it was clear he was asking her to leave as well.

Caelfel's whole body tensed at being dismissed, particularly over the subject of Brenin and Gwyndolyn marrying. She did not move until Brenin said, "Excuse us, Caelfel."

Caelfel did not bow, even though she probably should have. "Of course," she said shortly before following Dagwen outside.

Dusk was fast approaching, turning the sky to a ruddy pink, and a spring breeze chilled the air of the camp, bringing with it the odor of smoky campfire. Caelfel focused on these distractions as she struggled not to think of the conversation happening inside the tent. She realized she had no right to be upset if Brenin promised himself to Gwyndolyn, for she had intended on never seeing Brenin again. But now, faced with all possibilities, Caelfel no longer felt so certain. In the meantime, Caelfel entertained the idea of visiting Feraan. She still needed to finish healing.

Turre and Huwel had taken Feraan to a deserted tent near Brenin's. She found this out when she walked by Brenin's tent and heard the distinguishing tenor of Feraan's voice from the tent next to it. She entered with a sense of trepidation and saw Feraan sitting on a cot, muttering teasing remarks to his guards. Huwel greeted Caelfel pleasantly enough, and she gave him a small smile. Feraan sat up straighter when he noticed her entrance.

"Turre, Huwel, would you give us a moment?" She was relieved that they went outside without a word of complaint.

Feraan arched an eyebrow at her. "Champion *and* ordering soldiers around? You are quite changed since we last met."

Caelfel gave a thin smile and sat next to him. "I could say the same for you, but I don't think you've changed much. Just my perception of you."

Feraan looked puzzled. "I've never known you to be so hostile. Quite changed, indeed."

"Where have you been? Father said you left the Cromlech Palace and didn't go back to Honey Water."

"How would you know that if you've been out here?"

"I went home for a while," Caelfel said slowly. She turned her gaze to the ground. "My mother was killed."

Feraan breathed out a sharp sigh. "I'm sorry to hear that, Caelfel." She felt his hand on her arm.

"So what have you been doing? Reconnaissance on the Princess Gwyndolyn? Why?" Caelfel asked, quickly changing the subject.

Feraan ignored the question. "How has your perception changed of me?"

Caelfel looked him in the eye. "I'm not sure if I've ever really known you. I don't know but maybe I pretended I did. You always kept secrets from me. I shouldn't be surprised to discover a few more of them."

"Secrets?" he repeated.

Caelfel opened her mouth but then paused to think about how to phrase her thoughts. "You never told me about Fronia."

Feraan blinked at the name, and it was apparent to Caelfel that he recognized it. "Fronia? Fronia was a long time ago."

"I wouldn't say more than twenty and a few years," Caelfel said.

"How do you know this? How do you know about Fronia?" Feraan wasn't angry. He sounded curious.

Caelfel smiled, but she felt something hollow in the expression. "Shortly after your time with her, she married King Orrik of Umfeld. Now she's known as Queen Fronia. Brenin is her son. He told me of a story of how his mother fell in love with an elf. It was quite obvious to me after that."

"You couldn't have known it was me just from that," Feraan said with a small chuckle.

"I was highly suspicious after I heard of it," Caelfel admitted slowly. "My suspicions were confirmed when I met her firstborn son."

At first Feraan did not understand. "Her firstborn? You mean Brenin?"

Caelfel shook her head. "No, Brenin is her second son."

"But isn't he the Prince of the Vale?" Feraan asked.

"Yes, because he is King Orrik's firstborn son. Brenin has an elder brother, Fronia's firstborn."

She waited for this information to register with Feraan. He continued staring at her with a puzzled expression. "Who?"

"His name is Madoc, and he looks just like you."

Feraan's mouth fell open as he struggled to form words. "Are you saying Madoc is my—" But he shook his head, and Caelfel wasn't sure if it was because he didn't believe her or because he didn't *want* to. "Where is Madoc?"

The question made Caelfel realize that she had not seen Madoc for some time, not since before her fight with Feraan. "He was here at the camp, but I haven't seen him in a while."

Feraan nodded, his eyes losing focus as he absorbed Caelfel's news. She waited for him to accept the idea of having a son. After a few minutes, he blinked, returning his attention to her. "You still need healing?" he said in a choked voice, as though he was looking for a distraction to his currents thoughts. She nodded, and he said, "You shouldn't have pushed me away earlier."

Caelfel said nothing in protest, and Feraan's hand returned to her temple. She felt the warm energy flowing from his touch. She closed her eyes in weariness.

"How is Fronia?" he asked quietly.

Caelfel kept her eyes close, but her tone was gentle. "She's gone, for years now."

Feraan didn't retouch the topic. As Caelfel slowly regained her strength, his thoughts wandered in a different direction. "You look like you've been through a lot. Am I ever going to know what you've been doing?"

She sighed and began her own tale. "Garvanna and I were in Kanetalm, crossing the Pirinac Forest when we were attacked by werewolves, a pack led by Tarion. We were separated, and I was certain she had been killed. Prince Brenin found me and took me back to Palpses. It was there that I learned about my mother. Garvanna had gone to Haradrop and sent a letter to her to say that I was missing. Then my mother went looking for me and found Tarion instead. We went back to Honey Water for the funeral—"

"*We?*" Feraan repeated.

"Brenin and I," Caelfel clarified. "As we were leaving Honey Water, Tarion invaded the Fey Forest and kidnapped Brenin. Since then, I've been trying nonstop to get him back. I risked the wrath of King Orrik by freeing a prisoner on her way to an execution. I met Voten on Matron Mountain. I went to Sorasaen and then to Haradrop to meet with the werewolves there. I've only just rescued him from Tarion before we came here to meet Gwyndolyn's army."

"And Tarion?"

Caelfel opened her eyes to meet his serious gaze. "Dead, at my hand."

Feraan nodded. "You've had quite the adventure and gone to such great lengths for Prince Brenin."

"You could say I owed Brenin a life debt for saving my life."

There was a definable pause in Feraan's response. "*Prince* Brenin."

Caelfel held very still as she was reminded of another conversation she had had with Garvanna.

"As Prince of the Vale and son of King Orrik, that is his title, is it not?" Feraan pointed out.

"It is," Caelfel agreed slowly.

Feraan angled his head meaningfully. "So what's the story there? You don't even call him Prince Brenin in his presence, and even more surprising, he doesn't correct you."

Caelfel carefully arranged her features into a placid, unchanged mask. "What story is there to tell?"

Feraan scoffed. "Come on, Hen. I know you better than that."

"I do not know what to tell you," Caelfel insisted stubbornly.

Feraan stood up and began to pace around the tent. When his hand left Caelfel, her body grew familiarly cold at the absence of his aura. "You travel all over Kanetalm, climb Matron Mountain to face Voten, and fight against a pack of werewolves for him? You can't tell me there's not something there," he said pointedly.

"What is there supposed to be?" Caelfel demanded furiously, rising herself. "I'm not like you. I don't just flit from one love to the next. I don't want something so fleeting, so what's the point of even loving a human if they're just going to die anyway?"

Feraan gave a dry laugh. "Is he it, then? It sounds like it didn't take you long to move on."

Caelfel glared. "I suppose it never takes you long, once you set your sights on something," she replied icily. "You had made your own decision to move on, and I don't recall swearing myself to you, especially since you made no such promise to me."

Feraan sighed, and the fight left him. He deliberated on her words long enough that Caelfel almost felt like leaving. Eventually, he said "The only counsel I can offer is, as long as you are not bound to some higher cause, then you should pursue anything that makes you happy."

"Is that your excuse, then?" she asked. "Bound to some higher cause?"

He looked at her evenly. "You already know it's true."

Caelfel said nothing, and soon they were interrupted by Garvanna who poked her head into the tent. She only had eyes for Caelfel. "There you are. Reuthe is feeling better. She wanted to see you."

Caelfel nodded, briefly turning to Feraan to say, "I'll see you later. Don't get yourself into trouble."

Feraan gave a mischievous wink and declared he would make no such promise. But there was an edge to his voice. After discovering for himself that Caelfel harbored certain feelings for Brenin, he did not sound as relaxed around her, and Caelfel didn't know how to help that. Perhaps there was nothing she could do.

Then she left the tent with Garvanna.

24. Vain-Glorious

Once she stepped outside, Caelfel's anxiety lifted, and she found it easier to breathe. But the relief was short-lived when they were immediately approached by Brenin. Caelfel froze while Garvanna dipped into a quick bow. Thinking quickly, she decided to turn the attention to him before he could grow suspicious of her choice of whereabouts.

"How did your negotiations with Princess Gwyndolyn go?" she asked him suddenly.

The question was enough to distract him from whatever dark thought clouded his face, but Caelfel's whole body tensed awaiting for his answer, waiting to hear if some marriage between him and Gwyndolyn had been arranged. Her stomach twisted in fear of that occurring.

"She is returning to her camp at this moment and has agreed to not harm anything of Umfeld. We're to return to Palpses and let King Orrik decide about an alliance." It was this moment that his expression flickered to its original dark expression. "Now I'm to decide what to do with our prisoner, and you are free to do whatever you wish."

He sounded as though he intended his words to be harsh, but his voice only managed a regretful tone. Brenin pushed past her to enter Feraan's tent.

Caelfel exhaled and rubbed her face, feeling far from peace. Brenin's answer did not satisfy her curiosity. A jealous thought entered her mind, and Caelfel wondered if Brenin had any desire to marry Gwyndolyn.

"Everything should be fine now," Garvanna said, trying to break Caelfel's dismal silence as she led her to Reuthe.

"Yes," Caelfel said indifferently. "Tarion and the other werewolves are defeated, and Umfeld is presently safe from Gwyndolyn's wrath."

"And you are alive," she pointed out. "For such victories, you do not sound fine at all."

Caelfel took this opportunity to wash the dried blood off of her face before going to see Reuthe, and Garvanna helped in making sure her face was spotless. When they reached Reuthe's tent, Caelfel saw Aeliria and Geri standing just outside. They spoke to each other in hushed, irate tones, and Caelfel wondered if they were arguing. When Garvanna neared them, she placed a gentle hand on Geri's arm, and the conversation between him and Aeliria instantly ended. Aeliria excused herself, announcing she was going to find Forra.

Garvanna made no move to go in, staying by Geri's side. Caelfel took the liberty of watching them for a moment. There was no denying their attraction, but they were careful with each other. Garvanna would reach for his face then stop herself. Geri would angle his body toward her but then hesitate without completing the motion. Caelfel wondered what held them back, but she spared them from her staring and entered the tent.

Reuthe was wrapped in heavy woolen blankets, and sweat beaded the exposed skin of her arms, neck, and face. Freki was beside her with a bowl of water ready for when she needed it. Caelfel thought Reuthe did not look well enough to see anyone, but her features brightened considerably when she saw Caelfel.

"Caelfel! I'm glad that you came," she said. Fatigue was audible in her voice.

Caelfel hesitated. "Has Garvanna healed you?"

"She has done all that she can do—healed my skin and returned what strength she could. But I have acquired some new sickness that her magic cannot heal."

This puzzled Caelfel. Elves did not fall ill with disease, so it wasn't so outlandish to think a healer's magic was useless against sickness. Caelfel approached Reuthe's other side. "I am sorry for what happened to you."

Reuthe shook her head. "I wanted to tell you that it's not your fault, and I am glad you stayed with me for as long as you could until

Freki got there. *I'm* sorry I could not go with you to defeat Tarion."

Caelfel gave her a weak smile. "Do not trouble yourself. It is not your fault."

Reuthe's eyes became distant, and she nodded before slumping against the mattress, breathing deeply and eyes fluttering shut.

"She is better than what she was," Freki said quietly so as to not wake her. "She is really tired but was quite determined to see you."

"Do you think she should have stayed behind like Geri wanted?" Caelfel asked. The longer she stared at Reuthe, the more she felt responsible for convincing her to go into battle.

Freki shook his head. "No, this is what she wanted. She does not regret it, so neither will I."

With nothing left to say, Caelfel turned to leave.

"Thank you for being so kind to her," Freki said just before she left. "It has really helped her."

Caelfel paused at the tent flap. "Let me know how she is."

"I will," Freki promised.

Garvanna was still waiting outside the tent with Geri. They both straightened when Caelfel appeared.

"Can you find Madoc?" she asked Garvanna. "I haven't seen him since yesterday. I'm starting to get worried."

Garvanna nodded. "Now that you mention it, his absence has been a bit odd. Didn't he come here with us after we left the Pirinac?"

Caelfel shrugged. "I thought so. If you find him, don't let him near Feraan. I don't think they should meet yet."

Garvanna's eyes tightened, but she agreed. Geri joined her search, leaving Caelfel alone. She found herself wandering back towards Feraan's tent, hesitating just outside. She couldn't think of anything left to say to him, but she did wonder if Brenin was still with him. The sky was darkening, giving way to the illumination of torchlight and campfires.

"Is Brenin still here?" Caelfel asked Huwel who was standing guard outside.

Huwel nodded. "Aye, he is, my lady."

Caelfel stared at the tent uncertainly. Brenin was speaking to Feraan in private about his immunity. "Perhaps I should leave," she mused aloud for Huwel's benefit.

"Shall I tell him that you stopped by?" Huwel asked.

"I don't think that's necessary—" But as she was about to leave,

Brenin stepped outside.

He didn't look surprised by her presence, and his face took on a stoic expression as he gestured to the tent behind him. "You can go on in. He probably wants to talk to you."

Caelfel searched Brenin's face. "What about you?" she asked.

She saw an idea enter his thoughts as it played across his face. There was something he wanted to say, but he brushed it off. "I'm retiring for the evening. I am rather tired."

She couldn't deny it. Of the many things she saw pass through his face, exhaustion was one of them. "When will you leave for Palpses?" she asked.

"I hope to have the Company moving in the morning," he answered.

"Just the Company?" Caelfel asked, slightly surprised by this.

Brenin nodded. "The King's Army will stay here with Lycaon to make sure Gwyndolyn's army doesn't attack."

It made sense, and Caelfel took some small measure of satisfaction in that Brenin did not fully trust Gwyndolyn on her own. She hoped it was indicative of what he thought of the proposed marriage alliance with the princess. Meanwhile, Caelfel had no idea what she would do. "I hope you sleep well," she said softly.

Brenin started for his own tent, but something held him back. He turned to look at Caelfel. "Is this the last time—" But instead of finishing his question, he shook his head and continued on his way.

Caelfel stared after him long after he had disappeared into his own tent. A small breeze swirled through the camp, ruffling the canvas tents all around. She sighed and ducked through the tent flap to see Feraan.

He looked particularly amused with something, and his amusement only increased when he saw her visiting. "Caelfel," he greeted.

"Did he give you immunity?" she asked, getting straight to the point.

Feraan looked as though he deliberated on telling her, but he decided to give in to her query. "He did, though he does think my guards are a necessary precaution while Gwyndolyn is near."

"Are you not allowed to leave?"

"I am, but that's just while I am here. He said he couldn't promise me safety once I leave, so I don't think I will be leaving anytime soon."

Caelfel nodded at this information and having gotten her answer, she prepared to leave, thinking about turning in for the night as well. Feraan called her back with a small observation.

"Leaving already? He asked me a lot of questions about you."

Caelfel hesitated. "What sort of questions?"

"How long we had known each other, if you had changed since we saw each other last."

"And what did you tell him?" Caelfel asked, looking over her shoulder.

Feraan shrugged. "It doesn't matter, because you won't pursue him anyway."

Caelfel said nothing.

Feraan was undaunted. "You know, I never noticed it earlier, but he is *quite* tall for a human."

Caelfel snapped her head back towards the door, not daring to betray any sort of expression to Feraan's critical gaze. She had made a promise to keep Brenin's secret.

The cot moaned as Feraan pushed himself off of it. His voice sounded closer now. "What did you say happened to him? He was kidnapped by some werewolf?"

"Tarion," Caelfel clarified, holding very still.

Feraan waited for Caelfel to point out what he probably already knew. "You're not going to tell me?"

"Tell you what?" she asked innocently.

"You *know* me better than that. You know I've fought alongside werewolves in Amasel. I know what they're like, moreso I know what they *smell* like. You've been with werewolves for a while now, you should have noticed their distinct scent."

Caelfel nodded, her nostrils flaring as she recalled their sharp odor. "They smell like pine trees."

"Observant," Feraan noted. His mouth was right next to her ear. His breath tickled the strands of hair on her neck. "But new werewolves also carry the slightest hint of blood."

Caelfel hadn't noticed this about Brenin, but she had also reasoned with herself that the lingering smell of blood was a result of the battle. She remained silent, neither confirming nor denying his evident insinuation.

"Does the change bother you?" he asked, tickling her neck again. "Does it bother you that he's been turned into a werewolf?" She smelled his salty sweat and smoky clothes.

She shook her head. "No."

"He's a bloodthirsty monster and that doesn't bother you?" Feraan repeated.

"He's not a monster," Caelfel asserted staunchly.

Feraan stepped back. "Then you are lying about something if you're still holding back."

"I'm not lying about anything."

"So what is holding you back?" Feraan shot back.

"I already told you," she whirled to him. "I don't want to see him die!"

Feraan considered her for a long minute. "Everything dies, Caelfel. Even you and me. We don't age like humans and we don't contract illness, but elves are not impervious to the sword."

"It doesn't matter how," Caelfel said despairingly. "He will fall on whoever's sword much quicker than I."

Again, Feraan took a moment to examine her, as if he didn't quite understand what she was saying. He shook the confusion from his face and changed subjects. "Is Lycaon here? I suspect he is, since all of Haradrop is."

"Lycaon?" Caelfel repeated. She then remembered how Feraan and Lycaon were old friends. "He is here. Would you like to see him?"

It was arranged for them to visit Lycaon. Feraan was no longer a prisoner, so he could wander the camp as he wished. Huwel and Turre accompanied him, though, to make sure Feraan was safe, which Caelfel thought was a bit ridiculous. Feraan was far more capable of protecting himself than two humans.

Lycaon was in his tent with Aeliria, Forra, Nym, and a few other werewolves. When he saw Caelfel, he rose to greet her, but when Feraan followed in after her, Lycaon's expression changed. He was stunned for a frozen moment, surprised to suddenly see his longtime companion before him, and a huge grin stretched across his face. Feraan all but ran past Caelfel to embrace his old friend.

"Feraan," Lycaon said breathlessly. "My brother!"

Caelfel found the scene to be warmly touching. Feraan pulled back and held Lycaon at arm's length to study him. "How long has it been? Your beard has grown."

"Twenty years, I think," Lycaon said.

At this point, Feraan turned back to Caelfel to look at her

meaningfully. "Twenty years!" he said, keeping his eyes on Caelfel.

Caelfel gave the slightest shake of her head, not understanding his message.

Feraan continued with whatever point he was trying to make. He didn't look at anyone else. "Do you remember when you came to Honey Water? When we fought in that battle? I believe that was eighty years ago."

Caelfel remembered Feraan telling her that story. That was the fall of Amasel.

"Do you see how often he visits me?" Lycaon asked Caelfel. "I'm lucky to see my own brother every twenty years."

"Are you really brothers?" Nym asked suddenly.

Feraan turned to her with a lopsided half-smile. "Definitely. Actually, just half-brothers. And guess who is older?"

Caelfel blinked, and it took her mind a moment to process this revelation. "Who are your parents, Lycaon?" she asked slowly.

"The beautiful Refurinn and the infamous Saint Hubertus," he answered.

By now, Caelfel knew enough of those historical figures to know that both of them, including the father Lycaon and Feraan shared, had been dead for centuries. This put Lycaon at five hundred years old at least.

"Who is older?" Caelfel asked.

Feraan nudged his werewolf half-brother in the ribs. "He is."

Nym started asking them more questions, distracting the conversation to another tangent. Meanwhile, Caelfel turned her questioning gaze to Feraan. He angled his head toward her, waiting for her to figure it out on her own.

She knew Feraan was five hundred and thirty-six years old, and Lycaon was older than Feraan. Lycaon was over five hundred years old.

Both of Lycaon's parents were human, making the only explanation to Lycaon's longevity—lycanthropy. Werewolves could outlive humans, and, possibly, elves.

Since Feraan knew of Brenin's secret, there was only one thing he could have possibly been trying to get across to her. And, as she pieced it together, a small smirk came to Feraan's face. His work done, he turned his full attention to Lycaon and everyone else in the tent.

Caelfel became deaf to the rest of them as she came to the

shattering conclusion. Brenin was a werewolf now, which meant he could live as long as Lycaon had, possibly even longer. He could match the lifespan of an elf. There was a possibility that they could spend their lives together.

The conversation in Lycaon's tent had sufficiently veered away from her, picking apart the details of Gwyndolyn's campaign that Feraan had managed to discover. Everyone listened to his tale with rapt interest, so Caelfel slipped outside, unnoticed.

The night air provided a new clarity to her senses and her life's direction. Caelfel knew what she wanted, and she wasn't going to let it slip away from her. She headed back to Brenin's tent with her heart pumping at a thrilling pace.

She entered his tent with a strong sense of purpose that instantly evaporated when she saw him lying on his bed, the same dark, thunderous expression that he had recently adopted still plastered on his face. When he saw her, the dark mask lifted, revealing a tender curiosity at her presence.

Caelfel froze suddenly, wavering on the edge of uncertainty. Something inside of her crumpled and nearly pulled her back outside, insisting she was making a mistake. She had never felt so much doubt at something she had been so sure of moments ago.

"Caelfel?" he said, drawing her attention back to his face. She stared at it and thought of him being alone in his dark tent with nothing for company except his new angry thoughts and his boiling blood. She approached him cautiously and held his gaze inches away from him. She took in his face, the slope of his nose, the pale curve of his mouth, and she felt a warm pit growing in her belly as she realized her own intentions.

"I'm going to kiss you," she informed him.

His pale lips broke into a grin, and she felt more than heard his breathy chuckle. "Are you asking for my permission?" he asked, quoting some long ago, previously forgotten conversation they had shared.

Before he could finish the question, Caelfel leaned forward and pressed her lips against his. Brenin's fingers knotted through her hair, and she felt his fingernails scrape slightly against her scalp.

As she had expected, his kiss bore the qualities of vulnerable passion. If she did not know better, she would have been oblivious to the fact that he was a newly changed, angry werewolf. She felt the strength in his touch, but his hands were gentle as they caressed her neck and tipped her chin back. His hands explored the length of her body. Her fingers sought out the planes of his chest.

She tasted nothing but Brenin and wanted nothing other than her prince. She was dizzy and breathless, and as her whole body flushed with anticipation, Caelfel knew she had made the right choice.

***

Madoc had watched Caelfel's combat with the opposing champion, and though he thought her efforts were valiant, he did not wait with the others to meet her when she had returned to the camp. After Caelfel's victory, he had watched them all from a distance, but his eyes had rested on his brother. Half-brother. Werewolf brother. A range of conflicting emotions passed through him, and Madoc felt an overwhelming sense of not belonging. His whole life had been a lie. He was no prince of Umfeld. He was a bastard half elf, *quarter* elf.

He was too ashamed to face anyone—Caelfel, his brother. So as the others reconvened at the Commanding Tent, Madoc turned away. He went to his own tent and packed a few things. He would not take anything in the way of valuables or other luxuries being a prince afforded. The only item he dared to take was the greatsword given to him on his sixteenth birthday. He wrapped it in a thick cloth and secured it to his pack.

Then he left the camp, refusing to say his goodbyes to anyone. He slipped through the rows of tents, heading west for Onusal on his own as a rogue wanderer. And as he began to grow accustomed to his new despair, his thoughts repeatedly returned to one thing.

Saffir.

***

Dagwen did not return to the Crossroads Village with Princess Gwyndolyn. But Dagwen was acting on other instructions from Princess Gwyndolyn.

Dagwen's specialties were in the dark and deadly art of assassination, and Princess Gwyndolyn had finally seen fit to utilize Dagwen's area of expertise. It was exhilarating for Dagwen. She crept through the heavily populated camp undetected, and then she made her way straight for Palpses.

It took two days for her to reach the capital of Kanetalm on foot.

Sneaking into the city was an easy feat after nightfall, and breaking into the palace was child's play. The most difficult part was locating the king inside.

It was late at night, but King Orrik was up and about and roaming the palace. She found him in the main hall, the throne room, which she found to be an aesthetically pleasing setting for an assassination.

The guards and sentries were all outside, which suited her as she strode up to King Orrik who had his back turned to her. Dagwen had had plenty of experience from previous contracts to know that speaking to targets before eliminating them was a bad idea if she allowed them a moment to respond. But Dagwen had not murdered a monarch before, and so, with a smirk, she decided she better not waste this opportunity.

She waited until she was right behind him. "Your majesty?" came her smooth melodious voice.

Surprised, King Orrik turned to face her. His face was open, not yet alerted to his imminent demise. "And who are you?"

The small blade warmed in her grip. "I'm afraid your reign has come to end."

In a deft movement, she dragged the knife across the skin of his neck. Her incision was deep enough that he could make no sound other than a muted gurgling as he suffocated on his own blood. A wave of scarlet poured forth from his gash, staining his neck in a thick sheet.

Then, Orrik fell.

***

Nym watched Feraan carefully. When Lycaon was finally distracted and turned away from his brother, she felt it safe to approach this new elf.

"Why are you wanting to take down Princess Gwyndolyn?" she asked. Nym was not familiar with Princess Gwyndolyn or the ways of the woodland elves of Honey Water, but she thought this was a crucial question to ask if everyone was so readily open to grant him immunity. She did not know Feraan, but perhaps that was for the best, since everyone else around her seemed blind to the fact that he could quite possibly be dangerous.

He didn't answer her question but gave her a sideways glance. "You're not a woodland elf," he observed.

She gave him a thin smile. "No, I do not think so."

"Does that make you a mountain elf, then?"

"I am not familiar with mountain elves," she admitted aloofly.

"Perhaps because they are extinct," he mused. "But if you are truly a mountain elf, then I supposed they wouldn't be extinct. That means the real question here isn't about me. What is a mountain elf doing in Umfeld?"

"I was born in Umfeld, and I was raised here all my life. Where else would I be?" she asked.

"If I stayed where I was born and lived all my life, I would certainly not be *here*," he countered. His eyes went to her forged leg. "Were you born like that?"

"Hardly," she scoffed. "A werewolf chewed it off."

Feraan stared at her craftsmanship. "How old are you?"

"Over a thousand," she told him.

Her answer suddenly attracted all of his attention. He turned his body to face her fully, and he leaned closer with a scrutinizing look, as if he was solving some interesting puzzle. "A thousand years and you've lived in Umfeld all your life. How come we've never met before?"

She shrugged. "Do you come to Umfeld often?"

"Often enough that we should have at least encountered each other once."

Nym didn't see the point of his observations, so she supplied Feraan with one of her own. "Do you love her?"

"Who?" he asked, confused by the jarring subject change. But Nym had a feeling he understood who she meant.

"You know who. Caelfel. I've seen the way you look at her. You surrendered to her to save her life, even though you're bound to some secret mission of taking down Gwyndolyn. Caelfel still took precedent." Nym paused. "And you looked so *injured* when she left just now, like you knew where she was going."

She was successful at making him uncomfortable, and Feraan shifted his position to give himself more space away from her.

"It's not that hard to imagine where she went to," Nym continued when he said nothing. "She risked her life to stay with Brenin when he was turned."

"What are you talking about?" Feraan asked, no longer trying to hide his discomfort in the subject.

Nym kept her even gaze on him to watch for his reaction. "She was there when the prince first changed into a werewolf. You know what happens when you're around a new werewolf like that? They try to kill you. She knew that, but it didn't stop her."

She saw his jaw strain and his fist clench. "She did *what*?"

Nym smirked. "Relax, she obviously made it out alive. You must really have had a thing for the youngling, then."

His fist relaxed, but his jaw remained clenched. Nym was about leave the exchange when she thought of something he said.

"So what do you know about mountain elves?"

He looked at her closely, his previous discomfort gone. "Probably a lot more than you do."

"Do you know where they lived? Where they came from?"

"I do," he admitted slowly.

An ancient eagerness heightened her senses as she yearned to learn more about her people and heritage. "Can you take me there?"

He didn't say anything for a long time as he studied her closely. He seemed to place a certain scrutiny on her fake leg. Then, his face brightened with an idea. "I will, but you'll have to help me with something first."

Nymaaria folded her arms carefully. "What did you have in mind?"

Epilogue

It had been a month since Brenin's werewolf transformation. Now that the moon would be full once again, he would turn into his beast-form a second time, willingly or no.

A lot had happened in that month. Madoc had gone missing, and Brenin had returned to Palpses to discover his father was dead, murdered. Assassinated. Which left Brenin to assume his new title as the King of Umfeld. It caused an upset among the nobles. Not many had known Madoc was not the true son of Orrik, and many had insisted on the elder brother taking the throne. It helped Brenin's case that Madoc had taken off on his own, forfeiting a crown that was not his. It was two weeks after King Orrik's death before Brenin was coroneted.

Then came the matter of finding his father's assassin. Whoever it was, they left no trace of their presence nor any evidence behind. For all anyone knew, it might have been an apparition that had killed Orrik. After several investigative efforts, all Brenin could do was post a bounty and an award for any information regarding his father's assassin. And that was that.

But there were also happier things in that month. Despite any love that Brenin *should* have felt for his father, he had—in reality—despised the man. Taking up his mantle was not an overly grievous task. Brenin thought he did quite well as Umfeld's king. The matter of Gwyndolyn's army still put him at odds sometimes, but he had not heard anything new from the princess after he had sent messages alerting her of King Orrik's death. Even though they had had just the one conversation, it was enough for Gwyn to leave a lasting impression on Brenin. One that did not sit well with him. He had left the encounter with a new sense of anxiety concerning her army. She might have been silent now, but he knew that silence would not last.

Despite all of these things, Brenin could forget his grief and anxiety, even if only in stolen moments of the day or in the small, dead hours of the night.

Because now, Caelfel was with him.

He clearly remembered the night she had entered his tent after his conversation with Gwyndolyn. It was the night she had made her promise. She would never leave, not unless he asked her to, and Brenin had promised her that he wouldn't.

After that night, Caelfel had certainly stayed true to her promise. She had rarely left his side on the way back to Palpses, and once they had gotten back to the capital and he was swarmed by his new kingly duties, she was never far when he looked for her. She had written to her father back in Honey Water with her intention to stay in Palpses for a while until she could visit him. Brenin wished he could stay with her in Honey Water or make it so that they both could leave Umfeld for an extended period of time. He would give anything for her to visit her father. Rather, he would give anything for *her*.

But the duties of a new king were relentlessly demanding.

He had heard the word *marriage* being hissed among the nobles and other extended members of his family, accompanied by strong tones of disapproval. He hadn't thought about marrying Caelfel before hearing them, but he knew that if the conversation ever arose, many of those nobles would be staunchly against it, unless Caelfel could provide some noble influence from the elvish empire. But Brenin did not presently concern himself with those thoughts.

There were others brave enough to swear to his face that their bliss would be short-lived. That they had not known each long. That it had only been a month since she had started living at the palace. Brenin would learn; happy couples did not remain happy for very long, particularly where a king was concerned.

But Brenin paid no attention to these discouragements, and he looked forward to retiring every evening alone with Caelfel. He did not dictate her movements or actions, so she spent her time roaming the palace and the city and found many ways to amuse herself. Brenin noticed elves could keep themselves busy with any and all manner of activities. He regretted not spending as much time with her as he would have liked, and he loathed the idea of her being confined and lonely in Palpses.

But she would insist to him that she did not feel trapped and that she enjoyed her time in Palpses. The only thing that Brenin could do to put his mind at ease was to promise her better things in the future. He would take her around all of Umfeld so she could see Onusal and Atalon. But most importantly, he promised her a visit to the coast so she could witness the majestic vastness of the sea. Caelfel had laughed mirthfully at that, declaring that she would love to go to the coast.

The week before the full moon, Lycaon arrived at the palace with Geri and Garvanna. Brenin gave them a private audience and discovered that they knew of his werewolf secret. It did not bother him so much now, especially since Lycaon came to warn him about the full moon and how this second change would be much like his first—involuntary, possibly even painful.

"You will need to be prepared," Lycaon warned.

They arranged for Lycaon to return in a week with Geri, Freki, Reuthe, Aeliria, and others of the pack. They would take Brenin hunting in the Pirinac, away from the people in Palpses, to keep his people safe. After exchanging a glance with Caelfel, Brenin agreed to this.

"There's something else," Lycaon continued.

Apparently the wolves that had surrendered from Tarion's pack did not join Lycaon's pack. They weren't unwilling, just incapable. They claimed that their alpha was someone else, leaving Lycaon to believe that Brenin had become their next alpha.

"They will be running with us too," he said. "To see if it is true."

Brenin wasn't particularly comfortable about hunting in the forest with werewolves that previously kept him captive, but he saw little use in arguing with Lycaon's case.

"How are they incapable of joining your pack?" Brenin asked.

"Werewolves maintain a sensitive pack mindset. It's all about the strongest becoming their leader. Since you have royal blood and were changed by Tarion himself, it makes sense for you to become their next designated alpha."

So then it was decided, and Lycaon returned to Palpses on the morning of the full moon. The other werewolves stayed outside of the city so as not to raise suspicion. Brenin was still determined to keep his lycanthropy a secret from the rest of the kingdom for as long as he could.

When dusk approached, Lycaon told Brenin to say goodbye to Caelfel, which surprised Brenin. He had expected Caelfel to join them. After all, Caelfel had proven she could handle werewolves.

"It's not the place for her," Lycaon maintained. "You wouldn't want her to see you like that."

Brenin thought back to his first night as a werewolf. He didn't remember all that had happened, just enough to know he was ashamed of it, even if he had had no control over himself at the time. Lycaon left for the Palpses gate to give them some privacy.

Brenin turned to Caelfel, feeling a growing sense of trepidation at leaving her behind. They were on the palace steps, him standing a few steps below her, making Caelfel the taller one for the moment. He wore his cloak with the hood that he had used to attend the Festival of Strigi with her not long ago. He was using it now to slip out of Palpses unseen.

"I'll be fine," she promised. But he could tell she sounded miffed at being left behind. "I'll look after things while you're gone."

While Caelfel didn't hold an official position in the palace, the favor she held with the king was apparent to anyone who saw them. She could command things like she was a regular queen, and they would listen to her.

"I'll be back in the morning," he assured her.

She descended one step and cradled his head with her hands. She ran two fingers from his temple all the way down to his chin, to trace the shape of his face. She pressed her other thumb against his lips and parted them slightly to open his mouth. "Just don't forget about me when you're down there." She kissed him deeply then, and Brenin savored the taste of her as he smiled against her lips.

"Never," he promised loyally.

She gave another giggle and sent him on his way with the others.

They found shelter in an abandoned hut beyond Fort Wymdall before they stripped of their clothes. Brenin kept his neatly in a pile near the broken window. It felt strange to get naked with so many people, but the others were used to this and felt no shame in the act. Brenin pretended to be the same way.

Then they waited for Brenin's change.

Lycaon had explained that the werewolf change would not occur so unwillingly after this. He said werewolves would feel a strong pull to transform on nights of the full moon, but by that point, they usually maintained enough control over the transformations to prevent the change from happening.

Now that Brenin knew what to expect, the turn was not as painful as the first time. It still hurt when his body felt like it was ripping from its own skin, but Brenin bit down on the screams and suffered through it. It wasn't long before he felt the itchy fur cover his body, and his heavy breathing made him realize that he was on all fours.

Brenin gave a great, instinctive howl at his accomplishment, and pretty soon, the others joined him.

At Lycaon's indication, they all ran for the Pirinac at an unnatural speed.

They had called it a hunt, but Brenin realized they wouldn't be hunting anything. The point of the exercise was to keep him away from people so he wouldn't hurt anyone until he could acclimatize to his abilities. They would run all night in the Pirinac under the light of the full moon, and Brenin would learn his own limits.

It was an invigorating freedom he had never experienced before. He felt like a tightly bound coil that was now free to unwind. His tension and anxiety slipped away in the miles that stretched behind him. The rushing night wind ruffled his fur, and he felt the air of wildness emanating from the rest of the wolf pack. They were strong and dangerous. It was bracing.

But Brenin was lucid enough to know his own heart, his desires and fears. Inevitably, his thoughts turned to Caelfel, and he imagined her sleeping alone in their bedchamber that night. Perhaps she wouldn't even sleep while he was gone. The thought caused him to whimper.

Before he could dwell on this image any longer, a new scent entered his field of perception after they had entered the forest. Instinctively, he ran for it. The wolves behind him growled in protest, but something eerily enigmatic steered him towards the scent.

Suddenly, he saw a woman ahead, and he feared that he would not be able to stop before colliding with her.

"*Stop!*"

Brenin skidded to a stop just before her outstretched hand.

There was a long moment when they looked each other up and down. Brenin recognized the half-naked frame and the blank, milky eyes absent of iris and pupil. The Blind Seer was standing before him.

"I *told* you!" she told him sharply. "What did I tell you?"

Brenin only tilted his head in confusion at her words. By now, the other wolves had reached them, but they kept their distance from the Blind Seer.

"Have you forgotten already?" she asked. "I do not give my prophecies away so lightly."

Brenin recalled meeting her at the Festival of Strigi and how she had given him some prediction. He did not remember what she had said.

The Seer gave an exasperated sigh and recited, "*An era shall end when a king stops for a traitor in the wood.*"

Brenin blinked, trying to make sense of this prophecy. He gave a low, non-threatening growl to indicate she should explain herself.

The Blind Seer smirked, as if understanding the thoughts behind Brenin's guttural communication. "You want to know what it means. As you should, because it's happening *right now*." She paused, as if listening to some dead, silent wind. "No, I should say that it's already happened."

Brenin gave an impatient growl.

"You are a king," she pointed out. "This is the wood, and I am the traitor—Traitor of the World, as people like to call me. Something is changing. An era is ending."

She waited for him to realize her cryptic message. When he did not, she continued.

"Did you enjoy your era? Where is your heart, King Brenin?" she asked, sweetly condescending. "Where did you leave her? Unprotected? Arguably, not a very good idea."

Brenin's eyes widened as he thought of Caelfel. He gave a threatening bark.

"There's no use fighting me about it. Go on! See for yourself. You're already too late." She was smirking and shooed him away as if he were an annoying insect instead of the king of Umfeld.

Brenin did not wait for another dismissal. He turned and ran back towards Palpses, despite the obvious pleas from the others that he shouldn't. Brenin didn't care about any of that right now. He had to get back to get Caelfel.

He pushed himself to the extent of his strength and further. He would not stop until he saw Caelfel. He returned to the abandoned shack to retrieve his clothes, even though he felt like it was an irritating waste of time. But he deemed it necessary to enter the city in his human form. He didn't even waste a moment to pull his hood over his face as he ran down the street of Palpses. Let the people of Umfeld see their king running like mad at odd hours of the night, as long as Caelfel was safe.

The palace guards gave no indication that anything was amiss, but Brenin entered the palace warily. The rooms were drafty and silent.

He went to their bedchamber—the queen's rooms that they shared, despite the protests from others that the king should sleep in the king's rooms. Those squabbles were a distant memory now as he passed through the receiving room with the parlor and dining table. The door to the bedroom was open, which briefly registered upon Brenin as odd. But he continued through undeterred.

The scene in the dark bedroom was illuminated by the light of the moon. Cyrus lay unconscious on the floor, a small rivulet of blood running down his temple. The bed and other furniture were in wild disarray, as if an altercation had taken place. Then a breeze swirled through the room, rustling the bed canopy and the blankets, and Brenin noticed that a section in the wall of windows had been broken. Brenin stepped closer to peer over the edge of the cliffside. From his position, he could see nothing that might be below.

Caelfel was nowhere to be found.

A few of the guards had followed him into the bedchamber. Brenin turned to them now in a furious rage. "Search every room of the palace. Search the city. Search outside the walls, if you have to. *Find her!*"

They tittered their compliance, bobbing quick bows before scuttling away to their assignment.

Brenin's gaze returned to the bed, and for the first time, he noticed a small pool of blood that stained one of the pillows. He knelt to examine it and discovered that the blood had a slightly foreign sheen that distinguished it from human blood. He suspected it was Caelfel's, and the evidence that she had been harmed stabbed through him.

He would *not* lose Caelfel.

It was then that Cyrus groaned back to consciousness. Brenin rushed to his side as the steward looked around the room with terrified eyes.

"Cyrus?" Brenin said, trying to keep the panic from his voice. "What happened?"

"I'm sorry, your majesty," Cyrus panted. "I tried my best, but they took her."

Brenin's blood ran cold at this announcement. As he uttered his next question, his voice sounded strangled. "Who did?"

Cyrus struggled to describe them. "I don't know what they were. Damnable monsters of the night. As strong as elves and werewolves. There were two, and Caelfel fought against them."

Brenin's voice was thick, and he could not hide his rage. "Cyrus. Tell me who took Caelfel."

The color drained from the steward's face. "Your majesty, I believe they were vampires."

Glossary
be wary of spoilers

CHARACTERS
Main

Caelfel Gyssedlues—daughter of Eviat & Sylaera Gyssedlues, granddaughter of Lady Ellissara, victor of Strigi's Tournament, native to Sal'Sumarathar, 76 years old

Prince Brenin Orrikson of Eildon—son of King Orrik of Umfeld and the late Queen Fronia, half-brother of Madoc, Prince of the Vale, lord of Kanetalm, alpha werewolf, 22 years old

Madoc—son of Feraan and the late Queen Fronia, 25 years old

Cyrus Dering—steward to Prince Brenin, 37 years old

Garvanna Hunithrae—elf, native to Amasel, 431 years old

Feraan Auvrearaheal—most hated elf of Honey Water, member of the Chthonic Order, father to Madoc, son of Saint Hubertus and Lady Fawnrial, half-brother of Lycaon, 536 years old

Forra Ettln—native to the city of Kierm in Umfang, Enemy of the Kingdom before being pardoned by Brenin, 23 years old

Runa Snowaxe—daughter of Ralfric, native to Ruxcloke, The Raven's Hand, servant of the Mountain Sorcerer, 19 years old

Nymaaria Vulcaandatter—elf, daughter of Vulcaan, werewolf hunter & blacksmith, native to Sorasaen, 1,011 years old

Men

<u>King Orrik Loerson of Eildon</u>—King of Umfeld, son of the late King Loer, father of Prince Brenin, brother of Prince Orren, 55 years old

<u>Queen Fronia of Mirlykke</u>—late queen of Umfeld, mother of Madoc and Brenin, daughter of Lord Bared, sister to Barad, deceased

<u>Prince Orren Loerson of Eildon</u>—prince of Umfeld, second in line, son of the previous king Loer, younger brother to King Orrik, 32 years old

<u>Lord Bared of Mirlykke</u>—Lord of Akeonn, father of Barad and the late Queen Fronia, grandfather of Prince Brenin and Madoc, 76 years old

<u>Barad of Mirlykke</u>—brother to the late Queen Fronia, son of Lord Bared, father of Lady Anissa, 50 years old

<u>Lady Anissa of Mirlykke</u>—Lady of Akeonn, daughter of Barad and the late Eira, 13 years old

<u>Eira of Mirlykke</u>—previously Eira of Oledattar, wife of Barad, mother to Lady Anissa, deceased

<u>Saffir of Wrenne</u>—daughter of Onusal's Officer of Trade, native to Atalon, 26 years old

<u>Captain Lewod</u>—Captain of the Palpses Guard in Kanetalm, 45 years old

<u>Huwel</u>—soldier in the Company of the Prince, native to Palpses, brother of Ameala, 28 years old

<u>Edilon</u>—healer and soldier in the Company of the Prince, native to Ruxcloke, 33 years old

<u>Turre</u>—soldier in the Company of the Prince

<u>Melker</u>—soldier in the Company of the Prince

<u>Lovas</u>—soldier in the Company of the Prince

<u>Joen Nystrom</u>—Commander of the King's Men, native of Atalon, 46 years old

<u>Ólff</u>—temple keeper of the Saint Hubertus Temple, father of Reuthe, 45 years old

<u>Pren</u>—pyrotechnic, native to Dunnere in Umfang, 8 years old

Elves

Eviat Gyssedlues—Caelfel's father, 2,375 years old, greyling
Sylaera Gyssedlues—Caelfel's mother, daughter of Ellissara, estranged member of the Sal'Sumarathar Family, 589 years old
Thoroth Orletylar—healer, native to Amasel, 399 years old
Ellissara Ambrosius—head of the Family of Sal'Sumarathar, mother of seven daughters, grandmother of Caelfel, 981 years old
Adar Ambrosius—daughter of Ellissara, imperial blacksmith, 589 years old
Elaine Ambrosius—Eleanir, widow of Tristram, daughter of Ellissara, healer & alchemist, 589 years old
Guinervra Ambrosius—daughter of Ellissara, politician, 589 years old
Morwen Ambrosius—daughter of Ellissara, acolyte of the Sal'Sumarathar Temple, 589 years old
Liavyn Ambrosius—daughter of Ellissara, artist, 589 years old
Ruefel Ambrosius—daughter of Ellissara, Sea Captain of The Dirge, 589 years old
Rindur Faalingar—Chief Executor of Sal'Sumarathar, 231 years old
Uthruil Killelvris—Daerad's father, Head Councilor of Sal'Sumarathar, 591 years old
Daerad Killelvris—student of the College, 124 years old
Nimuath Killelvris—Uthruil's brother, Headmaster of the College of Sal'Sumarathar, 600 years old
Blaes Llychlin—husband of Empress Haelyn, previous General of the Elvish Imperial Army, ambassador of the Vinius Islands in Foreign Relations, 874 years old
Empress Haelyn of Ernmas—ruler of the elves, mother of Gwyndolyn, 844 years old
Empress Clytemeria of Ernmas—previous ruler of the elves, mother to Empress Haelyn & grandmother to Gwyndolyn, ruled during the Reign of Firescales
Turrelia—Empress Haelyn's stewardess, native to Yamalvon, 312 years old

Ghaenfal Malchrite—General of the Elvish Imperial Army, native to Elewyr, 682 years old

Fawnrial Auvrearaheal—mother of Feraan and Luewyn, member of Empress Haelyn's Elder Council, banished noble, native to Sal'Sumarathar, 739 years old

Nisseria Yvainol—Senator on the High Council, member of the Elder Council, native to Yamalvon, 1,062 years old

Galath Caerbannic—son of Lanslak, native to Rasaen, 63 years old

Lanslak Caerbannic—exiled diplomat, father of Galath, 609 years old

Travin Copperlyre (previously Travin Gyssedlues)—blood brother to Eviat, husband of Camilla, native to Sal'Sumarathar, 1,053 years old

Rebellion

Gwyndolyn Ernmas—illegitimate daughter of Empress Haelyn, Rightful Princess to The Cause, Warden of the Labyrinth, 100 years old

Lisiek Darkling—steward of Gwyndolyn, sorcerer & advisor, The Most Trusted, 26 years old

Markis Rilynnzea—advisor to Gwyndolyn, Captain in the Rebel Army, 293 years old

Dagwen Frumech—advisor to Gwyndolyn, assassin & spy, 577 years old

Fódla Danann—loyal to The Cause, native to Yamalvon, 298 years old

Winwaloe Lannvenec—forced loyalty to The Cause, cavalry officer & Courier, native to Sal'Sumarathar, 192 years old

Erryn Triblanur—forced loyalty to The Couse, cavalry officer, native to Elewyr, 364 years old

Sanddef Pyrd—Gwyndolyn's hostage, native to Yamalvon, 777 years old

Olwen—forced loyalty to The Cause, native to Yamalvon, 193 years old

Werefolk

Macha Morrígna—werebird (raven), Blue Eyed Sister, member of the Chthonic Order, 19 years old

Badb Morrígna—werebird (raven), Red Eyed Sister, courier, member of the Chthonic Order, 19 years old

Anann Morrígna—werebird (raven), Golden Eyed Sister, courier, member of the Chthonic Order, 19 years

Pippi—werebear, resides in Haradrop, 51 years old

Dirus Clan

Lycaon—werewolf alpha, head of the Dirus Clan, member of the Chthonic Order, 540 years old

Aeliria—werewolf, 47 years old

Geri—werewolf, twin brother of Freki, 119 years old

Freki—werewolf, twin brother of Geri, 119 years old

Reuthe—werewolf (turned), daughter of Ólff, 18 years old

Wurnsen—werewolf (turned), 24 years old

Benka—werewolf, 136 years old

Dorth—werewolf, 97 years old

Jalmer—werewolf, 17 years old

Pirinac Clan

Tarion—werewolf alpha, 36 years old

Skolt—werewolf, 198 years old

Gunilla—werewolf (turned), 172 years old

Viveka—werewolf (turned), 27 years old

Knotas—werewolf (turned), 53 years old

Other

Sibylla—the Blind Seer, "Traitor of the World", a feminine being who is physically blind but is able to accurately determine all possible futures and the choices that spur them, resides in the Center of the World, also called the Middle Tree

Geography

Ariang'ron—the Silver Crown World, the world that encompasses the Honey Water Empire, Umfeld & Umfang

Honey Water—empire of the woodland elves

Fey Forest—forest mainland of the woodland elf empire, primarily deciduous

Vinius Islands—cluster of islands in the Latrielle Sea, north of the Fey Forest, conquered by the elves over 5,000 years ago and then added to the Honey Water empire, originally home to the ormr before the Reign of Firescales which resulted in their extinction

Heather Tombs of the Nadeths—section of the Baetic Mountain range where it only borders the Fey Forest, reserved as sacred burial ground for the woodland elves

Latrielle Sea—body of water that borders the Fey Forest to the north, the sediment content in the water prevents natural underwater life

Baetic Mountains—long mountain range that primarily borders the Fey Forest but also extends into Umfeld and Umfang

Mount Ormr—volcano in the Baetic Mountains, close to Yamalvon

Ruxlitta Mountains—the southern portion of the Baetic Mountains that extends from the Farpass and into the Pirinac Forest and Umfeld

Farpass—mountain pass between the Baetic and Ruxlitta Mountains

Pirinac Forest—Umfeld forest in the kingdom of Kanetalm that connects to the border of the Fey Forest, primarily coniferous

Marsda's Mantle—mountain range in the northwest of Kanetalm, named after the human Mother Goddess Marsda, the three largest peaks are named after her life stages: Maid, Matron, and Crone

Myry Jungle—large expanse of jungle in the northwest of Umfang

Strigi's Run—forest in the east of Umfang, bordering the Baetic Mountains

Yamalvon—elvish capital of both the Fey Forest and the Honey Water empire

Sal'Sumarathar—elvish city in the Fey Forest

Elewyr—elvish city in the Fey Forest, also commonly referred to as the Port City, center of trade and shipping for the empire

Amasel—elvish ruins in the Fey Forest

Rasaen—elvish city in the Fey Forest

Frea—capital of the Vinius Islands, named after the Rebel Queen

Umfeld—realm of the humans, south of Umfang and west of the Fey Forest

Kanetalm—kingdom of Umfeld

Palpses—capital of Kanetalm

Fort Wymdall—fortress in Kanetalm

Sorasaen—religious center of Kanetalm, previous home to Hubertus

Haradrop—city of Kanetalm, only known residence of a high concentration of civilized werewolves in Umfeld

Onusal—kingdom of Umfeld

Akeonn—capital of Onusal

Or Embraer—fortress in Onusal

Temple of Donar—religious center of Onusal, maintains regular correspondence with Sorasaen

Rotariel—city of Onusal

Brakiel—city of Onusal

Atalon—city of Onusal, center of trade in Umfeld

Crossroads Village—village that sits on the very edge of the Amhsis Desert that marks the border between Umfeld and Umfang, giving it its name

Umfang—northern realm of Ariang'ron, governed primarily as a representative democracy

Amhsis Desert—desert of Umfang that separates it from Umfeld and the Fey Forest

Cromlech Fortress—fortress in the Amhsis Desert previously belonging to Grimault Cromlech, conquered by the Honey Water Empire before being conquered by Princess Gwyndolyn's campaign

Thrain—landmass of Umfang that includes everything north of the Amhsis, divided into three major principalities (from west to east):

Welt, Mitten, Est

Malanov—capital of Umfang, in Est

Lehyr—city in Est

Phracei—city in Mitten, port

Rackarn—city in Mitten

Dunnere—city in Welt

Kierm—city in Welt, port

Numen—city in Welt, stronghold

Ruins of Kierva—ancient ruins in the Myry Jungle

Chthonic Hall—ancient temple that sits on an island unaffiliated with any of the Silver Crown realms, base of the Chthonic Order

TERMS

life debt—sacred oath that binds an elf to another person in order to protect and guard their life, especially if the same service has been done for the elf

youngling—an elf child, an elf less than fifty years old

greyling—an elf that has breached their second millennia

nadeth—title given to the oldest elf in a certain region, usually over 3,000 years old

aura—slightly perceptual field of radiation that allows its owner to perform magic, each person has a distinctive color that may change or disappear over time, usually natural born among elves and rare in the case of humans

ormr—dragons

Reign of Firescales—a long war the ormr waged against all other races that resulted in the extinction of mountain elves and dragons and also the isolation of the Fey Forest from Umfeld and Umfang, the ormr were eventually conquered

Firescales—a special breed of ormr that took pride in terrorizing Ariang'ron

Ormr Masters—a mysterious race that tamed the ormr, were destroyed in the original conquer of the Vinius Islands

Daemona language—language used by the Ormr Masters

Chthonic Order—a secret and mysterious organization, members are usually identified with a unique tattoo behind their left shoulder with one given exception to their sole elf member

Voice of the Unknown—a magical spell used to cloak one's identity (up to user's discretion), the spell is normally detected by the user's voice when using the spell (a dark, rumbling voice that does not hint to the user's original), a typical characteristic of followers and servants of the Blind Seer

Family—as in, Family of Sal'Sumarathar, the nobility of a certain area, usually granted special favors and privileges from the empire such as having designated seats in the High Council, believed they were descended from the original Conquerors of Ormr that established all the elvish cities and as such are born with superior abilities, Caelfel's mother was born into the Family of Sal'Sumarathar

PANTHEON

Men

Voten—the Creator and Father of the World, Judge of Souls, champion of goodness, lives on Matron Mountain

Marsda—Queen of the Earth, wife of Voten, patron goddess of earth, trees, harvest, and childbirth

Strigi—Mistress of Animals and The Wilds, Lady of the Moon, goddess of hunting, the forest and rivers, mountains and archery, daughter of Voten, twin sister of Donar

Donar—Warrior of the Sun, god of truth and intelligence, soliders and military strategy, twin brother of Strigi, son of Voten

Ruxlitta—goddess of witchcraft and magic, change and healing, sister of Marsda, wife of Numen

Numen—Warden of the Never World, god of death, husband of Ruxlitta

Ewyn—Mistress of the Sea, goddess of grace and beauty

Samain—god of science and innovation, husband of Ewyn

Saint Hubertus—martyr werewolf hunter assimilated into the pantheon for his brave and valiant efforts against werewolves

Elvish

Ewyn—the Creator and Mother Goddess

Yamalvon—firstborn child of Ewyn, founded city of Yamalvon, warrior

Amasel—second child of Ewyn, founded city of Amasel, mage

Sal'Sumarathar—third child of Ewyn, founded city of Sal'Sumarathar, archer

Elewyr—fourth child of Ewyn, founded port city of Elewyr, sailor and bard

Rasaen—fifth child of Ewyn, founded city of Rasaen, clergy

Sidhe—foreign husband of Elewyr

Frea—rebel queen and patron martyr of the Vinius Islands

Acknowledgements

In a way, writing book number two was both easier and harder to do than book number one. Although *Prince of the Vale* is thirty-percent longer than *Archer of the Lake*, the writing for this book went by much faster, despite the fact that I was inundated with college work. But, things did not always just fall into place so easily. On December 11th, 2014, I lost my mother, and that was a devastating, traumatic blow I will never forget.

So I want to take this opportunity and quickly thank everyone who helped moved this project along. Some of these people were coerced (that's a nice word) into forming a group that I've dubbed as **KRM's Production Team**. Here they are:

Kelsa Warner
Arbor Winter Barrow
Olivia Cleveland
Halley Hampton
Andy Arnold
Alyssia Arnold
Laura Hooge
Amelia Honea

There was bickering. Tempers raised, personalities conflicted. Opinions differed. But each of you helped in some manner and I shall be forever grateful for your help. Thank you.

You might note the first name, Kelsa, who was also essential to *Archer*. She is my patient, thoughtful, witty, beautiful editor, cover model, and—most importantly—friend.

Arbor was someone I met after *Archer* was published. And she writes books too! (Check out her first book, **Kinetics: In Search of Willow**!) She is also an amazingly talented artist that designed the new map you should see included in the books. And of course, she is both a wise mentor and devious conspirator of all writerly and geeky things.

Olivia is a fantastic photographer who brought the beautiful new covers to you. (She's also the model on the cover for my other project *The Runewell Fairytale*, check it out!)

I was happy that Andy rejoined the team for another round of editing (and devoting his summer as such). And I am also grateful for the support of others—Halley, Alyssia, Laura, and Amelia.

There are others I would like to take this opportunity and mention— my dad, my grandmother Martha Jo, my grandfather James, Uncle Levoy, Aunt Debbie & Makayla, Mrs. Lisa, Brittany Moyers, Jon Mills (fellow college comrade and procrastinator), and James (the Brenin model you see featured on the cover!).

IN LOVING MEMORY OF
LADY KIMBERLY MICHAELS

About the Author

Kelly writes fiction and independently publishes books and novels under the imprint of Little Owl Publishing. Her first book of The Silver Crown Chronicles—*Archer of the Lake*—was released May 2014. The next book of the same series titled *Prince of the Vale* was released December 2015. She expects to release more titles in 2016.

Kelly lives in a small town in southern Tennessee where she graduated in 2013 with her Associate of Art (A.A.) in Foreign Language. After a gap year, she then proceeded to Athens State University to pursue a Bachelors in English with a minor in Education. Aside from school and her part-time job, Kelly usually spends time with her books and her publishing.

FOR MORE INFORMATION
ON KELLY R. MICHAELS OR HER BOOKS
YOU MAY VISIT HER WEBSITE AT:
WWW.KELLYRMICHAELS.COM

THE SILVER CROWN CHRONICLES
BY KELLY R. MICHAELS

Archer of the Lake

Prince of the Vale

Queen of the Pyre

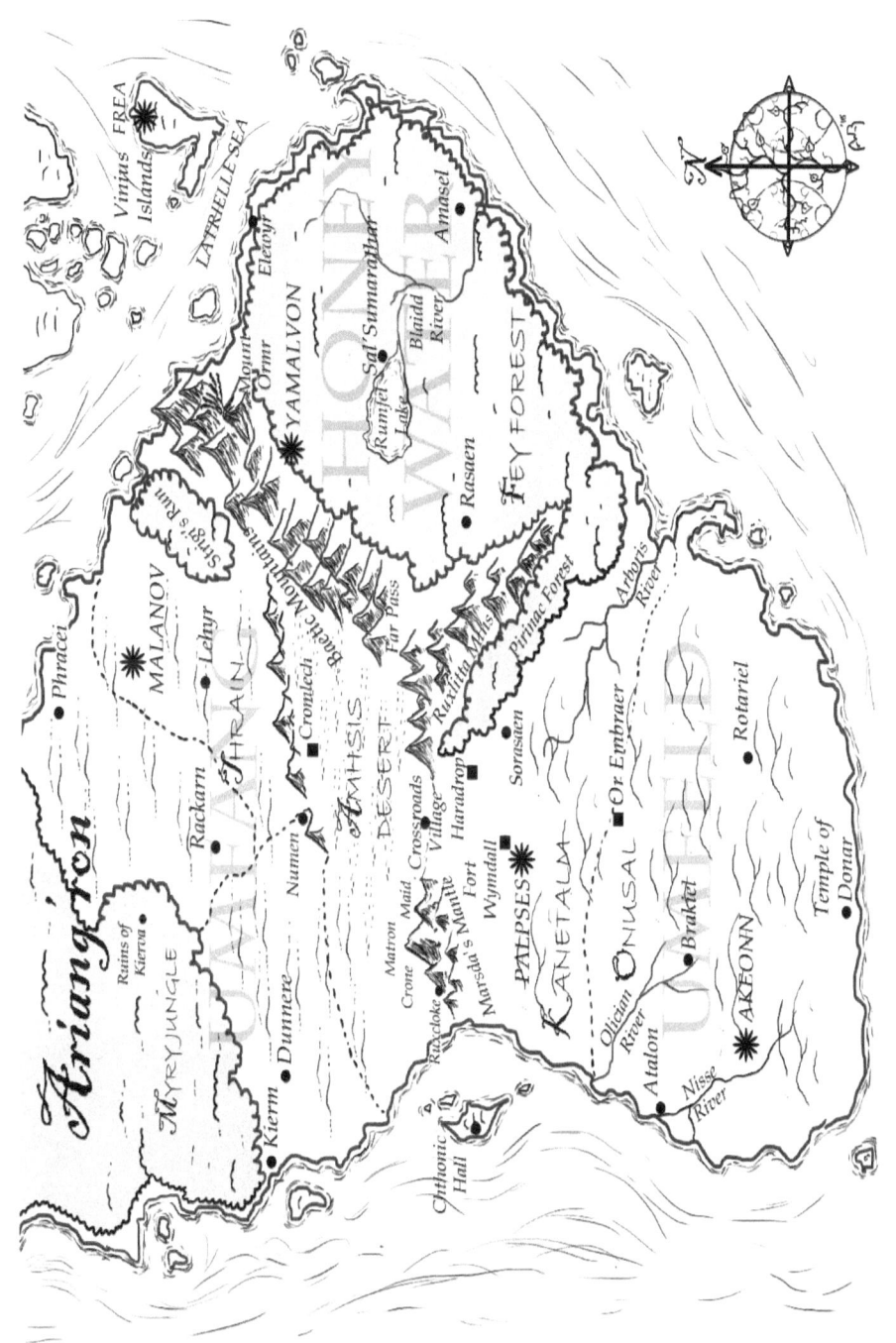

LITTLE OWL
PUBLISHING

www.ingramcontent.com/pod-product-compliance
Lightning Source LLC
Chambersburg PA
CBHW030401180626
46812CB00005B/1873